CAROLINE OF LICHTFIELD

Chawton House Library Series:
Women's Novels

Series Editors: Stephen Bending
Stephen Bygrave

Titles in this Series

FORTHCOMING TITLES

Isabelle de Montolieu,
Caroline of Lichtfield

EDITED BY

Laura Kirkley

Routledge
Taylor & Francis Group

LONDON AND NEW YORK

First published 2014 by Pickering & Chatto (Publishers) Limited

Published 2016 by Routledge
2 Park Square, Milton Park, Abingdon, Oxfordshire OX14 4RN
711 Third Avenue, New York, NY 10017, USA

First issued in paperback 2016

Routledge is an imprint of the Taylor & Francis Group, an informa business

BRITISH LIBRARY CATALOGUING IN PUBLICATION DATA

Montolieu, Isabelle de, 1751–1832 author.
Caroline of Lichtfield. – (Chawton House library series. Women's novels)
I. Title II. Series III. Holcroft, Thomas, 1745–1809 translator. IV. Kirkley,
Laura, editor.
843.6-dc23

ISBN 13: 978-1-138-23550-2 (pbk)
ISBN 13: 978-1-8489-3392-7 (hbk)

Typeset by Pickering & Chatto (Publishers) Limited

CONTENTS

ACKNOWLEDGMENTS

I came to the works of Montolieu on the 'recommendation', as it were, of Mary Wollstonecraft: her uncharacteristic delight in what modern critics had dismissed as a flimsy novel of sentiment intrigued me. I had been researching *Caroline de Lichtfield* for several months when Gillian Dow suggested that a new edition of Holcroft's translation was long overdue. I am grateful to Gillian for inspiring this project, and to the Chawton House Library Series Editors, Stephen Bending and Stephen Bygrave, for their expert advice and their patience in helping me to see it through to completion. Thanks also go to Mark Pollard of Pickering & Chatto for his guidance and efficiency at various stages of the project.

I completed the majority of my research as a Research Fellow at Trinity Hall Cambridge, and I will feel forever indebted to the Master and Fellows for the research time, resources, support and encouragement that my time in the Fellowship gave me. Special thanks also go to: Kate Tunstall for her invaluable and inspired suggestions for the translation of Appendix IV; Matthew Grenby for his comments on the introduction; and Jessica Stevens for her expert proof-reading of the copy text. I am also extremely grateful to my parents, Ken and Maureen Kirkley, for their unstinting encouragement, and to my husband, Tristan White, for his serenity and his support, which always goes above and beyond the call of duty.

INTRODUCTION

An international bestseller in its heyday, *Caroline of Lichtfield* (1786) is the site of a unique textual encounter between the Swiss author of the source text, Isabelle de Montolieu, and the English translator, Thomas Holcroft. At first glance, this encounter seems an improbable one. Apart from the fact that Montolieu wrote for profit, the patchy biographical information available to us suggests that she lived her life in relative privilege, a model of conventional womanhood. By contrast, Holcroft was 'sprung from the people',[1] a working-class political radical who, in 1794, was indicted on insubstantial charges of high treason. As this thumbnail sketch might suggest, his novels tend to be morally didactic or politically utopian; *Anna St Ives* (1792) is often called the first Revolutionary novel. Holcroft's corpus might seem strangely incompatible, then, with *Caroline de Lichtfield, ou Mémoires d'une famille prussienne* (1786), a light-hearted novel of sentiment that draws liberally on anti-mimetic genres such as heroic romance, pastoral and even fairytale. Furthermore, although no record of Montolieu's political views survives, Valérie Cossy observes that she often partook in a Swiss 'helvetist' rhetoric that was 'intrinsically reactionary'.[2] Why, then, did Holcroft single out *Caroline de Lichtfield*, the only novel he would ever translate, and one of very few translations he made from female-authored source texts? A closer examination of the respective cultural contexts of Holcroft and Montolieu will offer some answers to that question; more convincing ones, however, can be found in the text of the novel itself.

At first glance, *Caroline* epitomises a literary vogue for ardent sentiment which, while it endured into the nineteenth century on the European continent, in Britain degenerated into pastiche or darkened into Gothic melodrama. This might explain a tendency, amongst modern critics, to dismiss Montolieu as a populist writer who dealt in what are now clichéd sentimental conventions. Isabelle Bour, for instance, describes *Caroline* as 'featuring the most outrageous characteristics of sensibility – hyperbolic sentiment, extreme pathos, implausible situations, impossible dilemmas.'[3] And yet the overwhelmingly positive response of eighteenth-century readers and reviewers invites closer scrutiny of *Caroline* as an influential work of literature. Mary Wollstonecraft, ever an exacting literary critic, described Montolieu's novel as 'one of the prettiest things [she had] ever read' and brought elements of the plot to her first novel, *Mary, a fiction* (1788).[4] Anna Seward, Anna Barbauld, and Germaine de Staël all remarked on Montolieu's admirable treatment of moral sentiment. The *œuvres* of Wollstonecraft and De Staël testify to a Rousseau-inspired investment in the discourse and philosophy of sensibility, which might explain their enthusiasm; but Jane Austen and Maria Edgeworth, both of whom were apt to poke fun at the excesses of the genre, also read and admired *Caroline*. Austen, who found Montolieu's novel '*beautiful*,[5] may have had it in mind when she created Marianne Dashwood and Elizabeth Bennett, both of whom, like Caroline, fall in love with the virtues of a man they had previously shunned. Edgeworth records a family pilgrimage to the village of Bussigny, in 1820, to meet the aging but, by her account, still sprightly Montolieu. Edgeworth's delight in *Caroline* animates her enthusiastic account of the author; the family even imagine Montolieu's balcony, which commands views of the surrounding mountains and lake, as the prototype for Caroline's pavilion.[6]

As Bour points out, the sub-plot to Edgeworth's *Belinda* (1801), in which Virginia St Pierre falls in love with a portrait, alludes to Caroline, whose love for her disfigured husband germinates from an account of his virtues and a portrait of his former, handsome self. Bour claims, however, that *Belinda* is set apart from the works of Montolieu by its critique of sentimental conventions and its metafictional, self-consciously theatrical dénouement.[7] This analysis underestimates Montolieu. On one hand, *Caroline* is an unapologetic novel of sentiment, one that invites the reader to participate in the exquisite pains and pleasures of thwarted lovers, and to sympathize with the artless and intermittently swooning heroine. Such 'natural' women of feeling are evidently a target of Edgeworth's satire; but her metafictional approach may also derive, in part, from her reading of Montolieu, who punctuates her sentimental prose with episodes of playful irony. As we shall see, she not only treats the conventions of heroic romance to gentle mockery, she also highlights the fictionality of her narrative, making her characters periodically self-conscious about their place within her chosen genre. Moreover, at various points in the novel, she turns her critical eye on the attitudes to erotic love and virtue that run through the literature of sensibility, in particular the works of Rousseau. If contemporary readers were moved by *Caroline*, many also responded to a level of literary sophistication that modern critics have largely overlooked.

Isabelle de Montolieu and *Caroline de Lichtfield*

On 7 May 1751, Montolieu was born Élisabeth-Jeanne-Pauline Polier de Bottens in Lausanne. Her father, Antoine-Noé Polier de Bottens, was a friend of Voltaire, an enlightened clergymen who contributed articles to the *Encyclo-*

pédie. Her mother died when Montolieu was 17, leaving her impressionable and largely unsupervised daughter to find solace in the works of Rousseau. Against the advice of her parents, at the age of eighteen she married Benjamin-Adolphe de Crousaz. They had one surviving child, a son named Henri-Antoine, whom Montolieu adored. Crousaz died just six years later in 1775. During the ensuing eleven years of widowhood, Montolieu forged a warm friendship with the celebrated French pedagogical writer, Stéphanie-Félicité de Genlis; reportedly flirted with the English historian, Edward Gibbon; and, in 1778, took the first steps towards an elopement from Neuchâtel with a young English lord, which was foiled by his watchful tutor. She also became a prolific and highly successful author, beginning her literary career with *Caroline*, which she created from the raw materials of a German tale by Antoine Wall, published in 1783 in the periodical *Les Bagatelles*.

In conversation with Maria Edgeworth, Montolieu claimed to have written *Caroline* 'without the least thought of publishing it, for an Aunt who was ill,' a claim she reiterated in her preface to the 1815 edition.[8] In this preface, she explains that Jacques Deyverdun, the translator of Goethe's *Leiden des jungen Werthers (The Sorrows of Young Werther)* (1774), conspired with his close friend Edward Gibbon to have the novel printed without her knowledge. She comments good-humouredly that she was obliged to pardon these 'traîtres amis' (treacherous friends) when the success of *Caroline* exceeded their sanguine predictions and her wildest expectations.[9] Genlis encouraged Montolieu in her literary endeavours, promoting *Caroline* among her acquaintance and suggesting revisions for the second edition. Such denials of literary ambition, many of them disingenuous, were often made by women anticipating the charge of hubris habitually levelled at female authors. While Montolieu may have had one eye on her public image, however, in the provincial society of Lausanne amateur literary and artistic activities were a primary source of entertainment. It may be, then, that she began writing for pleasure before discovering that she could turn a profit.

Whatever Montolieu's initial intentions, *Caroline* was a phenomenal success. Anna Seward reports gleefully that Montolieu's second husband, the baron Louis de Montolieu, a wealthy widower who was twenty-one years her senior, was first drawn to her by the 'merits and graces' of the novel.[10] Whatever the truth of this claim, they married the year *Caroline* was published. Like Montolieu's hero, Walstein, Louis de Montolieu had an aristocratic background and a military career, before retiring to his chateau in the Pays de Vaud. He died in 1800 and, for the remaining 32 years of her life, Montolieu devoted her affection to her son and her energies to her writing, becoming as prolific as she was popular. In the course of her career, she published over a hundred volumes. With the exception of *Les Châteaux Suisses* (1816), these are predominantly adaptations or translations of existing texts.

As Montolieu acknowledges in her 1815 preface, many contemporary readers wondered why she consistently produced derivative works. She responds by protesting, in keeping with her habitual pose of feminine modesty, that she lacks 'ce don du génie, de cette imagination créatrice qui fait inventer des situations nouvelles, des événemens frappans ou intéressans, des caractères originaux' (that gift of genius, that creative imagination which invents novel situations, striking or interesting events, original characters).[11] To be inspired, she insists, 'il faut [...] que quelque chose, soit en réalité, soit en récit, me saisisse, m'électrise; alors je puis développer cette impulsion, l'étendre, y ajouter des incidens, la prolonger ou la modifier, enfin en tirer parti' (there has to be [...] something, either in reality, or in a story, that takes hold of me, electrifies me; then I can develop that impetus, extend it, add incidents to it, lengthen it or modify it, in the end make it partly my own).[12] Yet in this account of her creative process, it becomes clear that the line between invention and adaptation is a difficult one to draw; indeed *Caroline*, which has the status of an original work, had just such a genesis.

Traditionally, translation has been regarded as inferior to authorship, a defective shadowing of original texts. Accordingly, translations have often been figured as occupying a subservient 'feminine' position in relation to the creative authority of the source text. Where the translator rejected this bond of service to the original text, he or she was seen to 'betray' its style or meaning. Since the 1980s, however, there has been a paradigm shift in Translation Studies from emphasis on fidelity to a new appreciation of translational creativity. Evincing poststructuralist scepticism that any text might straightforwardly mediate 'original' meaning, the works of translation theorists such as Lawrence Venuti and André Lefevere have put author and translator on an equal footing.[13] 'Translation' can be understood literally, as inter-linguistic transfer, or metaphorically, as literary appropriation and transformation. In both cases, though, it constitutes a creative act commensurate with that of an 'original' author. This paradigm shift invites us to reassess the literary corpus of Montolieu who, after a century of neglect, is now emerging from her longstanding position as a footnote to the lives of more prominent writers. Before feminist challenges to the British canon, this was a fate shared by the now celebrated playwright Aphra Behn who, in common with many of her male contemporaries, re-worked material from a range of sources. Moreover, as critics such as Sherry Simon and Josephine Grieder have demonstrated, translation work often enabled eighteenth-century women to engage critically with the authoritative texts of the period without risking the stigma of authorship.[14]

Montolieu's most influential translation was undoubtedly *Le Robinson Suisse, ou, Journal d'un père de famille naufragé: avec sa femme et ses enfants* (1816), a creative adaptation of Johann David Wyss's *Der schweizerische Robinson, oder der schiffbrüchige Schweizer-Prediger und Seine Familie* (1812). Montolieu interpolated episodes of her own, extending the story in an additional five volumes between 1824 and 1826. *Le Robinson Suisse* was the source text for English translations of the work now known, by Anglophone readers, as *The Swiss Family Robinson*.[15] The recent revival of critical interest in Montolieu has, however, been largely due to the role she played in Austen's reception in continental Europe. Montolieu's translations of *Sense and Sensibility* (1811) and *Persuasion* (1818) were published as *Raison et Sensibilité; ou, Les Deux Manières d'Aimer* (1815) and *La Famille Elliot; ou, L'Ancienne Inclination* (1821). A detailed analysis of these translations can be found in Cossy's illuminating work, *Jane Austen in Switzerland* (2006), which places Montolieu's aesthetic values in the context of a specifically Swiss-French paradigm of moral sentimentalism. For Cossy, Montolieu's adherence to this paradigm gives her translational strategy a conservative tendency. She argues persuasively that Montolieu elides the subtle feminist potential of Austen's novels, reducing her idiosyncratic heroines to sentimental literary types complicit with patriarchy – types that Cossy identifies as distinctly 'Swiss'.[16]

In the latter part of the eighteenth century, Swiss 'helvetist' writers often used the novel of sensibility to define their homeland as a locus of moral sentiment. The 'moral' aspect tended to reinforce duty to family and social institutions, draining sensibility of its sensual connotations. Swiss countrymen and women were depicted as honest and artless, in contradistinction to French sophistication, vanity, and *bel esprit*. Integral to the moral health of the virtuous Swiss republics was an inherently conservative ideal of virtuous womanhood, one that holds sway over Rousseau's misogynist gender theory in *Émile, ou de l'Éducation*. Swiss women were held to a narrow definition of virtue by laws and customs that segregated the sexes and confined women to the domestic sphere. With the notable exceptions of Isabelle de Charrière and De Staël, few appear to have contested this patriarchal status quo.

For Cossy, Montolieu 'registers the conflicting and sometimes contradictory aspirations of the period through which she lived'.[17] Raised in a progressive and tolerant milieu but constrained by the growing moral and religious orthodoxy of her homeland, in *Caroline* she lauds Walstein as a benevolent patriarch worthy of her heroine's adoration, but also indulges in irreverent humour at his expense, most notably in her description of his appearance: 'his large black eye was fine; but alas! it was single' (vol I, p. 8). At the same time, although her novel is set in Germany, it plays out the Swiss helvetist construction of a cultural space set apart from the corruptive influence of Paris – the latter embodied by the shallow narcissist, De Zastrow. Similarly, through her characterisation of the Baron of Lichtfield, Montolieu subtly ridicules the duplicity and unscrupulousness of courtly life, often regarded as synonymous with the French *Ancien Régime*. By contrast, Walstein's estate is a pastoral haven in the tradition of Rousseau's Clarens, a rural idyll held together by sentiment, simplicity, and a patriarch of almost god-like wisdom and virtue. The King of Prussia, apparently Frederick the Great, is portrayed as a similarly benign despot, but Montolieu – evidently a good republican – also gives him flaws that stem from absolutism and hereditary rule.

The collective cultural identity of the Swiss had much in common with that of the British, who increasingly perceived themselves as stalwart guardians of common sense, but were also known in Europe for their sensibility.[18] De Staël brings this latter perception of the British to her portrait of Lord Oswald in *Corinne, ou l'Italie* (1807). Montolieu's typically Swiss Anglophilia is also evident in Lindorf's glowing descriptions of freedom and plenty in England. For Gibbon, Swiss history epitomised public spirit and political liberty. This perceived kinship of values between Britain and Switzerland, together with their strong religious, political and commercial ties, fostered an imagined transnational community that ran counter to the cultural hegemony of France. An analogous critique of monarchy and Frenchified aristocracy pervades the radical and Dissenting works of Holcroft's London coterie, as well as more conventional bourgeois writings of the period. As Holcroft scouted for works to translate, he may have recognised, in *Caroline*, a novel that would not only satisfy his target readership's demand for heightened sensibility, but was also underpinned by a value system in some ways congenial to his own.

Thomas Holcroft and *Caroline of Lichtfield*

Born on 10 December 1745 into a working-class family, Holcroft spent his early life variously as a shoemaker, a stocking-weaver, a stable-boy at Newmarket, and a strolling player. In 1777, he was hired by Sheridan as an actor at Drury Lane and began his career as a playwright shortly afterwards. An autodidact with a voracious appetite for knowledge, he taught himself French, German and Italian, and from 1783 until 1791, he was 'one of the best and most voluminous translators upon record.'[19] For Holcroft, translations were not simply pot-boilers; they were a form of apprenticeship to literary modes he strove to master, as well as an insight into different political and cultural systems. Many of his plays were adaptations from foreign sources, and in the course of his career, he also succeeded as a journalist, a periodical columnist, a reviewer, and a novelist. In 1783, he went to Paris as a correspondent for the *Morning Herald*. Moving in free-thinking intellectual circles, he formed lasting friendships with Nicholas de Bonneville, later a prominent Revolutionary, and the Rousseauvian thinker Louis Sébastien Mercier. He also sought out French works to translate or adapt. His selection criteria seem to have exceeded purely commercial factors, as many of his source texts outline the Enlightenment principles that informed his reformist moral agenda and increasingly radical politics.

In 1786, Holcroft formed a close friendship with William Godwin, which the latter cited as a major influence on his controversial work of political philosophy, *An Enquiry Concerning Political Justice* (1793). In 1791, both men joined a radical committee dedicated to publishing the first part of Thomas Paine's inflammatory *Rights of Man*. By 1792, Holcroft was an enthusiastic participant in the Society for Constitutional Information (SCI), which petitioned for parliamentary reforms under Pitt's increasingly reactionary government. When Robespierre's militant Jacobin faction seized power in the National Assembly, reports of escalating violence in France fuelled British paranoia about the contagion of popular revolution. In May 1794, Pitt's administration issued a warrant for the arrest of twelve members of the SCI and the London Corresponding Society. Among them was Holcroft. In the sensational 'Treason Trials' that followed, three of the accused were acquitted, after which the rest were released from Newgate without trial. Holcroft, incensed at being denied a courtroom speech in his own defence, lived the rest of his life marked as an 'acquitted felon'.[20] Until shortly before his death, however, he continued to write and enjoyed periodical successes.

Holcroft's translations often ran to several editions. Amongst his most successful were his comic opera *The Follies of a Day* (1785), an adaptation of Beaumarchais's *Mariage de Figaro* (1778), and the pedagogical works of Montolieu's friend Genlis. The latter seems to have favoured Holcroft as a translator and may have drawn his attention to *Caroline*. Genlis complained, however, about alterations Holcroft made to *Les Veillées du château, ou Cours de la morale à l'usage des enfants* (1782), published in English as *Tales of the Castle, or Stories of instruction and delight* (1785). In a letter to Genlis, Holcroft defended his translational choices, which were designed to domesticate the text for his British readership. In order to convey broadly universal truths, he claims, some concessions must be made to the local and particular: 'Truth and nature are the same in all countries, but the mode of decoration varies.'[21] This is an attitude he also brings to *Caroline*.[22] Holcroft's translations bear witness, then, to his judgments about the universality – or translatability – of certain ideological convictions or aesthetic modes, as well as his convictions about the literary preferences of his target readership.

In the eighteenth century, translators were often highly interventionist, censoring or radically revising large portions of their source texts to produce what the French called *belles infidèles*, beautiful but unfaithful translations. As the century wore on, a countervailing trend for translational 'fidelity' gained currency, but when *Caroline* was published in 1786, a growing enthusiasm for literary originality, or 'genius', was also furnishing new justifications for translational interventionism. In his *Essay on the Principles of Translation* (1791), Alexander Tytler privileges originality over imitation, proposing 'a perpetual contest of genius' between the translator and the author, one that is supposed to refine the source text.[23] Holcroft's translational prefaces suggest an effort to introduce a degree of otherness into the British literary system, but he also coloured his translations with idioms recognisable to the British target readership. Honed by his experiences as a playwright, his ear for dialogue gives *Caroline* what Mitford, seventy years later, would call 'the zest and savour of original writing.'[24]

As his friendship with Godwin would suggest, Holcroft placed a premium on reason, which he regarded as an essential antidote to the passions and prejudices that underpinned political and social injustice. His sympathetic portrayal of feeling individuals in *Caroline* is by no means unique to his *œuvre*, but he may also have seen, in Montolieu's novel, the 'great lesson' identified by the critic for the *English Review*: 'that passion, however romantic, however powerful, and in however young and undisciplined a mind, will yield to the still, but steady voice of reason and conscience.'[25] The critic cites Lindorf's selfless attempt, on discovering that Caroline is secretly married to his friend, to reunite the estranged couple by giving Caroline an insight into the virtuous man behind the disfigurement. At this point, Caroline performs a feat that Edgeworth's Lady Delacour would later deem impossible: she falls in love with good qualities.[26] As she has seen nothing of Walstein since their abortive marriage, this developing love grows out of her imaginative investment in his virtues. It is therefore a rational love that accords perfectly with her growth into a woman of conscious virtue as well as sentiment. The implication, articulated by Walstein, is that virtuous love 'is nothing more than a lively friendship founded on reciprocal esteem, and improved on a difference of sex.' (vol II, p. 94) To some extent, then, Montolieu redefines romantic love in order to advocate companionate marriages sustained by mutual affection rather than passion. As we shall see, however, the novel can also be read as a challenge to that very same doctrine.

Caroline de Lichtfield and Jean-Jacques Rousseau

At the age of seventeen, Montolieu read *Julie, ou La Nouvelle Héloïse* (1761), in which the eponymous heroine consummates her forbidden love for her tutor Saint-Preux. Although few unchaste heroines survive the eighteenth-century novel, a repentant Julie lives on to marry Wolmar, the man of her father's choice. As a devoted wife and mother, she grows into a paragon of virtue at the moral heart of Clarens, an idyllic estate in the Swiss Alps. Considering herself restored to virtue by her loveless marriage, Julie describes her partnership with Wolmar in terms of a mutual commitment to their parental and civic duties, implying that such clear-sighted philanthropy is incompatible with erotic love. Like Walstein, Wolmar is a figure of near-supernatural wisdom and benevolence, who invites Saint-Preux to live at Clarens. Set apart from human passions but capable of reshaping them, he stage-manages Julie and Saint-Preux's interaction, compelling them to value their social duties above their natural desires for each other. In this way, Saint-Preux and Julie carve out a measure of personal fulfillment within the parameters of their hierarchical society. At the end of the novel, Julie dies content that she has been a virtuous wife; but virtue has demanded that she constrain her desire for Saint-Preux until only the desire for death remains.

The complex moral life of Julie held potent appeal for many eighteenth-century women but was commonly censured in Switzerland, where readers claimed to prefer Rousseau's Sophie, the submissive Everywoman bred up to complement the eponymous hero of *Émile*. In her short story, *Le Serin de Jean-Jacques Rousseau* (1811), Montolieu gave readers an insight into her troubled fascination with her celebrated compatriot. She confesses that Rousseau was the focus of an intense adolescent passion, a fantasy of moral perfection later dispelled by his infamous *Confessions*. Her frame narrator makes a pilgrimage to Rousseau's monument at the Pantheon, where she finds a manuscript written by a woman called Rosine. It describes her childhood friendship with Rousseau, ultimately destroyed by his growing persecution complex. In a letter to her publisher, Amaury Duval, Montolieu claims to have drawn from life, having been acquainted with Rousseau when she was the same age as the Rosine of her story. The manuscript left at the tomb suggests an enduring, if ambivalent, love for the writer and his works that is reflected in *Caroline*.

Rosine visits the Pantheon with her two thriving children, named Émile and Sophie in tribute to Rousseau. This homage to Sophie, who often failed to beguile French readers, marks Montolieu out as a writer in the Swiss sentimental tradition. Her description of Caroline in the opening chapters of the novel also owes much to Sophie. Brought up in rural isolation, Caroline arrives at adolescence untouched by the corrupting effects of courtly life. She is naïve, lively, fond of finery, and blithely anticipating marriage to some unknown Prince Charming. As the novel develops, however, Montolieu gives Caroline a capacity for reason that distinguishes her from Rousseau's doll-like creation, and allows her to assert a right to independence that Walstein concedes. Like Julie, Caroline is torn between two men, Lindorf and Walstein, who ostensibly represent the irreconcilable claims of love (Lindorf) and duty (Walstein). In her account of Caroline's growing love for Walstein, however, Montolieu interrogates and challenges Rousseau's dichotomy.

From Walstein's perspective, Caroline's Sophie-like qualities make her an ideal candidate to fulfil his desire for a bride whose mind and body are blank slates awaiting his inscription:

> But, could I meet some young heart, such as I wish, and such as I shall incessantly endeavour to find, simple and innocent, unacquainted with love, and with little

knowledge of the world; if such I find, it shall be mine, even though I should oblige
her to marry me; for I would render her happy in her own despite. (vol II, pp. 100–1)

This uncharacteristic statement, in which Walstein justifies a scheme of male
domination with a fantasy of willing submission, aligns him with Rousseauists
of the period. Inspired by *Émile*, writers such as Bernardin de Saint-Pierre and
Thomas Day imagined a virgin brought up in seclusion and untainted by civilization, ready to be moulded by her prospective husband into his idea of perfection
– a formula later mocked in Edgeworth's *Belinda*. In one sense, Montolieu's
dénouement, in which Caroline and Walstein are united, triumphantly affirms
a conservative and patriarchal status quo, for Caroline conveniently comes to
delight in her marriage with a social equal selected by her father and favoured
by her king. Acquiescence costs her nothing because Walstein is a good man and
– once his scars heal and his hair grows back – an attractive one too. Arguably,
then, the novel is an exercise in wish-fulfilment for eighteenth-century women
readers, many of whom faced arranged marriage as a fact of life.

Yet Montolieu also challenges Rousseau's argument that loveless marriages
are the best marriages. Walstein may be capable of near-divine virtue but, unlike
Wolmar, he is also capable of passion. His attempts to overcome his desire for
Caroline invite admiration, but they are also part of a comedy of errors that
precedes a mutual declaration of love. Alluding to the consummation of the
marriage, Montolieu disingenuously exploits a well-worn eighteenth-century
conceit, whereby the novelist presents herself as the editor of a manuscript. The
convention gives her an excuse to hint teasingly at the taboo subject of sexual
initiation: 'Our history does not inform us whether long habit made the Count,
as usual, leave Caroline's apartment after supper; the reader must, therefore,
suppose what he pleases on that subject.' (vol III, p. 191) Although modesty
demands that the bedroom door swing shut, Montolieu makes it clear that
Caroline awakes to sexual pleasure: 'in the morning, Caroline made the Count
promise they should soon return to this charming estate; "for," added she, with
a softened voice and downcast eyes, "I shall love it as long as I live!"' (vol III,
p. 191) Walstein admits, moreover, that he owes his current happiness, in part,
to his wife's brief infatuation with Lindorf, for she would never otherwise have
come to admire his good qualities. As Joan Hinde Stewart points out, this comment subtly revises his belief in the desirability of a Sophie-like *ingénue* or female
tabula rasa.[27]

Following Wolmar's logic in *Héloïse*, Lindorf no longer looks upon Caroline
as a lover, but as the Countess of Walstein. This appreciation of Caroline's role in
the social idyll of the Walstein estate leaves him free to resume his engagement
to Walstein's sister, Matilda. This is the 'cure' envisaged for Julie and Saint-Preux
– and miraculously, in *Caroline*, it works. Furthermore, Caroline and Walstein

are inspired by their reconciliation to make a bequest, renewed annually in perpetuity, which gives six pairs of impoverished lovers the capital to marry. Unlike Rousseau, then, Montolieu makes love compatible with philanthropy, depicting it as a socially cohesive, rather than solipsistic, passion. And yet, even as she satisfies the conventions of her genre by rewarding virtue, punishing vice and uniting lovers, Montolieu laces her impassioned narrative with allusions to the disparity between reality and romance. This ironic element is most evident in the characterisation of Caroline's guardian, the Canoness. An avid reader of sentimental literature, she regards the Walsteins' marriage as 'a romance in which she was quite in raptures to be one of the *dramatis personae*,' (vol II, p. 134) and stages a dramatic reunion between Caroline and Walstein that backfires spectacularly when Caroline collapses from shock. A domino effect ensues, with Lindorf 'presently almost lifeless.' (vol II, p. 137) In the same vein, her characters' dialogue periodically anchors the text in a more prosaic reality. Hence the scheming Mme de Manteul mocks Matilda's novelistic vision of escape from her aunt's house:

> And so you thought I meant to send you to Berlin alone, and on foot, a fugitive heroine, in disguise, no doubt, with a bundle in your hand, and a large straw hat tied under your chin, beneath which should be discovered a certain dignified and noble air, which some piteous stage-coachman perceiving should give you a place on the box. (vol III, p. 206)

By highlighting the contrivance of her own narrative, then, Montolieu places her marriage of erotic love and philanthropic virtue in the land of fairytale, and has her characters recite their lines in full consciousness of their place within the genre.

Alternately a work of heightened sentiment and light-hearted irony, Caroline apotheosises and subtly critiques the eighteenth-century novel of sensibility. Constructing an apparently conservative narrative of moral sentiment, Montolieu alludes self-consciously to her literary predecessors to lament the frustration of female desire and to play out a self-confessed fantasy of its fulfilment. Holcroft's translation, which emphasises the moral elements of the novel while apparently revelling in its comic potential, offers a version of *Caroline* that is by turns whimsical and heartfelt, a complex blend of metafictional play, lively dialogue, and acute sensibility.

Notes

1. M. R. Mitford, *Recollections of a Literary Life, or, Books, Places, and People*, 2 vols (London: R. Bentley, 1852), vol.1, p. 111.
2. V. Cossy, *Jane Austen in Switzerland: a study of the early French translations* (Genève: Slatkine, 2006), p.52.
3. I. Bour, 'What Maria Learned: Maria Edgeworth and Continental Fiction', *Women's Writing*, 18:1, pp. 34–49, on p. 35.
4. M. Wollstonecraft, *Collected Letters*, ed. J. Todd (London: Penguin, 2004), p. 98.

5. J. Austen, *A Chronology of Jane Austen and her Family*, ed. D. Le Faye (Cambridge: Cambridge University Press, 2006), p. 344.

6. M. Edgeworth, *Maria Edgeworth in France and Switzerland: Selections from the Edgeworth family letters*, ed. C. Colvin (Oxford: Clarendon Press, 1979), pp. 237–41.

7. Bour, 'What Maria Learned...', p. 36

8. Edgeworth, *Maria Edgeworth in France and Switzerland*, p. 239.

9. Montolieu, 'Préface de l'auteur', *Caroline de Lichtfield, ou Mémoires d'une Famille Prussienne: par Mme La Bne Isabelle de Montolieu. 3ᵉ. édition originale, revue et corrigée par l'auteur* (Paris, A. Bertrand, 1816).

10. A. Seward, *Letters of Anna Seward*, ed. A. Constable, 6 vols (Edinburgh and London: 1811), vol. 1, p. 209.

11. Montolieu, 'Preface de l'auteur', p. viii.

12. Ibid., pp. vii–ix.

13. See L. Venuti, *The Scandals of Translation: Towards an Ethics of Difference* (London and New York: Routledge, 1998); L. Venuti, *The Translator's Invisibility: A History of Translation* (London: Routledge, 1995); A. Lefevere, *Translation, Rewriting and the Manipulation of Literary Fame* (London and New York: Routledge, 1992).

14. See S. Simon, *Gender in Translation: Cultural Identity and the Politics of Transmission* (London and New York: Routledge, 1996); J. Grieder, *Translations of French sentimental fiction in the late eighteenth-century England: the history of the literary vogue* (Durham, NC: Duke University Press, 1975).

15. See W. H. G. Kingston, *The Swiss Family Robinson* (London: 1879).

16. Cossy, *Jane Austen in Switzerland*, pp. 206–61.

17. Ibid, p. 183.

18. A. Alliston, 'Transnational Sympathies, Imaginary Comunities', in *The Literary Channel: the international invention of the novel*, eds M. Cohen and C. Dever (Princeton and Oxford: Princeton University Press, 2002), pp. 133–48, on p. 136.

19. Mitford, *Recollections of a Literary Life*, p. 130.

20. J. Barrell and J. Mee, *Trials for Treason and Sedition, 1792–1794*, 8 vols (London: Pickering & Chatto, 2006–7), vol. 1, p. xxxv.

21. Cited in T. Holcroft, *Memoirs of the Late Thomas Holcroft*, (London: Longman, Hurst, Rees, Orme and Brown, 1816), vol. iii, p. 284.

22. For more on Holcroft's translational strategy, see the 'Note on the Text' and the endnotes to this edition.

23. A. F. Tytler (Lord Woodhouselee), *Essays on the Principles of Translation*, (Amsterdam: John Benjamins B.V., 1978), p. 79.

24. Mitford, *Recollections of a Literary Life*, p. 130.

25. *The English review, or An Abstract of English and foreign literature* (London: J. Murray, 1786), vol 8, pp. 253–64, on p. 263.

26. M. Edgeworth, *Belinda*, ed. K. J. Kirkpatrick (Oxford: Oxford University Press, 1994) p. 339.

27. See J. H. Stewart, *Gynographs: French Novels by Women of the Late Eighteenth Century* (Lincoln and London: University of Nebraska Press, 1993) p. 143.

SELECT BIBLIOGRAPHY

Primary Material

Works by Montolieu

This bibliography lists a small, but pertinent, percentage of Montolieu's published works.

*Caroline de Lichtfield, ou Mémoires d'une Famille Prussienne. Par Mme de ***. Publiée par le Traducteur de Werther. Nouvelle Édition avec des Corrections Considérables* (Londres: n. p., 1786).

'Préface de l'auteur', *Caroline de Lichtfield, ou Mémoires d'une Famille Prussienne: Par Mme la Bne Isabelle de Montolieu. 3e. Édition Originale, Revue et Corrigée par l'Auteur* (Paris, A. Bertrand, 1816).

Le Serin de Jean-Jacques Rousseau, ed. C. Jaquier (Genève: Minizoé, 1997).

Les Châteaux Suisses, Anciennes Anecdotes et Chroniques (Paris: A Bertrand, 1816).

Le Robinson Suisse, ou Journal d'un Père de Famille Naufragé: Avec sa Femme et ses Enfants, 2e édition (Paris: A. Bertrand, 1814).

Raison et Sensibilité, ou Les Deux Manières d'Aimer, ed. H. Seyrès (Paris: L'Archipel, 2011).

La Famille Elliot, ou l'Ancienne Inclination (Paris: A. Bertrand, 1821).

Works by Holcroft

The Novels and Selected Plays of Thomas Holcroft, ed. W. M. Verhoeven, 5 vols (London: Pickering & Chatto, 2007).

Tales of the Castle, or Stories of Instruction and Delight. Being Les Veillées du Château, Written in French by the Comtesse de Genlis (London: G. Robinson, 1785).

Adelaide and Theodore: or Letters on Education: Containing All the Principles Relative to Three Different Plans of Education; to That of Princes, and to Those of Young Persons of Both Sexes, 3 vols (London: C. Bathurst and T. Cadell, 1783).

Other Primary Material

The English Review, or An Abstract of English and Foreign Literature (London: J. Murray, 1786) vol. 8, pp. 253–64.

European Magazine, and London Review (November, 1786) vol. 10, pp. 343–4.

Austen, J., *Cambridge Edition of the Works of Jane Austen*, 8 vols. (Cambridge: Cambridge University Press, 2013).

Day, T., *The History of Sandford and Merton*, ed. S. Bending and S. Bygrave (Buffalo, NY: Broadview Press, 2010).

Edgeworth, M., *Belinda*, ed. K. J. Kirkpatrick (Oxford: Oxford University Press, 1994).

—, *Maria Edgeworth in France and Switzerland: Selections from the Edgeworth Family Letters*, ed. C. Colvin, (Oxford: Clarendon Press, 1979).

Cavendish, Georgiana, Duchess of Devonshire, *The Passage of the Mountain of Saint Gothard* (London: n. p., 1798).

Cervantes Saavedra, M. de, *The History and Aventures of the Renowned Don Quixote*, trans. by T. Smollett (London: n. p., 1786).

Kingston, W. H. G., *The Swiss Family Robinson* (London: n. p., 1879).

Lennox, C., *The Female Quixote* (Oxford: Oxford University Press, 1998).

Rousseau, J.-J., *Émile, ou De l'Éducation*, ed. A. Charrak (Paris: Garnier Flammarion, 2009).

—, *Émile, or, On Education*, ed. A. Bloom (Harmondsworth: Penguin, 1991).

—, *Julie, ou La Nouvelle Héloïse: Lettres de Deux Amants, Habitants d'une Petite Ville au Pied des Alpes*, ed. R. Pomeau (Paris: Classiques Garnier, 1981).

—, *La Nouvelle Héloïse ; Julie, or the New Eloise: Letters of Two Lovers, Inhabitants of a Small Town at the Foot of the Alps*, ed. J. H. McDowell (University Park, PA: Pennsylvania State University Press, 1987).

Seward, A., *Letters of Anna Seward*, ed. A. Constable, 6 vols, (Edinburgh: Archibald Constable & Co., 1811), vol. 1.

Staël, G. de, 'Essai sur les Fictions', *Œuvres Complètes*, ed. S. Génand (Paris: H. Champion, 2013), vol. 1.

Wollstonecraft, M., *Collected Letters*, ed. J. Todd (London: Penguin, 2004).

—, *'Mary, a Fiction' (1788) and 'The Wrongs of Woman, or Maria (1798)*, ed. M. Faubert (Peterborough, Ontario: Broadview Press, 2012).

Secondary Material

On Montolieu

Berthoud, D., *Le Général et la Romancière : 1792–1798, Épisodes de L'Émigration Française en Suisse, d'Après les Lettres du Général de Montesquiou à Mme de Montolieu* (Neuchatel: Éditions de la Baconnière, 1959).

Broglie, G. de, *Madame de Genlis* (Paris: Libraire Académique Perrin, 1985).

Cossy, V., *Jane Austen in Switzerland: A Study of the Early French Translations* (Genève: Slatkine, 2006).

Russell, A., *Isabelle de Montolieu Reads Jane Austen's Fictional Minds: The First French Translations of Free Indirect Discourse from Jane Austen's 'Persuasion'* (Bern and New York: Peter Lang, 2011).

On Holcroft

Baine, R. M., *Thomas Holcroft and the Revolutionary Novel* (Athens, GA: University of Georgia Press, 1965).

Barrell, J. and Mee, J, 'Introduction', in *Trials for Treason and Sedition, 1792–1794* (London: Pickering & Chatto, 2006–7), vol. I.

Mitford, M. R., *Recollections of a Literary Life, or, Books, Places, and People*, 3 vols (London: R. Bentley, 1852), vol. II.

Rivers, D., 'Thomas Holcroft', in *Literary Memoirs of Living Authors of Great Britain, Arranged According to an Alphabetical Catalogue of Their Names* (London: R. Faulder, 1798), pp. 265–9.

Rosenblum, J., *Thomas Holcroft: Literature and Politics in England in the Age of the French Revolution* (Lewiston, NY: The Edwin Mellen Press, 1995).

Stallbaumer, V. R., 'Thomas Holcroft as a Novelist', *ELH*, vol. 15, no. 3 (September, 1948), pp. 194–218.

Wallace, M. L. and Markley, A. A, eds, *Re-Viewing Thomas Holcroft, 1745–1809: Essays on His Works and Life* (Farnham: Ashgate, 2012).

On Caroline de Lichtfield

Barbauld, A., 'An Essay on the Origin and Progress of Novel-Writing', *Select Reviews of Literature and Spirit of Foreign Magazines*, vol. 6 (Philadelphia, PA: John F. Watson, 1811).

Bour, I., 'What Maria Learned: Maria Edgeworth and Continental Fiction', *Women's Writing*, 1:1, pp. 34–49.

Le Faye, D., *A Chronology of Jane Austen and Her Family* (Cambridge: Cambridge University Press, 2006).

Stewart, J. H., *Gynographs: French Novels by Women of the Late Eighteenth Century* (Lincoln, NE: University of Nebraska Press, 1993).

Wallace, M. L., 'Holcroft's Translations of the 1780s and Isabelle de Montolieu's *Caroline de Lichtfield*', in *Re-Viewing Thomas Holcroft, 1745–1809: Essays on His Works and Life*, ed. M. L. Wallace and A. A. Markley, (Farnham: Ashgate, 2012).

On Translation and Transnational Literature

Alliston, A., 'Transnational Sympathies, Imaginary Communities', in *The Literary Channel: The International Invention of the Novel*, ed. M. Cohen and C. Dever (Princeton, NJ: Princeton University Press, 2002), pp.133–48.

The Literary Channel: The International Invention of the Novel, ed. M. Cohen and C. Dever (Princeton, NJ: Princeton University Press, 2002).

Grieder, J., *Translations of French Sentimental Fiction in Late Eighteenth Century England: The History of the Literary Vogue* (Durham, NC: Duke University Press, 1975).

Hayes, J. C., *Translation, Subjectivity and Culture in France and England, 1600–1800* (Stanford, CA: Stanford University Press, 2009).

Lefevere, A., *Translation, Rewriting and the Manipulation of Literary Fame* (London and New York: Routledge, 1992).

Simon, S., *Gender in Translation: Cultural Identity and the Politics of Transmission* (London and New York: Routledge, 1996).

Tytler, A. F., *Essays on the Principles of Translation*, Amsterdam: John Benjamins B.V., 1978.

Venuti, L., *The Scandals of Translation: Towards an Ethics of Difference* (London and New York: Routledge, 1998).

Venuti, L., *The Translator's Invisibility: A History of Translation* (London: Routledge, 1995).

On Sensibility

Barker-Benfield, G. J., *The Culture of Sensibility: Sex and Society in Eighteenth-Century Britain* (Chicago, IL: University of Chicago Press, 1992).

Brissenden, R. F., *Virtue in Distress: Studies in the Novel of Sentiment from Richardson to Sade* (London: Macmillan, 1974).

Ellis, M., *The Politics of Sensibility: Race, Gender and Commerce in the Sentimental Novel* (Cambridge: Cambridge University Press, 1996).

Jones, C., *Radical Sensibility: Literature and Ideas in the 1790s* (London: Routledge, 1993).

Kelly, G., *The English Jacobin Novel 1780–1805* (Oxford: Clarendon Press, 1976).

Porter, R., *Flesh in the Age of Reason* (London: Allen Lane, 2003).

Todd, J., *Sensibility: An Introduction* (London: Methuen, 1986).

CHRONOLOGY

CHRONOLOGY OF ISABELLE DE MONTOLIEU

1751   (7 May) Isabelle de Montolieu is born Élisabeth-Jeanne-Pauline Polier de Bottens.

1761   Jean-Jacques Rousseau publishes *Julie, ou La Nouvelle Héloïse*.

1762   Rousseau publishes *Émile, ou de l'éducation*.

c.1762   Montolieu meets Rousseau.

1768   Montolieu's mother dies; Montolieu reads and becomes enthralled by the works of Jean-Jacques Rousseau.

1769   Marries Benjamin de Crousaz.

1770   Montolieu's only surviving son, Henri-Antoine de Crousaz, is born.

1775   Benjamin de Crousaz dies.
Befriends Stéphanie-Félicité de Genlis

1778   Goes to Neuchâtel as part of a planned, but ultimately abortive, elopement with a young English lord.

1786   *Caroline de Lichtfield* is published by Georges Deyverdun without Montolieu's consent; a second, corrected edition appears in the same year.
Marries her second husband, the baron Louis de Montolieu, who is twenty-one years her senior.

CHRONOLOGY OF THOMAS HOLCROFT

1745   (10 December) Thomas Holcroft is born in Leicester Fields, London.

1765   Marries his first wife, with whom he has a daughter, Ann.

1770   Plays small parts at Samuel Foote's Haymarket Theatre.
Goes to Dublin as a member of Charles Macklin's theatre company.

1771   Returns, disillusioned, from Ireland; becomes a strolling player.

1774   Marries his second wife, Matilda Tipler, with whom he has a son, William, and a daughter, Sophy.

1777   Becomes an actor for Sheridan at Drury Lane.

1778   Marries his third wife, Dinah Robinson, with whom he has a daughter, Fanny.
The Crisis, or Love and Famine and *Rosamund, or The Dutiful Daughter*, are staged.

1778–9   Publishes a serial novella, *Manthorn, the Enthusiast*.

1780   Publishes his first novel, *Alwyn, or The Gentleman Comedian*.

1796	Publishes *La Sylphide; ou, l'ange guardian*, a translation of *The Sylph* (1779) by Georgiana Cavendish, Duchess of Devonshire.	1781	*Duplicity* is staged at Covent Garden.
1798	Napoleon's army invades Switzerland; the Helvetic Republic is established under French protection.	1783	Travels to Paris as a correspondent for the *Morning Herald*, where he befriends Louis Sébastien Mercir and Nicholas de Bonneville.
1800	Louis de Montolieu dies.		Publishes *Adelaide and Theodore*, a translation of Stéphanie-Félicité de Genlis's *Adèle et Théodore ou Lettres sur l'éducation* (1782).
1801	Publishes *Tableaux de famille, ou Journal de Charles Engelman*, a translation of *Engelmans Tagebuch* (1800) by August Lafontaine.	1785	*The Choleric Fathers* and *The Follies of a Day; or The Marriage of Figaro* are staged. The latter, adapted from Beaumarchais's *Le Mariage de Figaro* (1778), is a phenomenal success.
1803	French troops withdraw from Switzerland; end of the Helvetic Republic		
1804	Publishes *Aristomène*, a translation of Lafontaine's 'Aristomenes und Gorgus' from his *Sagen aus dem Alterthume* (1796).	1785	Publishes *Tales of the Castle, or Stories of instruction and delight*, a translation of Genlis's *Les Veillées du château, ou Cours de la morale à l'usage des enfants* (1782).
1806	Publishes *La princesse de Wolfenbuttel*, a translation of *Die Prinzessin von Wolfenbuttel* by Heinrich Zschokke. This work was then translated by Holcroft as *Christina; or, Memoirs of a German Princess* (1808).	1786	Meets William Godwin. Publishes *Caroline of Lichtfield*.
		1787	*Seduction* is staged.
		1789	The fall of the Bastille marks the beginning of the French Revolution.
	Publishes *Corisande de Beauvilliers, anecdote française du 16ᵉ siècle*, a translation of 'The Story of Corisande' from Charlotte Smith's *Letters of a Solitary Wanderer* (1800-1802).		Holcroft's son, William, commits suicide.
1808	Publishes *Saint-Clair des Isles, ou Les Exilés à l'Isle de Barra*, a translation of Elizabeth Helme's novel *Saint Clair of the Isles, or the outlaws of Barra* (1803).	1791	*The School for Arrogance*, an adaption of P. N. Destouches's *Le glorieux* (1732), is staged.
			Joins the committee to publish Part I of Thomas Paine's *Rights of Man*.
1812	Publishes *Agathoclès, ou, lettres écrites de Rome et de Grèce au commencement du quatrième siècle*, a translation of Caroline Pichler's *Agathokles* (1808).	1792	*The Road to Ruin* is staged and proves a hit with audiences. Publishes *Anna St Ives*, considered the first Revolutionary novel.
			Joins the Society for Constitutional Information.

1813 Publishes *Le Robinson Suisse, ou, Journal d'un père de famille, naufragé: avec sa femme et ses enfans*, a translation of Johann David Wyss's *Der Schweizerische Robinson, oder der schiffbrüchige Schweizer-Prediger und Seine Familie* (1812).

1815 Publishes *Raison et Sensibilité, ou Les Deux Manières d'Aimer*, a translation of Jane Austen's *Sense and Sensibility* (1811).
Publishes her short story *Le Serin de Jean-Jacques Rousseau* (1811) as part of the collection *Dix Nouvelles*.

1816 Publishes *Les Châteaux Suisses*, an original work which remains in print in Switzerland until the early twentieth century.

1819 Publishes *Amabel, ou Mémoires d'une jeune femme de qualité*, a translation of Elizabeth Hervey's *Amabel: or, Memoirs of a Woman of Fashion* (1814).

1821 Publishes *La Famille Elliot, ou l'Ancienne Inclination*, a translation of Jane Austen's *Persuasion* (1818).

1826 Publishes *Le Siège de Vienne*, a translation of Caroline Pichler's *Die Belagerung Wiens* (1824).

1832 Montolieu dies in Vennes, near Lausanne, aged 81.

1793 Godwin publishes his *Enquiry Concerning Political Justice and its Influence on Morals and Happiness*, in part the fruit of conversations with Holcroft.

1794 Publishes *The Adventures of Hugh Trevor, Part I. Love's Frailties, or, Precept against Practice* and *The Rival Queens, or, Drury Lane and Covent Garden* are staged.
Habeas Corpus Act is suspended. Indicted for High Treason but later released without trial.

1795 Publishes *A Narrative of Faces, Relating to a Prosecution for High Treason* and *A Letter to the Right Honourable William Windham*, who had dubbed him an 'acquitted felon'.
The Deserted Daughter is staged.

1797 Publishes *The Adventures of Hugh Trevor, Part II*.

1798 *He's Much To Blame* is staged.

1799 Marries his fourth wife, Louisa, the daughter of Mercier.
Travels to Hamburg; moves after one year to Paris.

1801 Returns to England.
Deaf and Dumb is staged.

1802 Holcroft's first melodrama, *A Tale of Mystery*, is staged.

1804 Publishes *Travels from Hamburg, through Westphalia, Holland, and the Netherlands, to Paris*.

1805 Publishes his last novel, *Memoirs of Bryan Perdue*.
Another melodrama, *The Lady of the Rock*, is staged; Fanny Holcroft composes the accompanying music.

1806 Holcroft's final play, *The Vindictive Man*, is staged.

1809 Holcroft dies on 23rd March.

1813	Fanny Holcroft publishes her first novel, *The Wife and the Lover*.
1816	William Hazlitt completes the autobiography Holcroft had begun, publishing it as *Memoirs of the Late Thomas Holcroft*.
1817	Fanny Holcroft publishes *Fortitude and Frailty: a Novel*, dedicated to her father's memory.

NOTE ON THE TEXT

Isabelle de Montolieu's French text, *Caroline de Lichtfield, ou Mémoires d'une Famille Prussienne*, first appeared in 1786 in Lausanne and Paris. It was published anonymously, although the title page, which stated that it was printed by the translator of Werther, led many readers to conclude that Georges Deyverdun was the author. This first edition was immediately followed by a second, corrected version, purportedly published in London later that same year. A third expanded edition was published in 1815 and bore Montolieu's name. It was followed by a fourth edition in 1821. Montolieu's additions to the text included an authorial preface and a fuller account of the romance between the Canoness and the Baron of Lichtfield. She also separated the dénouement of the Walsteins' romance from the subsequent account of Lindorf and Matilda, which in later editions bore the title 'Suite de Caroline'. In the fifth edition of 1828, Montolieu exploited this new structure to insert a false ending at the point of Walstein and Caroline's reunion, before stepping forward, as author of the tale, to flout the French commitment to unity of design and announce her intention of making both pairs of lovers happy. The later editions include illustrations and a musical score, also written by Montolieu, to accompany the songs of Caroline and Justin. The novel was reprinted well into the nineteenth century and was also translated for the English, German, Dutch, Spanish, and Portuguese readerships.

I have chosen as my copy-text the first English edition of 1786, which is held by Chawton House Library. It was published by the prominent London publishers G. G. J. and J. Robinson. A second edition was published in the same year in London and reprinted in 1797. Another slightly different version appeared in Dublin in 1786 and, in 1795, this edition was taken as copy-text for a Dublin reprint for P. Wogan, P. Byrne and W. Jones. The first American edition was published in 1798 for Evert Duyckinck & Co., and appears to have been taken from the 2nd London edition. It reproduces some of the minor variations of the 1797 reprint. Following Holcroft's death, a new edition was published by Richard Scott in New York in 1815, which appears to have been drawn from one of the virtually identical Dublin editions of 1786 or 1795. Another American edition was published by S. & D. A. Forbes in 1831. A Minerva Press edition appeared in London in 1817, which appears to take the 2nd London edition as its copy-text.

In this edition, superscript lower-case letters refer the reader to textual variants of Holcroft's translation published in his lifetime. Superscript arabic numerals denote endnotes that gloss persons, places, allusions, quotations, words or concepts likely to be unfamiliar to the modern reader. Where these superscript numerals are underlined, however, the note refers to a significant or illuminating disparity between Montolieu's source text and Holcroft's translation. These notes allow the reader to identify patterns in Holcroft's translational choices. Most commonly, his alterations are apparently intended to emphasise: Caroline's innocence or innate goodness; Walstein's god-like qualities; Lindorf's remorse and capacity to reform; and the courtly vices of the Baron of Lindorf. For readers interested in Montolieu's original text, I have included the French versions of the songs of Caroline and Justin in Appendices I–III. At the end of the novel, Holcroft cuts a substantial section, in which Montolieu alleges that she edited the novel from a manuscript given to her by Lindorf. She also claims to have met the two central couples of her novel in Berlin, and to have lived with them on their various estates. Holcroft may have excised this section because it undercuts Montolieu's metafictional sophistication in the body of the novel. Alternatively, his excision may testify to his commitment to unity of action, a principle he applied to his own novels. I have included the deleted section in Appendix IV. It appears in Montolieu's original French, accompanied by my English translation.

The punctuation and occasional orthographical peculiarities of Holcroft's text have been largely retained, but minor changes have been made to make the text accessible to modern readers. I have silently corrected typographical errors and changed the long *s* to the roman *s*. I have also eliminated running quotation marks and, in three sections of the text, I have taken further steps to standardize confusing and inconsistent punctuation. These sections are: Lindorf's long manuscript to Caroline; Matilda's account of her escape from Mme de Zastrow's house; and Lindorf's account of his experiences in Hamburg and England. These sections are remarkable insofar as they are punctuated by Holcroft as speech, but frequently contain dialogue which, in turn, occasionally also contains reported speech. Since Holcroft's erratic punctuation can make it difficult to ascertain who is speaking to whom, I have opted to apply the following rules of punctuation uniformly to these sections: in keeping with Holcroft's style in the rest of the text, the whole section is punctuated as speech with double quotation marks; dialogue within the section is punctuated with single quotation marks; reported speech within dialogue is italicized. Otherwise, the text has been reproduced as its first Anglophone readers would have encountered it.

CAROLINE

OF

LICHTFIELD;

A NOVEL.

TRANSLATED FROM THE FRENCH.

BY THOMAS HOLCROFT.

Idole d'un cœur juste, & passion du Sage,
Amitié, que ton nom soutienne cet ouvrage;
Règne dans mes écrits, ainsi que dans mon cœur,
Tu m'appris à connoître, à sentir le bonheur.

VOLTAIRE

VOL. I.

LONDON:
PRINTED FOR G. G. J. AND J. ROBINSON,
PATERNOSTER-ROW.
MDCCLXXXVI

CAROLINE

of

LICHTFIELD.*

The Baron of Lichtfield was High Chamberlain and Minister of State to the King of Prussia,[1] "Caroline," said he to his daughter, as they one day sat at breakfast, "tell me, (the Baron had an insinuating smile as he spoke, with somewhat of penetration in his look) tell me, dear Caroline, is thy heart free?"

"Sir!"

Caroline did not immediately comprehend his meaning.

"It is two months since I brought thee to court, from the retreat in which thou hadst been educated; and hast thou seen nobody, in that short space, no young courtier, to whom thy heart would give a preference?"

Caroline was but sixteen,[2] and the question was of that kind that usually embarrasses, when addressed to a virgin of sixteen. Caroline, however, might reply without dread or hesitation. Her young bosom, as pure and tranquil as in the serene and jocund days of infancy, had never sighed, except for pleasures innocent and pure as itself. A new blown rose, a favourite bullfinch, or a fairy tale, had, hitherto, been the general limits of her hopes and fears. These pleasures, indeed, since she had come to court, had been somewhat superseded by a ball, a concert, or a new fashioned cap but that man might influence the happiness of her life had never yet entered her imagination. Those who were the best and most indefatigable dancers, certainly, gave her the greatest satisfaction, while at an assembly; but, the ball over, Caroline could sweetly sleep twelve hours together, awake with a song, and prepare for a new appointment, without thinking of the partner with whom she last had danced.

Her father had therefore rather surprised than confused her; and, after a short silence, she replied, "Your question, papa, is very singular!"

"It is very natural, my dear," said the Baron: "and, moreover, I will endeavour to shew you it is likewise very important. Listen to me seriously, Caroline," continued he, drawing his chair closer to her's, and tenderly clasping her hand.

---

* Not Litchfield in England, but Litchfield a supposed Prussian title

– 3 –

"You have the misfortune to be the only daughter of the High Chamberlain of Prussia, and heiress to twenty-five thousand crowns a year."[3]

The mixture of irony and satisfaction visible in his countenance, though unseen by Caroline, while rehearsing his titles and estate, proved, too powerfully, that these his misfortunes were his supreme pleasures. But it was necessary to his present purpose to assume a philosophic, a disinterested, and a sentimental air, thereby to inspire awe, and, by affecting the passions, to read the heart, and induce obedience. This was the more easy for him to effect, in that he was not only perfectly a courtier, but had a degree of natural eloquence, which supplied the want of a sound understanding, or a feeling heart.[4] Besides, it is not easy, at sixteen, to discover the face of honesty from the mask, especially when a father speaks.

The word misfortune, however, had somewhat surprised Caroline; who, thinking she perhaps had misunderstood, repeated smiling, "Misfortune, papa!"

"Yes, misfortune, my child," replied the Baron, apparently affected. "I see, with pleasure, you know not as yet all the consequences of these seeming blessings, for this informs me you still remain such as I could wish you to be."

A thousand confused ideas were crossing and combating one another in the mind of Caroline. Misfortune and herself had never, before, been united, in her imagination: the idea, for a moment, made her melancholy, and she stood, with downcast eyes, unconsciously plucking the leaves of a rose, which she held in her white and virgin hand.[5]

"Yes, my dear daughter," said the Baron, rising, and gravely walking the room, "it is often one of our greatest misfortunes to be born of noble parents, and to be possessed of vast domains. The chain, I own, is gilt, but is not the less heavy, or the less a chain. (The Baron was charmed to hear his own wit.)[6] Yet I hope," added he, assuming a chearful smile of benignity, "I hope, my Caroline, the chains that thou shalt wear shall hang lightly, and be ever worn with grace and pleasure."

The Baron paused, and Caroline looked up, vainly endeavouring to comprehend to what this his preface tended.[a] He continued:

"My dear girl, the first wish of my heart has ever been thy felicity. Long have I foreseen (the Baron sighed, but the Baron was a courtier) long feared, that not on me, but on a Monarch, whose power is absolute, and must not be controverted, thy destiny would depend—no, not on a tender father! To avoid, therefore, heaping on thee the distress, the torment, of combating affections which may not be consulted, ever since the death of thy mother, I have committed thy education to a friend, whose care and retired situation have preserved thy heart free. I have sacrificed the sweet pleasure of living with my child, of super-intending her education, and being myself delighted with her progress, to her future happiness; and, if I have secured this happiness, my self-denial will be more than repaid."

"Ah, my dear dear father!" cried Caroline, kissing the Baron's hand, which she moistened with her tears, unable to express her sensations. Somewhat she would have added, but he interrupted her.

"The moment is arrived, my daughter, in which the success of all my precautions must be ascertained. Two months since (thou wert then at Rindaw) the King[7] told me he should with pleasure behold thee united to the Count of Walstein, his known favourite, and his present Ambassador to Petersburgh.[8] Notwithstanding that this marriage might even exceed the utmost wishes of a father, I alledged thy great youth, in hopes to see the ceremony deferred, and longer to enjoy thy company, longer to behold thee a part of myself.

"The King replied, thy society I might and should enjoy as soon as thou wert married. Caroline, said he, must now be sixteen; it is time she should come to adorn my court, and make my Walstein happy. He will return immediately from his embassy; send, therefore, for your daughter, and the nuptials shall as immediately take place.

"I could make no reply to a command so precise; and, as thou knowest, I directly came, and brought thee hither.[a] But scarcely had we returned before I learnt the Count was fallen dangerously ill on the road, and that his arrival and our intents were, for a while, suspended. I, therefore, thought it useless to speak to thee of a marriage which, perhaps, might never take place; and I was willing to see thee enjoy, for a moment, the sweet illusions of youth. Yesterday evening, however, the Count returned, recovered from his illness, and the King sent instantly for me, presented my future son-in-law, and bade me prepare for this marriage with all possible speed. Thou seest I could no longer delay to inform thee of the will of my Sovereign: thou seest, my child, thy destiny is fixed. My fear was that, during the two months thou hast been at court, thy young heart might, unfortunately, have selected some one of the youths thou hast seen there. Thus, what should have been thy happiness would, then, have been thy misery; but I see, with transport, thy heart is yet untouched; thy present simplicity and innocence are certain proofs, and my Caroline may now comply, may give me her promise, that she will willingly become the Countess of Walstein, and the Ambassadress of Russia.[9] Wilt thou not, my Caroline? Wilt thou not, my child?"

These fine titles, emphatically dwelt on, dazzled the young fancy of Caroline. Astonished, taken by surprize, and conceiving nothing so wonderful and so charming as all at once to become an Ambassadress, and a Countess, she raised her charming blue eyes, and looking at her father, while they sparkled with pleasure—

"What," said she, in the simplicity of her heart, "shall I be all that, papa? Indeed I am exceedingly glad to hear it."

Her natural good sense, for she had abundance, immediately reproved her: she felt she had rather spoken from the fullness of her heart than from prudent reflection; again her eyes were cast down, and the blood rose blushing to her cheeks, till they resembled the rose leaves she had just been scattering.[10] After a moment's silence, she timidly added, still with downcast eyes,

"But I have never seen the Count, papa; and if I should not love him?"

"You must marry him, notwithstanding, my child," instantly replied the Baron. "We only ask your hand; there is no authority, royal or paternal, which can command the heart."

This moral sentiment was, no doubt, a very strange one to come from the mouth of a father; but the Baron, we may well conjecture, had his reasons for being thus relax.

Caroline replied, with surprise, "Indeed, papa, I do not understand you. Give the Count my hand and not my heart! No, really, papa, I do not understand you!"

"You will do before you have lived six months at court," replied the Baron, as he rose. (Another proof, this, that the Baron was a courtier.) "But this is nothing to our present purpose. Give me thy promise, thy solemn promise, my Caroline, that thou wilt fulfil the engagement I have entered into in thy name. 1 am waited for at court; I will announce thy consent, dine there, and return, this evening, with the Count. Go, dress thyself, and prepare to receive the man who is shortly to be thy husband."

After having received the solemn promise of the gentle and tractable Caroline, and tenderly kissed her, he departed, well satisfied with his negociation.

The reader, perhaps, may expect that the sweet Caroline, left alone, would then, immediately, have abundance of serious reflections on all that had passed; and, particularly, on the approaching marriage. For six and twenty[11] these would have afforded sufficient subject for a whole morning's contemplation; but, at sixteen, the mind does not dwell so long on the same object. Truth, however, obliges us to remark that Caroline, after the departure of her father, remained full ten minutes in the same place and attitude; which, certainly, was a thing somewhat extraordinary.

At length, finding she had so many things to think on that she could absolutely think on nothing, and that the rushing ideas floated and whirled into confusion, she suddenly started up, ran to her piano forte, and played cotillions and country dances, *presto prestissimo*, for a full half hour.

Now, while she was playing, it happened, naturally enough, to strike her active imagination, how delightfully the Count would dance them all with her; "and it will be quite charming," said she to herself, "to continually have a partner at one's command."

Dance!—His Excellency dance!—Yes, to be sure; his Excellency dance: for the Baron had been very careful to inform her that, notwithstanding his high rank, great dignity, and that he was also an Ambassador, he still was not above thirty; which circumstance, it is very probable, pleased her full as much as all the aforesaid titles, dazzling as they were: for, though this was nearly twice the age of Caroline, she had remarked that men of thirty, and women of sixteen, are a kind of contemporaries.

Thus, forming the project of dancing every day, as soon as she should be the mistress of her own house, she ran to the garden to gather a nosegay. There, as she plucked the flowers, she saw several beautiful butterflies, wantoning from bud to bud; and, delighted with the restless vagrants, and their various hues and vivid tints, began, with ardour, to pursue them; till, somewhat heated and fatigued, without having had the good fortune to catch a single fugitive, she consoled herself with supposing the Count, more nimble and active than her, would catch them for her. "Besides," said she, skipping back towards the house, "we shall be very unfortunate, indeed, if we can't both of us entrap them."

The hour of dressing succeeded, and, while at her toilet, the idea of jewels, new dresses, equipage, balls, operas, and assemblies, presently made her forget the butterflies: for, with the lively, the innocent, and the happy Caroline, one pleasure came but to efface another.

"O yes," said she, "I well know Ambassadors ladies are invited every where, are dressed like Queens, and are envied by the whole world. Instead of simple flowers, I shall have clusters of diamonds adorning my hair; my dresses shall be all the most fanciful and elegant ever beheld, and I will put them on with a grace that shall charm every eye, and win every heart."

Thus, the conjugal felicity of Caroline, founded on dress, dancing, and butterflies, seemed to her the most certain of all certain things: she already beheld herself the happiest of women, employed every moment to embellish her person, and enchant her Ambassador, and expected him with an impatience unchecked by any fear, except that of not appearing sufficiently handsome in his eyes.

As for him, she was well assured he would please her infinitely: for, innocently thoughtless as she appeared, she still had her moments of reflection; and, all circumstances again and again considered, had fully persuaded herself the Count was the most charming man in the world.

He was the King's Favourite! Her father had told her so; and the word Favourite, was most extensive and significant to the imagination of Caroline. She, in the country, had likewise had her little court, and her little Favourites; there was her favourite bird, her favourite lap-dog, her favourite lamb, and these were all the prettiest creatures of their kind she had ever beheld; wherefore, there could be no doubt but the Favourite of a King must be the Phœnix of Nature.

Of all this she was so perfectly convinced, so happy, and so rejoiced to think she should see him, that, when her maid came to tell her he was come, and that her father was waiting for her, she made but one skip from the glass to the door; where, finding the High Chamberlain, who earnestly bade her remember her promise, he took her by the hand, which trembled with pleasure and emotion between his, and, exhorting her to be very prudent, and behave with great propriety, led her to the apartment in which was the Favourite of the King.

They entered, Caroline looked, and no sooner saw, than, instantly hiding her eyes with her hands, she gave a piercing shriek, and disappeared like a flash of lightning at midnight.

Now, while the father follows, while he employs the whole force of paternal eloquence to calm and make Caroline return, let us give the outline of the picture that thus had terrified; let us justify the young and innocent Caroline.

The Count of Walstein was, in fact, little more than thirty; but an enormous scar on one cheek, a countenance excessively meagre and of a livid yellow, round shoulders, and, instead of hair, a perriwig, made him appear at least fifty. His large black eye was fine; but, alas! it was single; he had but one, the other a bullet had extinguished. Nature designed him for a tall and well proportioned man, but a habit of stooping had prevented her intent. He had one very good leg; but this husband, who was to dance from morning to night, and aid Caroline to catch butterflies, walked with difficulty, and limped exceedingly on the other.

Such was the exterior appearance of Walstein, and we shall hereafter see how far the mind corresponded with the body: We have said enough, at present, to palliate the emotion and the flight of Caroline. Perhaps, we will not say but that, had she taken time to consider and examine, she might have found an air of grandeur, and a somewhat of benevolence, characterising this uncouth figure. But she saw only the scar, the one eye, the round shoulders, the perriwig, and the limping gait. She had received the first impression, and, almost fainting in her apartment, Caroline scarcely heard her father's menaces and prayers to return. Her only answer was a torrent of tears, and her struggles to overcome the shock rather increased than repelled her disorder.

Her father, finding it impossible she should appear again at present, left her, and went back to the Count. He reflected that this would even be the wisest course,[a] and that his daughter's sudden illness would be sufficient excuse.

He found his intended son-in-law exceedingly agitated at his reception, and too truly suspecting the motive. But the High Chamberlain was so eloquent, so persuasive, when he had any purpose to obtain, and his oratory was so powerful on the present occasion, that the Count was appeased; fully convinced that a violent head-ach, the consequence of the preparations of that busy day, which had suddenly seized Caroline, had been the sole occasion of her exclamation and her flight. It may be, even, that he feigned conviction. Who dare be responsible for courtiers? Historians, the most exact, by them may be deceived.

Be these things as they may, he took leave of the High Chamberlain, hoping to find the young lady recovered, and not liable to the same disorder, on the morrow; though, it is very certain, Walstein found himself a good deal affected by what had passed; not that we will suppose him in love with Caroline, whom he had scarcely seen, but that this marriage was in many respects exceedingly suitable to his wishes and his views; insomuch that he thought the future happiness of his life depended on it; not to mention the will and pleasure of the King. This latter might be as strong a reason for the Favourite as for the High Chamberlain; and the latter undoubtedly thought it irresistible. We must own he would have been wise to have pre-informed his daughter of the person of the Count. He felt all this, and deeply regretted his want of foresight, but it was too late. He imagined it best to extort a promise from which the timid Caroline would not dare recede.[b] Little had he foreseen the effect of the first interview, or the terror of Caroline, which was doubled by the imaginary and beautiful picture she had formed of the Count.

The moment he was alone, he returned, and found her just as he had left her. She had still, however, sufficient strength to fall at his feet and implore his mercy, conjuring him, by every tender appellation, not thus to sacrifice his child.

The High Chamberlain saw her emotion was too violent for her to hear reason at present.[c] We would not have the reader think it too strange, but he was even affected himself, raised her with tenderness, begged her to be calm, and to assure herself that her happiness was the utmost of his hopes, and that he would speak with her on the subject the next morning; and, again exhorting her to be tranquil, leave weeping, and go to rest, quitted her apartment.

The drowning wretch, 'tis said, will catch at straws. Caroline ardently seized this ray of hope, and her fears were almost hushed to peace. Ah! thought she, how good is my papa! How dearly he loves me! How desirous to see me happy!ᵃ— Surely, then, since it is his wish, he will not unite me to a monster who has but one eye, whose legs do not pair, who is hump-backed, and who wears a perriwig!

Caroline saw defects ten-fold defective; but such is the nature of youth; its propensities, its passions, its love, its friendship, its aversions are all extremes. At first she thought herself lost beyond recovery; at present she imagined herself freed, for ever, from the Count, and as suddenly recovered the gaiety that had so suddenly fled. Somewhat wearied, however, she went to bed, reflecting on the strange and singular taste of Kings in the choice of their Favourites, and protesting that, were she a Queen, Walstein never should be her's.

As sound was her sleep, and as gentle were her dreams, as if nothing had happened; and, when the morning appeared, no stronger impression remained than that which an ugly vision sometimes occasions. Presently her father entered, and found the same smile, the same sweetness, the same infantine graces with which he was daily received.ᵇ Nay, she was fonder, more attentive, more eager to oblige than usual; and thanks for his condescension, of which she entertained no doubt, were in every motion and in every look; though she dared not to retrace the past, her heart was all gratitude and joy for the future. Her father's behaviour increased it; for, instead of reproaches, his looks were all good nature, and kindness and smiles accompanied every expression.

Lovely girl! Sweet emblem of innocence, that, knowing not sorrow nor guile, knoweth not suspicion, enjoy the flattering illusion! Thou hast been but two months at court, and how shouldst thou be acquainted with the heart of a courtier? Thou, who art thyself all sensibility,[12] how shouldst thou suppose it shut to every tender feeling? Thou thinkest thou hast a father, a tender father; thou art to learn that he is only a Minister of State and a High Chamberlain!

Let us, however, be just: except his titles, his places, and his pensions, of all things in the world the Baron certainly loved his daughter the best. Not to mention that he really thought, for such was his manner of thinking, he was laying the foundation of her future happiness by so high an alliance. So magnificent a marriage! made immediately under the auspices of the King! and by order of the King! and to the Favourite of the King! and with the daughter of the High Chamberlain of the King!

Determined, therefore, to accomplish his purpose, by prayer or by power, he thought it best first to try how far affection and tenderness might win. Taking, therefore, his daughter's hands, and tenderly clasping them between his own—

"Caroline," said he, "dost thou love thy father?"

"Do I love him?" replied she, falling with enthusiasm on her knees, and kissing his hands, "Let him only permit me to live with him, and for him, and he shall then find how much Gratitude, Respect, and Filial-affection can perform!"

"Of all these I have no doubt: but thou wilt give me a farther proof?"

"Any! every! all you can desire, my dear, dear papa! except—

She was going to add, "marry the Count;" but the Baron, assuming a momentary and paternal austerity, put his hand upon her mouth.

"No exceptions, Caroline; and the first proof of love I shall ask will be to listen to me, silently and attentively.

"What wouldst thou do, my child?" (The Baron changed his countenance; it was, now, all sentiment; it was an appeal to the best affections of the heart.) "What wouldst thou do, Caroline, if the life of thy father were in thy hands?"

"His life! The life of my father! Save, preserve, cherish it, at the expence of my own. Can my father doubt it? But how —Wherefore my"—

"I expected no less, my dear girl," replied the Baron, taking care to stop her in due time; "and thou thyself shalt now decide between us.—Yes, my life, my very life depends upon the alliance. Think not I would survive my disgrace! and, unless my engagements with the Count of Walstein are fulfilled, that is inevitable!—Terrified by thy repugnance for this marriage, yesterday, I left thee, went instantly to the King, and threw myself at my Sovereign's feet, entreating, and even imploring him, to restore us our promise and our freedom. Thus daring had my affection for thee, Caroline, made me.

"'Your daughter is a child,' said the frowning monarch; 'a baby, who knows not what pleases or what is proper, and with whom you ought to act according to your own prudence, not her caprice. You *may*, however, act as you please. If she persist in this her refusal, you will re-conduct her to her country retreat; and you will, likewise, remain there yourself. It is impossible so feeble a father can be a good Minister of State.'

"He turned away, and spoke no more to me during the whole evening. Imagine, Caroline, what are my present feelings! I saw the malicious joy of my enemies, they had marked my Sovereign's frowns, and, with the smile of malignity, prophesied my approaching fall, disposed of my places, and, imitating their master, scornfully turned from me. Oh my child! my Caroline! wilt thou, the darling of thy father's heart, be the cause of this his misery? What talk I of misery! His certain, his instantaneous death!"

The trembling, the tender, the affectionate Caroline, a thousand times more terrified by this idea than she even had been by the aspect of Walstein, shuddering, flung herself into her father's arms.

"I will obey, I will obey," repeated she, sobbing. "Lead me to the altar this moment; lead me, if so it must be! Cause your death! I! God of Heaven forbid! Oh! my father, go immediately, tell the King to dispose of me as he pleases; only let him restore his favour and friendship to my father. Yes, I promise, solemnly promise, to submit to his will; but do thou, also, my father, promise me not to die."

So strongly had the idea of her father's death seized upon her imagination that she feared lest a moment's delay might make it certain. She would willingly have gone, even herself, and told the Count she was ready to be his; and ceased not to intercede with the Baron to depart, instantly, to the King; again engaging herself, by promises the most positive and unlimited, to be in all things obedient.

Once more left alone, she thought no more of court balls, cotillions, or chasing butterflies. With one hand hiding her eyes, mournfully resting upon her elbow, and agitated by a thousand struggling sensations, she remained motionless, incoherently dreading lest the least change or movement might precipitate her into the gulph that seemed gaping to receive her, and in which she were then eternally sunk. Filial affection, at length, came to her aid. Once more erect she sat, with self-approbation raised, when she recollected that, by suffering herself, she should save her father. "I shall preserve his honour, and, with his honour, his life," said she, with affection and admiration mingled: her own heroism inspired the latter; and which a sentiment so virtuous ever must inspire in a noble mind.

"Yet how dear must I pay for this!" continued she, "and what shall my life be?"

Strait the image and figure of the Count presented itself, and the father vanished. Caroline, shuddering, recoiled, and doubted whether yet she should keep her word.

In this attitude, in this agitation, she continued, when her father suddenly returned. Joy excessive brightened in his countenance. Scarcely could he tell, so out of breath with haste and transported was he, that the King himself and the Count were coming. "Yes, the King! the King in person!" repeated he, "publicly coming! and those who yesterday rejoiced at my disgrace, may now retire and weep. May their own envy be their only comforter. See, my Caroline, my child, my darling, what obedience is, and imagine what shall be its reward."

Caroline, alas! thought not of rewards, but of punishments, and of the confirmation of the fearful sentence she herself had pronounced. Her father reproved her for not having employed the time of his absence at her toilette. The day before, she herself would have been very sorry to have been caught by Majesty in her present dishabille; but, at present, this was become a trifle beneath thought; and she waited, in expectation of her august visitor, without once casting a look towards the glass.

The Baron was in his fourth repetition of the manner in which she should comport herself, when he was interrupted by the rattling of the coach wheels. Up he started, ran to receive Majesty, and left the trembling Caroline to the assistance of salts,[13] and as much fortitude as she herself could collect, for this interview of constraint and dread. The Monarch entered, followed only by his Favourite and his High Chamberlain, elate with joy, and inflated with self-applause.

"Beauteous Caroline," said the King, as he advanced and presented the Count, "be thou the recompence of the man who has rendered me so many important services; and do thou, dear Walstein, receive, from my hand, this lovely bride, whose worth, I am certain, thou wilt well know how to estimate."

The Count drew near, and, taking the half retiring hand of Caroline, begged her, with a low and timid accent, kindly to confirm his happiness.

Had the riches of the whole world, and all its Monarchs, been prostrate at the feet of Caroline, she could not have articulated a single word. Perhaps, had she raised her downcast eyes, and looked at the bridegroom, she might have had sufficient power to have said no. But this she very prudently avoided. She made a most respectful courtesy, and, at the King's desire, sat down in silence. This command was well timed; had she been longer required to stand, the scene of over-night might again have been repeated. A universal tremor had come over her; she was obliged to have recourse to her salts, and might still, perhaps, have betrayed her feelings by a fainting fit, or a deluge of tears, had not a glance of her father, himself almost fainting at seeing her agitation, restored her all her fortitude: she even forced a smile, to quiet his fears, and collected the resolution to answer the King's condescending interrogation, by saying, she was very well. Every thing was then placed to the account of country education and virgin timidity.

She hoped the company would retire, or, at least, change the subject of conversation; but she was deceived. To respect the feelings of their subjects is one of those things that Kings understand the least; and his Prussian Majesty, delighted with the marriage he himself had made, could talk of nothing else. Totally inattentive to the suffering Caroline, he dwelt circumstantially on particulars, first naming the day, then the hour, and then the place of performing the ceremony.

Unable to support this any longer, Caroline, at length, made another effort, and begged permission to retire. Her prayer was granted, and the Monarch did not neglect, as she made her reverence, to salute her by the title of the Countess of Walstein.

The youthful and wretched Countess, alone in her apartment, gave a full flow to affliction. Finding, however, that tormenting reflection could not change her destiny, *that* now being fixed beyond the power of reprieve, she wisely concluded submission was her only course; and to take such advantage as her present situation might afford her best expedient.

Let no one be astonished to hear that a young girl of sixteen could reason thus prudently. Misfortune is a most able master, and a few hours of affliction, trouble, and terror, had taught Caroline more than years of tranquility. She heard the coach of the King depart with much less emotion than she felt at its thundering approach; and her father had the satisfaction to find her tolerably calm and resigned,[a] when he came to acquaint her with the royal arrangements.

The marriage was fixed for that day week; the Count had desired it might be as secret as possible, and celebrated at his country seat, six leagues from Berlin[14]; and, moreover, that the rejoicings, visits, bride-favours, and presentation of the Countess at court, should not take place till the ceremony was over.

Caroline highly approved the Count's plan, and begged her father's permission to pass the intervening time in retirement. So well pleased was the Baron with her docility that, except breaking off the marriage, there was nothing she could have asked he would have refused; he therefore promised, and kept his word. Her solitude was uninterrupted, except by a few visits from the bridegroom; and him the Baron undertook to hold in conversation. Thus, while they were deep in politics, debating on matters of high moment, States, Empires, and Kings, Caroline was silently determining to execute the projects she had formed.

We shall not follow her through the many and melancholy ideas which occupied her mind, during this penitential week; it is sufficient for us to observe that she might, truly, be said to have thought more, in that space of time, than she had done in the whole course of her life. With the result of all this thinking we shall presently become acquainted.

Time passes away as well in pleasure as in pain. Behold then the redoubted day, on which the fate of Caroline was irrevocably to be fixed. She was prepared for it, and appeared perfectly resigned. Her father was in extacies, for he was now at the height of all his happiness and honours. Majesty, in person, intended to accompany his daughter to the altar. The High Chamberlain, good man, would have been happy to have had the whole world spectators; but two Lords of the court, and their wives, were, alone, appointed assistants. He consoled himself, however, with the idea of the many fine things he should have to relate on his return to Berlin. Off they set, for the country seat of the Count, and the tender bride, more thoughtful than melancholy, not only supported the jaunt exceedingly well,[a] but even the marriage ceremony, which was immediately performed on their arrival: the Baron, wondering at, and blessing himself for, the dexterity and address with which he had insured the obedience of Caroline, had, at length, the inexpressible gratification of presenting her to the King by the title of the *Countess of Walstein!*

This was the only moment in which the fortitude of Caroline had nearly forsaken her. Affected, agitated, by the caresses of the High Chamberlain, who was unbounded in his panegyric, she owned she deserved not all this praise, and earnestly supplicated him to spare her. Caroline had a delicate heart, to which every praise the Baron bestowed added a fresh pang.[b]

They were to return that evening to Berlin, there to install the young Countess in her new dignity, as Lady of Walstein House; and they were already preparing to depart, when, taking advantage of the moment when the Count was standing alone, concealed by the projecting of the window, she went up to him, presented a paper, entreated him to read it with indulgence, and went into an anti-chamber, where, she told him, she would wait for his answer, and his orders. Surprised as much as man could possibly be, the Count instantly opened the letter, and read as follows:[c]

"My lord,

"I have obeyed. The absolute commands of my father and my King have given me to you, and your's at present I am; wholly your's; I acknowledge no other master. You only have the right to dispose of me, and from you I dare expect and hope benevolence,[d] indulgence, and generosity. Yes, it is from him who just has sworn to make me happy, I now presume to ask what may ascertain my happiness, and, no doubt, his own. You know not, my lord, cannot imagine, how much the young creature, to whom you but this instant gave your hand, is unworthy of that honour; how little reasonable she is, and how much a child; how much it behoves her to pass whole years in that retreat where she has been educated, and with that dear friend who has been to her a mother. Oh, consent! I conjure you in mercy to consent and suffer me this evening to return to Rindaw; there to wait till my reason has so far conquered prejudice that I may submit, without expiring, to the engagements I have formed. By doing this, you will inspire gratitude inexpressible,[a] and, perhaps, accelerate that event. Your refusal, on the contrary–Yes, be certain, your refusal will equally, and for ever, deprive you of the wretched Caroline.

"I feel, most forcibly, the just reproaches you have a right to make me.[b] This letter should not have been sent now; but, had I explained what my sensations were before our union, I should have hazarded the life of my father: at present I only hazard my own. He swore, solemnly swore, he could not survive his disgrace; and his disgrace was inevitable if I did not become your's. Your's, therefore I am, and the King now will rest satisfied; for I dare hope that, should he make my father responsible for my conduct, and should this conduct offend him, you will have the justice to save my father, and inform him that I, alone, am culpable. But certainly the King cannot complain of his want of zeal, or the unlimited obedience with which he is devoted to his will; neither will I complain, if you, only, will have the goodness to grant my present request."

This letter, the offspring of a hundred, which had been written and torn during the preceding week, had been finished that very morning before they left Berlin. If ever man was astonished, confounded, thunder-struck, it was the Count of Walstein. He could not believe what he beheld. What! a young creature so timid, and so submissive! Had she a will of her own? And could she declare what that will was with fortitude like this?

Again he read the paper, and pity presently succeeded to surprize. He then saw she had been the sacrifice of despotism and ambition; and mortally reproached himself for being the object and the cause. Though we all may be somewhat deceived respecting our own personal attractions, and though the Count, like others, might not be wholly exempt from self-illusion, he still did himself the justice to imagine he certainly had not been married for his beauty; but, from the positive assurances of the High Chamberlain, and the apparent resignation of Caroline, he supposed, at least, it had been without repugnance, and without constraint. The moment that undeceived him, or, rather, that told him he had been deceived, was, no doubt, to him a dreadful one; but he did not hesitate an instant concerning how it was proper for him now to act. Desirous to relieve Caroline from her fears, he, with his pencil, wrote thus on the cover of her letter.

"Lovely and unfortunate victim of obedience; you, in your turn, shall be obeyed. Instantly I will go and obtain the King's compliance with your request; instantly will repair, as much as in me is possible, the wrong done you; the tyranny of which I am the cause, without being the accomplice. Should I be refused, depend on me for restoring you that liberty of which you have been so cruelly deprived. I feel the inestimable value of the confidence you place in me, and will endeavour to deserve it, by renouncing my own happiness! Though, not so; for still shall I be happy, if any conduct of mine can render me less odious to her by whom it would be felicity supreme to be"—

Beloved, Walstein would have added; but it was a moment of most trying affliction. A mirror was over the table at which he wrote;[a] he looked in it and durst not.[15] Half opening the door of the anti-chamber, where Caroline waited the sentence of life or death, he gave in his short answer, which she tremblingly received, and instantly disappeared.

The first sensation of Caroline, when she attempted to read, was dread; but this, as she proceeded, was presently dissipated, and when she had ended she was so surprised, so affected, so grateful, that she had almost an inclination to recall the Count; but, unfortunately for him, as she looked through the window, she saw him walking in the gardens with the King. Walking and broad daylight are little favourable to a man who limps in his gait, and whose face has been disfigured by wounds.[b] Could she have read his billet, and forgot his person, the effect would have been different; her favourable ideas would not have been so easily effaced, nor would she, so instantly, again have felt that impatient desire of returning to her former retreat. Besides, indeed, she recollected it was too late; that she had gone too far to recede, without appearing capricious and weak. While thus she reflected, still looking through the window at the Count, his billet crumbled away between her fingers, and, like the impression it had made, was no more.

While Caroline was thus employed, the generous Walstein was using all his influence with the King, over whose mind he had a wonderful ascendancy, persuading him to consent to the request she had made. He shewed his Majesty the letter, who, instead of anger, found himself interested and affected by the stile and resolution of a girl so innocent and so young.

"There is energy in this young lady's character," said the Monarch, as he ended, and looking at the Count as he returned the letter.

He looked, and could not help acknowledging that his Favourite did not, altogether, possess that kind of form which the hoping fancy of sixteen loves to contemplate. The recollection came a little too late, but the moment was favourable to Caroline, and he added—

"You are right, Walstein. You must overlook this whim. She is a child, whom it will be best to indulge. She will soon be tired of her retreat; and as to the thing essential, the fortune, it is your's. A man has always enough of his wife's company."

The Monarch was frank; but, state secrets excepted, Monarchs take little trouble to disguise their thoughts.[16] Accordingly, the sentence pronounced, the High Chamberlain was sent for, this new project communicated, and his daughter's letter shewn. He was, certainly, in a very high passion, but the presence of Majesty made him, apparently, somewhat calm; and, after hazarding a few objections, which were silenced, he was all acquiescence. The King, indeed, who had never before seen him of a different opinion, thought it exceedingly strange, and, likewise, somewhat presuming, he should be so at present; which thoughts he did not take the least trouble to conceal. Whereupon the High Chamberlain, a little affrighted, made a most profound and reverential bow, supplicated pardon, and begged his Majesty would dispose of his daughter just as his Majesty should please.

The conclusion of this consultation was that Caroline should return, that very evening, to Rindaw; where the Baroness and Canoness of that name, by whom she had been educated, lived. Here she had permission to remain as long as she pleased, concluding she would soon be glad to return. A clause was, indeed, annexed, which seemed to render a long stay impossible; and this was that the most profound and absolute secresy must be kept concerning the marriage. The King did not give his reasons; indeed, Reason to Kings is a superfluous thing, Will is sufficient.[17] It has, moreover, been said, he was fearful lest this history should cast some kind of ridicule either upon his High Chamberlain, or his Favourite, or, perhaps, even upon himself; but, we must own, this assertion is too improbable to be true.

Leave we these matters in the uncertainty in which we found them, and let us add that it was his Majesty's command Caroline should still pass by her own name, and that no individual should know she was the Countess of Walstein. He went so far as to declare that, the moment the least breath transpired, she should again become subject to conjugal power, and that her indiscretion should ensure the loss of his favour. All this he said, looking stedfastly at the High Chamberlain, who could not get the words out fast enough to inform his Majesty of the eternal silence he himself should keep.

The King, likewise, pressingly recommended secresy to those who had been present at the ceremony; who readily promised obedience, and who really did not tell it—to above some thirty of their friends; and that under the most solemn promises it should go no further. Ah, happy Berlin! that thus, for a whole week, was plentifully supplied with behind-fan whispers and corner conversations!— "Do *you* know that Count Walstein has married the High Chamberlain's daughter!—Is it possible?—Oh! the King himself was present!—Indeed!— Fact, I assure you! I had it from the first hand; but don't mention it; don't let my name appear," &c. &c.

Thus ran Rumour, or rather, thus she flew; but as there was no farther confirmation of these whisperings, as Caroline did not appear, as the Count returned quietly on his embassy to Russia, as the High Chamberlain was discreet, and as, moreover, new secrets made the old forgotten, it was, at length, either not believed or not remembered.

Behold, then, the nuptial day concluded in a very different manner from what might have been imagined. The Baron was required to inform his daughter that her request was granted, and that she had leave to live retired at Rindaw. He was, likewise, to have conducted her thither himself, but Walstein, fearing he should vent upon her that wrath which had been so much curbed by the King, was desirous to bereave his young bride of so disagreeable a travelling companion. He, therefore, easily persuaded his dear father-in-law that it was most essential to his interest not to leave the Court, in this critical conjuncture; and, as the High Chamberlain had not the same taste for retirement with his daughter, he thought proper to confide her to the care of trusty servants, and to send a letter by her to his dear friend the Baroness and Canoness, for she was both, of Rindaw.

This Canoness, with whom we shall soon become acquainted, was a most excellent lady, in her way.[18] She had formerly been deeply in love with the High Chamberlain, who, likewise, had himself been as much in love with her as it was possible for him to be; but reasons of convenience, wealth and ambition, ever decisive with the High Chamberlain, had determined him to marry the mother of Caroline. The affectionate, the tender, and constant Baroness, thus crossed in love, had vowed celibacy, became a Canoness, retired totally from the fashionable world, and lived privately at her chateau. To meditate on her perfidious High Chamberlain, renew her vows of eternal fidelity, read novels and romances from morning till night, imagine parallels between herself and the heroine of the tale, and to saunter in her gardens, and muse for hours in lonely arbours, had been her mode of life for several years.[19] This passion, so strong, might be said, at last, to perish of inanity and want of food.[20] Therefore, when her dear High Chamberlain, become a widower, offered to recompence her constancy by marriage, she was prudent enough to refuse, alledging she had totally lost the habits of high life, and all relish for courts; which, indeed, was very true, but, pleased with the proposal, she promised eternal friendship, offered to take his daughter under her care, and educate her till the time of her marriage. We have before seen the motives which determined the Baron to accept this offer, and the rather, modestly added he, because he really understood nothing of the education of a daughter.[a]

It may be presumed, our romantic Baroness understood, perhaps, as little as himself of the matter; but, a few ridiculous singularities excepted,[b] she did not want understanding, and was really, and earnestly, desirous to fulfil the duty she had undertaken. She had read much, had addicted herself to various useful studies, and had become very capable of instructing her pupil, of forming her heart and mind.

Some remains, we own, there were of ancient habitudes; of a sentimental and Quixote imagination:[21] and this was the more pleasant by being a singular contrast to her natural character, which was Indiscretion personified; though she had an inexhaustible goodness of heart. But it has been remarked that these two qualities are very frequently companions, and the Canoness was an instance of its truth. She was so frank, so unsuspicious, so confiding, and loved so much to talk, that it was not possible for her to keep a secret above half an hour. And, as for friends, every person she saw instantly became her dearest intimate.[a]

Her reputation was so well known, even at court, and her indiscretions so indubitable, that there was an absolute prohibition laid on Caroline not to tell her the secret, as well as on the High Chamberlain. Caroline, who dreaded daily remonstrances and persecutions, was happy at the interdict.

The obedient Baron, ever submissive to his Master's will, wrote, by his order, to the Canoness, that, the projected marriage of his daughter being deferred for some time, he again confided her to the care of his dear friend, the Baroness.

Caroline, provided with this letter, took leave of her father kneeling for pardon and benediction. The High Chamberlain, well satisfied High Chamberlain to remain, granted both the one and the other with a tenderness that did not come truly from the heart. He saw her depart for Rindaw, which was only seven or eight leagues thence, and, soon after, returned himself to Berlin, with the King and the Ambassador.

Caroline could not help being somewhat surprised, at first, at seeing herself alone in one of the Count's carriages. Affected by her father's farewell and the quick succession of events, it would be difficult to describe exactly what passed in her mind; all there was tumult and disorder, and she herself knew not whether it were better to rejoice or weep:[b] all things had happened as she herself had desired; but, perhaps, though she did not confess that to herself, she expected to meet with more resistance; and Caroline was not the only person to whom the facility of obtaining a blessing has diminished its value.

Perhaps, too, her self-love, or her vanity, if any such quality could reside in a breast so pure,[22] would have been more flattered, had a greater desire to detain her been demonstrated. "Here I am," said she to herself, (and with a small tincture of sorrow was it said) "Here I am, all alone, left by myself; I said but a word, and my father, the King, and the Count, all three are agreed I may go as soon as I please. Is this indifference, anger, or generosity?"

In the midst of these meditations she recollected the short billet she had torn, and endeavoured again to recall every expression, and every word. She saw the action of the Count, at last, in the most amiable, the most generous point of view; a tear started into her eye, and she sighed, and said, what a pity it is he should not be handsome!

Her thoughts, mingled with regret, turned, occasionally, towards her father also, whom she had forsaken, whom she had afflicted, and a little, likewise, on the pleasures she had abandoned, and the sounding titles she might have borne. My Lady, the Countess of Walstein! The Russian Ambassador's Lady! The Lady of the Favourite of the King! All these she might have been: she was simply Caroline. At certain moments her head was half out of the coach to bid them drive back to Berlin; but these might be called moments of forgetfulness; the image of the Count returned, presented itself, she shrunk back, hid herself in the corner, and congratulated herself on her escape. "No, it is impossible," said she, "it is impossible I ever could support it! I should die with apprehension: and to see him every day, and all the day, and all the night! Oh! no, it is impossible! Then did she applaud her fortitude, and the manner in which she had fulfilled her duty, saved her father's life, and preserved her liberty.

With these ideas, and such as these, was her full heart occupied for two thirds of the rout; but the nearer she approached to Rindaw the feebler grew her regret; she, presently, thought only of the pleasure of again seeing her dear Mamma, for thus she called the Canoness, who, really, to her, had been a mother, and a tender mother.

This Lady idolized her pupil, and seemed to have transferred the tender affection she once felt for the father to the child. When the Baron had come for Caroline, and had told the Canoness his intention to marry her, so great was her despair, and so violent the efforts of separation, that her health was injured; she had been ill ever since; mirth, pleasure, happiness fled with Caroline. Farmers, peasants, servants, the whole village, whose darling and friend she was, ceased not to speak of her, to sigh for her, and to say they had lost their angel and their protector.

Imagine, then, what was the joy of all these good people, when, one evening, by the clear light of the moon, a coach drove through the village; a thing that seldom happened, at Rindaw, and stopped at the chateau, and as it stopped, and as the eager inhabitants crouded to see what and who it was, Caroline, their beloved, their adored Caroline, appeared. Enraptured to behold her, for the smile and the flush of joy on Caroline's countenance acted with sympathetic magic on them all, they knew not what to say, how to testify their feelings.

"Are not you glad, my dear friends," said she, "that I am come again to live among you; again am one of yourselves? Are you not glad to see me once more?"

Eager Enthusiasm and tumultuous Rapture spoke, but they spoke in confusion, and their cries reaching the ear of the Canoness, she ran out to see what all this noise meant. She ran and she beheld—Yes, it was Caroline—Her beloved! Her child! Her darling! she was in her arms, and the sweet tears of sensibility, unrestrained, flowed plenteously.

"Mama! Mama! My dear mama, your happy Caroline is returned, never to leave you more!"

The Canoness was the daughter of Sensibility: her frame was slender, her habit sickly, and her nerves delicate. Caroline was alarmed to see her so much affected, her joy amounted almost to suffocation; but the effects of joy are not often fatal.[23] She recovered, by degrees, and began to enquire of her beloved pupil what enchantment had conveyed her thither. Caroline, without further explanation, gave her the letter of the High Chamberlain; she read it, and wanted further information concerning this marriage deferred just at the moment of its conclusion.

"The last post," said the Baroness, "brought me a letter from thy father, which informed me the day was fixed—The day fixed!—Yes, it was this very day, I believe—Let me see—Yes, it was this very day—This is very strange!—I declare it is the most singular adventure I ever heard of, and I delight in singular adventures—Tell me, tell me the whole, how was it?—Thou knowest thou mayest rely on my prudence, I'll not say a word; if there is any secret in the affair, depend upon me."—Caroline knew just the contrary, yet was she obliged to use considerable effort over herself, not to tell her dear friend every thing she thought, who, till then, had ever been the partner of all her joys and griefs; her innocent heart, unaccustomed to dissemble, ill could perform the task, and, had it not been for the severe, the absolute prohibition imposed upon her, and the fearful condition annexed to her imprudence, she certainly had told all.

To come as near the truth, however, as possible, for falsehood and Caroline were natural foes,[24] she confessed that she herself was the cause of delay, that she could not endure the deformity of the Count, for which reason, said she, "they have granted me a respite, but I am certain I shall never change."

She then, by way of excuse, gave her friend a portrait of Walstein, which she certainly did not greatly embellish.[a] The Baroness scarcely could let her finish, so highly was she provoked that they should ever once think of marrying her sweet Caroline to such a monster.

"The High Chamberlain has certainly lost his understanding!" said she, "But be comforted, my dear child, thou knowest I have some ascendancy over him, and either this ascendancy is entirely gone, or this absurd marriage never shall take place. I give thee my promise, depend upon me, make thyself easy, thou never shalt be Countess of Walstein. The wife of the lame and the blind! What, thou! No, no, we will find as good a husband as he who shall be able to see thy beauty with both eyes; aye, and they shall be fine eyes too, and I warrant thee he shall walk upright. A charming spouse they had chosen thee, truly! It was just the same with me, when I was thy age; I must be married without ever being consulted; but they were mistaken; I saw my gentleman squinted most frightfully, and never would hear another word on the subject. I own, I loved thy father to distraction at that time, and there is nothing inspires fortitude like love. My grand system is that young people should be most passionately enamoured with each other before they marry, for what else can make us support the duties, fatigues, and pangs of the marriage state? Yes, my child, marriages of pure passion are the only happy marriages; for which reason, I refused all other: and though I likewise refused to marry the High Chamberlain, after thy mother's death, it was in support of my system, and because I felt I had only a tender friendship and not a passionate affection for him, which is so essential to happiness. Love, love, mutual love, 'tis that, that makes the house of Hymen the house of joy."[25]

Caroline, embarrassed, and burthened with her secret, with downcast eyes, silently listened to this inundation of words, and the happy Canoness, who for three months past had been deprived of the pleasure of speaking at her ease, took ample revenge, and did not wait for an answer; she only paused a moment for breath, and then, with an air of penetration in her eye, thus continued:

"But I believe, my child, it is not love that gave thee this fortitude and this resistance—Is it?—Tell me, make me thy confidante, come, own thou hast seen some one who has found the way to please thee better than the Count."

"Alas!" replied Caroline, with innocent simplicity, "all men can please me better than the Count."

"All! that is saying a great deal, indeed. But didst thou never distinguish any one in particular? Hast thou never seen the man for whom thou wouldst wish to live, and with whom thou wouldst wish to die? Has no one yet found a place in thy heart?"

"No, indeed, mama," said Caroline, sighing, "I am in love with nobody nor is any body in love with me."

"Well, that is very singular! There are certainly, then, no longer men so handsome as thy father at court. But have patience, my dear, all in good time, the man will be found, I warrant; as for this Count, never let me hear his name mentioned, for thou never shalt be his wife, that I am determined."

The poor young Countess again replied only with a sigh, kissed her dear mama, said her friendship was all she asked, and retired to her old apartment to repose after the fatigues of a very trying day.

In the morning she awoke, looked round, and scarcely knew where or what she was. "Good God!" said she, collecting her ideas, "Is it true, or is it a dream? Am I a wife? Is my faith plighted, my hands chained, never more to be free? Do I but enjoy the shadow of a liberty of which the very next moment I may be deprived, and for which I am indebted to the generosity, only, of him to whom I appertain? Appertain! Do I then appertain to some one, and have I for ever lost the hope of disposing of myself!"

Not all the flow of spirits natural to her age, not all that sweetness and happiness of temper natural to herself,[26] could, for some time, banish this corroding idea from her mind: it empoisoned her pleasures, it robbed her of that gaiety and those enlivening graces with her, formerly, so habitual. The indulgent Canoness, attributing her melancholy to the privation of town pleasures, feigned not to perceive it, and redoubled her cares and caresses to make her retreat supportable. Not only the Canoness, but the servants, individually, and even the very animals, testified their joy at the return of their Favourite, and the reciprocal attachment they felt for her who had so often felt for them. The tender heart of Caroline was the very opposite to insensible, and the secret charm which fancy affixes to those haunts in which the sports of childhood have past, added to the soft delight of being beloved by every person around her, soon had their usual effect, she fell into her former habits, and her daily occupations became as pleasant, now, as before her residence at Berlin. Her flower garden, neglected while she was absent, again flourished under her eye, and was enamelled with a thousand various buds and ten thousand tints and dyes. Again her aviary was re-peopled, and the new-mown hay, the yellow harvest, the distant mountains covered with flocks of sheep, the browsing cattle, the sports of the green, and the rustic flageolet[27] amused and delighted her as much as ere she had seen the spectacles of Luxury and the feasts of Pride.[28] These far fetched pleasures had been but momentary, and had rather dazzled than intoxicated, while those of Nature, simple but real, and always preferred by the unadulterated heart and the elevated mind, ever various and ever sublime, are beheld without weariness, and enjoyed without self-detestation.

She seldom heard from Berlin. Her father, whose cherished anger was only smothered, and who was, besides, totally occupied by his court dignities and state employments, seldom wrote, and her husband never. The High Chamberlain had another motive, indeed, for his silence; he hoped dulness would soon make her tired of her retreat; and Walstein, remembering only how much pain it must cost her to reply, was silent lest he should distress. Neither did he well know in what manner to treat a lady so young, whom he knew not, by whom he was unknown, and who, he might well suppose, thought him little less than an odious tyrant. Hoping every thing, therefore, from time and maturity of reason, he patiently waited their effects, and returned to Petersburgh and his duty. There, multiplicity of business and affairs of great importance, occupied him so entirely, that we will not pretend to affirm he did not think the caprice of his young bride a very unfortunate one,[a] since, without laying a constraint on her inclinations, it placed her in that kind of retreat, during his absence, which he himself would most have desired without, perhaps, daring to ask.

The result of all this was, that Caroline had scarcely remained three months at Rindaw before all that had passed appeared but as a dream which she scarcely could, and never wished, perfectly to recollect. She was even careful to banish all ideas from her mind that were any way relative to the Count, and no one sought to make her remember them.

Her friend, perceiving that at the very name of Walstein her countenance was clouded and her mind disturbed, was careful never to pronounce it, and thus, at length, was this union so far effaced from her mind that, had any one asked her if she was married, the probabilities were that she would, in the first moment of forgetfulness, very sincerely, have answered no.

None of the ideas she brought from court remained, except an earnest desire of becoming equal in knowledge, and in grace, to some few distinguished ladies she had there beheld; and to effect these purposes the winter was employed in music, drawing, the study of English and Italian, for the French she had already been taught. In these, by the help of good masters, she made great progress. Undisturbed by passion, much time, a strong desire for instruction, an unincumbered memory, and a genius of the first order,[29] were advantages by which she profited surprisingly. Reading was not neglected, and her natural good taste led her to a proper choice of books. Her person kept pace with her mind, and advanced to angelic perfection. Each succeeding day seemed to bestow some new grace, and, all beautiful as she was one month, she was evidently more beautiful the next. She grew taller, and her shape was so fine, each limb and feature so proportionate, her colour was so blooming, the white so pure, the red so transparent, her eyes so mild, so large, so expressive, so innocent and yet so animated, that it was a delight to look upon her. Virgin timidity she had, but no ill-timed bashfulness that makes even the form of beauty unmeaning: if the sympathetic tale of feeling were told, the precious pearls of sensibility would brighten in her eve, and fall on her cheek; and if the poet, with sublime hand, touched the lyre, genius would instantly rush on her imagination, animate her form, and illuminate her countenance.[30]

Her voice too she learnt to modulate, and it acquired a sweetness and flexibility that, when she sang to the harp, or Spanish guitar, it was not possible to resist those mild emotions, those delicious sensations, which she so well could feel, and so powerfully inspire.

To these, her talents, her graces, and her gifts, she added another; which, though perhaps not so esteemed, is still more uncommon, and not less captivating. There was an elegant simplicity and an air of dignity in her dress that seemed to make grace itself more graceful. These, added to her bright auburn ringlets, profuse in growth and flowing on her neck and shoulders, made her a creature such as the imagination scarcely can conceive, and such as tongue, or pen, must never hope to describe.[31]

Yes, such, and still more beauteous, was Caroline, at sixteen, while all these blooming sweets seemed doomed to wither in the desart air, unseen, except by the homely village swains, unadmired, except by the good Canoness.

She, it is true, was all extacy, and never ceased regretting the happy times of knighthood and enamoured chevaliers, when Caroline would have, undoubtedly, been the paragon of courts, the arbitress of tilts and tournaments, and the reward of valour that never had been equalled. How often did she vow, as she beheld her, silently appealing to every sacred power, that the Count of Walstein never should be master of such a profusion of charms! How unappeasable, how enraged, how furious would she have been, had she known she was already his, and that Caroline was thus improving, thus embellishing, for him alone! A Prince, at least, she deserved, but, might the Canoness have chosen, it should have been a husband of romance, beauteous as Astolpho,[32] faithful as Amadis,[33] and tender as Celadon:[34] neither could she help being astonished to find that they did not come in crouds to Rindaw, to dispute the hand of the lovely Caroline.

As to Caroline herself, she was astonished at none of these things, and only desired to remain as she was.[a] Ever peaceable, and ever busy, happiness seemed incapable of increase, except that, sometimes, when she was alone, and even in the midst of those occupations she most delighted in, she would feel a kind of mild melancholy come over her, or rather a dream, a revery without subject, and without end, of which she knew not nor sought the cause. This was a very different kind of sensation from that which her marriage had occasioned;[b] the one was painful and oppressive, the other so pleasant that, were it not for the efforts she occasionally made, she could have remained whole hours in that kind of gentle trance which the guests of heaven only are supposed perfectly to enjoy.[35]

In these happy occupations and still happier dreams did winter glide away, for nothing makes time so short as employing it well; and the return of spring began to add to her pleasures, which, however, were cruelly interrupted. Her good mama, who so long had been languishing, at last, fell dangerously ill. To know how sincerely she was attached to the Canoness, to express the greatness of her fears, and to imagine all the duties, cares, and attentions she paid her, one must have the heart of Caroline. During her illness, which lasted almost a month, she never quitted her bedside, and it was with difficulty they could get her to repose a little while, occasionally, in the same chamber. Let no one imagine that the fear of again falling into her father's or her husband's power, if her friend should die, occasioned this severe grief. No, however natural such a thought might be,[c] it never once entered her mind. Harrassed by apprehension, absorbed in sorrow, wholly occupied by nursing, and solacing, and fearing for her friend, Caroline never once thought of herself.

No; had it been necessary to restore life to the Canoness, that Caroline must have yielded her's to the Count, she would not have hesitated a single instant. But, happily, to this cruel proof she was not put. Heaven, touched by her tears, attentive to her prayers, which never saint offered more sincere, preserved the life of her friend; the good Canoness recovered by degrees, to which recovery the tenderness of Caroline did not, perhaps, contribute less than the prescriptions of the physician; at least, so the Canoness thought, and so said, and therefore redoubled, if it were possible, her former attachment to the lovely girl who gave such unequivocal proofs of affection.

During her illness she received a visit from the High Chamberlain. Alarmed, as he protested, at the danger of his dear friend, he had flown to Rindaw. Some people have pretended this was not his motive, but that he had hoped to take back his daughter, and with her own consent. Continually controverted in all his schemes, he, unfortunately, found the sick lady somewhat better, and the attentive Caroline never out of her sight, never leaving her for a moment, more powerfully fixed at Rindaw by her love for the Canoness than even by her fear of the Count. This, certainly, was not the time to mention returning, nor yet the place, wherefore not a hint was dropped, nor was the name of Walstein once pronounced, who was still at Petersburgh.

The Canoness, indeed, would have pronounced it if she could, that is, if she had been able to express all the indignation she felt at this marriage; but, alas! she was too weak, she only just told the High Chamberlain that his daughter was an angel, that her life was preserved by her affection and care, and that she would, therefore, consecrate her life to her happiness. The Baron soon departed, informing them he should pay them a second visit in autumn. It was then he expected the return of the Ambassador, and he told his daughter he hoped to find her perfectly reasonable and prudent.

At any other time a visit from her father would have most powerfully brought to mind what Caroline most wished to forget, but she was then too much occupied by her cares for her friend, and had lately been too much agitated concerning her to think of any thing else. Present danger effaces or, at least, enfeebles the fear of future, and Caroline was too happy to see the Canoness recovering to imagine she ever could be miserable.

Not but that, at the Baron's departure, the autumnal visit he announced with so much solemnity occasioned a kind of dread she could not overcome, and without remembering the emotion she might cause her convalescent, she fell on her neck, kissed her cheeks, bathed them with her tears, and exclaimed, "O my dear, dear mama, now you are restored to me, never will I leave you more, but live and die with you." Her friend, affected even to excess, returned her caresses, and promised that, if possible, they would never separate.

The fear of the moment over, peace again took possession of the soul of Caroline. She presently forgot the autumnal visit which was at so prodigious a distance. Is it for sixteen to fear a whole six months before it shall happen?[a] Not to mention that she had something else to do than think about any such thing. As soon as the Canoness was sufficiently recovered she ran, morning and evening, about the garden, from flower to flower and from arbour to arbour, enchanted and amazed at the progress which Nature had made during her month's retreat, that the sorrows of a suffering friend had not contributed to enliven. Never before had the return of spring made such an impression upon her: for, indeed, this was the first time of her life she had remarked and felt the growing charms of the reviving earth in all their infant varieties; then, when each returning day Nature assumes a newer, and still a fresher face; still bequeaths other, and more abundant, blessings to man; and, with her pure breath, inspires pleasure, plenty, and gladness of heart!

What a contrast, this, to the close chamber, the bed of pain, watered with tears, the distracting complaints of her dear friend, and the dread of being left desolate; for, if her friend died, who should comfort Caroline! Yes, these mournful objects, these fearful apprehensions were exchanged for the cowslip meadow, the budding grove, the lilac, the violet, honeysuckle, and the rose of May, to which succeeded the hiacinth, the ranunculus, the anemone, and the tulip, enamelling the earth and perfuming the air. At day-break was heard the warbling of ten thousand birds, and at the setting sun the nightingale and the linnet again began their song, responsive from tree to tree, in sounds melodious, wild, and sweet.

Nothing was indifferent to, nothing lost, nothing unobserved by, Caroline. She felt all, all enjoyed, enjoyed with rapture; believed she inhabited an enchanted world, and her happiness remained uninterrupted. The season, reviving to Nature, gave new life and health also to her friend, and she recovered rapidly. A weakness in the hams and a disorder of the eyes made her still keep her chamber, but she could breath the pure air of spring in the balcony; she could see her Caroline course along the gardens, collect the flowers, support those that drooped, and water and preserve them from weeds; she could hear her sweet voice mingle with the song of birds, and thus enjoyed the pleasures and the sports of Caroline.

Another very interesting incident was added to this rural happiness of the youthful Countess. She wished to raise some monument consecrated to her friend, and the happy epocha of her recovery. Desirous of causing an agreeable surprise, she took advantage of the time during which the Canoness was still held recluse in her chamber, to erect a small temple without her knowledge. For which reason, she chose her spot in an angle of the garden, and at the far end of it, towards which the windows of the Canoness did not look. On this spot was a wild irregular arbour, full in foliage. The beech tree, the hazle, the woodbine, and the jessamine, were there abundant; among them the path that led to the arbour winded, and beside them a small clear brook ran murmuring.

The Canoness had planted this arbour during the time her unfortunate passion was at its heighth; the name of the perfidious High Chamberlain had been traced on every tree by her beauteous hand; and she had always preserved her former predilection for this spot, the scene of her sorrows, her tenderness, and truth.

Caroline was pleased with it, likewise; the thick shrubs and uninterrupted security made it the delighted haunt of the red breast, the wren, the finch, and the linnet, and the Baroness and Caroline had, many a summer, passed delicious moments amid the refreshing foliage. At the farther end, therefore, of this favoured asylum did she resolve to erect the Temple of Friendship. Caroline informed her father, secretly, of her project, which he willingly forwarded by sending her the necessary workmen. A door which opened to the road gave them free egress and regress, without being perceived from the chateau, and Caroline was too great a favourite among the servants to fear their indiscretion. The Canoness, confined to her apartment, suspected nothing of all this; Caroline might, perhaps, have betrayed herself, had this happened six months sooner, but she had learned to keep one secret, and the second was certainly far less burthensome. Neither care, assiduity, nor money were wanting; her zeal communicated itself to the workmen; she furnished ideas, drew plans, and was always the first in the morning at the building, which went forward with excessive rapidity, and which was finished in less than a month.

As soon as the temple was ready for the reception of her friend she was most earnest in her entreaties to go there. "The air of your arbour, Mamma, is so cool, so refreshing, so pure, the foliage is so abundant, and the flowers so sweet, you will be delighted."

"I have no doubt of it, my dear, but thou knowest I cannot walk so far."

"If that be all, I will carry you thither myself, Mamma."

Caroline was so pressing, that the Canoness, who could deny her nothing, suffered herself, at last, to be carried in her arm-chair, and was well rewarded for her condescension, by the surprise, the pleasure, and the new mark of affection thus testified by her adopted daughter.

This little temple, or pavilion, was an octagon; the architecture was exceedingly simple. Eight columns of white stucco left an open space, which was paved, in Mosaic, with black and white marble. In the middle was an altar of white marble ornamented with festoons of most elegant sculpture; upon the altar stood a bust of the Canoness, modelled after an exceedingly good portrait in the possession of Caroline. In her youth she had been beautiful; and, when the High Chamberlain was her lover, he had more than one rival. It gave her pleasure often to remark that she was thought greatly to resemble the statue of Cleopatra. Though grief and years had stolen the roses from her cheeks, and destroyed somewhat of this resemblance, her features were still sufficiently regular for a very agreeable bust.

Caroline was very desirous of engraving some verses on the base of the altar, indicating to whom it was consecrated, but, as she determined not to borrow, it was necessary to write them herself, and, as the talent of poetry is not, however it may be supposed, intuitive, but requires long application and severe study before it can be good, Caroline was not a good poet.[36] She made the attempt, however, for when the feelings are strong and the ideas flowing in abundance, the expression of them seems, before trial, to be exceedingly easy; but, when the essay is made, is found to be exactly the reverse. Caroline wrote and effaced, interlined, tore, began again, and, at last, wrote some verses which might be, once, heard with pleasure, but which did not deserve to be engraved in marble. At first she was enchanted with them, but presently recoiled at recollecting they should always remain there, and would be read by every one. Renouncing poetical fame, therefore, she caused a simple inscription, in letters of gold, to be written, beneath the bust, indicating the day, the month, and the year in which the Canoness was snatched from the grave, herself restored to happiness, and this Temple dedicated to Friendship.

A double stair-case of white marble led to an upper apartment of the same dimensions and form with that beneath, that is to say octagonal, but walled in and lighted by four large windows. The cieling was a lofty dome, painted with such art that it perfectly imitated a most serene and chrystal sky. Round the walls, between the windows, were paintings, emblematic of the person to whom the temple was dedicated. In one of the partitions was Caroline, kneeling to Esculapius,[37] ardently invoking his aid, and pointing to her expiring friend. In the second Caroline was assisting her as she rose, while little Genii sported around her,[38] scattered flowers, overset the table on which phials and physical remedies were placed, and broke the javelin of Death who was seen flying in the back ground.[39] In the third a pavilion was building, Caroline placing the bust upon the altar, and the Genii of friendship and gratitude engraving the inscription. In the fourth, and last, Caroline was leading, and sustaining with one arm, the Canoness, whose attitude expressed surprize and joy, and extending the other towards the temple she had been building, and which she there presented to her.

The partitions were wainscot, and had doors, behind each of which was a recess for a small library; a table stood in the middle, and cabriole chairs round the room.

In short, nothing was forgotten, yet all was planned and conducted by a young girl of sixteen; but this girl was inspired and informed by Friendship: her heart overflowing with this affection, and, totally ignorant of any other, loving by nature, without other object of attachment than this her dear and only friend, to her the effusions of sensibility were all directed, and the dread of losing her had rendered them still more creative, more powerful, and more profuse. Genius likewise begins to show itself at her age, and the mind and imagination have then an ardor that must find employment, a fire that will have fuel. Independent of the pleasure she should give her friend, that which pertained to herself, alone, was far from small. To build was in some sort to create, each new idea was a new enjoyment, the execution and the effect of which gave her momentary rapture. Caroline, perhaps, never enjoyed greater felicity than while she was thus employed; so has she since frequently acknowledged, and never, afterwards, beheld this monument of affection and friendship without emotion.

Let the reader, if the reader can, imagine the extacy of the sentimental Baroness. It was the denouement of a romance, an incident of surprize so unexpected, and so perfectly conformable to her ideas and taste, that it seemed imagined and contrived purposely for her. A temple built by inchantment by the wand of a Fairy, or the talisman of a Genius.[40] Behold her clasping the lovely Sylph in her arms to whom she is indebted for this prodigy![41] and lo! Caroline kneeling, kissing her hands, and expressing her multitudinous sensations by looks and silence incapable of speech! see them mingle their tears, each contending for superior gratitude and love!

This was the moment in which Caroline felt happiness unmixed, free from the slightest shade of pain, and as pure as it was innocent. Happy age! existing but for the present moment, forgetful of the past, and regardless of the future! Rindaw was the world to Caroline, and her pavilion the Temple of Felicity. So enamoured was she of it, that she passed her whole time there, when she was not with her friend. The moment she left the Baroness she flew to the pavilion, and she scarcely could quit it without regret. The lofty dome was most excellently adapted to music, the sound was echoed, lengthened and increased, and, accordingly, all the instruments were carried thither, so that, presently, it was impossible to play or sing any where but in the pavilion.

The clear light was equally excellent for drawing; for, by means of the four windows and Venetian blinds, the light might be disposed in what manner the painter pleased; and pencils, pallets and colours were all transported thither.

The place was so tranquil, so undisturbed, so free from noise and interruption, that it was the properest in the world for reading, and Caroline's whole library stole thither by degrees. Caroline scarcely had any other apartment; she never entered her own room, except to sleep or hastily arrange her dress, and often in that of her dear mamma she felt a kind of impatience to be gone. Novelty is a pleasure which habit soon renders absolutely necessary.

Let us, however, do justice to Caroline. She was all impatience that her friend should so far recover her strength as daily to come and live with her in her dear pavilion; and so charmed was the Baroness to see Caroline thus happy, that she contributed every thing in her power to continue the sweet delirium. How long it was to continue, how long she was to love her pavilion for itself alone, we shall presently see.

Hitherto, the tranquil existence of Caroline has glided away untroubled in its progress, except the now forgotten week at Berlin, unmolested by love or hatred; for her repugnance to Walstein, her dread of living with him, was not hatred; and if, by chance, she thought of him, the remembrance inspired gratitude for the present liberty in which she lived. But this was, indeed, a kind of chance that seldom happened; seldom, indeed, did the recollection of the Count intrude itself, and the enjoyment of present pleasures effaced his image from her mind almost to total forgetfulness. Her freedom she enjoyed as though it had been absolute, and did not ill resemble a bird secured by a thread, winging the air, warbling, and fancying itself as free as the feathered songsters that vault from bush to bush: its forgotten captivity is not perceived till the hand that retains it draws gently back, catches, and carefully again incloses it within the cage.

Caroline had lately received some new music from Berlin; among it was a collection of lyric compositions, some of which she was delighted with, and one in particular. The air suited her voice, and the words her feelings; she sang it from morning to night, accompanying herself alternately on the guitar, the harp, and the piano forte, and each time of repeating it, finding a wish and a pleasure to repeat it again.

It is necessary to this our history that we should insert this song; and, perhaps, our readers will not be displeased to see words that gave Caroline so much delight.

I.

Gentle Eugenia, lovely maid,
Supine on flow'ry bank was laid,
She and the year alike were in their spring;
Of Love she oft had heard the name,
Of Love she ne'er had felt the flame,
Gentle Eugenia thus was heard to sing:
"Peaceful Indiff'rence, let me know,
"Of Bliss art thou the friend, or foe?

II.

"Love lives and breathes in every part
"Of Nature's works, except my heart;
"Each bosom heaves, save mine, with melting sighs:
"Ah why this apathy, this calm?
"If Love be Nature's sov'reign balm,
"Why should not I with Nature sympathize?
"Indiff'rence, thou, if this be so,
"No friend of Bliss art, but the foe.

III.

"Yet, lo, the butterfly and bee,
"From bud to bud, inconstant, flee;
"On sweets they surfeit, first, and then forsake;
"And, thus, to rove and riot prone,
"Has Love, like them, been ever known
"Of selfish pleasures eager to partake.
"Ah! dear Indiff'rence, thee I know
"The friend of Bliss, and not the foe.

IV.

"Disloyal, and devoid of truth,
"Full many a virgin, many a youth,
"Thou, Love, to sighs and tears, untold, dost doom;

"While I can peaceful sit and smile,
"As free from sorrow as from guile,
"Can view the young lambs sport, the flow'rets bloom.
"Yes, dear Indiff'rence, thee I know
"The friend of Bliss, and not the foe."

V.
Thus sang the maid, and Love, who, long,
Had angry listen'd to the song,
Strait vow'd revenge, and seiz'd the pointed dart;[42]
And, ere the sound had well expir'd,
'Twas whirl'd, and as it fled it fir'd;
The virgin felt it glowing in her heart:
Eugenia sigh'd, "Yes! now I know
"Indiff'rence is of Bliss the foe!"[43]

As she was singing this song, one day, in the pavilion, and, as it this time happened, accompanying herself with her guitar, she expressively repeated

Yes, dear Indiff'rence, thee I know
The friend of Bliss, and not the foe,

when she heard another voice, as sweet and melodious as her own, but deeper and more sonorous, that sung, as a second,

Listen to Love, and thou shalt know
Indiff'rence is of Bliss the foe.

The accent, the voice, the expression, were very different from the rustic songs to which she was accustomed, and gave her infinite surprize. She left singing, listened, but heard the voice no more; she then again began to sing, but in a softer tone, and an accompaniment less loud, and distinctly heard, as she wished, the voice once more. With her guitar in her hand, she ran towards the casement to look towards the high road, where she saw a youth, beauteous, finely formed, and arrived at full manhood, in a hunting dress, leaning on his fowling piece, with his eyes fixed on the temple. This, no doubt, was the person who sang. Caroline, however, had but a glance of him; for the moment she beheld him, confused and ashamed of having been heard and seen, and of her own curiosity, she instantly retired to the farther side of the pavilion, where, standing on tip-toe, and stretching forwards, she looked, with all her might, through the window from which she had fled; but it was too far distant, she could see nothing. She would have begun again to sing, only to see if she should again have been accompanied, but her voice failed her, she could not, or durst not, force out a single sound, and scarcely, and but lightly, could she touch a few chords on her guitar. Thus she remained for some time; at length, no longer able to subdue her curiosity, after having advanced eight paces and retired four, she took courage, and went up to the window. Alas! the beauteous sportsman, the youth, was gone; she saw him slowly proceeding along the road, and turning his head, every moment, anxiously towards the pavilion.

This was a very trifling adventure, to be sure; perfectly, at least apparently, insignificant in its consequences. A sportsman passed, by chance, near a pavilion newly erected, and decorated with taste. He saw, remarked it, and heard most sweet music as he stood; he listened, and yielded to the desire of joining in sounds so delightful. He then beheld a charming virgin approach the window, and it was very natural he should look at her. What, indeed, could be more natural? And yet was Caroline occupied, the whole day, by reflecting on these incidents, as if they had been the most extraordinary possible.

We own that to Caroline, who saw each succeeding day but like the day before, a common incident might seem strange, and any being who should interrupt solitude, so continued and so absolute as her's, might well appear singular. Of this youth, therefore, she often thought, and as often wondered who he might be, or why he should travel a road where beings like himself were so seldom seen. Of these her cogitations, however, she said not a word, for she felt some vague idea of dread lest her dear pavilion should become an interdicted place, and this, to her, would have been worse than death.

On the morrow, therefore, she flew with more early haste even than usual, and, after having passed an hour, looking through the window towards the road, and well assuring herself, by examining every way, that no one could either see or hear her, she took her guitar, sat down with the sash thrown up, and sang her favourite song from beginning to end; and, though she always had liked the last verse the least, it, this time, so far took her fancy that it was repeated: she next sung it to her harp, and afterwards to her piano forte. At this, however, she did not long remain, for it stood at the far end of the pavilion, and Caroline found the air so pure, so mild, so refreshing, that she could not possibly sit any where but at the window. She had written down the second that she had heard, and repeated in every kind of mode

> Yes, dear Indiff'rence, thee I know
> The friend of Bliss, and not the foe;

which, alas! no one came to contradict.

Tired, at length, and, for aught we know, somewhat chagrined to sing so long by herself when there were people in the world who so harmoniously could bear a part, she threw down her music, laid by her instrument, ran into the garden, plucked some flowers which she tossed without order into her flower basket, and, for want of other amusement, again returned to the pavilion, took up her pallet and her pencil, and carelessly began to imitate the tints and beauties she had been collecting. It was with difficulty, at first, she could any way fix her attention, and she looked oftener toward the window than the pannel on which she painted; but her work, by degrees, drew her attention and wholly occupied her. The flowers, which from her traces took birth, pleased her, each new touch was happy, and gave a new effect; the powers of genius were roused and high in action, when, suddenly, the clattering of a horse's hoofs were heard at a distance.

This noise, though of a very different nature, was little less surprising than the melodious sounds of the evening before; it bore no resemblance to the slow and heavy step of the beast of burden or the village horse. Accordingly, the pencil was thrown by, and Caroline, in a moment, was at the window, looking every way. She presently beheld, and not far distant, a fine handsome man, mounted on a grey horse that champed the bit he seemed to disdain, and foaming obeyed the restraining hand of his graceful rider.

How observant, how piercing, how exact is the female eye! Scarcely had Caroline seen the stranger of over-night, who was in a green sporting dress, the present youth wore a uniform, the one was on foot, the other on horseback, the first sung, the latter galloped. How little did these things resemble each other! and yet did Caroline, instantly, recollect these two to be one and the same person. It was not possible to resist that curiosity that desired to know if this youth could ride as well as he could sing. He, or rather his horse, advanced, for the proud animal was difficult to detain and not easy to manage; yet was he forgotten the moment his rider had a glance of Caroline: the hand quitted the bridle for the hat, for what cavalier would forbear to salute an angelic creature who appeared to be the goddess of the temple?[44] and the impatient steed, profiting by momentary liberty, and, perhaps, somewhat frightened at the sudden motion of the rider, gave a prodigious plunge, which would have unhorsed a rider less firm and daring, and set off, full speed, regardless of every effort of the cavalier, and, quick as lightning, was out of sight.

Caroline, greatly terrified, gave a piercing shriek, and followed the horse and his rider with looks of anxiety and dread as long as she could, which, however, was but a moment; they were gone, but her fears remained, and again, and ardently, she looked, though nothing was there to be seen. Fear, like other beings, propagates and multiplies, and Caroline saw the noble cavalier falling from his horse, rolled in the dust, wounded, and trampled on.—If the dangerous beast would but run towards the village, he might there, perhaps, be stopped, the people might come to his master's aid, and they might bring him back, if wounded, to the chateau. For a moment she thought to have sent the servants after him, but after whom? She herself knew not. And which road? for there were several at leaving the village. Besides, it was not easy to overtake a horse full speed. And then how could she give these orders? It seemed so particular, at least so she feared it would seem. No, she never could resolve, and, therefore, remain she must with all her fears and inquietudes.[a]

These she endeavoured to calm by recollecting how firm, how graceful, the officer sat, and how certain he seemed of his power before that vexatious saluta-tion, for which she wholly reproached herself; having no other person to salute she hoped the horse would lose his fears, and the cavalier regain his command; and even that she should be happy enough to see him again, on the morrow; "and really," said she to herself, "he ought to come merely to quiet my apprehensions."

The agitation of Caroline had totally deprived her of any desire any longer to sing or paint; so, after a few turns in the garden, still thinking on the youth who, like an apparition, had twice suddenly appeared and twice as suddenly van-ished, she returned to keep the Baroness company; to whom, however, she did not mention a syllable of what had happened; fearing, no doubt, to terrify her as much as she had been terrified herself. She went to bed impatiently wishing for the morrow, and ardently hoping she should either see the stranger or, at least, be certified he had escaped unhurt. Yesterday, simple and pure curiosity had engaged her to think of him; to day, humanity was added, for the life of a man was endangered. After many reflections on the subject, and after being very angry with unruly horses, that won't suffer cavaliers to be polite, and take off their hats to ladies, Caroline, at last, fell asleep.

On the morrow — Why on the morrow it rained, in torrents, from morning to night; it was a day that might well have been a day during Noah's flood;[45] it was as impossible to go to the pavilion, as it was to suppose any one could ride out on such a day. Caroline, baulked in all her expectations, found the day intol-erably tedious, and, tired, and vexed to death, could find no mode pleasantly to employ her time; her books, her music, her drawings, all were at the pavilion; her heart was at the pavilion also, and she herself most impatiently wished to be there, but, ah! it was impossible.

Conversations with her dear Mamma, concerning rain and fine weather, and most sincere wishes for the return of the latter, singing the burthen of *Peaceful Indifference,* and imagining the second, remembering the galloping horse, and again hoping for the morrow, were the best means Caroline could find of pass-ing the day. The morrow — why this good for nothing morrow was as bad as the former one; the rain was worse and worse, and the clouds seemed all to have made an appointment to meet at Rindaw. It was too much for nature to bear, and Caroline, for the first time in her life, was really out of temper, and shewed she was so. "Is it not intolerable, Mamma, that one cannot so much as step into the pavilion? There is my flower-basket, which I had begun to paint! The flowers will be all faded, and those in the garden will be beat down and deluged by this good-for-nothing unceasing rain! I shall find the leaves all torn from the roses, and nothing but the thorns remaining."

Alas! poor Caroline! the thorns already are in thy heart; thy gaiety, before so uniform, is now no more; that chearful void of care, happily improvident, which gave thee smiles and songs, as well beneath the gloomy as the golden and the azure sky, these all are fled.[a]

So impatient was Caroline once more to behold the dazzling brightness of the sun, that she consulted, on this second day, every barometer and every servant in the house; every moment was looking to see if the clouds were likely to disperse; but, no, they seemed for ever emptying and for ever increasing. At length, however, in the evening, a purple cloud, streaking the horizon, gave some small hopes; a fresh wind sprang up, and they were confirmed; and in the morning, when Caroline waked, she had the pleasure to perceive the sun's rays illuminating her curtains, and the shining ardor of day enlightening her apartment. The disappointment of the time past augmented the pleasure of the time present, and scarcely would she wait till the path was dry before she flew to the pavilion.

Not her flowers, so much regretted, not her books for which she seemed to sigh, nor yet her music, which might enliven the dullness of dark and cloudy weather, were the things that first drew her attention: it was the window and the road; uniform and inanimate as such an object may seem, that attracted and rivetted the eyes of Caroline. She looks this way, that way, and every way; she listens and fears to breathe; yet nothing sees, nothing hears; she examines the humid green swerd,[46] and the gravel path, trying if she can discover the new-made traces of a horse's hoof. "Ah! could I only know he had passed this way, that he were safe, that no accident had happened, how tranquil, how perfectly contented should I be! For, certainly, I was the cause of his misfortune. If I had left the window, he would not have pulled off his hat, and his horse would not have been frightened;[b] but only let me get the least glimpse of him, once again, and I will withdraw instantly, that he no more may be tempted to salute me." Thus to herself said Caroline.

Now, so it happened, just as thus she had said, she not only had a glimpse, but a full view of a cavalier, wearing the same uniform, mounted on the same grey unruly horse, and advancing, full trot, towards the pavilion, from which he was yet at some distance. Well, then, there he was, safe and unhurt, and Caroline, *no doubt*, was made perfectly easy; and, *no doubt*, she will retire, as she promised herself, and think of him no more.

But wherefore the tremor which suddenly has seized her? Wherefore this quickening pulse, this palpitating heart, this spreading suffusion that dyes alabaster scarlet, and gives the rose of the cheek a deeper hue? I know not wherefore these things were; I only know they were, and that Caroline was all agitation. She was going to leave the window, but just at that moment, for things will sometimes happen oddly, her handkerchief, on which she had been leaning, fell, and was borne, (no doubt by Zephyrs, for they are apt at wanton and malicious tricks)[47] yes, it was borne into the middle of the highway.

Caroline was absolutely in despair: the act was most surely involuntary, yet so it might not seem; not forgetting that this was still more dangerous to the cavalier than the salute she meant to avoid; for it is certainly less difficult to take off one's hat, on horseback, than to pick up a handkerchief from the ground. This was a very just conclusion, but so was not the next she made; she supposed the cavalier still so far distant as to give her time to run down, open the pavilion door, sally forth, pick up her handkerchief, and re-enter before he should arrive. The idea she thought excellent, it seemed to be the only possible expedient of clearly demonstrating that the handkerchief had not been purposely thrown out of the window for the cavalier to pick up; nor was there time to lose in reflection; away, therefore, she flew to the door, opened it, and was stepping out at the very moment that the young officer, after alighting from his horse, was himself in the act of taking up the handkerchief.

With a graceful and dignified manner the youth approached, and, in an elegant compliment, returned his prize; while Caroline, disconcerted, and unable to reply, extended her timid hand. The youth, with infinite modesty, begged permission to see the garden and the pavilion, which, he said, appeared most charming. Understanding the silence of the trembling Caroline as consent, cavaliers will so understand, he presently hung the bridle of his horse to the pavilion door and followed her.

The latent feelings of Caroline told her she ought to have denied his request; but which way? Caroline was naturally all benevolence, and there is something painful in denial. Neither did she perceive any infinite evil which could thence result. Her own innocence, her total ignorance of the world, concealed the danger that might lurk thus under the form of a youthful soldier. Beside, his uniform spoke him a gentleman, and the noble ease of his manner of no mean birth; his politeness was so natural, so graceful, so familiar, the tone of his voice, his modest confidence, all confirmed him perfectly well bred. The symmetry and beauty of his form made not all that impression which might naturally be expected, because Caroline durst not look at him; and yet she had seen sufficient to find that his full fine eyes were most expressively intelligent, and she very soon could have informed us that his teeth were white and regular, his smile enchanting, his nose aquiline, his visage oval, his eyebrows markingly arched, his stature tall, his dark complexion animated by the warm glow of youth and health, and that his open and frank countenance inspired confidence and friendship the moment they were beheld. All these things had the furtive glances of the beauteous Countess presently remarked.[a] This might, perhaps, in part, excuse that facility with which she suffered him to walk up into the pavilion; unless it should be thought more natural to cast the whole blame on absolute Innocence, too secure in its own simplicity. But whether this or that excuse were best, there he is, there looks, there admires, there praises with ecstacy, and yet with propriety, void of exaggeration, the taste and the talents which had decorated the temple. The altar and paintings particularly fixed his attention. He asked an explanation; it was given, and thus he gained a happy opportunity of learning to whom the place belonged without the indelicacy of interrogation, though neither the names of the Baroness of Rindaw or the High Chamberlain Lichtfield made him more polite, more attentive, or more respectful; for that was impossible.

The song and the guitar were laying on the piano forte, which, with a gentle but submissive smile, led him to mention the second, and to ask pardon for that temerity which had suffered him to mingle his voice with the harmonious sounds he had heard, and which, he added, he should be most happy again to hear. He saw the proposition augmented the confusion of Caroline, he said not a word more concerning it, therefore, but spoke of music, its effects and charms, like one who felt them, and was the first to propose quitting the pavilion and walk in the garden.

The fortitude of Caroline began to return; the stranger's conversation was so agreeable, so unaffected, and yet so animated, that it could not long leave her under any constraint; and, after a turn or two in the garden, Caroline spoke to him as naturally as if they had been acquainted all their lives. With the most perfect simplicity did she relate the terror with which she had been seized at the impetuosity of the unmanageable horse, and tell all her fears and inquietudes during those two dreadful days of rain.[b] Desirous, however, as she was to learn the name of the cavalier, this was a thing she durst not ask; she only understood he was captain in the guards, and her country neighbour, which both gave her pleasure; for the one informed her he was a proper visitor, and the other that she should certainly see him again.

A quarter of an hour, which, short as it was, seemed still infinitely shorter, they thus conversed; when the steed, neighing and pawing at the door, became so impatient that his master was obliged, however unwilling, again to mount. "Really," said Caroline to him as he threw the bridle over his neck, "were I in your place, Sir, I should not like a horse that would neither permit one to take off one's hat nor walk in a garden."—Ah! how infinite are the charms of Innocence![48] The stranger, with a smile half restrained, assured Caroline his horse should be better taught, and that, indeed, he had played him too many malicious tricks, of which he should be corrected; then, lightly vaulting into the saddle, after a thousand repeated thanks to Caroline for her condescension, he departed, as slowly as possible, curbing the haughty animal to obedience. Caroline, as slowly, returned to the pavilion; as soon, that is, as he was out of sight; her head, aye and her heart too, wholly occupied by the departed cavalier.

"How amiable his person! How soft, how attentive his manners! Oh that Heaven had given me a brother like him! How dearly would he have been beloved!—But wherefore may I not love this youth as I should love a brother, or as a friend, sent by Heaven to make solitude chearful? Yet how do I know if I ever shall behold him again?"

Thus meditated Caroline; and what the thought was which, added to this latter, so might move her we know not, but Caroline felt a sudden oppression at her heart, and the tear rose glistening in her eye. Sensible of this, and somewhat alarmed, she was desirous to divert her attention to other objects, and sat down to her music; but the two days rain had put her harp and guitar out of tune, and she was obliged to lay them by; the piano forte was less affected and she played an adagio, which but augmented melancholy. To painting she had next recourse, but with no better success; and reading was still less amusing than either: she opened books, but they seemed dull and ill written before she had finished a period. Some change must certainly have taken place, for objects that before gave pleasure, at present gave distaste, or painful lassitude at best.

Caroline returned to the garden, and took the same round she lately had gone with the cavalier, stopped at the same places, and recollected every expression, every attitude, and every look. The grand question now remained to be determined; that is to say, whether she should, or should not, tell all that had happened to the good Canoness. Silence was disagreeable, and to mystery Caroline was naturally averse; yet she seemed more averse to speak on the present occasion. She knew not how to speak, nor what to speak; and, supposing there to be nothing wrong in keeping the secret, there was nothing difficult in it; for secresy was, at present, become habitual, and she herself, it may be, less communicative.[42] Beside, what should she say? Why mention a person who, perhaps, I shall never see again, whose name I know not? It will be time enough if he should return. And then should the Baroness blame me for having admitted him into the garden, forbid me the pavilion, and not suffer me any more to look out of the window!

Caroline half shuddered, as thus she meditated, and resolved not to tell what had happened. When, however, she returned to her friend, she could not forbear asking a thousand questions concerning the neighbourhood, for two leagues round. As the Canoness never was visited, Caroline knew none of the neighbours; nor had she ever, before, made the least enquiry; though her good friend made a merit of knowing the genealogy of all their families through every branch. To question her concerning the characters and affairs of her neighbours was taking her on her weak side; and poor Caroline had a hundred histories to hear, while the only one to which she could have listened with pleasure was unrelated. Not the least circumstance could she learn that had any reference to the stranger. Here lived an old Baron who had retired from the army, with his wife as old as himself, shut up in their chateau; there a young couple, with several children, but they were infants, and all girls. Yonder, as you entered the village, an ancient Commander of the Teutonic Order; very infirm, very avaricious, and on very good terms with his Gouvernante.[50] A little farther, an old dowager, with an only son of five and twenty.

Caroline, who was half asleep, no sooner heard of the only son of five and twenty, than she was as perfectly awake as ever she had been in her life; but to little purpose was she disturbed, for this only son was deformed, and half an ideot, with no other employment than what hunting and drinking afforded, and who, notwithstanding his great riches, could persuade no woman to become his wife. Ah! thought Caroline, that is not my cavalier.

The Baroness continued, for it was not easy to interrupt her, and she was inexhaustible. At last, Caroline, quite wearied, and learning nothing of what she most desired to know, wishing to be alone, took advantage of a slight head-ach, and retired sooner than usual. "He is not my neighbour, then," said she, sighing. "And has he deceived, could he deceive me? If so, I shall never see him more. Well then I must forget, never think of him more."

Moncrief has said that the very act of determining to forget makes us remember.[51] Thus Caroline, fortifying herself in this her noble resolution, forgot the cavalier by recollecting every word that had passed; and, thus ruminating, dropt asleep. No doubt the project of thinking on him no more was her first on waking the next morning. She rose, and resolved not to go to the pavilion all the forenoon; habit was very strong and was with difficulty vanquished, yet vanquished it was: she raised her drooping flowers, examined her aviary, and sat down to her embroidery, every moment repeating, "I must think of him no more," and as often looking towards the pavilion. "Dear pavilion," said Caroline, sighing, "I am never happy but when I am there; I must pay it a visit, but it shall be very very late, when I am sure no person is walking. I will not go, at soonest, before four o'clock in the afternoon."

The day appeared exceedingly long, and Caroline persuaded herself it was already far advanced, as she sauntered towards the pavilion,[a] when she heard, in the very court yard of the chateau, the trampling of a horse, and the sound of hoofs she began to think she recollected, which made her heart palpitate. In a moment a servant enters and announces the Baron of Lindorf. The astonished Baroness recollects to have heard the name, and gives orders for his admission; when the charming stranger of the pavilion, with all his grace and gentleness, appeared.

Poor Caroline, what was thy emotion! How bitterly didst thou reproach thyself for not having mentioned him to thy friend! How deep are thy blushes at thy own dissimulation! For, whether he speak or whether he do not, thou art, equally, afraid of his indiscretion and his silence.

Lindorf chose the latter; a glance at Caroline, who, tremblingly confused, alternately pale and red, had courtsied to him with downcast eyes and timidity in every feature, in a moment informed him how it was proper to act. He returned her salutation as if it had been the first time he had seen her; and, addressing himself to the Canoness, congratulated himself on the happiness of being her neighbour, with self-reproaches for not having sooner profited by this advantage.

The Baroness, to whom this youthful cavalier was a total stranger, asked an explanation, and learned that the Commander of the Teutonic Order had, like herself, been ill, but had not, like her, recovered; for he was lately dead, and the Baron of Lindorf, his nephew and heir, was come to take possession of the mansion and estate of Risberg, which was adjoining to the Barony of Rindaw. He had at first intended not to make a long stay, but the country had pleased him infinitely; and he had very lately come to a resolution to pass the remainder of the summer there. His first wish was to be acquainted with his lovely neighbours, to present them his duty and his homage, and to solicit permission these occasionally to renew.

All this was said looking towards Caroline, who, with her eyes fixed on her work, which she was very industriously spoiling,[a] kept a profound silence. Thanks, however, to the good Canoness, the conversation was not therefore interrupted; she gave the history of her whole illness, then reverted, with great pity, to that of the Commander, and lamented his death, of which she had been wholly ignorant. "It was but yesterday," said she, "I mentioned him to Caroline, who had asked me who were my neighbours."

Lindorf did not recollect himself soon enough totally to suppress a smile, and Caroline was absolutely ready to faint with shame and vexation.

The Baroness proceeded with compliments to the heir, and enquiries concerning the estate and property, which must, from the character of the Commander, be considerable. After which came interrogatories concerning the degree of kindred in which the deceased and the youth stood, all which she answered herself. "Oh! I am acquainted with every branch of the family. Your name is Lindorf, is it not? Yes, yes, your name is Lindorf; and you inherit in right of my Lady, your mother. She, yes, she was Baroness of Risberg, own sister to the Commander, as I think; yes, yes, I am sure she was. To be sure, I was not personally acquainted with her, but one of your lady aunts was educated in the very convent I was, and she told me of this marriage of her sister with your father. Aye, with the Baron of Lindorf, I remember it as well as if it had only happened yesterday. There was a mutual passion, real and true love, and I was exceedingly affected by the story. Your aunt was in my confidence also; I told her of my passion for the High Chamberlain. Upon my word all this seems as if it had happened last week, and here I see a fine young gentleman—the eldest of the family, I suppose—Were there many children?—Is your father still alive; and my Lady your mother too?—Ah! they still adore each other, no doubt. Love, love only, can give happiness; and my dear friend, your aunt, whom I just now mentioned, is she dead? Is she married? It is so long since we saw each other, and I have lived retired here so many years, that I have quite lost sight of former friends."

These questions succeeded each other with such rapidity that Lindorf, surprised at the voluble haste with which they were delivered, scarcely could find opportunity to come in with a yes; or no; I am an only son; I had the misfortune to lose my parents; with like answers, as concise as possible. But his eyes, continually fixed on Caroline, would have said many things to her if Caroline would have attended to them. She, seemingly observant of nothing but her work, had not ventured a single word, when the Canoness, desirous of doing honour to her friendship and affection, asked her to show the young cavalier her pavilion; and, not foreseeing the least obstruction, began, without waiting her reply, to give him its history; why it had been built, who by, the altar, the bust, the inscription, the painting, the surprise, and every thing; all which he knew as well as herself; though, by his manner, it might well have been supposed he had never heard it before.

To a heart undisguised and sincere by nature, a heart like Caroline's, this was too much;[52] she could support it no longer, and when her friend, surprised at her backwardness to go to the pavilion, repeated her command, she scarcely could articulate that a sudden and strange indisposition had seized her, and that it was impossible she should go. In reality her voice was so affected, her face so pale, and her whole form so altered, that her indisposition was sufficiently visible, and made the Baroness very uneasy.

"Dear child, what can be the matter?" said she, laying her hand on her forehead. "Yesterday evening I particularly remarked, when you came in, you seemed absent, and your mind wholly occupied; and, for several days past, you have not only retired sooner than ordinary, but have been particularly melancholy and agitated. My Caroline, Sir, certainly has a fever; 'tis that vile pavilion that kills her. I assure, you, Sir, she is quite infatuated with it; and, lately, more than ever; for, notwithstanding the humidity of the earth and the air, the moment it had ceased raining she would be gone, by which means she has caught cold."

Lindorf, without being remarkably vain, had heard sufficient to imagine himself a party somewhat concerned; but, suffering with the suffering Caroline, and most desirous of relieving her from pain, he shortened his visit, took leave of the ladies, and hoped the indisposition of Caroline would have no bad consequences.

Caroline made no other answer than by courtesying, and the Baroness, repeatedly, entreated Lindorf to take advantage of their near neighbourhood and come frequently to the chateau of Rindaw.—"It is but a step," said she. "The poor Commander was gouty, and, during three parts of the year, never stirred abroad; but you, Sir, are young and agile, and it will be only a short walk to our house. Miss Lichtfield will not always be indisposed, and some other day will show you her pavilion: she tells me it is most excellently adapted to music; you, no doubt, are a musician, and you may play and sing in concert."

It only wanted this last trait to compleat the confusion of Caroline, and the Baroness seemed not willing any thing should be wanting. At length the cavalier departed, and the Canoness was silent. Caroline, however, was not greatly relieved; leaning on her great chair, her face hid by both her hands, with difficulty she restrained the tears and fobs that rose thronging for a passage. The Canoness attributed all to her indisposition, and begged her to go and lay down; and Caroline was glad to profit by the permission. Her chagrin, however, went with her; but, being alone, she could now abandon herself to grief, and again and again repeated, "Good God! what must he think of me!"

The Canoness, alone also, was occupied by ideas much less melancholy; the handsome, the amiable Lindorf had absolutely gained her heart; he was precisely the husband she wished for her dear Caroline. And how happy should she be to have her near her, at least for a part of the year; and to see her so well, so properly, and so highly married. The young officer united in himself every thing she wished; youth, beauty, wit, birth, fortune; for, without mentioning his own wealth, of which he was before in possession, being an only son and his parents deceased, the inheritance of the avaricious

Commander must have been immense. Already high in rank in the army, every thing that ambition could hope he seemed formed to obtain.

The advantages of Lindorf were great, yet her dear Caroline was in no respect inferior; first, Caroline was an angel, and as to fortune, that of the High Chamberlain was not to be disdained; to which she should add all her own; and, together, they would be vast. No match, in short, could be every way more proper; and she protested Caroline should be Baroness of Lindorf, or her endeavours should be strangely frustrated. She even fixed on the epocha for celebrating the wedding; the autumn following she determined on, when the High Chamberlain was to pay his promised visit.

In thinking all this she resolved carefully to conceal her projects and ideas even from Caroline. It would, certainly, be very difficult to be silent, but her passion for every thing romantic was still stronger than her inclination to talk. She imagined what a pleasure it would be to observe the effects of sympathy; to follow it through the progressions of two young hearts; day after day to see passion augmented by hope and fear; and, at last, to make them happy at the very moment when they expected to be eternally miserable. Oh! what delicious pleasure, this, for the Baroness! But this she could not obtain except by keeping her secret.

As to the projected union with the Count of Walstein, she troubled herself little concerning it; she thought it impossible not to make the High Chamberlain understand reason; for he, most certainly, knew, by his own heart, the influence of mutual passion. "I need only (the Baroness was almost as simple and innocent as Caroline)[53] I need only recal to memory how much we suffered for each other, and he will yield, with melting tears, to the happiness of a pair of true lovers. On this condition, too, I will leave Caroline all I possess. Beside, when the High Chamberlain shall see the youthful Lindorf, all perfect as he is, can he, for a moment, make comparison between him and a monster? No, no; leave we sympathy, love, and paternal tenderness to their natural effects, and the happiness of my dear Caroline is for ever fixed."

While the good Canoness was composing her little romance, and enjoying, by anticipation, the tender scenes at which she should be present, and the sweet delight of making two beings happy, Caroline was abandoning herself to grief and self-reproach, for having acted so imprudently, and given Lindorf an idea so much the reverse of her real character. Every word the Baroness had said, though unintentionally, had made a wound, and every word a thousand times recalled the blushes and confusion of Caroline. "I will leave Rindaw," said she, "never more to return. Yet to fly would be to confess my guilt; and to confirm the idea, the cruel, distracting idea, that I am dissembling, false, and artful. Oh! impossible!"

Then did she search for and imagine all imaginary means of self-justification; but found not one which did not increase, instead of eradicate, suspicion. So troubled were her thoughts that all night long she lay, restless, and disturbed by ten thousand fears and suspicions; and, for the first time in her whole life, sleep fled from the eyelids of Caroline. How long, how painful was this night, and yet how much was her agitation encreased, the next morning, when a letter, addressed to her, was brought by servant of Lindorf's, who was waiting for an answer! The offended Caroline had almost instantly returned it unopened.— "What," says she, "does he write to me, purposely to demonstrate how much he despises me? Nothing but the idea he must have entertained of me, for my reprehensible conduct, could have emboldened him to take such a liberty. Yet is not this his excuse? And am not I alone guilty? How polite, how respectful was he before the unfortunate visit of yesterday! Yes, I myself, alone, am to blame."

But what was to be done with the packet? To open it was impossible; to return it unopened was very severe. Beside, who could tell what his thoughts, or what his stile might be? The letter was held and turned in the hand, and looked at again and again, in every possible form, as if the eye wished to penetrate the paper and purloin the contents. At last, a ray of light broke in upon the mind of Caroline; she determined to run to the chamber of her dear mamma, open her curtains, fall on her knees, and there, with tears and penitence, make a full confession of all that had passed between her and Lindorf.

The execution was as prompt as the resolve; the second, the run-away horse, the handkerchief, the walk in the garden, every circumstance was related, even to the avowal of the secret reasons of her silence, for which she had been so severely punished.

"Judge, mamma," said Caroline, "what I suffered during his visit! I really thought I should have died! And he to be totally silent, as if it had been a plot agreed on between both; while you, mamma, every moment, unconsciously, was piercing my very heart! Can you, can you forgive me for having acted thus? No, load me with your reproaches; I well deserve them all, and they will be less cutting, less painful, than those with which I load myself."

Alas! the good Canoness, all emotion, all tenderness and tears at her recital, thought of nothing less than reproach. She had been dreaming all night on her projected marriage, on which the more she thought the more she was enchanted; her sole fear had been that Lindorf, so long an officer, so long in commerce with the gay world, might have formed other engagements; but the history of Caroline, and the manner in which she had related it, had quieted all her fears; the *Baroness saw, or imagined* she saw, that sweet sympathy of souls which re-*established all her hopes*, and gave certainty to all her schemes: she raised Caroline, tenderly kissed her, and declared she never, in her life, had heard any thing so interesting.

"Ah! if I had but known it!—To be sure, I should not have said many things I did say; for these men are so self-sufficient,[54] so ready to believe well of them-selves, and that we women are enamoured of them!—However, I must do

Lindorf the justice to say he is very different from men in general; his modesty, his politeness"—

"Ah! Mamma," said Caroline, shaking her head and interrupting the Baroness, "I have but too much cause to fear he is like the rest. Has not he had the audacity to write to me this morning?"

"Write to thee, child! Quick, quick, quick, show me the letter, read it, let me hear his stile, his sentiments; I can imagine all his ardour."

"Alas!" said Caroline, taking the packet from her pocket, "here it is; it would not have been proper, mamma, for me to have opened it. You will do with it what you please." And the pleasure of the Baroness was, instantly, to break the seal; for her curiosity was stronger even than that of Caroline, which was much diminished by fears of what might be the contents of the letter. The first thing they came to was a polite card, in the usual stile, in which the Baron of Lindorf "presented respectful compliments to the ladies, enquired after their health, and, in particular, concerning the indisposition of Miss Lichtfield."

But all this was a mere pretext; and, certainly, needed not to have been so closely sealed up; wherefore, this laid by, a paper, folded up and placed under the card, was eagerly seized and opened. Caroline, trembling as she unfolded it, after slightly running it over to herself, read aloud as follows:

"I am about, Madam, to commit a new impropriety, to aggravate former errors, and, perhaps, encrease anger, which I had but too justly raised, by a new offence. Now, while I write, I imagine your indignation, feel the effects of your resentment, behold myself punished for my temerity, yet have not the power to forbear. If, Madam, you will but deign to read this letter, and surmount that first emotion which should bid you tear or send it back unopened, you then, at least, will understand my motives, and confess that to you, alone, could I, with propriety, address myself.

"You know not all my offences. No, Madam, you know them not; and yet you treat me with as much severity as if you were acquainted with my whole guilt. Since, then, I am not benefited by your ignorance of it, I will make a free confession; hoping that my sincerity may obtain a generous pardon.

"Four times did I, yesterday, pass your pavilion, each at a different hour, hoping to find you there and ask permission to pay my respects to you and the Baroness; but continually were my hopes deceived; you appeared no more in that pavilion so dear to you, and in which you had before that time unceasingly dwelt; while I, far from suspecting the truth, far from accusing you as the cause of this absence, cast the whole blame entirely on Madam the Baroness; she, thought I, informed of my temerity, not knowing who the person was who had dared to obtrude into your asylum, had forbidden you to go there any more. Vain and weak as I was, I even imagined you might obey with regret; I thought myself certain that, when I was known to Madam the Baroness, she would no longer lay you under the like restraint, and, therefore, did not hesitate to come and pay her my respects in the afternoon. Alas! Madam, how severely, and how justly, have you punished my presumption! Your reception of me, so very different from her's, instantly informed me how much I had been deceived; and that it was you, alone, who thus had renounced the unfortunate stranger. You did not permit me to enter-tain the least doubt, the least hope; the illusion was wholly destroyed; I instantly saw that Madam the Baroness, whom I had imagined so severe, was ignorant even of my existence, and that the youthful, the beauteous Caroline, whom I had supposed obedient to her commands, to the counsels of, perhaps, a too rigid friend, had been subject only to her own prudence, uncommon and unex-pected as it was in a lady so young. I had been happy had this prudence only been extended to a stranger who might himself have been an improper person, or have had improper designs; but, though this doubt was removed, though I was named and known, I could not obtain so much as a look of pardon. Your determined silence, Madam, your refusal to show me the pavilion, your apparent anger at the invitation of the Baroness, all informed me that I, personally, had given irrepa-rable offence. However, Madam, whatever my errors may have been, whatever I may endure, I will not again offend by visiting at Rindaw without your permis-sion; yet suffer me to supplicate this permission, and be assured, Madam, I will endeavour hereafter to deserve it. You were a witness to the obliging manner in which Madam the Baroness was pleased to desire I would frequently visit at Rindaw. What answer am I to make to a request so kind, and which I so earnestly wish to profit by? You, Madam, must decide. On you my conduct must depend. Must I neglect the civilities of Madam the Baroness, and submit to that sentence of condemnation which you have silently pronounced; or may I dare entreat you to revoke it? I wait your commands, and solemnly vow, whatever they be, to me they shall be sacred. Yet, permit me, for a moment, to hope you will not be inexorable; and that him whom your respectable friend has deigned to honour with her protection will,[a] being thus protected, obtain a pardon which is become absolutely necessary to the future happiness of his life."

While Caroline was reading this letter, which was dated from the chateau of Risberg, she felt a confused mixture of sensations so opposite to each other as to be almost indefinable. At first, utter astonishment at perceiving, without ever suspecting, herself to be thus consummately prudent; afterwards, that kind of shame which a sincere mind feels at receiving praise it does not merit; and, next, joy of the most pure and perfect kind to learn that she was still esteemed and respected.[b] Yet, on reflexion, she was somewhat uneasy concerning the poor young gentleman, the embarrassment he was under, and the means of removing it, without destroying the high opinion he entertained of her.

These different affections were alternately visible in her countenance; pleas-ing sensations, however, were predominant, and her heart felt eased of a most insupportable burthen. When she had finished the letter she could have pressed it to her lips; but she forbore, laid it on the pillow of the Canoness, seized one of her hands, and on that bestowed her kisses and her tears. Again the Baroness took the letter, again desired Caroline to read it, and again was in raptures.

"Did not I tell you this young gentleman did not resemble other men? I saw it instantly. What a delicate turn has he given to your silence and embarrassment, which he had understood to proceed from anger! Is it possible to be more modest, or more respectful? One of your court fops would have interpreted the whole of your behaviour to his own advantage, but Lindorf! Well, really he is a most charming youth, and we must instantly put him out of pain. Get the pen and ink, my dear, sit down and write; come, come, make haste."

"I! Mamma," said Caroline, blushing. "I thought you would have been kind enough to answer his letter."

"You know, my dear girl, it is with difficulty I can write, at present: (the Baroness had a disorder in her eyes, the consequence of her illness, and her sight daily became worse) but no matter; you shall write in my name, and I will dictate." Caroline obeyed, and, having taken pen, ink, and paper, the Canoness, after considering a moment, thus began to dictate.[a]

"Sir,

"Your letter came most seasonably to the relief and consolation of Caroline, she had all night lain in the most desperate affliction"—

"Really, mamma," said Caroline, stopping her, "I cannot write what you bid me; for, though I own it is partly true, it would absolutely contradict all his present favourable thoughts concerning me."

After a short contest, the Baroness owned Caroline was right; the paper was torn, another sheet taken, the Baroness again began to think and to dictate.

"Sir,

"Miss Lichtfield is most exceedingly glad to find you entertain so high an opinion of her, her joy cannot be expressed" —

"Upon my word, mamma," said Caroline, throwing down the pen, "this is worse than the other; let me beg you will neither speak of my joys nor griefs."

The Baroness was now absolutely vexed, and said she would have nothing at all to do with her answer; and that she might write it herself. Caroline began to think this the wisest way, and after considering in her turn, and, in her turn, tearing two or three sheets of paper, she had the good sense, at last, to recollect that the simplest and most unaffected mode is always the best; she therefore wrote,

"We thank you, Sir, for the concern you are kind enough to take in the health of your neighbours; my indisposition is gone off. Madam the Baroness is deprived, by the disorder in her eyes, of the pleasure of answering your letter, the contents of which I have just communicated to her; she has therefore desired me

to write in her name, and to inform you, Sir,[a] that your visits will always be well
received at Rindaw;[25] the Baron of Lindorf, when known, never can doubt of a
proper reception

C. L."

The Canoness thought the stile of this exceedingly common and trivial; there
were a thousand things to say, a thousand sensations to communicate,[b] according to her; but Caroline was firm, and would not change a word; and, at last, by
caresses and coaxing, prevailed on the Baroness to let the letter be sent.

As to the epistle of Lindorf, we have been assured, from the best authority,
that it was read and re-read at least a hundred times a day; and that, before the
evening, there was a person in the world who could have repeated it by heart.
It is likewise affirmed that these repeated readings had dissipated every remaining trace of the overnight's chagrin. Yes, Caroline, by being thus frequently told
of her uncommon prudence, at last believed it real; still, however, owning that
she never could have imagined her absence from the pavilion, and her secresy
with her friend, could have been productive of such excellent effects. It was very
certain, nevertheless, that the thought was her own; wherefore, gaining her own
self-esteem by degrees, no longer having any reason to blush for her mysterious conduct towards the Baroness, and being assured of the respect of Lindorf,
Caroline lost both her sorrows and her fears.

Nobody will doubt but that Lindorf was very careful to avail himself of the
permission granted, and to pay his respects in the evening. Caroline had foreseen
this, expected him with somewhat of impatience,[c] saw him arrive with joy, and
not without emotion. He himself was rather disconcerted, but a gentle smile
from Caroline presently restored him all his former ease; they both became perfectly unconstrained, to which the Baroness did not a little contribute; she, with
pleasantry which she highly enjoyed, ran over every incident of the stranger, the
secret, and the letter; and thus saved Caroline explanations which she was most
happy to avoid.

Lindorf was cautious and penetrating: he read the feelings of Caroline: they
went together to the pavilion, and he said not a word that had the slightest reference to what had passed, except that he entreated Caroline to sing the song on
Eugenia. She consented, and Lindorf accompanied her on the piano forte; but,
though he was an excellent musician, he was often out of time; and Caroline
herself made several mistakes. Notwithstanding this, the song pleased him so
much that he asked permission to take and copy it; which granted, Lindorf, on
receiving it, had the courage to kiss the hand by which it was presented, and to
pronounce, in a half whisper, "How good, Madam, are you to-day, and how different are my present feelings from those of yesterday!" The ingenuous Caroline
was on the point of declaring that she herself was much easier and happier, but

she just had the recollection to refrain. They returned to the Canoness, and Lindorf, shortening his visit, begged permission to repeat it on the morrow.

The morrow and the morrow, and every succeeding morrow, each resembled the other; and this was the history of their lives. Again Caroline inhabited her pavilion in the morning; and again Lindorf took his usual ride. The horse, formerly so unmanageable, was become quite docile; so that he would sometimes stand quiet, for half an hour, under the window of Caroline, with which he began to be acquainted, and which, when he came to, he instinctively would stop at. Every afternoon Lindorf came betimes to Rindaw, where he often remained to sup; and, every night, after he was gone, the Canoness, more and more transported with his conduct, spoke of him with enthusiasm. Caroline listened, and modestly approved, and each went nightly to bed declaring he was the most amiable of men: nay, Caroline, it is said, would sometimes repeat it in her sleep; and as for the Baroness, her nocturnal dreams were all concerning the marriage she had imagined, and which she thought nothing could frustrate.

Well but Lindorf?—Why Lindorf had his dreams likewise; for he loved with an ardour which he sought not to oppose, and with a sincerity that gave dignity to affection, which every day grew stronger. Born with great sensibility and strong passions, he had not lived till five and twenty without a knowledge of love, or, at least, without a supposed knowledge. But how different were his former tumultuous sensations to those he at present felt! His thoughts all tender, delicate and pure, had no other object but Caroline; happy in her sight, happy to hear the sweet sound of her voice, infinitely happy in her presence and that sweet familiarity which country retirement authorizes, he could not imagine superior bliss; and if, when alone, which walking, music, and the infirmities of the Baroness occasioned them often to be, he sometimes were like to betray himself, and risk an avowal of his sentiments, timidity, respect, and dread of destroying that share of felicity of which he was in present possession, always made him silent. Such ever are the effects of true and sincere love. Caroline too confided all her thoughts to him with such innocence, such security, he was so perfectly convinced that she no way suspected either what passed in his heart or her own, that Lindorf, whose delicacy equalled his affection, would likewise have thought it a crime to disturb that happy ignorance before the moment in which he himself should be at his own disposal, which he could not then be perfectly said to be.

Beside, what could he gain by the confession? A knowledge that his love was returned. And could he doubt of that? Certainly not; for, though the penetration of man equals not that of woman in this respect, Caroline was so frank, and so little understood the art of dissembling, of concealing her feelings, that it was impossible for him to doubt. She alone was ignorant of them. She supposed her love for Lindorf was the love of a sister,[56] and her affection the affection of friendship; she even applauded herself for daily finding fresh occasion to love him more, nor had the slightest idea that an attachment so pure, as she felt her's to be, could, in the least, become injurious to engagements which she held sacred, but of which she seldom thought. How, indeed, could she? Was there time to think on any thing but Lindorf, when Lindorf was present? And he was ever present, either ideally or really; for the moment he was gone, either the pleasure of having seen him, impatience to see him again, or his image in every attitude, under every aspect in which it had so lately been beheld, occupied her whole thoughts. Lindorf to Caroline was every thing, and, the Baroness excepted, she knew not of, thought not of, any other being in the universe.

This imprudent Baroness still added, by her enthusiasm, to the fascination of Caroline. From infancy accustomed to think as she thought, and to see as she saw, her authority would have been fully sufficient to fix the attachment of Caroline on a person for whom the Canoness had a predilection so absolute, and so continually augmenting. Often did the Baroness, when she could find opportunity by being left for a moment with Lindorf, suffer her secret half to escape; clearly enough did she give him to understand that it depended on him, only, to obtain the hand of Caroline; and that she already looked upon him as her son.

Thus the happy Lindorf, encouraged by one, adored by the other, and, perhaps, in more full and delicious enjoyment of happiness than if he had been a declared lover, thought himself certain of prevailing the moment he should speak; and for which moment he waited a little impatiently. Engagements he had, by which he had been restrained; and from these it was necessary to be free before he could honestly avow his passion for Caroline, and make an offer of his hand and heart. He had been very busily employed in removing these obstacles; and, for some time past, his agitation and short symptoms of melancholy betrayed something of his inquietude and fears.

One evening, as he left Rindaw, he informed the ladies he was fearful lest he could not have the pleasure of seeing them on the morrow; he was obliged to go, himself, immediately to Berlin, where he expected to find letters that were to him of the utmost importance.—"But," added he, with a tone more than usually animated,[a] "I hope, in compensation for a day thus lost to life, I shall be permitted to return early the morning after."

The Canoness immediately invited him to breakfast, and Caroline accompanied him to the garden, where they took leave of each other as if it were a long farewell, and separated, impatiently wishing the morrow over. The next day, which for two months had been the only one passed without Lindorf, appeared exceedingly tedious to both the ladies. The good Baroness loved Lindorf so entirely that, had not her friendship for Caroline intervened, which we must do her the justice to acknowledge was always predominant, he might, in all probability, if so he had pleased, have even banished the High Chamberlain from her bosom. She acknowledged that Lindorf continually brought him to her recollection, and made her remember the happy days of their former loves. "Yes," said the Baroness, "the High Chamberlain was just so fine, so sweet a youth."

"My father, then, is surprisingly altered," said Caroline.

"Ah! yes, my dear," replied the Baroness, "whatever he may be at present, he was then a most charming man—If thy mother had not been so rich—But, alas! my dear High Chamberlain was ever ambitious."

"And is still," mournfully thought Caroline; "he is not altered in that respect; his poor child is the victim of that unrelenting ambition, to which every other feeling has been sacrificed."

This conversation, this gloomy retrospect, naturally led her to think of the Count, and of her union with him. The absence of Lindorf, and the certainty of not seeing him all the long long day, had disposed her mind to languor and melancholy: in the evening she walked in the garden, where these sensations and gloomy ideas accompanied her; the image of the Count, particularly, tormented her; in spite of every effort to remove it from her imagination, and to think on something else, it continually recurred, and with increasing pain and disgust. A dry and yellow leaf fell from one of the trees at her feet, and approaching autumn immediately rose to memory; her heart shrunk at the thought, and an oppressive weight, almost to suffocation, came over her; tears at length began to flow.

"And is the summer, this happy summer, already passed? It has endured but a moment, and it will return no more: with it ease and content are fled from Caroline. Autumn approaches, it is here, and my father is coming to tear me from these beloved haunts, to separate me from my good mamma; and, if the Count my husband pleases —My husband!—My husband!—O Lindorf! friend, brother, every thing that esteem holds most dear, must I never see thee more!—Alas! poor Caroline, wherefore hast thou known him if thou must so soon be separate from him!"

This was the first time she had ever made the reflection, and it was so cutting, so dreadful, and affected her so much, that it absorbed every other afflicting thought.

Intent on this idea, and absent to every other, she walked till she came to the door of the pavilion that led to the road. It was open: opposite was a wood. Caroline was alone: the thick foliage was adapted to the present temper of her mind; it was dark and gloomy and almost shut out day. During the summer she had often wished to walk in this wood, but with Lindorf it would have been improper; the recollection of this wish slightly returned; there was no present restraint, and she crossed the road. As she entered the wood she felt herself highly affected by objects which were new to Caroline. It was a glorious evening; the rays of the setting sun with gold and purple decorated the horizon,[a] through an immense space of clouds, which seemed almost on fire, and the red and ardent colours of which were seen through the branches of oaks, whose antiquity appeared almost coeval with Nature. The evening song of the birds was loud, melodious, and universal; to which the monotonous chirping of the swarming grass-hopper gave variety.

If it be impossible for a feeling mind ever to enter a forest with indifference, what emotion must the young heart of Caroline, and in its present disposition, receive from objects so vast and so magnificent! She took the first path she saw, and which apparently led through the wood; she followed it, for a considerable time, without thinking or perceiving how far she had strayed; at length, some noise suddenly drew her from the profound revery in which she was plunged;[a] she looked up and saw before her, at no great distance, a grand and elegant chateau; she had not much time for reflection; there was an avenue that led to that chateau, and in that avenue was—Lindorf.

The lover instantly leaped the wall that separated them, for he had seen Caroline; and already he is by her side, already he is testifying, more by looks than words, his astonishment and joy at finding her almost at his own habitation. Caroline confused, amazed, blushed even to the finger ends, and durst not look on Lindorf, but, stammering, said she had lost herself! —She was absolutely ignorant of! —She had supposed Risberg lay another way!

Lindorf saw, by her manner, she had supposed so, and, far from pressing her to stay, far from desiring her to walk into his gardens and repose herself, he had the delicacy to offer to re-conduct her to Rindaw immediately. The offer was instantly accepted, and Lindorf, to vary the walk of Caroline, took another path, still, as he said, more agreeable, still more pleasant.

Lindorf, undoubtedly, by the pleasantest understood the longest, and the distance was doubled. Caroline could not but remark it, and was so fatigued at last as to be obliged to accept an arm she had at first refused.

"This way must be greatly round about, Sir?"

"It is; I ask pardon, but I was willing you should know what I do every day."

"How do you mean, Sir?"

"When I go to Rindaw, I take the shortest way, through the wood; but when I return home I go this, which is the most round about."

Caroline blushed, and made no reply.

Whether it was a continuation of the reflections of the day, or whether it was her embarrassment at finding herself at Risberg, the presence of Lindorf had failed of its usual effect; far from dissipating, it but increased her present dejection of spirits; tears stood brimful in her eyes, and she felt that if she had but spoken a single word they must have overflowed.

Lindorf, on the contrary, had, when they first met, seemed more than usually pleased and contented; joy unmixed enlivened his countenance, and gave animation to every feature and every expression. He had spoken with rapture of the beauties of the country, and the delight of living there with the person on earth the most beloved. Caroline scarcely could give the shortest answers, such oppression was there at her heart; Lindorf could not help remarking the change; he was silent, and observed her with eyes alternately expressive of tenderness, hope, and fear.[a] He appeared as if he had something to say which he durst not utter. The moon rose, and her soft clear beams, glimmering on their silent path, still increased their mutual emotion.

At last, Caroline, having recovered herself sufficiently to pronounce a few words, asked Lindorf if he had received the letters he had so impatiently expected.

"The letters! The letters!" repeated Lindorf, with passion in his words and looks, "O, yes! I have received them!—You know not, dear Caroline, cannot imagine, how essentially these letters may influence my future happiness!—To-morrow morning I will come, will communicate their contents.—Yes, charming Caroline, gentlest and dearest friend of my heart, to-morrow you shall read that heart which burns with impatience to expand, to unburthen itself, and pour its most secret thoughts into your bosom—Every thing I think, every thing I feel, all I have thought, and all I have felt, to-morrow you shall know; and my destiny shall be eternally decided!"[b]

These words, and particularly the tone and manner in which they were uttered, roused and terrified Caroline: they tore off the veil which had already been half raised. Without the power of replying a single word, she still had the force to disengage her arm, which Lindorf pressed with ardour, and, looking up, found herself precisely opposite the garden door, which she precipitately entered; saying, with words that almost choaked her as they obtained passage, "Farewell, Lindorf! — To-morrow—I will, also,—tell you something—You shall hear"—

She could contain no longer; her head fell on her bosom; her tears, too long withheld, streamed down her cheeks; a universal tremor seized her, and she was obliged to sit down on a grass bank.

And Lindorf?—Why Lindorf follows. Lindorf is at her feet. Lindorf is pressing with transport her lilly hands, and stooping to kiss them, while Caroline is unable to resist; he dares even clasp her in his arms; and the languid head of Caroline, reclining, droops upon his shoulder.

"My dearest, my best beloved," said Lindorf: "Oh! suffer me to assuage, to dry those precious tears, pledges of my approaching happiness.—Adored lady! Oh calm thyself, fear not; 'tis thy friend, thy lover, thy future husband who thus conjures thee."

This word, this dreadful word, recalled Caroline to animation and herself. She rose, terrified, broke from Lindorf, would have spoke, but could not articulate a word, and, shuddering at her present danger, felt that flight alone could retrieve, could save her. Lindorf remained, for a moment, half amazed at the terror of Caroline, and doubting to what motives it ought to be attributed; while she escaped, ran to her chamber, threw herself into the first chair she found, and was so affected, for some time, that she lost all coherency of thought.

She remained not long in this state; and that which succeeded was much more dreadful. Happily for her, the Baroness had gone to bed before supper, as she sometimes did, and was in a sound sleep: her appearance, therefore, was dispensed with; and, that she might with freedom yield to her present feelings without a witness, she, likewise, determined to go to bed and dismiss her maid.

As soon as she was sufficiently collected to reflect, not with apathy but something more calmly, on her present situation, she felt the absolute necessity of informing Lindorf she was no longer free, and of determining never to see him more. The sentence was indeed most severe. Virtue pronounced it; but her heart could not forbear weeping while it was pronounced.[a] Caroline no longer could, in the least, deceive herself respecting the nature of her feelings. Love stood confessed, arrayed in all his tyranny; his arm was pitiless and his power unbounded. Sorrow sharpened his arrows, and Despair shot them[57]; yet Despair itself only confirmed Caroline in her resolution; Dishonour threatened her, and she did not hesitate a moment.

But how was she to inform him?—How speak the dreadful tidings?—The scene of the evening was too recent and too painful to risk renewing, and she felt it impossible to be herself the narrator. A letter was the only means, and she was all night mentally occupied in writing it; but a letter, on such an occasion, and with sensations like her's, was not easily written; each word, each phrase appeared either too cold or too passionate. At length, when she had imagined nearly the manner and the turn she should give it, she was impatient for day break, that she might rise and write. Every minute did she open her curtains, hoping to discover the first rays of morning, and no sooner had she discovered them than she left her bed, put on a morning gown, and prepared to begin this most painful task.

We have already seen that every thing Caroline most delighted in had found the way to the pavilion; and so had her ink-stand, and writing-desk, along with the rest. There was nothing in her chamber wherewith she might trace a single line; patience, therefore, was her last resource, and waiting till the servants were up and should open the doors. But, as none of these had a lover to dismiss, they slept a full hour longer. This hour Caroline passed at her window, and it depended wholly on her to have enjoyed the most sublime of sights, and, no doubt, for the first time in her life. The retiring of darkness, the gradual increase of light, and the sun rising in all his splendour and animating great Nature,[b] made no impression on the wretched heart of Caroline. Lindorf, whom she was for ever to forbid her presence, whom she was to render miserable; Lindorf, whose love she had been ignorant of, and ignorant also how dear he was to her till the very moment when they must separate for ever; Lindorf obscured every object, she thought of him only, him only she saw. The bright colours of the morning, the sun's rays, and the revival of Nature, were to her all dark and inanimate.

No sooner could she go out but she ran to the pavilion. It was necessary that Lindorf should receive her letter before his arrival at Rindaw; and Caroline had no doubt but he would be there as soon as possible.— Mournfully, then, she took her way towards the pavilion; but what were her thoughts, what her emotion, when, as she entered, she saw, or thought she saw, Lindorf himself, seated at the far end, pale, dejected, his hair all in disorder, leaning on his elbow, and apparently plunged in the most profound revery!

We say thought she saw, because, for the moment, she supposed it to be an illusion of a mind that had lately been most liable to illusion, and of an imagination that beheld no other object. She looked and shrieked, but she could not any longer doubt it was Lindorf himself when, as she shrieked, he rose, flew to catch her, fall at her feet, and utter,[a] with an impetuosity it was not in her power to stop, "Oh! pardon, pardon, Caroline, pardon one who adores you! Think not I have forfeited my word. Yesterday, when I left you, I went home, but, think not I passed the night in sleep; no, at day-break I rose; hither my wishes bore me; the door was open; in short, I scarcely know how I came in this place, but this place never will I leave, Caroline, no never, by every sacred power I swear, never, till you have told me what my destiny is to be;[b] or, at least, Caroline, till thou hast suffered thy happy lover to interpret thy silence and emotion in his own favour. A smile will suffice. Certain of thy consent and the consent of our dear friend the Baroness, I will fly to obtain that of thy father.—To-morrow, yes, perhaps, to-morrow, thou mayest confess, without blushing, thou lovest!"

This, no doubt, was the moment to have spoken. A word would have been enough, would have instantly destroyed the lover's dearest, sweetest hopes; but, oh! how painful was it to pronounce a word like this! It stopped short as it rose to the lips; Caroline wished but could not utter it. Lindorf, prepossessed by former appearances, interpreted this silence in his own favour; it was attributed to modesty, embarrassment, timidity; and, wishing to oblige her to speak, he precipitately rose, ran and snatched his hat as it lay on the piano forte.

"Dear Caroline," said he, as he seized it, "I would not lose a moment when happiness so supreme is in question! I will no longer demand a confession which I see distresses you so much to make: I will fly, instantly, to Berlin, and as instantly return; I hope, with a better claim to request this confession."

Longer delay was now impossible. Caroline, terrified, collecting all her force, stopped and held Lindorf. "What are you going to do?" said she. "Alas! you know not—But learn"—

Lindorf himself now partook of the terror of Caroline. "Learn what?" said he. "A secret."

"What secret! Speak, Caroline, release me from this dread."

"I—I—I am"—

"You are"—

"Married."

The bolt of thunder could not have struck more effectually—"Married!" repeated he, with the accent, or rather with the shriek, of terror.—The most profound silence followed.—Caroline, trembling, sat down, and hid her face with her handkerchief. Lindorf remained petrified; at last, starting wild, and striding about the room, he repeated again, "Married!"

Silence again ensued.—And again, striking his forehead, "No, it is impossible, absolutely impossible; you deceive me, Caroline, you impose upon a wretch whom you have driven mad. Ah! cease, cease a sport so cruel. Say, tell me, you are not married."

"It is but too true that I am," replied Caroline, almost fainting.

"But the Canoness?"—

"She is ignorant of my marriage. I told you it is a secret."

"Oh! Caroline, Caroline,—Fatal secret! And I a confirmed and everlasting wretch!"

For some minutes he was in an agony that approached the wildest phrenzy; he sat down, rose, tore his hair, groaned, gnashed his teeth; every action denoted the fury and tempest within.

"Be calm, Lindorf, dear Lindorf, be calm! In the name of Heaven be calm! Do not thus give way to passion! Am not I, also, still more unhappy?"

"You! You unhappy! Caroline."

Affection and tenderness rose at the supposition, and tears—ay, bitter tears scalded the manly cheek, and gave a little ease to the heart.—"Caroline," said he, in a softer tone, "explain this secret, the discovery of which is thus fatal. Who is this unknown, this inconceivable husband; who thus can leave, thus neglect, the supremacy of mortal bliss?"

Caroline, who scarce could speak, somewhat, however, consoled, to see Lindorf more tranquil, gave a succinct relation of her marriage with a nobleman whom she did not name. She respected the secret of Walstein, and gave not any indications by which he might be known. She only said that invincible repugnance for a match to which she had submitted, in obedience to her father, had occasioned her to intreat a separation, at least for some time, which had been granted her, under condition of keeping it secret. "Perhaps," said she, "I forfeit one of my duties now by revealing it; but I trust I shall carefully fulfil every other, whatever pangs it may cost my heart. Farewel, Lindorf, we must see each other no more. Fly this fatal place, and, if possible, forget the unfortunate Caroline."

"Fly, forget you!" replied Lindorf, whose countenance was somewhat changed by a ray of hope during the short recital of Caroline.—"No, never, never!—I still see a possibility, I still dare hope for happiness!"

"Lindorf!—Be careful what you say; grief certainly has disturbed your reason!"

"No, if thou wilt deign but to consent, bliss may still be mine—My dearest Caroline, hear me—I know thy heart pleads in my behalf, in vain wouldst thou forbid it; to me it appertains, by the ardour, the purity of affection have I deserved it, and my rights are far more sacred than those of a tyrannical husband, who thus has abused paternal authority: grant me but thy permission and these hated bands shall be broken; yes, they shall; I dare affirm they shall. The King is just, he loves me, will listen to me. Beside, I have a certain resource, a friend, a support that cannot fail."

"Unhappy Lindorf!" interrupted Caroline; "yield not to these chimeras. The King himself has forged the chains which no power can break; for who is there whose interest may, for a moment, outweigh that of the Count of Walstein?"

Again Lindorf stood the statue of amazement and dread, again the moment he could respire he echoed—Caroline!—The Count of Walstein!

"The name has escaped my lips," said Caroline, "and my only dependance is on your discretion. Judge, then, what your hopes must be, since it is he, Lindorf; yes, it is the Count of Walstein who is—my husband!"

Lindorf stood with his eyes fixed on the earth, his arms crossed, his faculties wholly absorbed, and in thought so deep as to seem almost lifeless; long he stood,[a] but recovering, at length, from apparent stupor, "Caroline," said he, fetching a deep and almost endless sigh, and without looking at her, "I must leave you, Caroline, but I will return to-morrow morning; it is essentially necessary that I should speak to you once more. To-morrow, here, in this same place, at this same hour, tell me, will you meet me?"

"Yes," answered Caroline, scarcely knowing what she said.

"To-morrow, then," continued Lindorf, making a step to approach Caroline, but instantly recoiling and seizing his hat—"To-morrow"—He could say no more, but suddenly fled.

Imagine what the condition was, what the feelings were of Caroline,[b] and what the crouded and confused ideas that assailed her heart. The first, however, was the promise that she should see him once more. What could he have to say which he might not then have said? Wherefore, so earnestly, and with such solemnity, intreat an interview to-morrow? She almost repented of the consent she had given; and, yet, could she have refused? Beside, it was possible he had not abandoned the hope of obtaining a divorce, for he did not say he had; it therefore was necessary to meet him again that she might dissuade him from all useless efforts, which could only end in discovering their affection, and in rendering the miserable Caroline still more miserable.

The reflection determined her to be punctual to the appointed time and at the appointed place. She afterwards began to think how difficult it would be longer to conceal the truth from the Canoness. What would the absence of Lindorf lead her to suppose? Caroline felt, too, how great the consolation would be of giving her sorrows vent, and shedding her tears in the bosom of a friend so tender and so indulgent. Yet the promise they had required of her had been so strong, so positive, and the menaced punishment was so terrible that, without permission, she durst not speak. Her having betrayed it to Lindorf was enough, nay, too much; and nothing but the motives on which she had acted could justify her to herself. Yet the more she reflected the more she saw the necessity of informing the Baroness; she therefore determined, be the consequence what it might, to write to her father, and beg permission to inform her. "It was no longer possible," she said, "to dissemble with her dear mamma, or to conceal her marriage. The ignorance of the Baroness, concerning that event, exposed her to most painful conversations, and which were continually repeated. Every moment ready to betray herself, she most humbly supplicated permission to confess a secret which lay too heavy on her heart, and which was an offence to the gratitude and the friendship she owed the Baroness. And what was there to fear? The ill health of the Baroness, her love of retirement, her absence from all society, made discretion certain; for to whom could she speak, since nobody she saw? Beside," added Caroline, willing to prevent the visit and the persecution she dreaded, "determined as I am not to leave her, so long as she lives, is it not a shocking thing to be forbidden to speak truth, and to open my heart to the dear friend who has been to me a mother?—Believe me, dear, dear Sir," continued she, "to afflict you will doubly afflict myself, or to deprive you of a child who, if so you had pleased, never would have forsaken you, but to you would have consecrated her life, in proof of her affection; but, you, Sir, thought proper otherwise to ordain: permit me, dear Sir, in my turn, to enjoy that liberty which my Husband and King have granted, which was that *I might remain at Rindaw as long as I pleased;* for such was the sentence, which I shall never forget. My resolution, Sir, is to remain here so long as my only friend shall live, to whom my cares and attentions may be useful, and so long as my heart and my reason shall revolt at the ties I have formed."

Such was the substance of the letter, which after having copied and sent, Caroline found herself somewhat relieved; her secret became less burthensome by the hope of being permitted to reveal it; and the idea of not beholding the Count, for years to come, somewhat consoled her for the dreadful one of never beholding Lindorf more. It was, indeed, too much to feel the double torment of renouncing the man she loved and living with the man she hated; persuaded that her fortitude would rid her of the latter misfortune, she felt recovering strength to support the former.

"I shall see him no more," said she; "but, though I see not him, I shall be troubled with the sight of no one else; and of him I may think unceasingly, here, in these groves, in this pavilion, which his presence has rendered so dear to memory."

Thus fortified, Caroline was able to support the conversation of the Canoness and her questions, afflicting as they were; for she every moment was enquiring if Caroline did not imagine Lindorf would come to-day, every moment was repeating her astonishment that he had not been punctual to his promise. The disorder in her eyes, which still increased, prevented her from seeing the effects of her enquiries on the countenance of Caroline, whose cheeks were flush and pale and continually varying, affected by a continued variety of distress, but this the Baroness saw not; she spoke of nothing but the dear youth, was fearful lest some misfortune had happened to him, and, in the evening, determined to send the next day to make enquiries.

At length she retired to her chamber, as did Caroline gladly to her's, in which she passed the night as she had done the night before. At the appointed hour she was at the pavilion; but Lindorf was not come. She waited half an hour, which seemed half an age, and yet he came not. She opened the window, went out on the road, went to the entrance of the wood, and looked every way as far as look she could; at length, she beheld him coming. She just had strength enough to gain the pavilion, where she sat herself down, unable to rise when he entered, and could only return his salutation by a slight inclination of the head.

Lindorf observed her excessive paleness and dejection:[a] he advanced, tremblingly, and without speaking a single word. When he was near her, he kneeled on one knee and presented her a packet, sealed up, and a box containing a miniature picture. He bowed and, rising, recovered sufficient strength to say, in a low and half suffocated voice, "Accept these from a friend.—Farewel! Caroline, farewel! may you be happy!" Then, respectfully, though not without passion, twice kissing her hand, he rose, put his handkerchief to his eyes, and left the pavilion.

Had not the packet and the box remained, Caroline would have imagined she had seen an apparition; so suddenly and so strangely had he disappeared. With wild stupor her looks followed Lindorf, and no sooner was he gone than, her arms instinctively extending themselves towards the door, Caroline exclaimed, "Oh Lindorf! Lindorf!"

Lindorf heard her not, Lindorf saw her not, Lindorf, alas! was no longer there. She rose precipitately, let the packet and the box fall from her lap, on which they had been placed, and ran to the window, where she saw Lindorf as if flying from an enemy, or struck with panic fear. He was presently out of sight, and the tears of Caroline began abundantly to stream down her cheeks. It was well they did, for, in all probability, they prevented fainting, and, perhaps, worse consequences.

"It is past," said she, "I shall see him no more. To me he is for ever lost."

Her sobs interrupted speech, and almost respiration; and again her tears began to course each other with greater violence. At length she remembered the packet and the box, which Lindorf had left, and which were lying at her feet. In these, no doubt, she would find something that might explain this singular and mysterious farewell: she took the box up first. It is his image, the portrait of Lindorf, thought she, as she was endeavouring to open it. And thinkest thou I have need of such aid to recollect thee, Lindorf?

Yet was it a consolation to possess his picture, the value of which she fully felt, and the recollection made her open the box with eagerness.—How great was her surprize!—It was the uniform of Lindorf, it was a Captain of the Guards, it was a most handsome man, but it was not her lover; a person entirely different from Lindorf and to her entirely unknown. She instantly shut the box again, threw it with anger on the table, and took up the packet.

"Let us see," said she, "if this incomprehensible man has explained what this may mean. Whose is this portrait? Wherefore leave, why give it me!" The seals of the packet were presently broken, and in it she found a manuscript in the hand-writing of Lindorf. Caroline was so much affected that she began to read without at all comprehending what she read; at length, however, her scattered thoughts were somewhat collected, and, seating herself at the window, she took up the manuscript, and again began to read.

The MANUSCRIPT *of* LINDORF.

Dated at the chateau of Risberg, the evening after he had quitted Caroline; and at the conclusion was written,

Finished this morning at nine o'clock.

"GENERAL WALSTEIN, father of the Ambassador, having travelled to England, in his youth, he there saw Lady Matilda Seymour, whom he loved, whose hand he asked in marriage and obtained, and whom he brought to Prussia, where he made her the happiest of women. Two children were the sole fruits of this union; the first a son, the present Count, and the only remaining male of the family, which, if he dies childless, will, with him, become extinct. This son was, therefore, the greatest blessing Heaven could bestow on his parents. Twelve years after he was born they had a daughter, whose tardy and unexpected birth was the death of her mother. The event threw the General into the deepest melancholy; he had adored his lady and remained faithful to her memory; for, though still young, he vowed never again to marry, but to consecrate the remainder of his days to the service of his country and the education of his children.

"The daughter, to whom the name of Matilda had been given, was committed to the care of the General's sisters, one of whom had married the Baron of Zastrow, a Saxon gentleman,[58] but living then at Berlin; so that the child was still under her father's eye. His son, conducted through the paths of honour and virtue by himself, gave signs, in earliest infancy, of what he should one day become, and inspired his tender father with the sweet and certain hope of hereafter fully recompensing all his cares.

"But, alas! this happy father lived not to the full enjoyment of a pleasure so supreme. War broke out between Austria and Prussia.[59] The General commanded a part of the victorious Prussians, and the King had already distinguished him as one of his greatest Generals, when he had the happiness to prove his unbounded attachment and zeal, to his Majesty, by sacrificing his own life, at the battle of Molviez,[60] and saving that of his Sovereign. The King, depending wholly on his courage and neglecting his safety, was in the utmost danger; pursued by several Austrian Hussars,[61] his horse had been wounded and could not fly, and himself ran the risk of either being taken or killed. General Walstein was the sole person who saw the danger, attended by his son, then in his sixteenth year, and making his campaign, in the company of his father, as a simple volunteer. The General intercepted the Hussars; the young Count flew to the King with his horse, while his father wounded, or put to flight, the pursuers, and himself received the mortal blow which, else, perhaps, had descended on the Monarch.

"Some officers came up, among whom my father was, who was the General's most intimate friend, and they and young Walstein bore his father to his tent. The King, in consternation, followed; and the surgeons, having examined the wound, declared he had only a few moments to live. His son, kneeling by his bedside, gave way to grief the most unbounded; and incessantly repeated, 'Oh! my father, my dear father, why was it not me they killed!' The General collected the little remaining strength he possessed to console and recommend his son to the King. 'I remit him, Sir,' said he,[a] 'into your hands; he has partook my peril and my glory,[b] and he, like me, will learn to live and die in the defence of his King and country. You will be to him a father, he faithful to you as I have been, and thus both to you and him I shall be replaced.—And for you, young man, weep not; shew more fortitude, and envy the glorious death I die. Instead of grieving, think of deserving, by your courage, the august father to whom I dying confide you.'

"'Yes,' said the King, exceedingly affected, clasping the young Count in his arms, 'I will be a father to him, and never so long as I live will forget that for my sake he lost his own. He shall henceforth be my son and friend; and, to prove it, I now, instantly, give him a commission in the guards, which will fix his residence near me, during his youth, and which is but the beginning of the good I intend.'

"The young Count, wholly devoted to affliction, answered not; perhaps, did not hear what the King had said. Gratitude and happiness however again were visible in the countenance of the expiring General, and animation once more rose to those eyes which the shades of death had half obscured; he stretched out one hand to his King and the other to his son, and, making a last effort, said to the latter—'My son—your sister—my dear little Matilda[a]—to you I confide her and the care of her future happiness—Poor girl!—But you will love, you will be a father.'

"He could say no more; the young Count would have replied, but incessant sobs choaked up utterance; he only could kiss the General's hand, which he did with such an enthusiasm of affliction as might well assure the dying father of the love and obedience of the son. Alas! that hand was already cold, and the next moment the breath departed from the general, who lay reclined in the arms of *my* father, to whom, likewise, expiring, he said, 'Lindorf, you love my children. Oh! my King, my son, my friend grieve not for me, for I die the happiest of subjects and of fathers.'

"Perhaps, Madam, these affecting incidents are not unknown to you, but, if so, I still thought it my duty, on the present occasion, to recal them to your memory. Yet I have reason to suppose you wholly unacquainted with them, and that they will make the same impression on you they did on me when my father, a witness of this affecting scene, has taken pleasure in recounting it to me. How has it warmed my heart! How has it incited admiration and a desire to emulate the young hero who, at so tender an age, had saved the life of his King, and discovered so much courage and sensibility! With what ardour did I desire to become acquainted with him, attach myself to him, and imitate his virtues as far as for me imitation was possible! How often have I intreated my father to take me to Berlin, that I might solicit the King to permit the young Count of Walstein to come and pass some months at our house!

"My father's ill health had obliged him to quit the service a few years after the death of the General; since which time he constantly remained at an estate which lies in the farther part of Silesia.[62] Several years were past there before the passionate desire I had to see the Count could be gratified; I was too young to appear at court, and being engaged in my studies these could not be interrupted; nor could my father, notwithstanding his frequent solicitations, prevail on the King to suffer his adopted son out of his sight, for whom his attachment daily increased.

"Never, perhaps, was there so great a favourite, and never, perhaps, was there so deserving a one. Far from profiting by the partiality of his master, and accumulating wealth and honours to himself, he sought only to make others happy; and, instead of being envied, was adored. The name of the young Count of Walstein was never pronounced without affection and praise; every father proposed him as a model to his sons, and every mother wished him the husband of her daughter; though few, indeed, might flatter herself with such a hope. The King openly said he himself would give him a wife, and the King destined the most amiable of women for Walstein.

"Oh, Caroline! Caroline!—Yet, have I a right to murmur?—No, you ought to appertain to the best of men; you, only, could reward the virtues of Walstein, and Walstein, only, could merit you.

"At last, the long wished for moment of meeting the Count arrived. Returning from a most fatiguing campaign, young Walstein, having need of rest, added his entreaties to those of my father, and supplicated permission of the King to pass a part of the summer at Ronebourg, the estate at which my father resided. The King had not the power to refuse him any thing, and his request was granted, though with pain.[a] I heard the news with transport. He came, and I found that Fame, instead of having exaggerated, was still far beneath the truth. The Count was in the very prime of life; he was then four and twenty, and to the most dignified figure, and features the most beautiful, he added a countenance incredibly expressive; his eyes were the very mirror of his mind;[b] in them were painted benevolence and sensibility, and, whenever any trait of virtue or of courage was related, they perfectly flashed with animation and pleasure; he was tall, his leg was remarkably handsome, nor is it possible to convey the pleasing sensations that the symmetry of his person and his whole appearance inspired.[c]

"I see your surprize, Caroline—Yes, such was your husband, and such your husband would still have been, if—O, Caroline, I implore your pity; never did wretch stand in greater need of compassion.—You cannot imagine the horrible tale I have to tell; you cannot have the most distant conception of the pangs I feel at recollecting that, perhaps, in a moment, you will detest me—Yet, no; the good, the gentle, the tender Caroline will weep over my destiny, will pardon, and, I hope, forgive; for, though great have been my crimes, yet, surely, great is my present punishment."

Tears and contending passions took possession of the soul of Caroline, obliged her to rest, and the manuscript dropped from her hands. She cast her eyes on the box that contained the portrait, comprehended whose it once was,[d] reached out her arm to take it, and, without daring to touch it, as suddenly drew back. The palpitations of her heart were violent, her ideas disordered, her imagination bewildered, and it was necessary to recollect herself, for a moment, ere she could again begin reading. She sighed profoundly, dried up her tears, once more glanced at the box, again turned her eyes away, took up the manuscript, and continued with an emotion that augmented at every line.[e]

"I was in my nineteenth year when Walstein came to Ronebourg, and, notwithstanding the difference of age and situation, his kindness outran my hopes by the most delicate offers of friendship, which, to me, was as necessary as it was flattering; for I then stood in the utmost need of a friend. My heart panted after some one who could understand it, to whom it could open itself, and who could participate its feelings. I was distractedly in love—Yet, no, it is profanation so to use the word. I loved not. I have since too well known what love really is, so to confound the two sensations—But I was ardently, inordinately, desirous of obtaining a young woman of absolutely obscure birth; yet, whose beauty might have placed her on a throne. Yes, Caroline, Louisa was indeed beautiful; she must have been, otherwise, I could not think her so now, could not tell you so at this moment."

The heart of Caroline had undergone such variety of trials, and so severe, that it is not wonderful she felt herself affected at this place. She leaned back, for a moment, on her chair; had recourse to her smelling bottle, and, when she was somewhat recovered, again went on.

"Louisa was the daughter of an invalid serjeant (my father held it a duty to maintain a certain number of invalids) and of one of my mother's maids. The old couple lived a quarter of a league from Ronebourg, on a small farm, which my parents had given them as a reward for past services. During my childhood I was continually with them, continually in the arms of the good Cicely, who had nursed me, and who loved me as dearly as she did her own son, Fritz; who, in these my boyish days, was my intimate friend. Louisa, younger by some years than he, was still dearer to me; for I could not quit the farm of the good Joselin, her father, nor live separate from her a moment; and when they sent me to the University I shed as many tears at taking leave of Cicely, Joselin, and, particularly, the little Louisa,[63] as in quitting the house of my father.

"I obtained permission to take Fritz with me. I was ignorant, then, that this lad was, naturally, as vile and deceitful as his parents were honest; or, I should rather say, his baseness was not at that time come to maturity. I saw him acute, active, faithful, and zealous for my service and my interests. He was the son of my nurse, the brother of Louisa. How many claims, therefore, had he on my confidence and love! They were not forgotten, and he was more on the footing of a friend than of a domestic.[a]

"Some years stay at Erlang[64] greatly enfeebled the remembrance of the farm, and the pleasures of childhood; yet were they occasionally revived by letters that Fritz received from his sister, and shewed me. These always contained some short article concerning her young master, which was so tenderly expressed, and she recommended Fritz so urgently to love him, to serve him faithfully, asked so earnestly concerning his health and welfare, that I melted while I read them, and felt great impatience again to see her by whom they were written.

"Among them came one which informed Fritz of the death of his mother, my good and dear nurse. The grief of Louisa was real and affecting, and painted, with so much sensibility, an energy so powerful, and so native to a noble heart, that, at hearing it read, the most rugged nature must have been moved. I, too, was sincerely afflicted for her who, ever since my birth, had bestowed the most tender attentions on me. I wept her death more than Fritz, and was far less easily consoled. I have since recollected that one day, when I spoke of my sorrow for the death of his mother, a phrase escaped him which I did not then interpret as I do now. 'You may see Louisa with much less difficulty,' said he. Had age and experience better taught me, this would have sufficiently unveiled his odious character; but I, at that time, preserved that sweet innocence which suffers us not to suspect evil.

"A short time after I was recalled home. I returned to Ronebourg, and arrived there some months before the visit of the young Count of Walstein took place.— The very next day I ran to the farm of Joselin, accompanied by Fritz; but, good God! what were my feelings when I beheld Louisa, and saw the amazing change which a few years had made in her person! Never before had I beheld a being so beauteous. She was in mourning, and her black gown,ᵃ while it marked her elegant form and shewed her slender shape more slender, gave a fine contrast to one of the finest complexions Nature ever bestowed. Her cheeks glowed with animation and pleasure at the return of her brother, and young master; her large dark eyes were powerfully and affectingly expressive, and her hair, black as the ribband by which it was decorated, falling in large tresses on each side, made freshness look more fresh, and added brightness to the vivid colours of youth.

"Pardon me, Caroline, for thus dwelling on circumstances which, to you, cannot be very interesting; and which, now, to me, are become only indifferent, except as they may prove some alleviation to excesses into which a most ungovernable passion hurried me; for never can my crime find forgiveness, unless in the superiority of that beauty by which it was inspired; its effects, alas! were the most sudden and the most deplorable!

"When I set out for the farm, I had resolved, in the gaiety of my heart, to let Louisa guess which of the two was her brother; and had, therefore, dressed myself nearly like him; but the ecstacy, the trouble, the desires of my soul, presently betrayed me. Fritz laughed, and saw, with joy, the impression his sister had made on me. Louisa ran with open arms and pleasure in her eyes, but, suddenly stopping when she came to me, she made me a rustic courtesy, which I thought all grace, and, falling on her brother's neck, melted into tears.

"I was as much affected as she, and the good old Joselin came to add to our emotion. He received me with tenderness and respect; we went into the house, and there he spoke to me of Cicely, the manner of her death, the greatness of his affliction, and recited all she had said, in her dying moments, relative to Fritz and me. I wished to answer, but I could only behold Louisa and weep with her. Joselin, afterwards, talked of his children, and asked if I was satisfied with his son. 'As for Louisa,' said he, 'she is a good girl; she takes care of me, and the household affairs, and supplies the place of her mother better than could be expected: so long as she continues prudent, and her brother behaves well, I shall be easy and happy, and, after a while, shall, in my turn, again go and meet my dear Cicely.

"'When I am gone, I trust to God and my Lord the Baron to take care of my small family, in whom, my children, I hope you will find consolation for the loss of your poor old father.'

"Louisa ran into his arms. Fritz, also, approached, but he appeared to me but feebly moved; or, rather, I beheld only Louisa, the beauteous, the affectionate, the tender Louisa; and I could have wished, like her, to have kneeled to the old man, to have called him my father, also, to have taken his hands and have pressed them to my lips. The father of Louisa was to me, at that moment, the most respectable of beings.

"It was time that a scene so affecting should finish. My heart was overcharged and might not contain all these thronging sensations, and I left the farm, bearing, in this captivated heart, the image of Louisa and the fever of love. Fritz perceived all this, because he waited and wished it all. A connexion between his sister and me made him suppose my favour certain, and his own fortune made. Perhaps, his ambition went farther still, and flattered him he might become the brother of his master. His base and interested mind regarded not the dishonour of his family, or of mine, if he only could receive benefit thereby; he, therefore, took every means in his power to blow up the flame by which I was devoured, and in which he succeeded but too well.

"'Is not Louisa well grown and exceedingly handsome, Sir?' said he. 'What a pity would it be if some stupid lout should possess such a treasure of charms! For my part, I verily believe I should rather see her the mistress of a great Lord, like you, than the wife of a rustic who would never know half her worth.'

"This, and other similar conversation, disgusted me not, though it would have done, no doubt, before I had seen Louisa. The dear idea of possessing her, no matter by what means, transported me; and I, every day, swallowed deeper draughts of the poison by which my feeble heart was infected; every day went to the farm, under the pretext of coursing or shooting, and was always kindly received by Joselin and his daughter, when they were together. As soon as I arrived, Louisa would run to the dairy, fetch me a bowl of milk, cut me some brown bread, and, sometimes, eat with me. The good Joselin would recount his ancient exploits and campaigns, while emptying his bottle of beer. I feigned to listen while my eyes were continually searching Louisa and devouring her beauties; and never could I leave the place without an increase of passion.

"If I found her alone, all her former pleasing attentions, all that air of friendship and satisfaction were gone, and a marked embarrassment was ever apparent. She began a sentence and left it unfinished; sometimes seemed affected, and ready to weep; then, no longer master of myself, would I approach her with extacy, venture some little liberties, and recal to her mind the sports of our infancy. But she ever repelled me with so firm, so serious, so decided a tone, that it awed my audacity, and inspired headstrong passion with fear.

"When I returned home I would complain to Fritz of his sister's reserve, conjure him to see her, to speak in my favour, and to prevail on her to grant me more of her friendship and confidence. He would laugh and assure me I was beloved, passionately beloved, that he knew it well from the confusion in which Louisa always appeared when we were alone, which was a certain proof. 'But these young girls,' said he, 'who, in fact, only wish to yield, wish to have some excuse for yielding.'

"Emboldened by this hope, I would return to the farm. If Joselin was present I was received with every possible kindness, if not, the same continual embarrassment took place, and, if I became pressing, the same resistance. This conduct drove me to despair, and my love, at length, knew no bounds.

"Such was the trouble and effervescence of my passions when the Count of Walstein came to Ronebourg. Louisa was the whole world to me, for Louisa only I existed, and Louisa I must possess or die was the continual exclamation of my heart. The very reputation of the Count for prudence was sufficient to deter me, for some days, from making any avowal of my passion. At first I was afraid of his over powerful reason, but the Count knew so well how to conceal his own superiority, that he himself seemed unconscious of it. His mind, while it was strong and sublime, was so gentle and affectionate, and, to a ripened wisdom of age he so naturally added all the graces and vivacity of youth, that, after a short acquaintance, all fear and constraint were gone.

"His indulgent nature was so conciliating, so winning, that, one day, as we were walking together, and he was rallying me on the absence, the apparent distraction of my thoughts, I ventured to inform him of the cause, and to open my whole heart. To him I made a recital much like that you just have read; I omitted no circumstance, and all was repeated with that warmth and enthusiasm which well were descriptive of the passion by which I was devoured, while he seemed to listen with the utmost emotion and concern. When I had ended, he took me by the hand, and clasping it with all the sympathy of affection, 'O Lindorf,' said he, 'my too youthful, too tender friend, what a mountain of affliction art thou heaping on thyself!'

"He was proceeding to give me some advice, but I interrupted him. 'It is not advice,' said I, 'dear Count, that I ask; it is compassion and indulgence, it is your consent to see my Louisa, and, till you have seen her, not to pass judgment on me.' So saying, I forcibly drew him towards the farm.

"Louisa was alone, and very melancholy. She appeared as if she had been weeping, but this only made the greater impression on me; the surprise of seeing a stranger, as we entered, spread her beautiful face with modest blushes; and her timidity and embarrassment heightened her charms. She recovered herself, and received us as well as possible. I observed she often looked at the Count, and that sighs occasionally escaped her which she endeavoured to repress. As for

Walstein, he beheld her with astonishment, and turned, afterwards, and looked on me with eyes of affliction.

"We took a walk round the little kitchen garden of Louisa. There were a few flowers, intermingled, and she gathered each of us a violet. I could not help observing she gave the finest of them to my friend; but, certainly, this was nothing more than politeness, and I could not be jealous of the Count, whom she had never seen before; no, I was only pleased that she behaved so as might best obtain his good opinion. Nothing, I observed, escaped him; the good order of her little garden, the neatness of her person, and the cleanliness of her house; he saw them all, and felt them all.

"We took our leave, and, at a little distance from the house, met Joselin, who was returning from the fields. His long white hair and venerable figure struck the Count. 'This,' said I, 'is the father of Louisa.' Joselin came up, and spoke some time with his usual good sense; after which we parted and continued our way. I walked beside the Count without uttering a word, my anxious and inquisitive eyes endeavoured to penetrate his thoughts, but he likewise kept silence. At length, I could forbear no longer—'Well, my dear Count, tell me, am I so very culpable for adoring Louisa?'

"'Not, at present,' replied he; 'you are yet only unfortunate; she deserves to be adored'—Then tenderly embracing me, 'No, you are not culpable,' added he, 'but, perhaps, another day, and you may be—Fly, dear Lindorf, fly that dangerous girl; there is no other possible resource. If the most sincere, the most tender friendship may any way soften the pangs of love, mine shall be wholly your's. I will not forsake you, will go with you to Berlin, or take you to my own estate, or, in fine, wherever you please, provided it be far enough from Ronebourg.'

"'Fly!' said I, 'Fly Louisa! Live without Louisa! No, never, never.'

"'And what, in the name of God,'ᵃ replied the Count, with ardour, 'do you think of doing? What are your hopes? Do you mean to *marry her*?—Remember your parents, and think whether you also mean to *murder them*.—Do you wish to seduce her? I cannot suppose you would entertain an idea so dishonourable, so abhorrent. Louisa is the picture of virtue and innocence. And her respectable aged father, who esteems, who loves you, who receives you as if you were his own son, would you betray the confidence he reposes in you by bearing that from him which of all things on earth is to him the most precious? No, Lindorf, you never can be guilty of an act so atrocious. Lindorf will listen to the voice of honour, of reason, of true friendship, and, if he shed tears, they shall not be the distracting tears of guilty remorse.'

"The features, the voice, the eyes of the Count assumed an expression and energy which are impossible for me to convey; and with conviction irresistible assailed the heart. A Deity seemed speaking! A supreme Intelligence, descended from Heaven to enlighten and save! Every word he pronounced was so different from what I daily heard from Fritz, and I had been so little accustomed to behold my passion under so criminal a point of view, that I was absolutely struck speechless, and stood before him abashed. The Count observed, and saw what was passing in my mind,[a] and, tenderly taking me by the hand, 'I see,' said he, 'the reasons I have urged have made some impression on you, and that virtue will soon regain her empire. Come, my friend, come with me, and ask your father's permission to travel awhile. We will depart to-morrow.'

"'To-morrow!' cried I, in all the pangs of returning passion, 'depart to-morrow! from Louisa! See her no more! Ignorant whether I am beloved, whether I ever may see her again! No, Walstein, no; hope it not; it is too much; it is at once to plunge a dagger to my heart.' Then, leaning my head against a tree, and shedding tears, I added, 'I feel the force of what you have said, it is but too true. Ah! wherefore had I not a friend like you in the beginning of this fatal passion? But it is now too late, a devouring fire scorches me up, and now I feel, too powerfully for me,[b] there is no alternative but Louisa or death—Yet will I endeavour, in part, to follow your advice; to remain some days without seeing her, without going to the farm; but let me have the consolation of being near her.—Alas! dear Sir, I am a sick man, to whom nursing and precaution are necessary, and whom a remedy too violent would immediately kill.'

"The Count owned I was right, and mildly endeavoured to calm and console me. He remained satisfied with the promise, which I repeated, of not going for some days to the farm, and, no doubt, hoped, by degrees, to bring me to consent to a longer absence.

"In the evening I complained of not being well, that I might thus impose an obligation upon myself of keeping my chamber; for I felt, if I should leave it, my feet would, instinctively, conduct me to Louisa, but a feigned sickness would deprive me of the liberty of going. Yet could it not be said to be feigned, for I, for several days past, had had an inward fever, the usual consequence of violent passions. I slept little, and eat less; this excessive change alarmed my parents, but I assured them that a few days of rest and proper care would presently restore me. Walstein failed not highly to praise my fortitude, left me but seldom, and, while with me, took every means to encrease and give force to reason, and greatly relieved the torment of passion; but the moment he left me it as suddenly resumed its empire, to which Fritz, indeed, continually was aiding, by his insinuations and discourse.

"He had perceived, from some few words he had heard, and even from what had escaped me myself, that the Count opposed my love for Louisa; and this fellow was, therefore, only the more industrious to keep it alive and enflamed. Nor were any great efforts necessary; for no sooner was I ever alone with him than I began, in spite of all my endeavours to be silent, to speak of his sister. He assured me she secretly moaned my absence and my indisposition, and that, for four days, during which she had not seen me, she had done nothing but weep. 'Poor girl! it's quite piteous to see her, my Lord;[a] she loves you to distraction; and then she keeps it all to herself; no soul but I knows it, but I does all I can to comfort her; I tells her she is not the first country lass that has loved a great Lord, and I says, how happy she would be with you; for, to be sure, you are so good, and so generous, that, certainly, you would never forsake her.'[65]

"These kind of conversations, continually repeated, too potently contributed to encrease passion and enfeeble fortitude. One day, the fifth or sixth of my retreat, the Count having left me to go a shooting, and Fritz having spoken for a whole hour of Louisa and her love for me, unable any longer to resist, I broke loose, like a child whose guardian had left him to himself, and flew to the farm, hoping to be back before the return of the Count.

"Joselin was gone to the field, and Louisa left alone in the house. Her wheel stood by her, yet was she not spinning, and, leaning on her elbows, she had covered her eyes with her handkerchief.[b] At first she did not perceive me, but, hearing the noise the shutting-to of the door made, she looked up, and exclaimed, blushing, 'Good God! my Lord, is it you? I was told you were very ill, and am exceedingly glad to see that'—

"I did not give her time to finish her sentence; the affection which I imagined these few words contained, her blushes, and her eyes red and humid with tears, all confirmed me every thing Fritz had told me concerning her love was true. Enchanted, in extasies, at seeing her again, and at seeing her thus soft and tender, I flung myself at her feet, and know not what I said. No longer master of my reason, I expressed myself with such enthusiasim and fire that Louisa was terrified, but she could neither stop me nor break from me; I had seized both her hands, which, with great agitation and force, I held, while I covered them with kisses.[c]

"Just at this instant the door opened, and in came the Count—I know not which of the three seemed most confounded. The surprise of being thus caught made me quit Louisa's hands, who, the moment she was free, fled precipitately; I rose, but durst not look up at Walstein—At length, 'Are you here, Lindorf?' said he. 'I left you in your Chamber, and I find you at the feet of Louisa.'

"'Then you did not come to seek me,' replied I; with amazement still superior to his own.

"I know not what passed at this instant in my mind; I certainly did not suspect the Count; no, I did not; and yet could I no way account for this his unexpected arrival at the farm. I had, at first, supposed that, having been home and not finding me in my chamber, he had mistrusted where I was gone; but the surprise he discovered had wholly eradicated that idea.

"'No,' said he, recovering himself, 'it was not you I came to seek; I wanted to speak to Joselin; I will tell you on what subject.' Then, taking me by the arm, he brought me away before I could again see Louisa.

"As soon as we were out of the house, he told me his serjeant was recruiting at the neighbouring village, that he had just been speaking to him, and finding he had enlisted several young men, with whom he supposed Joselin to be acquainted, he had come to make enquiries concerning them. This appeared plausible, and half dissipated the vague kind of inquietude I had involuntarily felt.

"'And now,' said the Count, 'permit me to ask you, in your turn, what you were doing there; and what saying, to Louisa, in an attitude of such supplication, and a tone so vehement? Forgive me, Lindorf, but you have granted me your confidence, and of this confidence I should be most unworthy if I did not endeavour to protect you from this worst of dangers. You promised me to remain a week without seeing Louisa; what then could be your intention by this secret visit?'[a]

"'To convince myself that I am beloved, and in that case'—

"'Well; what then?'

"'Why, then,—to sacrifice every thing to Louisa; to renounce all for her; family, country, fortune, friends: she to me would be all, with her would I fly to the end of the world, if so it were necessary. I have offered her the choice of a secret marriage or an elopement; and I am determined on the one or the other. I ask not the Count of Walstein to assist me in this enterprize, but I depend upon his discretion.'

"'And has Louisa consented?' said he, with emotion.

"'She has not answered me; you, suddenly, came in; but she was greatly affected; her tears, her manner, every thing spoke her tenderness; beside, I am very certain I am beloved.'

"'It is possible you may deceive yourself,' said the Count. 'I think I am more certain that Louisa loves another.'

"'Loves another,' repeated I, with phrenzy—'But, no, it cannot be; Louisa is all innocence; she never is from home, she sees only her father, brother, and me.'

"'And one more,' replied the Count; 'a young peasant, called Justin, as I believe; nay, I am assured he and Louisa have been lovers these three years, and that Joselin has refused his consent to the marriage only because Justin is poor. If, however, he be beloved'—

"Unable any longer to listen, my blood boiling in my veins, and jealousy maddening in my eyes, I seized the Count by the arm, looked steadily at him,[b] with wild distraction, and demanded from whom he had his information—My countenance was so frantic, to which my voice was so correspondent, that Walstein was alarmed.

"'In the name of Heaven! Lindorf,' said he, taking me by the hand, 'be calm; dear Lindorf, recover yourself; I may have been misinformed or deceived; I will enquire, however, and particularly; that I promise; ere long I will let you know from whom I received my information, and whether it be or be not exact. But, indeed, Lindorf,' added he, in a tone of the deepest affliction, 'you rend my very heart; there is nothing I would not do, or suffer, to restore you to yourself and happiness.'

"'Happiness!' said I, in a low voice, 'happiness exists not without Louisa.'

"The Friendship, however, of the Count, and his affecting and tender manner made me somewhat more composed. I fancied he had been ill informed; I knew this Justin, and never had had the least suspicion of him; he was a poor orphan, whose sole advantage seemed to be a good person hid under a dress so mean that it was an attestation of his extreme poverty. Educated by charity in the parish, he had been made shepherd to the village. I had often heard speak of the activity, honesty, zeal, and even courage with which he did the duties of his place; the flocks all prospered under his care, and he knew how to cure most of their diseases; he could defend them likewise, and had, already, killed several wolves which came to attack them. The country people vaunted of his talents. He worked prettily in osier,[66] and carved with his knife, for he had no other tool; his voice was fine, and he played exceedingly well on the flagelet, untaught, except by nature, and perhaps love. I had often, while out a shooting, stopped to listen to him; but never had it entered my imagination that the poor shepherd, Justin, could be my rival. Louisa had appeared to me so very much above him; though, indeed, to me, she had appeared above the whole world; yet, led now to reflect on these circumstances, I could not help remembering their birth was equal, and a trifling difference of wealth the only distinction. Justin, too, was a handsome lad, and I well recollected that, in my continual visits at the farm, I had often met Justin and his flock in that vicinity; but he was always with them, and never had I seen him at the farm; nay, I had often spoken of his songs and flageolet to Louisa and her father, but they always had appeared not to pay the least attention.

"Thus, by turns, tortured and relieved, I knew not what to think; though a rival like Justin was too humiliating not to make me endeavour to doubt. No sooner was I alone than I called for Fritz, who, intimate with his sister, and very often at his father's, ought to know something of this affair. I interrogated him, very seriously, concerning Justin, his intercourse with Louisa, their pretended love for each other, and the secrecy with which it had been kept from me.

"At first, he appeared greatly confused; but, afterwards, denied every thing; spoke of poor Justin with the utmost contempt, assured me his sister thought, like him, and would be exceedingly offended at such reports; and concluded by asking me from whom I could hear such a falsehood. I had the imprudence to name the Count!

"'My Lord, the Count,' answered Fritz, shaking his head, 'knows very well what he is about; he takes care not to tell you it is he himself who loves Louisa; and that this very morning—but one must not tell all one knows.'

"He pretended to be going to leave the room, but I commanded him to stay, and, after pressing him a good deal,[a] he told me that, ever since the first day I had brought the Count to the farm, he had become passionately in love with Louisa; that, while I kept my chamber, not a single day had passed on which the Count had not come to the farm and endeavoured to seduce her by the most flattering and advantageous offers; nay, that very morning, that he, Fritz, had caught him with her, and that the Count had tried to bribe him to secrecy. 'Perhaps,' added Fritz, 'I should have said nothing, because, to be sure, I don't like to vex my Lord; but since I see he wishes to scandalize[67] my sister, by pretending to talk of her loving a beggar, like Justin, I can no longer hold my tongue. To be sure, I would wish to consult my Lord thereupon; for, though I know Louisa is a very virtuous body, and that she loves my Lord too much to love any body else, yet who can answer for these young girls? My Lord the Count is so rich, and so pressing; and, besides, he is his own master; he has neither father nor mother, and these are plaguy great temptations. Then, if he should go about to run off with her, for he loves her so desperately that he would do any thing to get her, would it not be better for us to be before-hand with him? If my Lord pleases, we will put her out of his reach in a twinkling; for my part, I have always said, and always shall say, I would rather my Lord had her than any body else.'

"My agitation while Fritz was speaking was excessive; I walked, or rather strode, about my chamber, not knowing what to think of the Count; my esteem for him was so rooted that I could not persuade myself he might be guilty of such perfidy. Were what I heard true, his persuasive, his affecting, his powerful eloquence, which seemed the effusion of the purest friendship, would have been nothing more than deceitful artifice to remove me from Louisa, and snatch from me this object of my adoration. I could not support the horrible idea; it appeared wholly incompatible with the known character of the Count, and, sternly looking at Fritz, I commanded him to leave my presence, and no longer insult my friend by falsehoods totally undeserving belief.

"I did more, I intended to go to Walstein, and undisguisedly inform him of what I had heard; certain that a single word from him would presently efface every remaining trait of suspicion. I went, but I found my father with him, who did not leave us the whole evening, and before whom such a conversation was impossible. Their's turned on the duties of society, morality, and true honour. The Count said many things, on these subjects, so strong, with such natural conviction, expressed himself with such a noble energy of mind, and such a purity of heart, that I inwardly blushed for having a moment doubted of his virtue, and promised myself never to doubt more. I resolved, likewise, not to speak to him on the subject; for to suspect a man like him of such an action, I was convinced, was equally foolish and disgraceful. Beside, to have mentioned it I must, in some measure, have made my footman his accuser, which was too degrading; I was, therefore, determined to be silent myself and to make Fritz silent also, whom a false zeal for my service might have deceived.

"But, while repelling from my memory all his accusations against the Count, I still was resolved to profit by his assistance in carrying off his sister. I admired the principles of Walstein without the power of imitating them; or, rather, I wilfully shut my eyes on the consequences of the act. I imagined my benefactions would console the aged Joselin. Madman, that I was! as if gold could console a father for the loss of his child; and a child, too, like Louisa. But I was incapable of reason. Fatal and terrible effect of the passions, how much are they to be feared since they can lead a naturally upright and virtuous heart thus dreadfully astray!

"Walstein came the next morning to my chamber before I was up; he was dressed and booted. 'Lindorf,' said he, 'I am going to the village to meet my serjeant and examine my recruits. I do not ask you to go with me, because I intend to call at the farm. I want to speak with Joselin. After your scene of yesterday, I suppose both you and Louisa would be equally embarrassed in the presence of a third person; and I inform you that I am going,' added he, smiling, 'in order that, should you once more escape from yourself, you may not be once more surprised.' After affectionately pressing my hand, he left me.

"This visit to the farm, of which he spoke so openly, ought rather to have removed than confirmed my fears. He could not know what Fritz had been saying to me; therefore, there could be no insidious mystery; and yet I was very uneasy; tormented by suspicions of I know not what; suspicions which, notwithstanding, I could not wholly subdue. I rang my bell, Fritz was not to be found, but one of my father's servants came in his stead; he was a native of the village where he went every day, and I asked him, with all the indifference I could assume, whether the serjeant of Walstein was there, recruiting. He answered in the affirmative, and, moreover, that one of his own brothers was enlisted; as, likewise, was that Justin, whom the Count had pretended was the favoured lover of Louisa. 'My Lord the Count,' said he, 'is so good a nobleman, and so kind an officer, that all the young men wish to serve under him.'

"This simple panegyric made me blush at my own doubts; tranquil, therefore, respecting the Count and this Justin, I thought of nothing but carrying off Louisa, and living and dying for her.[a] This idea was for ever fermenting in my head and my heart; and, at twenty, when devoured by a passion so unconquerable, youth is not apt at imagining reasons which should counteract it, nor at foreseeing difficulties; seconded by Fritz, all things appeared possible, and I waited for him, with impatience, that we might hold consultation together. Fritz, however, came not, and the Count returned. Wholly occupied by my own projects, and held in restraint by his presence, he observed the difference of my manner, and very unaffectedly told me so. I saw he wished to penetrate my thoughts, and, unwilling to deceive him more than necessary, I spoke as little as possible, yet enough to let him understand I persisted in the design I had mentioned the evening before.

"After dinner, he left me, as he said, to go to his apartment and write some letters; and, after they were finished, we were to ride out together. Anxious to take advantage of the moment, the only one, perhaps, I should have to myself, I would have instantly flown to Louisa to have obtained the so much desired consent to go off with me;[a] but I might find her father with her, and my going would have been fruitless. A letter, therefore, which I could privately convey to her, would remove this inconvenience, and I immediately sat down to write. The disorder of my mind was visible in every line. My propositions of flight were renewed; eternal love was vowed; promises of compliance to all her wishes repeated and sworn to with all the exaggerations of passion. I requested an answer, and referred her to her brother for our mutual arrangement.

"I had folded up my letter, and was got to the door, when Fritz, whom I had not seen all day, entered my chamber, hastily. 'You, yesterday, Sir' said he, 'treated me as an impostor. Where do you suppose my Lord the Count this moment is?'

"My blood instantly ran cold—'In his own chamber,' answered I. 'Why that question?'

"'Not in his own chamber, but in my sister's, where I just have seen him with my own eyes.'

"'Take care what you say—Walstein!—Impossible!'

"'You may convince yourself, Sir; only go, and you will find him, either there or in the garden, waiting for Louisa, for she was not at home, nor my father either. The Count sent a boy to seek Louisa, instantly; I heard him, he did not see me, and came, immediately, to tell you, Sir, that you may be convinced I am no lyar.'

"As Fritz proceeded, my rage increased, till it was soon ungovernable. To be imposed upon with so much perfidy and baseness!—And by whom? By the man I venerated, the man in the world I most respected, and the friend to whom I had confided the secrets of my soul!— I sent Fritz away, and, almost mechanically, seized my pistols, loaded them with ball without perceiving they were loaded before, and, putting them in my pocket, went out with a fury that approached madness, and was presently within sight of the farm.

"It was necessary to pass by the far end of the garden, where, the hedge being low, I saw the Count, impatiently walking, and incessantly looking towards the garden door, which was opposite to where I stopped. Before I had time to determine how it was proper for me to act, the garden door opened, and Louisa, the timid, the modest Louisa, from whom I never could obtain the smallest favour, ran, with open arms, to the Count, who opened his to receive her, kissed his hands, pressed them between her's, and on him fixed her fine eyes, sparkling with love and pleasure.

"I scarcely know how I recovered, for I felt as if I had received the stroke of death. A cold, a mortal cold, froze up my blood; my strength abandoned me, and I was obliged to support myself by leaning against a tree. Rage presently again brought me to life; again my eyes were cast towards the fatal garden; the lovers, for I no longer doubted they were so, were expressing themselves with all the warmth of sensibility; the countenance of Walstein shone, as it were, with bliss, and never had I beheld it so illumined. I could not hear their discourse, but, by their gestures, it seemed as if he ardently entreated something which Louisa feebly refused. At last, the Count took out a purse, which appeared full of gold, presented it, which, after another moment's hesitation, Louisa received with a half confused half tender air.

"The Count kissed her, and both together re-entered the house, just at the very moment I was going to leap the hedge, and, perhaps, immolate two victims to revenge. I was no longer master of my actions, and should certainly have taken away my own life, if I had not immediately seen the Count leave the farm, with all the tranquility of innocence and virtue, which I interpreted into the triumph of successful love.

"'Defend thyself,' said I, 'traitor,' running up to him with my pistols; presenting him the handle of one and the muzzle of the other to his heart; 'Deprive me of the life which thou hast rendered miserable, or let me rid the world of a perfidious monster!'

"He would have laid hold of my arm, and have spoken to me. 'I will hear nothing,' said I, 'defend yourself! I am capable of any mischief!'

"So saying, I clapped the mouth of my pistol to my own forehead. Happy, most happy, had I been had I drawn the trigger! But the Count prevented me, and, taking the pistol—'You are determined,' said he; then, drawing back a few paces, fired it in the air. Mine was discharged at the same moment; but mine, for ever cursed be that moment, took a fatal, an abhorred direction. I saw my friend stagger, and fall, bathed in his own blood, and saying, 'Alas! Poor Lindorf! when you shall know—Ah! how much more will you be to be pitied than I.'"

CAROLINE

OF

LICHTFIELD;

A NOVEL.

TRANSLATED FROM THE FRENCH

BY THOMAS HOLCROFT.

Idole d'un cœur juste, & passion du Sage,
Amitié, que ton nom soutienne cet ouvrage;
Règne dans mes écrits, ainsi que dans mon cœur,
Tu m'appris à connoître, à sentir le bonheur.

VOLTAIRE

VOL. II.

LONDON:
PRINTED FOR G. G. J. AND J. ROBINSON,
PATERNOSTER-ROW.
MDCCLXXXVI

CAROLINE

OF

LICHTFIELD.

"ALL my rage instantly vanished. I cast the murderous pistol from me; and, running up to my friend, endeavoured, with my handkerchief, to stop the blood that bubbled from the wound. One ball had struck him in the face,[a] and, he said, he thought he felt a wound in the knee, but was convinced that neither of them were mortal.[1] I dragged him to the tree, and placed him against it, where I gave him all the succour in my power, for I was so totally beside myself, that I had even forgot the farm which was not forty paces distant. I remembered not so much as the cause of this miserable affair; at that moment of horror the danger of Walstein was all I remembered: I kneeled behind him; he leaned against my breast, and, notwithstanding the universal tremor of my limbs, I bound up his wound with our two handkerchiefs.

"No sooner had I finished than recollection suddenly returned. 'Oh God,' said I, 'Wretch! accursed wretch that I am! it is I who have committed this dreadful, this murderous act.' My groans could not find utterance. I hid my face in the dust, and added nothing but inarticulate cries and exclamations.

"'Lindorf,' said the poor wounded Walstein, 'Dear Lindorf, be calm, listen to me. There is one way, still, of repairing your wrongs, of preserving, nay, even, of augmenting my friendship. Yes, dearer shall you be to me than ever, if you will pledge your honour to perform what I am going to request.'

"I had no doubt but it was to renounce Louisa, but the atrocious crime I had committed had wrought so instant a revolution in my feelings, that I did not hesitate a moment to promise, by the most sacred oaths, to perform all he should require.

"'Well, then,' said the most generous of men, I require, absolutely, without reserve, that this affair, for ever, remain a secret between you and me; happily, no one has seen us; let me tell the story my own way; and, beware, Lindorf, how thou contradictest me. Thou hast sworn, and I repeat on this condition, only, can I pardon and love thee still. A sole word will for ever deprive you of my friendship.'[b]

"I would have spoken, but sobs and groans prevented me. I could only take his hand and press it to my heart, which was rent by the most cruel remorse. In despite of all my cares the wound continued to bleed; Walstein, with my aid, endeavoured to rise, but he soon perceived the wound in his knee was much worse than he had supposed. One of the balls had taken a different direction, and, we feared, the knee-pan was wounded, for he could not bear the least weight on it, but again sunk down on the ground.

"I detested, I cursed, I prayed, I almost shrieked with agony, I prostrated myself at the feet of my friend, while he continued to yield me every consolation.

"At last, said he, 'go to the farm, and endeavour to get assistance; you will there find a proof that I was not, as you have supposed, the basest of men. Go, but remember your oath; if you break it, I never will see you more.'

"I could not reply, but ran to the farm, and, as I precipitately entered, immediately, beheld an explanation of the conduct of Walstein, and irrefragable reasons for holding my own in still more utter, more damnable abhorrence!— O! pardon—Mine was the guilt of fiends! The shepherd, Justin, new cloathed, was seated beside Louisa, holding one of her hands between his, while she was leaning on his shoulder, and looking up at him with every speaking sensation that tenderness and happiness could inspire. The old man, Joselin, sat opposite to them contemplating a scene so affecting to the heart, and holding the purse the Count had given Louisa, and which I had supposed the price of her dishonour. On the table was another, equally large. Every circumstance was a dagger to my heart, and, insensate as I had been, devoured by passion, I can solemnly attest that remorse, bitter, inexpressible, and almost intolerable, was the only feeling of which I was conscious, or capable.[2]

"'Oh! my friends,' said I, as I entered; 'come with me, fly to succour the Count, he is here, just by, wounded; come, instantly.' My sudden appearance, my paleness, the blood on my cloaths, and the intelligence I brought, were each the subject of terror.—'Good God!' exclaimed Louisa and Justin, 'our dear benefactor wounded!'

"I led them to the place where I had left the Count. Pain, and the loss of blood, had so enfeebled him that he was almost insensible. Louisa ran for water and vinegar. He came a little to himself, and, with difficulty, related that a pistol, with which he had been amusing himself, having burst as he fired it, had occasioned all this disaster, and that my coming by was the effect of chance.

"It was necessary to bear him to the Chateau, and Justin flew to the farm, and brought back a kind of hurdle, and a matrass on which he was laid. Justin, in the prime of youth, and animated by gratitude, not, like me, weighed down by guilt, was most useful and active. Louisa and her aged father gave us all the assistance in their power, and we began our march. It was long, and most painful; and, as we proceeded, several things that Justin and Louisa said to each other gave me to understand they had long been lovers, and that the Count, that very day, had removed every obstacle to their union, by giving Justin a considerable farm, at his estate of Walstein, under the sole condition that they should marry, immediately depart, and that Joselin should go with them.

"Criminal, indeed, most criminal, did this relation make me; but my passion for Louisa was so perfectly cured by this dreadful event, that I heard, even with a kind of horrid pleasure, she was to be gone, and that I should see her no more![2]

"We arrived, at length, at the Chateau; and the hurdle being placed in the hall, and servants called to assist, my first care was to take a horse, and ride, with all possible speed, to the next town in search of surgeons. It was more than three leagues distant. I made, however, so much haste that I returned with them by dusk. I found every person in the most fearful consternation. The manner in which my father received me, tenderly embracing, melting in tears, and praising my zeal, proved that he was totally ignorant of the part I had had in this dreadful affair. His despair was such that, had he known it, he certainly could not have survived such tenfold addition of misery. The recollection of this, more than my oath, kept me silent; but I may truly say the silence was a burthen to my heart, and that nothing could so effectually have given it ease as to have proclaimed my guilt, and thus have rendered me as detestable to the whole world as I was to myself.

"The surgeon, after the operation of extracting the balls, and probing the wounds of Walstein, declared they were not mortal, but that, it was to be feared, he would lose one eye, and the use of his leg; and they even spoke of amputation. The Count, who somewhat doubted of their skill, resolutely opposed this, and sustained, with fortitude almost incredible, the dressing of the wounds, and the afflicting intelligence they had communicated. I could not support being present; but, when the surgeons had done, I again entered his chamber, and solemnly swore never to quit it but in company with Walstein. I know not how it happened that my excessive grief did not betray our secret. It was, indeed, most profound. My tears flowed continually; while the suffering victim of my hateful crime, unceasingly, endeavoured to calm and comfort me. He said, and protested, that he looked on the event as fortunate; that his inclination and abilities had always rather led him to study than to a military life; that he had devoted himself to the latter in obedience to his father and his King; and that he should be exceedingly glad of so fair a pretext to forsake it, and yield to his love of literature and political and legislative researches. 'Beside,' added he, 'you are now cured of your passion; the remedy, it is true, has been somewhat violent, but it has had it's effect, and I most unfeignedly return Heaven thanks for all that has passed.'

"Yes, it had its effects; but I should ill deserve the sublime friendship of Walstein if I did not lament and execrate them everlastingly.[4] I was cured of my love; for, three weeks after this misfortune had happened, I heard, without the least emotion, unless it were an emotion of joy, from the mouth of Justin, who came every day to enquire concerning the health of his benefactor, that he had married Louisa, and that they were ready to depart for their new habitation.

"The Count now entered circumstantially on that subject: delicacy had, hitherto, kept him silent; but, solicited by me, he informed me that the morrow after the visit we had together paid at the farm, alarmed by the violence of my passion, he most seriously reflected on the means of avoiding effects so fatal; that his serjeant brought him a young man whom he had just enlisted; this was the poor Justin; his handsome person, intelligent countenance, and profound melancholy, gained the attention of the Count, and he questioned him concerning what induced him to enlist. The sincere and simple Justin did not endeavour to disguise his motives.—Passionately enamoured of Louisa, her lover for several years, but without the least ray of hope, rejected by Joselin, menaced by Fritz, he wished only to die; but he wished to die like a brave fellow, combating the enemies of his King.—'I should die all the same,' said he, 'with grief, at seeing Louisa the wife of another; and this misfortune must be mine, for her father has sworn I shall never be her husband.'

"The Count asked him if he was beloved by Louisa. 'To be sure, I certainly am,' answered he; 'if I were not, I might not, perhaps, have been true to her for so long a time. But, poor dear Louisa! I yesterday saw her never to see her again, and we both wept so much at parting that we thought we should have died with grief.'

"'I recollect, dear Lindorf,' said the Count, 'that when you first took me to see Louisa her melancholy struck us both.'

"'But, I hope,' continued Justin, 'that, when I am gone, Louisa will be less unhappy; her father, and her brother in particular, ill treat her every day on my account; and that is the reason why I am determined to become a soldier. I wish, indeed indeed I do, she may forget me; but her I shall never forget; no never never to my dying day.'

"Walstein was extremely affected by the sincerity, honest intentions, and passion of Justin; and, instantly, conceived the project of rendering two lovers happy, and rescuing me from the worst of dangers. He mentioned nothing of his intentions to Justin, being first desirous to speak to Louisa and know if he had told him the exact truth. He went twice to the farm before he could find her alone, but watched his opportunity so well that at last he spoke to her in private. He had little difficulty in bringing her to confess her love for Justin; her heart was full of nothing else; and she had done nothing but weep since he had enlisted. She was desirous of recommending him to the Count; and, therefore, glad of finding him alone, she told him their love for each other had commenced long before the death of her mother; that ever since she had each day gone to meet him at the pasturage, and Justin had taught himself to play on the flagelet, purposely that he might not only give her the signal to come and join him, but accompany her likewise when she sung. To gain her favour, also, he had learned to make basket-work, spinning-wheels, bobbins, to twine the osier, and to carve in wood. Louisa shewed the Count two little groups of his sculpture exceedingly well carved, the one representing Louisa, and the other Justin himself, seated at her feet; both the figures were sufficiently like to be known. In another carving, still better executed, the young shepherd was combating a large wolf; for it was for the sake of Louisa, also, that he had first given proofs of his courage, by killing the wolf which was bearing off one of the sheep of Joselin.

"How might the tender and grateful Louisa refuse yielding her heart to him who so well had merited the gift! 'Yes, my Lord,' said she, to the Count, with all the enthusiasm of sensibility, 'I love him with my whole soul, and shall for ever love him, though I never should see him more.—One hope, alas, we had, one sole hope. I often said to Justin, when he bewailed his poverty, *be comforted, dear Justin, only wait till our young master returns, he will speak for us to his father, and, I am well pursuaded, will have us married.* Our young master is returned, but—'

"Louisa stopped—'Finish what you had to say,' said the Count.—'I very well perceive,' said she, blushing, and looking down, 'I was wrong; and I should even be very sorry, at present, if he knew I loved Justin; for my brother has assured me he would kill him, immediately. When Justin is out of his reach, I then will tell him, the first time I see him; and, if he wishes to kill one of us, let it be me.'

"Walstein comforted Louisa, promised her she should soon be happy, that Justin belonged to him, at present; he might dispose of him, and he would make him the husband of Louisa. Scarcely could she believe what she heard, and the very hope appeared but like a dream. Walstein, however, assured her it should be realized, immediately, for that he had spoken to Justin, and that he would directly speak to Joselin.

"'It was that very day, dear Lindorf,' continued the Count, when, after having arranged every thing with the young shepherd, after having enjoyed the purest of pleasures, and spoken to Joselin concerning the marriage of his children, that I found you kneeling to Louisa. The poor girl, conscious of what I had been doing, and who was waiting for me with all the impatience of love, was exceedingly ashamed of being surprised with you in that manner. I confess, I, also, was disconcerted, insomuch that I scarcely could conceal my feelings; which, perhaps, first gave rise to your suspicions. I myself was not free from them; I was fearful lest Louisa had deceived both Justin and me; lest you and she understood each other; and, anxious to know the truth, questioned you. Your answer was but half satisfactory; it, however, convinced me of the great danger you were in, and that, at all events, it was necessary to tear from you the object of that passion to which you were ready to sacrifice every moral duty. You may remember, Lindorf, I, in part, informed you of the love of Justin for Louisa; imagining that, perhaps, your passion would decrease if you knew the love of Louisa was divided. Had you received this intelligence with more moderation, I then should have told you all; but your phrenzy was too visible. Reason had lost every hold over your mind, and your actions had somewhat convulsive about them that made me shudder. I saw this was not the proper opportunity to proceed further. I had said too much, and all I had to do was to smother the fire I had kindled.

"'I, therefore, endeavoured to calm your mind, bring you to yourself, and promised to make farther enquiries; hoping, there by, to gain time for Louisa and Justin to depart, and thus prevent your rash projects of marriage or elopement. In order to hasten the wedding, I went the next morning to Joselin; after having told you where I was going, purposely that you might not come and interrupt our conversation. I was alone with Louisa only for a moment,[a] but this was enough to convince me of the wrong I had done her, by suspecting any concerted treachery between her and you. The idea had tormented her all night, and her inquietude, grief, and ingenuous answers removed every remaining doubt.

"'She left the room as her father entered. I spoke first of my recruits; and, taking out the list, read over their names. When I came to that of Justin, I saw the old man was highly pleased.—"Ah!" said he, "is that knave enlisted? Heaven be praised! We shall now be rid of him."

"'Knave! what knave, Joselin?" said I. "I will have no knaves in my regiment; and I will give him his discharge."

"'Oh! do not do so, by any means, my Lord," replied Joselin. To be sure, I ought to speak with more respect before you, and not have called him a knave, for there is not an honester lad in the whole village, nor is the King himself a braver fellow. He will make nothing of killing you a wolf, you may suppose then what he would do with a man; and you cannot have a better soldier; but to tell you the truth, added he, lowering his voice, he has taken it into his head to fall in love with our Louisa, and the poor little fool, with consent or without consent, would fain marry him; a fellow without a shilling, educated by charity; but, no, I would rather follow her to the grave.[5] God be praised! He must, now, soon leave the country, and I hope we shall never hear of him more. And, yet, it is a pity too; for he took great care of all our flocks; he saved me a fine sheep; and the lad wants neither courage nor ingenuity.—If it was not for that devilish love.

"'And do you not wish to marry Louisa, to console her for the absence of Justin?

"'Ah! would to Heaven she was married. Girls are nothing but torment. I no sooner find myself relieved, on one hand, than I am attacked, on the other. Our young Baron is always haunting, now, about the house: so long as she had her Justin she was well guarded. I did not stand on ceremony with him; but, at present, I do not know what may happen; for I cannot forbid my young master my house as I did Justin; and, then, one cannot always be at home. I should be happy if I could but see her once well settled, but there is not the least appearance of it. The people of our village are all poor, and Louisa is not rich.

"'Well, Joselin, if you consent, I myself will marry her to one of my farmers; an honest young man and above want. He possesses a good grass farm, on my estate at Walstein; some days journey from this place; larger, I believe, than this of your's; and, as I esteem him very much, I will give him a purse of fifty ducats, on the wedding day, and as much to your daughter, to defray the expence of the nuptials, and begin house-keeping. If you think this a proper match say so, and it is a bargain.

"'Joselin, all amazement, would have fallen prostrate. A proper match! my Lord, said he; I cannot forbear weeping with joy and gratitude. All my fear is lest he should not fancy Louisa; and if he should hear of her love for Justin—

"'Fear nothing, he will not be jealous. Justin is his friend, and the more Louisa shall love her husband, the happier will Justin be.

"'The good old Joselin opened his eyes, staring, as it were, after the meaning of what I had said. An explanation, therefore, was necessary; and this threw him into still greater astonishment. But he the more joyfully confirmed his consent because his daughter, by this means, would be happy.

"'The only thing I stipulated for was that they should immediately depart for my farm; and to this there was no objection. Joselin proposed even to remove himself, and live with his children. I desired him to inform Louisa of what had passed, and left him to go down to the village. I there gave Justin his discharge, signed the gift of the farm, and left him the purse of fifty ducats which I had promised. After this I returned to you. Your air and manner, sometimes absent, sometimes agitated, sentences half pronounced, and the absence of Fritz,[a] who had been away from the castle all night and all day; these, collectively, made me fear you had concerted some project; the execution of which might, perhaps, be more prompt than I suspected.

"'I resolved, therefore, to hasten the marriage, and the departure of the young people, as much as possible; and, for this purpose, I again returned to the farm. This was the only injunction I had to lay on them, for the benefits already conferred, and the purse I intended to present to Louisa.

"'What followed, dear Lindorf, I need not relate. You know how much you was deceived by appearances. Louisa had been, all the day, at the village with a relation,[b] in order, most likely, to avoid another visit from you. Her father, impatient to inform her of her happiness, had gone in search of her. They had met the happy Justin, who came along with them; he had shewn them all his treasure. A boy, whom I had sent in search of Louisa, told her I was waiting for her; she, unable to repress the first emotions of her joy, ran, out of breath, to testify her gratitude in the manner by which you was so cruelly deceived.

"'Yes, Lindorf, I can imagine myself in your place, during this terrible moment; can suppose all the dreadful ideas and sensations by which you were assaulted. Surely you cannot doubt, then, that I can forgive you. A little more openness on my part, a little less passion on your's, and this misfortune had never

happened; and, let me add, it will be no real misfortune to me so long as you shall
remain unsuspected of being in any manner an accessary.'

"This recital was made at various times, as his strength permitted, and continually excited in my bosom the most painful remorse. I listened, and, in my
turn, informed the Count how entirely that vile fellow Fritz had deceived me.
I never saw him since the fatal day on which he disappeared from the chateau,
and I learned from his father he had listed for a soldier; since when I have never
heard of him more.

"The day after these fearful events, my father thought it his duty to go himself
to Berlin and inform the King; and, leaving Walstein to my care, he undertook
this melancholy journey. The King was most sensibly affected when he was told,
and immediately sent his own surgeons to Ronebourg, informing my father he
would come himself as soon as Walstein should be out of danger. The surgeons
of Berlin confirmed all the others had said; except that they hoped the wound of
the knee would be less prejudicial than had been supposed, and that the Count
might preserve his leg, though he certainly would be somewhat lame."[a]

"I had a bed brought into his chamber, never leaving him a moment day or
night, and incessantly endeavouring, by attention and care, to prove how deeply I
repented; and Walstein seemed as sensible of, and as grateful for, these my attentions as if I had not been the person who occasioned him to stand in need of
them. To amuse and divert his mind I read to him, as soon as the surgeons would
permit me. Till then, my youth, vivacity, want of thought, and the fatal passion I
had conceived for Louisa, had prevented my application to study. I now learned
the charms of this kind of occupation,[b] which communicates knowledge, amends
the heart, and ornaments the mind. I could easily perceive that, in his choice of
books, his purpose was rather my instruction, and a wish to give me a taste for
reading, than his own amusement. When I had ended he made the most just and
profound reflexions on what had been read; which, to me, were so many rays of
light. Whenever the subject happened to be the duties of a soldier, he described
them with energy, proved how they were compatible with morality and true honour, and how far courage might be allied to humanity and sensibility.

"Excellent Walstein! If, at present, I have any virtues, to thee am I indebted
for them. Thou hast made me such as I am, and the two months I lived in thy
chamber, after a crime for which any other man would have held me in everlasting abhorrence, and have been appeased only by my blood,[c] by thy benevolence
and wisdom, I gained more knowledge, and was better taught the duties of man,
than by all my preceding education."

We have forborn to interrupt a narrative so interesting by any remarks on
what the feelings of Caroline were; and our reason for this forbearance was that
every reader might judge from his own heart, and imagine the passages at which
the manuscript was laid down or taken up; or where it dropt from the hands of

the wife of Walstein; those at which her heart palpitated more or less, or where some strong exclamation was involuntarily uttered. It is very certain, however, that she did not read thus far without interruption; and, moreover, that, at this particular place, an emotion, prompt and instinctive, made her snatch up the box. She only half opened it, and shut it again, with a kind of respectful fear, as if it had been profaned by her looks: then, laying it close to her elbow, she again took up the manuscript.[a]

"A month after the accident, the King, learning that his Favourite could rise, came to Ronebourg, with few attendants. Walstein, then, presented me, for the first time; and the King gave me assurances of his good will and future protection. Alas! what was my confusion, what my shame, when I heard him praising me for the proofs of friendship I had given, on this melancholy occasion, and the uninterrupted attention I had paid the Count! Had it not been for my father's presence and the recollection of the pangs he must have suffered, I really believe, I should have fallen at his feet, have confessed how little I deserved his eulogiums, and have owned the whole enormity of my guilt.

"The King, after remaining a few moments in the chamber, desired to be left alone with the Count. They were together for some time. At last, my father was called in; and, presently afterwards, I, also. As I entered, I found my father kneeling to the King, and kissing his hand. 'Come hither, my son,' said he; 'come, and kneel, with me, to thank the best of Monarchs, and the most generous of friends.— The Count has resigned his commission in the guards, and, at his entreaty, his Majesty has graciously bestowed it on you. Lindorf! my son! if it be possible, merit this distinction, by equalling your predecessor!'

"To Walstein I would have kneeled, in his bosom would have hid my confusion, if I might; and so strongly was I affected that my father, thinking me half distracted with my joy, was obliged to recal my attention to the King, who raised me with affability, and, like my father, exhorted me to imitate the Count.

"'Imitate him!' said I, approaching him, and seizing his hand, which he held out to me. 'Is it possible for men to acquire virtue so sublime—Can I wretch!—'

"Walstein looked at me! and, immediately, put his hand on my mouth!

"Oh, Caroline! such is the man to whom you are united; such is he to whom, no doubt, you are proud, at present, to appertain, and whom you are now wishing to make happy—And, oh, how exquisite must be his felicity! so exquisite that he alone, I confess, can be worthy of it!

"The King departed, the same day, for Berlin, and, soon after, sent me my Captain's commission. At length, I found myself alone with Walstein. My heart was full, almost to suffocation, and I wished to express some part of what I felt. But, no! Expressions could not be found! Words were too feeble! and I could only testify my gratitude as to a Deity![7]

"His friendship for me seemed to encrease every day. 'Good young man,' would he often say, holding out his hand,[a] when he saw me stand with my eyes fixed on his wounds, 'do not suppose these a misfortune. Believe me, for it is a truth, we both are gainers; and I, especially: a friend, such as thou wilt be, merits well to be purchased with the loss of an eye. Had I a mistress,' added he, smiling, 'perhaps, I should be less a philosopher; yet, such as I shall be, I do not despair of finding a woman rational enough to love me. Love has been the cause of my misfortune, and love ought to make me reparation.'

"Behold, how just Heaven is, Caroline. Love will make him reparation, and I alone, as I ought, shall be unhappy.—Yet, no! I ought not, I shall not be, while I am a witness of the felicity of two persons so dear to my heart! Oh! that I may but accomplish the ardent wish I have that these two persons, so worthy, should be fully known to each other!

"As soon as he was sufficiently recovered to travel to Berlin, I joined my regiment, which lay there, and which I found most excellently disciplined. Walstein, yielding to his inclinations, retired to continual and severe study; which, added to want of exercise, was detrimental to his health. He became meagre, and his incessant application to reading and writing gave him that stoop in the shoulders which you, no doubt, have observed; but he had no longer pretension to beauty, and he was become passionately fond of study. The laws and policy of nations, which require knowledge so extensive, were the researches to which he was most addicted. In two or three years he was capable of undertaking the most difficult negotiations, and of filling, with the greatest dignity and success, the brilliant employment he now holds.

"When we arrived at Berlin, he introduced me to his aunt, the Baroness de Zastrow, with whom the young Countess Matilda, his sister, had been brought up. Long a widow and without children, the Baroness looked upon her niece as her daughter, and sole heiress. The Count, also, was fond of his young sister, and was as careful of her education and future happiness as the most tender father could have been. He often spoke of her to me,[b] at Ronebourg, and made it no secret that he should behold with pleasure a probability of our union, and, thus, add another tie to friendship. I thought her charming, but she was scarcely thirteen. She was still but a lively girl with whom I could play with pleasure, but who did not inspire the same sensations I had felt from the company of Louisa.

"My heart, however, being perfectly free, and the company I found at the Baroness de Zastrow's exceedingly agreeable, I went there, regularly, every day; where I was received as the intimate friend of Walstein. Matilda, particularly, took a thousand opportunities of doing me little favours. She called me her brother, and told me, laughing, she hardly ever saw her own, since he was become so ordinary and so learned; therefore, she thought it was my duty to come in his stead. I, in the same kind of sport, called her my dear little sister, and behaved as if she had really been so. Altho' she was very handsome, and daily became more formed, I felt no other sentiments for her than those of friendship, or brotherly affection. The kind of beauty she possessed, however seductive it might be to others, was not, precisely, that which I should prefer. It was neither the regular and striking features of Louisa,[a] nor the enchanting countenance, the look celestial, which penetrates the hidden sentiments of the soul, the lip of innocence, the angelic voice, the—

"Another word, Caroline, and you must never behold this manuscript! Let me speak only of the Count, him only see, think only of him; let my mind be wholly occupied by that sublime idea, and forget every other.

"Where was I?—Speaking, I believe, of the young Countess Matilda. You, I suppose, have never seen her. She was at Dresden,[8] when you were at Berlin, where she still remains, with Madam de Zastrow, who has there fixed her residence. She no way resembles what her brother was before his misfortune. Instead of his benevolent and dignified presence, Matilda's features are delicate and small; the character of her countenance is that of mirth and vivacity. The symmetry of her person is exact; her arm is round; her feet exceedingly pretty; her waist small; her nose turned up; her eyes blue, and intelligent; her rose coloured lips are always ready to laugh, and add dimples to her cheeks; and her whole form conveys the idea of what we call sports and smiles; but never any thing of tender sentiment. She seems even incapable of such sensations; so that one may play with her without the least danger either to her or one's self.

"Yet, however, did she, sensibly, begin to lose a part of that thoughtless gaiety by which she seemed to be characterised. She still laughed, but the laugh often seemed forced, and was sometimes followed by a sigh. By degrees she ceased to call me her brother, or let me assume the privilege of one. If I offered to kiss her, she would draw back and blush; and, when I called her my dear little sister, she very gravely would reply with a *Sir;* which, at times, she had some difficulty to pronounce. The Count perceived the change sooner than I did. 'Either I am much deceived,' said he, 'or the heart of our young sister begins to take part in my project; but tell me, dear Lindorf, what says your's? May I soon call you brother?'[b]

"I was too sincere to endeavour to conceal that I had, hitherto, felt nothing farther than friendship; 'but, certainly,' said I to the Count, 'my heart, already exhausted, is no longer capable of love, and since the charming Matilda fails to inspire passion, I shall never feel it more.' Ah, Caroline, how much was I deceived!

"'You are mistaken,' replied he, 'Lindorf; at three and twenty the heart is never satiated with love: nor have you ever known love; for your passion for Louisa was rather an effervescence of the senses than love itself; its excess was a proof of my assertion, and I desire no better than your meditated elopement. When a lover, Lindorf, prefers his own enjoyment to the interest of the object beloved, you may be certain his heart is but feebly affected. My utmost wish is that my sister may make you feel the difference between your passion for Louisa and the delicious sentiments of refined love. She is still sufficiently young to give me hope that this may happen; and, perhaps, it is her great youth that retards the desired event. You think her only a girl; but, when this girl shall discover sensibility, there will be but another step to inspire you with similar sensations.'

"I embraced the Count, and assured him I had already love enough for Matilda to think with pleasure on the time when I should love her more, and when I might add the name of brother to that of friend; but that I had still many errors to repair and to efface, and that his charming sister merited a heart wholly hers, and capable of feeling her worth.

"A short time after this conversation happened, Walstein was appointed Ambassador to Russia. Our farewell was tender, and affected me greatly. Since the commission of my crime (for what other name can I give it?) I never could behold the Count without a renewal of affliction and remorse. That countenance, so beautiful, that walk and figure, so noble, that look, which expressed so much, all incessantly haunted me. The Count seemed to recollect nothing of all this, nor to entertain the least regret. Before we parted, I entreated him to give me his picture, such as it was when he came to Ronebourg. I knew he had one, and I wished he would bequeath it to me; that my own fault and his generosity might continually be recalled, and that I might be certain time should not enfeeble the remembrance of them.

"This he absolutely refused. 'No, dear Lindorf,' said he, 'you shall have no portrait of mine, neither past nor present. I would have them forgotten as totally by you as they are by me. I never would have them mentioned more. I wish you only to remember our friendship, which is, and ever shall be, inviolable.'

"I did not persist in my request, because I saw him determined, and because I had another resource. The young Countess, Matilda, had a miniature picture in a bracelet; but which, after his accident, she no longer wore; and which, I believe, he himself had forgotten. I had no great difficulty of obtaining it from her, and, under the promise of secrecy, of taking a copy.[a] It is this which I have now left with you, Caroline, and which I beg you to accept. You are the only person to whom I would have given that picture; but you, I am certain, will know its value. Look at it often; and, while you look, remember the beauteous mind which once animated that beauteous form still exists,[b] with still improving beauty, and increasing purity. Yes, the change of his features gives Walstein new lustre, nor should the remaining scars make you hold your husband in horror.—Yet, Caroline, should you detest his wretched assassin, forget not his remorse;[c] remember his repentance! Think on what he suffered while he was making this his confession, and conjuring you to love another; banishing himself for ever from your presence. An expiation like this ought, almost, to make the crime forgotten, and to obtain a generous pardon.

"The Count, at parting, promised to write to me, as often as the multiplicity of affairs in which he was going to engage would permit.ᵃ Wholly devoted to his duty, he had little time for a correspondence of pleasure, or even friendship. Soon after his arrival, however, at Petersburgh, I received the letters which I enclose in this packet; you will find them numbered according to the order in which they came. Read them, Caroline; your spouse is a much better painter of himself than I am."

Caroline took the letters, looked for No. I. and hastily opened it. The handwriting recalled to recollection the short penciled billet of the antichamber; the only one she had ever received from Walstein, and the impression of which had been so strong, yet so little durable. She felt the anguish of remorse; and, for some moments, her tears impeded her sight. At length she began to read. The letter was dated from Petersburgh, the Year before her marriage, and was as follows:

Number I.

The Count of Walstein *to the Baron of* Lindorf.

Petersburgh, July 7, 17—

"The letter I received, yesterday, from Matilda, confirmed what I had long suspected. Yes, you are beloved, dear Lindorf: her innocent and pure mind is itself astonished at the new ideas which affect it, and has not had the art to conceal them from the penetrating friendship of a brother. Each phrase, each word, in her letter, betrays her secret; and I think myself guilty of no treason in revealing it to her husband—Yes, her husband, dear Lindorf!—In vain would your delicacy longer decline what friendship so ardently desires; it now ought to yield to what I shall say, or rather to what I shall repeat. I have reflected a good deal on our last conversation. Because you do not love my sister with the same transport, the same burning raptures you felt for Louisa, you imagine yourself unworthy of her, and conclude you never shall love her. Yet, you acknowledge, and I believe you have, the tenderest friendship for Matilda, and that she is the woman you at present would most prefer, and the only one concerning whom you are any way interested.—What more is necessary, dear Lindorf, to happiness? Does a sensation so sweet to the soul leave any thing farther to wish? And, when to these are added the gratitude you would feel for the love she bears to you, do you suppose it possible you should not make her perfectly happy? For my part, I think her happiness much more certain, this way, than if you had a violent passion for her, which consumes itself in its own flames, and leaves only regret and a painful void. Ever since I have thought of this union, which to see accomplished would, I own, be one of the greatest pleasures of my life, I have studied the characters of you and Matilda much more attentively than you imagine; and each remark I

have made has confirmed and even convinced me you were born for each other—
Without perhaps being so beauteous as Louisa, or, even, as many other women,
my sister has somewhat in her figure which every day pleases more, because it
every day is gaining some additional grace; and because it consists in that varied
and animated play of countenance which is more pleasing than a regularity of
features, that are but too apt, by their sameness, to lose their charm. Perhaps,
you will tell me she wants sensibility, and that you have too much. But shall I
surprise you, nay, shall I not vex you, dear Lindorf, when I say I believe Matilda
has at least as much feeling as my young friend?[a] Under the apparent thought-
lessness of childhood, if I mistake not, I have discovered the tenderest, the most
affectionate heart, and the most capable of a strong and lasting attachment. You
see, already, this little insensible has understanding enough to know your worth,
to love you, and, I think, Lindorf, you will never have any complaints to make
of her want of tenderness. Her mind, likewise, has those propensities which best
please and fix the attention of yours. Her amiable vivacity, her uninterrupted
gaiety, are qualities that will preserve you from dulness; which, of all the plagues
of a conjugal state, is one of the worst. Her gentleness and good temper will
meliorate that natural warmth which so often overpowers you, and, in your own
despite, carries you beyond the bounds of moderation. I hear your reply, dear
Lindorf. 'Yes, my own happiness, I see, will be certain; but what will become of
that of Matilda?' Be not unhappy on that account, my friend, for, once again I
tell thee, I am not; and that, when I press thee to marry my sister, I foresee how
thy heart, perhaps the most excellent I have ever known, will act. Yes, Matilda
must be happy, and I defy thee to prove the contrary. Besides, she loves thee, and
therefore without thee, Lindorf, must be wretched; and, whatever thou mayst
say, thou hast more love for her than thou supposest. Love, my friend, is nothing
more than a lively friendship founded on reciprocal esteem, and improved on a
difference of sex. Matilda has inspired this friendship, already; and what shall it
be when mutual interest and children give it additional strength? Lindorf, thou,
like me, must feel how dear to a man must be the mother of his children. Oh! my
friend, that kind of sensation which you experience when thinking of my sister
will, then, daily increase, daily acquire new powers, and confirm you both in
happiness. Renounce, therefore, these vain scruples, and prepare every thing for
this happy union. Speak to Matilda, speak to my aunt; with the first your efforts
need not be very great. My aunt, perhaps, may not be so complying. She wishes
her niece to marry a nephew of the late Baron de Zastrow, the heir of the title
and estates; but I will write to her, and she loves my sister too well not to yield
when she thinks her happiness at stake; besides which, she is acquainted with
you, Lindorf, and your reception at her house may well make you suppose she
will not reject you for a nephew.

"Adieu, write to me immediately, I am impatient to know whether I have convinced you you are such as it is requisite you should be to become the brother, the beloved brother, of your dear friend

'EDMUND, Count of Walstein.

"P. S. The steward of my estate at Walstein being lately dead, it has given me pleasure to bestow his place on the honest Justin, who manages his farm excellently. I yesterday received his answer, which is written with such simplicity of heart,ᵃ and affords so fine a picture of happiness that, I am certain, you will be pleased to see it; for which reason I have enclosed it.— Perhaps you would rather have seen that of Matilda: if so, dear Lindorf, be certain you may marry her without dread or apprehension."

Whether the letter from Justin was by chance inclosed in that of the Count, when sent by Lindorf to Caroline, or whether purposely put there, does not greatly matter; but there it was, and we imagine our readers will be glad to read it, and once again recollect the beauteous Louisa, whom certainly they have not yet forgotten.

The LETTER of JUSTIN.[2]

"To his Excellency, my Lord, the COUNT of WALSTEIN, Ambassador to the Court of Petersburg.

"My Lord,

"I AM certain, for I know my Lord's goodness, his heart would have been right glad if his Excellence had seen how happy his Lordship's letter made us all; nay, more happy than we were before, which, if any body had told us that such a thing might be, I am sure we should have said it was impossible. To be sure, I did not think that ever the poor Justin could have arrived at the honour of being my Lord the Count's Steward; though, at present, I feel, I am sure, I can do my duty in the discharge of that high office, of which I am as proud as if I were a King; and, though I be not learned, I am certain I can do any thing to serve my good and dear Lord; and I hope, when it shall please God to send him back, that he will be satisfied, and find every thing in good order.

"We have been in the Steward's apartment, at the Chateau, for these two days past. My dear Louisa, at first, was sorry to leave the farm; but she tells me, now, she finds as she shall be happy every where with me; though be this said with all respect to my Lord the Count, for I know one should not brag of one's self; but when one is the husband of Louisa, and the steward of my Lord the Count of Walstein, one may well be a little proud. Our good old father, too, is as proud as I am, and so gay of heart that he seems younger by ten years. He calls me nothing but my Lord the Count's steward; and he drinks a glass of wine more, every meal, to the health and honour of my Lord. All of us, even to our two dear little poppets, are quite overjoyed at being at the Chateau; and they are so pleased to play in the gardens of my Lord the Count; the eldest can go any where, the sturdy little rogue; and his young brother, who is not yet weaned, already begins to lisp the name of my Lord the Count, for that is the first word we teach them; and when his grandfather drinks the health of my Lord he always takes off his bonnet. To be sure they are two charming little knaves, and almost as beautiful as their mother.

"I should never dare to presume to tell all this to my Lord the Ambassador if he had not commanded me to write him word of every thing that concerned our good old father, my dear Louisa, and our little boys.—I had almost forgot the flageolet, but Louisa, who knows my Lord the Count's letter by heart, made me recollect it; and so I continue, as aforetime, to play to Louisa, to amuse her while she gives the breast to the little one, and so the biggest dances all the while I play, for this your Lordship knows is like the birds in their nests; the male sings while the female is sitting: and so my Lord the Count will very well perceive I am the happiest man this day on God's earth. Every thing goes its gait; all we undertake succeeds; and when we are in the meadow we see our four calves, three hens, and their broods of chickens, and I know not how many sheep, goats, and lambs, without reckoning our little boys, all playing around us; and all this my Lord the Count has given us, and so it is my opinion that my Lord the Count is as happy, or perhaps even happier, than we are, because he has done the good, and we have only received it; but it ought to be so; he wants nothing but a Louisa which may the good and bountiful God give him. We pray every day for my Lord the Count; for, truly, my Lord has, after God himself, the first place in our hearts. Wherefore, may God grant my Lord all his wishes and a long life to enjoy them in, which is the most sincere prayer of his most humble servants and superin- tendants of his estate at Walstein."

At Walstein this 12th
Day of June, 17–.

JUSTIN and LOUISA.

"You hear the prayers of these good people, Caroline, and Heaven has been pleased to hear them likewise. Walstein has a Louisa! No, not so; he has a still superior angel![10]

"I answered the Count's letter by the next courier.—Gratitude, the pleasure of being still dearer and nearer related to him, an ardent desire to merit the good opinion he entertained of me, certitude of my own happiness, and a promise to make Matilda happy, these my letter expressed, and these my heart dictated.— The only thing omitted was love; but the Count had just shewn me love was not necessary to happiness, but that it would be more certain from that kind of attachment which I felt for his sister. Walstein had too great an ascendant over me not to convince, and I was the more easy to persuade from the belief of being beloved, which gave a degree of force to the favourable sentiments I had for the lovely Matilda. I no longer saw her without emotion; and this became sufficiently strong to make me perfectly easy when, after a conversation of some length held with her, she gave me permission, though not without deep blushes, to ask her aunt's consent, and endeavour to gain her over to the views of her brother.

"I thought it best, however, to wait, before I spoke to the Baroness, till I had written to the Count, and received his promised answer. This I told Matilda, who thought it very proper; and we no longer endeavoured to conceal an affection thus authorized by fraternal authority.

"I continued, therefore, my daily visits at the Baroness de Zastrow's, and very assiduously paid her my court, though with very little success. After the departure of the Count her conduct to me had been wholly changed; always polite but always distant, she affected to receive me with great ceremony, and took her measures so well that I seldom had an opportunity of speaking a word in private to Matilda. These impediments and contradictions might naturally have been expected to augment love; and, I own, I was secretly vexed, which did not pass unobserved by Matilda, and which consoled her for her aunt's behaviour by persuading her she was beloved; and so, no doubt, she was; friendship, gratitude, attached me to her, and, had I then obtained her hand, I might myself have been well persuaded my affection was much stronger than it has proved.

"I waited, however, without any violent impatience, the effect of the Count's promises and letter to his aunt. He wrote me word 'he had not yet been able to gain the consent of that lady, for she tenaciously adhered to her design of marrying Matilda to the young Baron de Zastrow, then on his travels. Yet that he, however, was still more tenacious of his own, which certainly should be effective; for which reason he conjured me not to take offence, but to wait with patience. A considerable estate,' he said, 'depended on this aunt, which required some caution; but that, by one means or other, he would obtain his end, and that he already regarded me as his brother.'

"I wished to shew Matilda this letter, and immediately went to the house of the Baroness. I found it shut up. No porter, not a single servant, was there to whom I could speak. This circumstance appeared extremely singular; for, the very evening before, I had been received as usual, without the least mention of a removal. I enquired in the neighbourhood, and was told the coach had set off very early in the morning; but could learn nothing more. While I was remaining in the utmost astonishment, I saw Matilda's maid coming to me. I ran to meet her, and was going to question, but was prevented by her telling me to ask nothing, for that nothing she knew. 'I cannot tell you where they are,' said she. 'Yesterday, as soon as you were gone, I heard my lady speaking very loud, and Miss Matilda weeping. All night long there was nothing but packing up, scolding, and crying; and, at last, I was paid my wages, discharged, and they set off in a coach; but Miss Matilda, when she bade me farewell, slipt this into my hand.'

"The maid then gave me a rumpled paper, addressed to me, which, taking, I directly opened, but without, at first, being able to comprehend a word of its contents. It seemed an inventory of chairs, tables, and furniture. At last, I discovered that what regarded myself was interlined, and was as follows.

"'Oh! Mr. Lindorf, we are going to depart for Dresden, presently; and we are to stay there a long, long while; perhaps, for ever. What will you think when you shall come to-morrow and find your poor young friend gone? Will you grieve as much as she does? I hope you will be a little sorry; yet do not afflict yourself too much; for I promise you my thoughts will be the same at Dresden as they were at Berlin, and so they will for ever continue to be. Besides, have I not a brother, a dear good brother? Write to him immediately; and, should you wish to send a word in answer to this, let it be under cover to him, for there are no other means of its arriving at me. No, if you write to me, your letters must first go to Russia. But what of that, if I but get them at last?—I wish I were as sure this would come to your hands. I could contrive no means of writing to you, but, luckily, my aunt gave me an inventory to copy. When she looks at me, I set down a figure, and, the moment she is gone, write a line. When it is done, perhaps, I may give it to poor Nancy,[11] whom my aunt intends to turn away, because she might assist us, and because she loves you. I am sure she will give it you, faithfully.—I am vexed to be obliged to write thus clandestinely and deceive my aunt; yet she has had no remorse at deceiving me. Till this very night I knew not a word of our departure: no, I protest to you, I did not know a word of it. Is it not a shocking thing to be obliged to set off without seeing you?[a]—I scarcely can write for crying, and I hear my aunt coming. My paper is no more like an inventory, so I must hide it, and begin another. Farewell, Mr. Lindorf, I will remember you, and pray for you continually, and do not forget the poor Matilda, and do not think ill of her because she has written to you first.'

"Such was the letter of Matilda, on reading of which it was impossible, without any violent love, not to be affected at the native simplicity of the niece, and piqued at the behaviour of the aunt. I felt both these sensations in their full force, and returned to my chamber, where I immediately wrote an account of all that had passed to Walstein, and of the unworthy artifice that had been used. I believe anger was stronger than regret, for I insinuated to the Count that I looked upon our project as impracticable; and, since Madame de Zastrow was so determined, to renounce it appeared to me the wisest way. I inclosed a copy of the letter from Matilda, and my answer, desiring her brother to send it to her; and I received a letter from the Count, by the return of the post, as follows."

Number II.

The Count of WALSTEIN *to the Baron of* LINDORF.

Petersburg, July 18, 17—

"I am exceedingly angry, dear Lindorf, at the trick our good aunt, de Zastrow, has played us; but her efforts are fruitless, Matilda shall be your's. I declare, nay have sworn, my sister shall not become the victim of her obstinacy. I have nothing to alledge against the young Baron de Zastrow, whom I have not the honour of knowing, and to whom I wish all manner of happiness, except that of being the husband of Matilda. You, Lindorf, has she selected, and you, already, doth her young heart prefer. No, that innocent and open heart, which spoke all its secrets with such ingenuous confidence to me, shall not be deceived in its wishes; shall not have to combat a passion to which I myself may be said to have given birth; nor shall she have to blush for having first written to any other man than her husband. Poor dear girl! how much did her billet affect me! I will write, immediately, to console her, and afford her no very distant prospect of felicity: a little perseverance and we shall conquer. I will inclose your letter, likewise, which, I believe, will be more effectual than mine. By the same post I will write to my aunt, and, if necessary, assert the rights a dying father bequeathed to me over my sister. *To you I confide her and the care of her future happiness*; nor, oh! my father, will I betray this trust. Matilda and Lindorf shall be one, and your dear girl then cannot fail of being happy. Take courage, therefore, my friend, and be assured our project shall succeed. Matilda is yet but fifteen; in three or four years she will be more formed, more capable of happiness, more worthy of herself and you. My only fear is that, you being separate from her, that heart, so suddenly become cold, insensible, that heart, no longer susceptible of love, as you have supposed, may, in the mean time, stand convicted of it's error, and find that it never yet knew the passion. If, dear Lindorf, this misfortune should happen, promise me, swear to me, you will neither sacrifice yourself nor my sister to engagements which, from that moment, will cease to exist. I am desirous of this union no farther than as I am persuaded it will not be a misfortune to either party, and would rather have to comfort Matilda for the loss of a lover than for the indifference of the husband of her heart. Therefore, Lindorf, the very moment she would no longer be the wife you would prefer to all others, the very moment you feel certain some other woman may render you more happy,[a] have the fortitude to inform your friend of this change, and be assured that, instead of diminishing, by this conduct, you will redouble his esteem. I think violent love no way necessary to conjugal felicity. I have said so in my former letter and I persist in the opinion; but I am still more effectually convinced that a husband and wife ought, at least, mutually to prefer each other to the whole world, and never know regret at the remembrance of being united for life. I think it necessary that that agreement of taste and feeling, that entire confidence, that bond of affection, should be found, which cannot exist if one of the two love another and be obliged to conceal the thoughts by which he or she most is occupied.—These considerations, I own, have hitherto hindered me from marrying and yielding to the wishes and entreaties of my family, which, with me, will become extinct. I dread lest my present rank and favour might engage some woman, to whom I might address myself, to marry me, though she really loved another. I fear acquiring rights which I shall find are usurpations, and over a heart that has other engagements. I dread being the unconscious cause of misery to two lovers, and being myself still more miserable when I shall have made the discovery. You know me too well, dear Lindorf, ever to imagine I can mean to reproach when I thus speak my secret sentiments. You know my manner of thinking relative to the accident that has altered my person; it is ever the same; and, I again protest, I every day congratulate myself on the present opportunity I enjoy of indulging my most prevalent inclination, and following the studies in which I most delight; happy in having had the means, in my former station, of giving those proofs of courage and zeal in the service of my King which most I wished; and, in my present, of serving him, as I think, much more effectually. A good minister, Lindorf, is still a greater character than a good general. It is my greatest pleasure to fulfil the duties of the office to which I am appointed; and this office, I repeat it, is much more agreeable to me than the life of a soldier;[12] therefore I *can* have nothing to regret; nothing, nothing– Yet I must do myself justice. I may not now hope to inspire love, nor do I make any such weak pretences; and, perhaps, it may be for that reason I persuade myself that love is not necessary to happiness. But I wish, at least, to find a woman who has no partiality for another. I do not even shrink from a slight repugnance, at first; that is natural, and what I ought to expect. My endeavours must be to dispel it by degrees, and make myself first beloved, through gratitude, and afterwards from habit. The eye would soon accommodate itself to my person, and my sole study should be to make it forgotten by my actions. Is it possible that a woman must not, at last, love him who exists but to render her happy; who would prevent[13] her wishes, to which his own would be ever subservient, and who would be grateful for the smallest marks of attachment which she might bestow? Such, my friend, are the loved illusions of my heart, and which I yet, one day, hope to behold realized. I foresee all the obstacles, but they discourage me not. I know how difficult it is to find a woman whose heart is entirely free, without which my whole scheme would be frustrate; for comparisons would incessantly be made between me and the regretted, beloved object. I should be looked upon as a monster. Partiality and bitter remembrance would poison life. But, could I meet some young heart, such as I wish, and such as I shall incessantly endeavour to find, simple and innocent, unacquainted with love, and with little knowledge of the world; if such I find, it shall be mine, even though I should oblige her to marry me; for I would render her happy in her own despite. I am sensible that I should at first be accused of want of delicacy; but my secret motives would justify me in my own eyes. I have no other means of enjoying a felicity my heart most ardently desires; that of being a husband and a father, and ending my days in the arms of my children. Sacred ties! Connexions of the soul, which double existence! without which man is desolate, alone, in the wide world, as in a desart; dragging a useless life and dying without regret!—Yes, such intimate relations will constitute my happiness. Never can I think of them without emotion, never can read the letter from Justin, a copy of which I sent to you, without shedding tears. How happy are those good people! *He wants nothing but a Louisa, which may the good and bountiful God give him!*—Yes, honest Justin, the prayers of a heart so pure as thine ought to, and no doubt will, be heard. I shall find this companion, whom, already, I adore; though I know her not. She and Walstein, Lindorf and Matilda, Justin and Louisa, and there will be three happy couples in the universe! What say you, Lindorf, to my prophecy? For my part I am in raptures at the idea, and have faith in perfect bliss.—But what is it you mention about the loss of inheritance? Should my aunt be unjust enough to deprive Matilda of hers, is not she sufficiently rich at present; and does more or less influence happiness when we have more than sufficient for the enjoyment of life? Will not your wealth and hers be enough? However, as plenty is not an evil, and as it is best that what is done should be done with a good grace, let us wait awhile, my friend. I would not affirm I should not be jealous were you happy while I remain single: and my dear wife is not yet found. I shall soon, however, seriously begin the search. At present, I have too many affairs on hand. I fear I shall not often have the pleasure of writing to you, for which reason I take full revenge of the present opportunity"—

The remainder of the letter related only to political affairs, and accounts of Russia, which Caroline skipped over, or read unconsciously; her thoughts had other employment, and her heart was not capacious enough for her own affairs. She seemed as if transported into another world, of which, till then, she had had no idea. This last letter particularly struck her. She read it again, and with sensations somewhat painful. The prediction of the love of Lindorf, the excessive fear of Walstein, lest he should marry a woman whose heart was pre-engaged, made a severe impression on her. When she came to Walstein's projects of happiness, and to the motives which had induced him to marry her, she found herself, notwithstanding her repugnance, so affected, that, at the moment, she thought she loved him only in the world; or, rather, she did not herself understand her own feelings. She remained with her eyes fixed on this letter, without remembering that the manuscript was not ended. Her enthusiasm, at length, vanished by degrees; the idea of the Count was effaced, and the image of Lindorf regained a part of its former empire. The letter was laid down, and the manuscript once more taken up.

"Time fails, Caroline, and the four and twenty hours I have dedicated to this painful work are almost ended. I already perceive the first rays of day, of that day on which, perhaps, for the last time I shall behold her to whom, yesterday, at the same hour, I hoped to devote my life. How happy was I then! How did the sweet chimæras of hope and love flatter my heart! A single moment has destroyed them all, has plunged me into an abyss of despair!—Yet what complaints are these? Ought I thus to employ the few remaining moments in which I would conduct you to happiness,[a] by pointing out the road? Yes, Caroline, you will be, must be, happy; and the certainty of this will be the sole consolation of my future existence.

"The whole year passed without the least change of circumstance or situation. Matilda remained at Dresden, the Count in Russia, and I at Berlin. An uninterrupted correspondence maintained our mutual connections, but that of Dresden, passing first by Petersburg, was neither very frequent nor very animated. Matilda, educated in restraint, and even with severity, durst not indulge her feelings; and, at the utmost, expressed friendship only. My answers nearly assumed the same tone; yet, determined to espouse her as soon as her aunt would consent, and preferring her to all the women I then knew, I carefully avoided every occasion of meeting objects who might eradicate these ideas, and take place of her in my heart.

"To deprive myself of the pleasures of courts cost me but little. Ever since the unfortunate adventure of Louisa and the Count I had preserved an habitual melancholy, which well accorded with my future intentions. Wholly devoted to my military occupations and paying my duty to the King, I employed the remainder of my time in riding, music, or reading.

"An unfortunate event happened which disturbed my tranquillity and increased my melancholy. My father, who remained at Ronebourg, had an apoplectic fit;[14] my mother, who had long been in a feeble and ill state of health, scarcely could support her grief and terror. I was instantly sent for, and found them both, on my arrival, in great danger The sight of me appeared to animate them; my mother especially, who loved me with most affectionate tenderness, found herself sensibly better,[b] which she attributed to my presence and cares; but the state in which she still remained required every attention I could bestow. I wrote to Court, to obtain leave of absence. My motive was too sacred for me to be refused, and I devoted my whole time and faculties to my parents.

"It was during this absence, Caroline, that you came to embellish the Court I had quitted; and it was then also the Count had that unfortunate sickness which detained him so long on the road, and which I heard of by accident. At any other moment I should have flown to his assistance; but I was then detained at Ronebourg, by duties too sacred, and too dear, to admit even the idea.

"Some time after, I had the pleasure to learn, from himself, he had recovered and arrived at Berlin. His letter had an enigmatic and mysterious turn, which struck me at the moment of reading—[a] 'He would have given, he said, the whole world to see and speak to me. The cruel event, which detained me at Ronebourg, was the more distressing to him because he absolutely could not come thither, on account of the distance (Ronebourg is at the farther end of Silesia, and four long days journey from Berlin) and the little time he had to remain in Prussia, during which every moment would be occupied. He then spoke of Matilda, was grieved at the perversity of her aunt, but was determined, he said, the instant I should be at liberty, to leave Ronebourg, to exert his authority and terminate[15] our marriage.—He had a new motive for hastening the affair.—Perhaps he was himself on the point of being happy—of obtaining what he so ardently desired; but he could not enjoy perfect content unless I enjoyed it also.

"I paid less attention to this letter than I should have done at any other moment;[b] for scarcely had I time to read it, nor have I, till now, hardly recollected it since. I received it on the very day on which my father, after having languished four months, expired in my arms, recommending my mother to me, and commanding me not to leave her.

"Alas! my heart had already forerun the command, which was itself to me a law. Already had I sworn, to the tenderest of mothers, that her son, her only son, would not abandon her in the hour of her affliction!

"As soon as I had rendered my father the last duties of humanity, I wrote to the Count to inform him of my loss, and to entreat he should obtain a renewal of my leave of absence; and the King not only permitted me to remain at Ronebourg, but deigned likewise to approve the motive that made me wish to stay.

"The Count, in his answer, wrote in a stile of melancholy that did not surprise me. I knew how sensibly his heart was affected by, and partook of, the afflictions of his friends; beside, he himself had a strong attachment to my father. He made no references to the subject of his former letter, which had been mislaid in the grief of the terrible moment in which it was received, and I had almost forgot its contents. He only said he should go immediately to Dresden, being desirous to see his sister before he returned into Russia; he added that, if it were possible, he would also come to Ronebourg, but durst not promise; and, in fact, did not come.

"Wherefore, Oh! wherefore did he not then confide to me the fatal secret? — Yet, no doubt, his delicacy would not suffer him to encrease my present pangs by informing me of an event of which I could not help knowing myself to be the original cause.

"Three months more passed away, still more sorrowful, still more painful than the preceding. I had but one object of attention; filial affection was, now, solely attached to my mother, whom I beheld daily decline, without other hope, other consolation, than that of soothing her last moments. At length, I lost her, also. Her pure soul quitted its terrestrial residence, and rejoiced at the hope of once again meeting her husband, and expiring in the arms of her son.

"Pardon, Oh Caroline! this gloomy narrative. I have need of the support of former misfortunes to enable me to endure the present; and am obliged to retrace antecedent losses, now, when I suffer one which might have consoled me for them all. It is necessary for me incessantly to remember that man is born to be unhappy, and that misery is his portion; that he is successively to lose every object he held most dear, and for whom he only wished to live. No, happiness is not for man —at least only for one man—and his virtues, perhaps, make it his right. I, certainly, ought not to murmur.

"After the death of my father, I fled from Ronebourg; it was become a hated place, as well by the double loss I so lately had sustained as by the act of barbarity I formerly had committed there. I returned to Berlin and Potsdam,[16] where I passed the remainder of the winter, and lived still more retired than the year before. The Count wrote seldom, and, when he did, his stile seemed embarrassed and gloomy; and, at length, I began to perceive there was something which lay heavy at his heart. I told him so, he owned it, but deferred a full explanation till he should see me in person. This was to be in the following autumn, which was the time, also, he had fixed for my marriage with his sister. 'Thy destiny and mine,' said he, 'Lindorf, will then be finally determined. Oh! may they be happy! Or, if I myself am obliged to renounce bliss, may, at least, the felicity of my sister and my friend supply the loss of what I dare not hope!'

"I supposed he had a passion for some Russian lady, to which he found insurmountable obstacles; but, respecting his secret, I ceased my enquiries. I likewise occasionally received short letters from Matilda, which always were first sent to her brother. Her aunt remained fixed in her opinion, and had written for the young Baron de Zastrow to return from his travels. Her inheritance was only to be Matilda's on condition this marriage took place; but the generous girl was ready to forego every advantage, and asked me, with an affecting openness of heart,[a] whether I was not of her opinion; and whether I were not a thousand times better to have less riches and more happiness. For my part, I little regretted the loss of Madame de Zastrow's fortune; for my own, by the death of my parents, had become considerable, and was very largely increased by the decease of the Commander of Risberg, my maternal uncle. He lived, like a hermit, on the estate I at present inhabit; would never see me while living, and left me all his wealth at his death, under the condition, however, that I should marry within two years, and give the name of Risberg to my eldest son. My engagements with Matilda made the fulfilling of this clause apparently easy; and, perhaps, too, this motive might have contributed to decide Madame de Zastrow in my favour.

"Since that time, Caroline, how kind have I thought the obligation laid on me by my uncle's will! How sweet has the idea been of marrying within much less than the time prescribed! How many future joys did I dare expect, and how sincerely did I bless my uncle's memory! —At present, I renounce, for ever renounce his gift. I pretend not to wealth to which I have no right; and will quit an estate, to-morrow, to which I am never to return. What to me are riches and estates? Or what, alas! can I suffer now?—I have nothing to lose!

"Oh pardon! pardon! Caroline! How may the vows of a wretch whom it is your duty to forget affect you? I add to my crimes by continuing to adore you; and the purpose of this writing is to make reparation.

"Determined no longer to remain at Ronebourg, which retraced sorrowful thoughts, only, and heart rending recollections, and which, beside, is too far distant from the capital, I was delighted with the acquisition of Risberg, and came to take possession, at the beginning of the summer, a short time after my uncle's decease.—Caroline —It is here, at this place, at this moment, that I have need of all my fortitude to continue the fatal recital.—Angel adored! can I speak to you of yourself, and of what my feelings were, and are, and not expire!

"Sacred and pure Friendship! Thou who shouldst expiate the crimes Love hath committed, thou who, henceforth, only shouldst find place in my heart, return and animate, my zeal; once more return, and sustain relapsing Nature !

"I was charmed with my new abode, yet did not intend to stay here long; and was, therefore, desirous of examining the neighbourhood. The evening before that day on which I first beheld you, at the window of the pavilion, I had accidentally passed and heard those sweet and harmonious sounds, that affecting and angelic voice, the impressions of which have since been so powerful, and the effects of which, indeed, I felt the very moment they first were heard. Never before had I heard a voice of so much sensibility. I listened for some time after you had ceased to sing, and still thought I heard sounds so correspondent to the feelings of my heart. Nay, I continued to hear them, even at a distance; and, the next day, impatiently visited the same place.

"Passionately fond of music, to that alone did I attribute that irresistible attraction by which I was led thither. I will, however, confess I was, indeed, most desirous to see the person of her whose power over the heart I found so great; but this I attributed to curiosity. I imagined that, by singing with you, I might bring you to the window; and the stratagem was successful. I beheld you! Though but for a moment; but that moment was sufficient. The impression it made never can be forgotten; and my first wish was I might have beheld you ever.

"Wherefore, Oh! wherefore may I not dwell on incidents once so dear to memory? Wherefore not retrace each circumstance, recount each rapturous event of time which fled so swift away, and which has left mementos so fatal in my heart! Ah! Happy I! when, my soul absorbed by sensations of bliss so pure, sensations of which, till then, I had been wholly ignorant, I existed only at Rindaw, forgotten of the world beside! Ah how happy! when, leaving you in the evening, my sole idea was that of seeing you again on the morrow; and while that idea was so vast, so perfect, that it excluded every other! Not those burning, resistless, and tumultuous sensations that Louisa inspired; nor yet that monotonous tranquility, that indolence of heart, and apathy of sense, Matilda gave, did I feel. No; the charm was new, delicious, exquisite! It was another world which Caroline embellished! I beheld her in every surrounding object; or, rather, I beheld no other object but her. The only letter I wrote, during two months, was to ask permission to pass the summer at Risberg, which I obtained, and I thought those two months an eternity! The past forgotten, to the future blind, the present was Heaven, for Caroline was present!

"Yet wherefore seek to redouble my torments, by painting happiness foregone? Alas! I had forgotten that I ought no more to speak of myself; forgotten that Caroline is the wife of the best, the sublimest of mortals!—Yes, of him I will speak; of him only.

"About a month since, I received a letter from him; and this letter first awakened me from this inebriety of pleasure. He complained of my silence, at which Matilda, likewise, was not less surprised. Matilda!— The very name rent my heart, and made me feel it was wholly Caroline's. —I laid down the letter, and it was long before I had the fortitude again to read. At length I took it up once more, and the following passage restored me to life.—'Have you,' said Walstein, 'changed your opinion, either respecting Matilda or our future destinies, and do you fear to own it, Lindorf? All you have to fear is to leave us either in incertitude, or error. I refer you to the letter I wrote, last autumn, relative to this subject: read it again, and recollect well that the only thing I never could pardon would be your having deceived, and sacrificed your happiness to me. Write to me, immediately, Lindorf, and be careful to let me know the true state of your heart, as the only means by which you can prove it has suffered no change in friendship,' &c.—This was a ray of light to my bewildered mind, and at once informed me what my sentiments for Caroline were, and what my duty towards the best of friends. Alas! I thought to fulfil them all by placing the most entire confidence in him; by relating the truth, and entreating him to dispose of me at his will. How might I know that this very confidence was an outrage, and that I asked his consent to rob himself of the most precious of Heaven's blessings?—Impelled by some dreadful fatality, I seem destined to offend in every manner, and at all times, this most noble of men. Oh Walstein! Walstein! might thy greatest enemy have injured thee as I have done!—Yet should this writing have the effect which I expect, and even hope—Yes, hope— If she who reads it can feel the inestimable value of a soul like thine, what shall I then have to lament?

"I here add a copy of the letter, No. III. which I sent to the Count, the very day I received his. Condescend to run it over, it will be the last time you will have occasion to remember an unfortunate man who himself entreats you would for ever forget him; yet, as some small alleviation, wishes you to see how infinitely you were once adored."

Number III.

Copy of a Letter from the Baron of Lindorf *to the Count of* Walstein, *Ambassador at Petersburg.*

"You have but too truly divined, my dear Count, what are the present feelings of my heart. I have a secret to relate, the relation of which is become the more painful by having been so long delayed. Yet, believe me when I declare, it was your letter that first informed me what my feelings truly were; and that, till the moment I received it, I remained in unconscious security; or, rather, in the enjoyment of sensations the most congenial my soul has ever known, without once enquiring whence they originated—Love, that true that pure love, of which you, my friend, have so often spoken, and which I never felt before; love is the secret, love the source of this my happiness; the only happiness of which man is capable! Ah! did you know how the two last months have glided away! They have been but as a moment, and yet have I volumes to write concerning them, though not a single incident which Walstein will not approve.—Oh, my friend! in her are united every talent, every grace, and every virtue. Beauty is the least of her advantages; for, infinite as that is, it is remembered no more when the sound of her voice is heard, when her fingers touch the chords of harmony, or animate the lifeless canvass. She alone seems ignorant of the wonderous pleasure she herself creates. Did you hear her sing, Walstein! Oh! did you listen while she reads our best poets, adding a meaning more profound, and feeling superior even to what they themselves imagined; did you, especially, see how she is adored by all around her; were you a witness of her affectionate attentions to an infirm and blind friend; what a blessing she renders life to one who, else, might find life her severest affliction; were you where I am! — Yes, I might have my fears, but not that you would blame my choice.

"I feel too well any longer to doubt that, without her, for me there cannot be happiness. She only taught me to know what it was, nor, till her I knew, had I any conception of that sweet peace of mind which I imagined so incompatible with love. I am no longer the same. It is she who has wholly changed me. The head-strong, impetuous Lindorf, happy in her sight, happy when she speaks, most happy in the progress he daily makes in her affections, dares hope he is beloved though he has never dared to ask, having been too much enraptured with present enjoyment. Thus might I have passed a whole life away had not your letter awak-

ened me from this trance of beatitude! I feel, at present, without the consent of
my friend, without the certitude that my felicity will not be injurious to that of
others, this my vision of bliss must end! Can Matilda, the generous, the tender
Matilda, preserve esteem and friendship for one who could see yet not adore her;
and who, certain of being blessed in her possession, if so his wayward heart had
pleased, knew not to defend himself against tyrannic love? And can you, dear
Walstein, pardon and esteem me still; me whom you had beforetime so much
reason to detest, whom yet you destined to be your brother; and who renounces
a name so endearing? Yet, no, I do not renounce it, but refer the decision of what
I am to be to you. Be you umpire; for, here I vow, whatever you determine that
will I become. If the husband of Matilda, I cannot promise to forget my passion, it is too much a part of myself; but it shall remain for ever hidden in the
most secret corner of my heart. Ay, so that even yourself shall forget its existence.
This involuntary and concealed wrong, far from injuring, shall but increase your
sister's happiness.—Remember this and reflect on it well, dear Walstein, before
you write, however impatient I may be for an answer. Yes, Walstein, remember it
is the sentence of your friend, and that, after it is pronounced, I will either never
see her more, or kneel at her feet, and consecrate to her my future life! Till then I
will be silent, till then she shall remain ignorant of how much she is adored!—If
seeing her every day, and every day still more beauteous and more enchanting, I
have yet been able to keep my secret, think you not, if you require it, I shall keep
it when I behold her no more? While life remains it never shall escape my lips,
if I find it necessary to renounce her; not even you, Walstein, shall ever know
her name; it shall remain buried in my bosom, and never once rise to my lips: if,
on the contrary, I obtain your consent, with transport will I inform you of one
who merits the adoration of the universe. And most delighted shall I be to hear
a friend, like Walstein, applaud my choice and participate my joys; but, again I
repeat, these joys cannot exist should they cost Matilda a tear, or her brother so
much as a sigh."

"Such Caroline was my letter, and thus did every thing contribute to blind
me, even to the omitting informing my friend of your name; one single word
and you had been known to the Count, which at least would have prevented the
declaration I have made to you of a criminal passion. I had been less guilty, but I
thought this a respect due to yourself; for what right had I to name a person to
whom I was not certain of being at liberty to offer my hand? Another motive,
also, made me silent. Your immense fortune, at the remembrance of which I have,
more than once, grieved, and which would even have prevented me from declaring my sentiments had my own been less considerable, might have influenced
the Count in his decision, and I wished him to be wholly free from influence. It
was enough, nay, indeed, too much, to own that my future happiness depended
on this decision, and I waited in expectation of his answer with excessive anxi-

ety. Sometimes, relying on his generosity and principles, my heart yielded to all the flatteries of hope; at others, knowing how tenacious he was of the project he had formed, and his great affection for his sister, I dreaded he would require the sacrifice of my passion; and this sacrifice, to the performance of which I had pledged myself, seemed beyond my strength.

"Yet, so powerful were the mild sensations you inspired, it was only when absent from you I ever found myself tormented by these apprehensions of horror. The moment I beheld you they disappeared; and the same tranquility, or, rather the same dreams of bliss, again recurred. To these every inquietude gave place, and it seemed impossible this happiness, so pure, so permanent, could suffer interruption. The tender friendship which you, with ingenuity so unreserved, testified for me; the evident and partial goodness of the Baroness; the discourse she herself held in your absence; all aided the deception, and contributed to make me fancy myself the most blessed of mortal men. But so, indeed, I was, and three months of joys so heavenly, so unspeakable as these, well might compensate for an age of torments, did not the certainty that they never can return empoison the remainder of a wretched life. —Yes, whenever this wretchedness shall become too oppressive for nature to support, then will I return to Rindaw, and say, here did I pass three months with Caroline, and can I complain of being miserable?

"At length I received the answer so much dreaded and so much desired. My impatience, too, daily had become so great that I was every moment in fear lest my secret should escape my lips. I rode, therefore, myself to Berlin, to enquire at the post-office, and found the letter lying there. So great was my tremor, at receiving it from the postmaster, that he imagined I was ill, and asked if I wanted aid. I begged him to let me retire to a chamber and read it, and, when alone, I remained almost a quarter of an hour without daring to touch the seal. Yet how could I justify this excessive emotion? Did not I know Walstein? How, indeed, unless presaging Nature was informing me of my involuntary crime? In fine, my agitation increased so much that I left the room without opening the letter, resolved not to read it till I came home. I therefore mounted my horse, but had scarcely got a hundred yards out of town before I suddenly alighted, hung my horse to a gate, and broke the seal which enclosed my sentence, resolved, had it been such as I feared it might, never to return to Rindaw more. My project, in such a case, was immediately to depart to the Count, at Petersburg, and seek from him that fortitude I found not in myself. But Fate, to make my punishment the greater, suffered my delusion to continue and increase. Oh! Caroline, imagine what my raptures were when I read the letter I have here inclosed."

Number IV.

From the Count of Walstein *to the Baron of* Lindorf, *at Berlin.*Petersburg,
Aug. 15, 17—

"Love, dear Lindorf, of her and Love: think of these, and remember not ought
else the universe contains. Or, should Love grant a moment to Friendship,
employ that moment to assure thyself that a friend participates thy joys.— Happy
Lindorf! Thou lovest and art beloved! Thou hast found the mate of thy heart,
the sympathizing mind which the supreme Creator modelled after thy own; his
fiat formed you for each other.[a] And fearest thou then I should oppose a decree
so immutable; that I should tear thee from her who was written thine in the first
records of eternity? Thy letter has removed all doubts; not a phrase, not a word
is there which does not breathe love. It is a passion thou knowest too well how
to describe not both to feel it and inspire. In thee I behold that supreme felicity
the seeds of which have been deposited in my own heart, and of which I have
sometimes doubted the actual existence. Something of it I beheld in the loves
of Louisa and Justin, but this I attributed to country simplicity, and supposed
it impossible to be found elsewhere. Oh! how grateful is it to my heart to know
that this felicity has been realized by my friend, to have proof it is not wholly
banished this earth;[17] and of these proofs thy letter is full; even to that sacrifice which thou with such sincerity offerest, but which I should be a barbarian
to accept. My affection for my sister, were your's, Lindorf, out of the question,
would ensure my refusal. You are a man of honour, and I know you sincere when
you assure me you would be careful never to let Matilda perceive she was not the
wife of your heart; but how might you keep this fatal secret? Alas, my friend,
I am convinced it is impossible so to deceive a woman, and the misery of both
would be the inevitable consequence of a discovery.

"No, Lindorf, I wish your delicacy and conscience to be wholly at ease,
respecting our dear Matilda. I own she is strongly attached to you, and that you
are the first and only man who has made any progress in her affections. But,
whether it be the effect of character, education, or of youth, her sensations are
not of that profound and determined species on which the happiness or misery
of life depends; nor am I certain that we ought to give them the name of love.

"It has seemed to me that her feelings are rather the effect of a fervid imagination than of the heart, which, perhaps, have been heightened by opposition;
and that friendship has been mistaken for love. During my late visit, at Dresden,
I was struck with the levity, and even gaiety, with which she supported your
absence and her own chagrin. It is true, she always speaks of you with infinite
tenderness, but she laughed and cried both in a breath; and, a moment after she
had vowed eternal love for you, would begin to sing and dance. I was not uneasy
on this account, because, I own, I partly foresaw what has happened; and, sup-

posing I had been deceived in this, I, for my own part, was well pleased with this kind of passion; if you were united it might become every thing you wished, and, if not, Matilda might easily receive consolation, and be glad to hear of your happiness elsewhere. The young Baron de Zastrow is returned, and, as I am informed, is a handsome youth. He, perhaps, may contribute to her tranquility; but, be it as it may, make not yourself uneasy; rest assured that both brother and sister will find their happiness in yours. I, therefore, release you from every obligation, dear Lindorf, and only have to blame you for having supposed it possible I could do otherwise. Fly, the moment you have received this letter, and pay your homage to the lady you love, and who, if I may judge from your description, so transcendantly deserves to be beloved; nor have I any cause to doubt it, for, with all the enthusiasm of passion, you seem to have preserved the coolness of reason. How impatient am I to judge for myself! To see, hear, and, as you yourself say, to applaud your choice! Nor will it be long before I shall enjoy this pleasure. Preparations are made for my return to Berlin; you must direct no more letters to me at Petersburg. I shall be on the road when you receive this, and soon afterwards in your arms. We shall then, dear Lindorf, no longer have any thing to conceal from each other, for hitherto we have mutually had some reserve. I shall learn who your beloved is, and you will then be informed of a secret which, hitherto, a combination of circumstances has obliged me to keep; nay, indeed, to have afflicted you would but have added to my own grief, for my sorrows were of a kind that admitted not of alleviation. When I return they, perhaps, may cease, and, perhaps, also, I may then be destined never to enjoy that felicity which I do not envy you, Lindorf, but which yet I most ardently wish to partake. Oh! my friend, there is another *She,* another beloved, in existence, who, when you shall know, will not a little surprise you.—But not a word of this till I see you. I hope to find you either happy or on the point of becoming so. This, at least, is a certain bliss; and with this, if so my destiny should decree, I must endeavour to rest content. Farewell! Should you mention your friend to the mistress of your heart, should you tell her she has superseded his sister, tell her likewise she has gained a brother, nay, perhaps, a sister also, of whom may she become the friend, and whom may she render as much alive to love as she herself is. That she may, however, love you, Lindorf, equal to your deserts, is the ardent prayer of

WALSTEIN.

P. S. "Were you not in love I scarcely could pardon you two thoughtless omissions; the first, not having dated your letter, so that I neither know how long it has been coming, nor where you at present are; I suppose at Berlin, and, therefore, have directed as usual; the second, your not having said a word of your late uncle, the commander, nor of his will. You find I have heard of it, though, and I congratulate you on this addition to your fortune. The clause by which you are obliged to marry within two years will not be the least impediment to your succession. Once more, farewell, I am impatient till we meet, and till I have said the thousand things I have to say."

"You know the rest, Caroline: I have done. It is not for words to tell you either what I felt, after reading this letter, or after finding how presumptuous and culpable my hopes had been. I began this manuscript the moment I got home, yesterday. The time has been short; my wearied hand and eyes scarce have power to trace an adieu which my tears would efface; or to supplicate your pardon for an unfortunate man who has disturbed your future tranquility. Oh! may he be wholly forgotten by you, and may you recover that peace, that serenity of soul without which happiness may not be. Oh! Caroline, believe the friend who knows your heart better, at this moment, than you yourself, and who knows, also, the man to whom, henceforth, it is your duty to consecrate this your heart, your life; it is with him, only, by making him as happy as he deserves, that you can find happiness yourself. But you have read, and justice and love by this must have passed sentence. This sentence cannot but be in favour of Walstein, and I have nothing more to add.

"I have not yet come to any determination respecting myself; I neither know what I shall do or what say, to Walstein. I ought, perhaps, to tell him all; but a word, which escaped me in my letter, a word I would redeem with my life, has for ever sealed my lips.

"No, Caroline, never shall these lips, or this heart, pronounce your name. I will even deprive myself of that consolation. Farewell, Caroline farewell—For ever!—Ay, for ever; for never more must I see you unless I could cease to love you. Oh might this love become so sanctified, that I might only behold, in you, the wife of Walstein. Oh! might I restore each of you a friend worthy of yourselves!— This or death is all I have to hope!—Adieu, adieu! I fly to give you this; once more to behold you—No, not to behold. I will not look on Caroline! You are the wife of my friend; the Countess of Walstein. Yes, to the Countess of Walstein I am bringing these papers, this picture. Caroline is no longer in being; not Lindorf's Caroline!—You are now at the pavilion, I fly. Oh! Heaven grant me fortitude, sustain me in this fearful moment!"

We shall not attempt to describe what were the sensations of Caroline after what she had read. Who may express all that passed in a heart divided between love, remorse, admiration, and, perhaps, even a tincture of jealousy? Louisa and Matilda, by turns, drew her attention; she read again the passages that related to them. What fire, what enthusiasm did she find in Lindorf's expression of his passion for Louisa, compared to the feelings she had observed when in company with herself! She was tempted to believe that the latter were little more than the result of tranquil friendship. As to the young Matilda—how happy was she, who dared love Lindorf and own her passon!—Ay, but how much to be pitied;

not to be beloved again! Charming Matilda! Generous Walstein! Ye merit not ingratitude from others!

Caroline well recollected that, during the week preceding her marriage, the Count had mentioned his sister, and the hope that Caroline and she would become friends; but, as she was then wholly absorbed in meditating on the means of separation, she had paid little attention to his discourse. But ah! how bitter was the remembrance of having injured this Matilda, this sister; injured her beyond reparation; robbed her of a heart over which her claims were so numerous, and so legitimate! It was true she did not seem sufficiently to know the value of this heart, thought Caroline, as she again perused the letter of the Count to Lindorf; and though the apparent want of sensibility in Matilda was in every respect a subject of consolation to Caroline, yet could she scarcely pardon her.

Deep in thought, on the many and strange events she just had read, sat Caroline, and perceived not that it was noon, when a servant came from the Baroness to seek her. She hastily gathered up the papers that were spread open around her, and locked them up in her bureau; but, as she was going, she perceived the box, containing the portrait, still on the table; this she slipped into her pocket, and ran to the Baroness.

Caroline found her with a note she had received from Lindorf, which she could not read. "Here, my dear," said the Canoness, as she entered, "open this, and let me hear what our dear young Gentleman says, whom we have not seen for these two days; we shall learn why he is absent; I cannot tell thee how much I miss him." The melancholy Caroline, expecting what the contents would be, sighed, raised her eyes to Heaven, and took the note. It contained compliments to the ladies; informed them he, Lindorf, was forced to depart, immediately, on very essential and pressing business; could not have the honour of seeing them again; assured them, however, he never could forget them, and earnestly hoped a continuance of their esteem and friendship.

Yes, certainly, Caroline knew, before she read, the contents of this note; it was no surprise to her; yet was she so affected as scarcely to be able to pronounce a word. The conviction she should see him no more, that all intercourse between them was over, the cold and studied contrast of this billet, compared to the manuscript she just had read, the words esteem and friendship, traced by the same hand that so lately had painted, with such enthusiasm, the strongest sensations of the soul, the constraint she was under by the presence of the Baroness, all conspired to render her situation almost insupportable. Might one easily suppose her distress could suffer augmentation? Scarcely had she finished the note, suppressing her sobs, tho' the tears ran incessantly down her cheeks, when, taking her handkerchief out of her pocket, the box, which she had just put in it, and which was then far from her thoughts, fell at her feet, and, laying open on the ground, presented that form, and those features which she had before feared to look on. The accident was a very trifling one, yet did it make an incredible impression on Caroline; ay, as great as tho' the Count himself, in person, had stood before her and reproached her for infidelity. Her exclamation was almost a shriek. She stooped for the box, turned away her eyes, as she picked it up, and hastily ran from the chamber, without knowing why or from whom she fled— she presently recovered, returned, and found the Canoness surprised at the cry she had uttered, and her sudden flight; and still more affected at the farewell billet of Lindorf, and this his so unexpected departure.

The disorder in her eyes was a cataract; which, daily increasing, had too far injured her sight to see the picture. Caroline might say what she pleased, and it was much more easy to avoid an explanation concerning that than to answer the questions, suppositions, and lamentations of the Baroness on the departure of Lindorf, which were unceasing. It broke all her measures, disconcerted all her projects, and absolutely threw her into despair! Caroline, afflicted as she herself was, yet was obliged to exhaust her imagination to comfort her friend. The best mode, no doubt, would have been to have proved, by confessing her marriage, how chimerical all these her projects were. Caroline, who, at last, perceived what her views had been, in encouraging the visits of Lindorf, wished to make this confession; but it was now become so painful, so difficult, she had not the power. How might she so much as pronounce the name of the Count! How relate his wrongs! I am the source of misery to the most virtuous of human beings, the most sublime, most worthy of felicity; and then, when I ought to have held myself blest, beyond the lot of women, then did I yield to antipathy, the most unreasonable, the most unjust.

Thus reasoned Caroline; nor was this antipathy the only sensation for which she had cause to blush. The name of Lindorf was as painful to pronounce as that of Walstein; she resolved, therefore, to wait the answer of her father, and the effect of time, ere she spoke, and to support, as well as she was able, the regret of the Baroness for the absence of Lindorf. In fact, she regretted it too much herself not to find her heart in unison with that of her friend; and, however painful this continual subject of conversation might sometimes be, yet was she so interested in it that she seemed to listen as though it were fascination to her ears. She became still more assiduous in her attentions to the Baroness than before, who, being deprived of sight, had still more need of her cares. She went no more to the pavillion; her books and treasures were, one after another, brought back to her apartment; though her musical instruments and painting utensils were the last. The mind must be at ease before it can wholly devote itself to, and cooly consider, any subject. Caroline, whenever alone, was constantly reading her manuscript and letters, ruminating on the beauteous Louisa, the young Matilda, and the Count; sitting lost in a multitude of unconnected ideas, which were usually succeeded by a flood of tears. She, likewise, became so familiar with the picture that, at last, she was never easy but when looking at it, and never beheld it without emotion; nay, even not without pleasure. Great God! would she say, with her eyes fixed on the features, if, to so many virtues, a person so noble and a countenance so expressive were added, what mortal might be worthy of him? If!—Why do I say if? Who at present is worthy of Walstein? Am I? Oh! no, no; the best of men deserves the best of women; deserves a heart devoted to him, and him only!

Leave we, for a time, the lovely Caroline to reflect, weep over and, alternately, read the manuscript of Lindorf and the letters of Walstein; and let us see what became of the two friends. Indeed, the profound solitude of Caroline, the monotony of her present life, and the struggles of her heart, would but weary the reader. Not that it was dulness by which she was tormented; no, it was a state of continual agitation; the least noise she heard made her whole frame tremble and her blood run cold. Her imagination, incessantly employed on Lindorf and the Count, persuaded her that one of the two would arrive at Rindaw. What! might she think that Lindorf, who had banished himself for ever from her presence, would return? No: when she reasoned with herself, read his manuscript, and recollected the obligations he was under to Walstein, she would exclaim, with conviction, Never, never shall I see him more. But love and imagination do not always reason; and, unconscious of it herself, perhaps she thought, more than once, he would not have the fortitude to keep his resolution.

She was deceived. At the farther part of Silesia, in his melancholy mansion of Ronebourg, Lindorf repented of his involuntary crime with tears and groans, and thought the expiation of a life scarcely sufficient atonement. Alas! how often was he tempted to terminate that life he no longer could consecrate to Caroline, and which had, hitherto, been so fatal to the best of friends! But he knew them both too well not to be certain that such an act would for ever destroy their happiness and tranquility. He read the Sorrows of Werter,[18] but they produced a very different effect to what might have been expected. The despair of Charlotte, of Albert, the friend of Werter, were terrible; and, more generous than the latter, Lindorf would rather live and suffer than empoison the felicity of those he loved.

During the first part of his residence at Ronebourg life was become so odious to him, and the pain of supporting it appeared so great, that he thought thus, by enduring this pain, to make some reparation for his wrongs, which idea was his only consolation. We must likewise observe if his passions were violent they were the less likely to be eternal. Notwithstanding his subtle distinction concerning the different species of love, he had adored Louisa; and, though he had not the same extreme passion for Matilda, yet had she, certainly, begun to make a considerable impression on his heart, when she was carried off. We have since seen to what excess he loved Caroline; hope we then that time, or some other passion, may cure him of this unfortunate love. His heart is too honest, his affection for

Walstein too sincere, to make him endeavour to cherish sentiments he knows to be criminal.

He had been a recluse, more than a month, at Ronebourg, and his cure was not very far advanced when, one day, attempting, a second time, to write to the Count, without well knowing what to say, he beheld the Count, himself, enter his chamber, and run into his arms. Surprised, at his arrival from Petersburgh, not to find Lindorf at Berlin, and learning from the servants he had left there, he was gone to Ronebourg, where he was alone, Walstein, who dreaded some unexpected misfortune, waited only to pay his duty to the King and his good father-in-law, the High Chamberlain, and immediately departed to learn what might be the motives of this his singular retreat, at the very moment he supposed him in the full enjoyment of happiness. No sooner were the first transports of surprise, emotion, and joy over, than the Count began his interrogations. They were dictated by the fears and affections of friendship. "Tell me, instantly, dear Lindorf," said he, "wherefore do I find you here, alone, melancholy, with some secret malady at your heart, which your countenance but too plainly betrays? Unfold the cruel mystery, my friend. What is become of the lady you loved? Why is she not with you? Why not united to you? Wherefore is not my friend happy?"

The Count might have continued speaking; for Lindorf, ignorant of his coming, unprepared to answer questions so terrible as these, kept a mournful silence. Walstein was silent also; but he pressed the hand of Lindorf, while his countenance, expressive of the feelings of his heart, seemed to demand his confidence. At length, "What!" said he, "Lindorf, will you not tell me? Am I no longer your friend; the faithful guardian of your bosom secrets, and have I not a right to read what passes there?"

"Yes, yes," cried Lindorf, "you have every imaginable right over me; you are my friend, the best of friends, and never did I feel it more powerfully than at this moment, in which I am obliged to refuse you what you ask." The Count, amazed, fell back some paces. Lindorf continued, "Oh! my dear Walstein, recoil not from your unhappy friend, condemn him not too lightly. Silence is not my choice but the effect of absolute necessity; and, did you know, you must approve my motives. Restrained by honour, oaths, every thing most sacred, I may not betray a secret which regards not me alone. Ask no more concerning this unfortunate affair, but pity him who is deprived of the melancholy resource of dividing his griefs."

The Count again went up to Lindorf, again took him by the hand, and his looks proved how much he was affected. "Restrained by honour and oaths!" said he; "my questions, then, all are ended; too well, myself, I know how far a secret promise is obligatory, and I am answered—Yet, is the misfortune without a remedy? Have you no hope?"

"None, none," replied Lindorf, with vehemence. "I have for ever lost her whom I adored; she exists no more"—Lindorf stopped; he was going to have added, *for me*, but was fearful of saying too much, and the Count exclaimed, "Good God! Lindorf, exists no more! What has death deprived you of her? Ah! dear and unfortunate Lindorf, how infinitely do I pity you!"

Lindorf wished to undeceive him, yet his fears again kept him silent; he dreaded lest Walstein should divine the truth, and, on consideration, was not sorry he had thus misunderstood him. His silence, therefore, confirmed this idea of death, and would destroy every supposition that might have alighted on Caroline. Walstein, however, had none: never had it entered his thoughts that his own wife was the woman so much beloved, so much regretted. He had been absent from Prussia, was equally ignorant of the situation of Rindaw, where he had never been, and of Risberg; nor did he even know that Lindorf had lived there, or there had formed the connection so fatal to his repose. He knew, likewise, Caroline was living, and well, and remained persuaded that some tragical event had robbed Lindorf's mistress of life. The gloomy despair in which the latter remained, after this conversation, confirmed the idea. Walstein endeavoured to calm and console him, and asked if he would not return with him to Berlin.

"To Berlin!" cried Lindorf, with terror; "No, no, dear Walstein, never, never. —I must quit this country; I must travel for some years: oppose not a resolution absolutely necessary and fixed. On your friendship I depend to obtain permission, and the conclusion of peace makes me hope it will not be difficult to obtain. Should the King refuse, I must resign my commission; I must depart, I must leave this country."

Ignorant of his real motives, the Count judged he had very urgent reasons for quitting Prussia, and was the less ready to search for objections because he thought a few years travelling might remove his anguish. He, therefore, promised to obtain the leave he desired; and, a few minutes after, added, "It is very possible, dear Lindorf, I may go with you."—"You, Walstein?"—"Yes, I, my friend; I, as well as you, perhaps, may have reasons for wishing to quit my country. We will go together, and we shall be the less unhappy."

"Unhappy!" cried Lindorf; "may you, may the Count of Walstein, speak of unhappiness!"

"I understand your surprise," said the Count, drawing nearer, "but it is time it should end; time it is that I should reveal a secret I have too long kept hidden. Can I, Lindorf, blame you for mysterious conduct, when you shall know that I have been married these six months?"

Lindorf affected not surprise; it was impossible, on such an occasion especially, to feign what he did not feel; but his embarrassment, the red flushings of his countenance, and his real sentations, there so marked, gave him the appearance of surprise. The Count continued.

"Yes, my friend, I am united to the most angelic of women; and yet am I far from being happy! I will relate all my mournful story; at present, it will be some consolation, and may I bring that conviction home to you which I myself begin to experience; that in friendship, only, man ought to seek felicity."

Then did the Count enter on a narrative, bitter to the soul of Lindorf, which he had foreseen, and which, of all tortures, he most had dreaded. The recital confirmed his misfortunes, his remorse, and lacerated his heart. What must be the impression, on that agitated heart, of the name of Caroline, repeated every instant; a name so deeply engraven there, and of which he was obliged to dissemble ignorance? Surely, if Lindorf had been guilty of involuntary wrongs, to this the most worthy of men, what he now suffered was sufficient to expiate all his errors.[19] The Count began his narrative far back; told Lindorf it was the King who, knowing the rich inheritance of Caroline, first had the idea of this marriage,[a] and had written to him concerning it while in Russia. "The motive," said Walstein, "and even the will of my Sovereign, who was very warm on the subject, less influenced me than the age and the kind of education of the young lady.

"Caroline of Lichtfield, still very young, having lived recluse in the country, and never seen any man who had made an impression on her heart, seemed exactly the woman I had so long desired. You know my system was founded on an ignorance of the world, and of love. I certainly shall find means, said I, to allure and attach this young heart; if not by love, at least, by friendship so powerful and gratitude so tender that they may well supply the want of this passion. First appearances will be against me; but succeeding trials and better acquaintance will ascertain our mutual happiness. Full of this dear, this flattering idea, I answered the King with rapture, assuring him I should esteem myself too happy might I but obtain the hand of the young Baroness of Lichtfield. His Majesty delayed not to reply that he had obtained the promise of the High Chamberlain, and commanded me to return, immediately, and conclude the marriage.

"I began my journey, but was obliged to remain at Dantzic,[20] ill of a violent fever, which brought me to the brink of the grave; while you, dear Lindorf, were then fulfilling the first and most sacred of duties to an expiring parent. It was two months before I was well enough to continue my journey. I arrived at Berlin, and had the disappointment to find you were not there. I heard also, with anxiety, that my young bride had passed the two months of my illness at court. Ah! how many impediments might these two dreadful months have thrown in the way of happiness![b] How might they have deranged my whole plan!

"I strove not to conceal my fears from my sovereign, who consoled me with his usual goodness: He had often, himself, observed Caroline, and had always found the same air of innocence, and chearful sprightliness, which shewed the heart to be at ease. 'At leaving her retreat, I gave sufficient intimation,' added he, 'of what my intentions were, purposely to keep all our young courtiers at a respectful distance; and, though your bride is an angelic young lady, not one of them have attempted to pay her the least attention, more than politeness required; and Caroline, herself, without distinguishing one man above another, has sought her own amusement only.' The same evening I was introduced to the Baron of Lichtfield, my future father, and, on the morrow, to the lovely Caroline."

Here the Count related the manner of his first visit, which we have before circumstantially described; the aversion of Caroline, which she could not dissemble; and confessed that, no doubt, it would then have been more generous, more delicate, to have abandoned his intents, and that he even had thought so to have done; "but," added Walstein, "it is easy to delude one's self. Imagine, my friend, that this very flight, this emotion, so natural, so open, so unrepressed, which ought perhaps to have terrified, gave me, on the contrary, great pleasure; and, on full reflection, made me more ardent to obtain her. In them I thought I beheld indubitable proof of that candour, that innocence of early youth, which I had feared lest her residence at court might have tainted.ª Had she been more artful she would certainly have better concealed this first sensation of terror, and I inwardly thanked her for flying me thus. The moment I beheld her, the moment she entered, led by her father, her ingenuous, open and beautiful countenance, and the graces that were in every motion and in all her form, made their full impression. She was exactly the person whom, had I had the beauties of the world assembled, I should alone have selected.

"If I did not absolutely believe that I no way contributed to the sudden fear and flight of Caroline, it was not the fault of the High Chamberlain. I listened, however, with pleasure, to his protestations; and, particularly, when he declared, on his word and honour, she had, that very morning, assured him her heart was free, and that she was very willing to be mine. I have laid no constraint on her, said he, and confirmed it with an oath; and tomorrow, if her health permit, she herself will tell you so.

"Alas! my friend, how readily does the heart believe what it ardently desires! I departed, almost convinced; and the morrow, and the future morrows, confirmed the illusion. I observed the young lady; she appeared exceedingly timid, but shewed not the least repugnance. Our marriage was fixed, by the King, for that day week, and she consented without asking any delay; nay, once, when delay was mentioned, she begged it might not take place. (The reader will no doubt here recollect the artifice of the High Chamberlain, and the fears of Caroline for her father's life.)[21] I should have employed the intermediate time in endeavouring to gain her confidence and friendship; but, during the few visits I made, the Baron supposed etiquette required he should not leave us alone. (Here Walstein likewise mistook the High Chamberlain's motives.)[22] She spoke little; but that little had meaning, and was well timed, and discovered a mind that made me more and more enraptured with her, till I imagined myself the most fortunate of men.

"The evening before the ceremony was to be performed, I thought, however, I perceived marks of grief on her lovely countenance. Her eyes were red, her heart seemed heavy, and one might see she endeavoured to stifle her feelings. I was much affected at observing this, and, seizing the opportunity of a moment when we were unobserved, I, tenderly approaching her, said, 'beauteous Caroline, am I any way the cause of grief to you? Is it in my power, by any means, to give you ease?'[23] She, timidly, looked down, and was silent. At last she softly answered, 'an engagement for life will occasion fears; but I believe you, Sir, to be good and generous, and that hope cheers me: on you, alone, my happiness will depend.'

"I knew not how to interpret the manner in which she said this, and was going to reply, but her father came up; she then assumed her natural tone and manner, and seemed no longer to dread the approaching moment. How, then, was it possible I should divine her meaning; or presage the dreadful stroke that awaited me?"

The Count, then, relating all that had passed on the day of the marriage, took from his pocket-book the letter which Caroline had given him, and which has before been read. "Here, my friend," said he to Lindorf, "take this; read, and see the dreadful reverse; behold the fearful traits of the fallen thunderbolt."

Lindorf had occasion for all his fortitude. With a trembling hand, and with vague and absent eyes, he took and ran over lines traced by her he adored, in characters most affecting,[a] natural, and eloquent. He would have said something to the Count, as he returned it, but could not articulate a word. He flung himself into the arms of Walstein, pressed him to his bosom, and a tear, he could no longer detain, fell from his cheek.[b]

Had the Count had the least suspicion of the truth, this excessive emotion might well have given it confirmation; but none he had, for none he sought; his heart was a sanctuary too holy for a guest so vile,[24] and he beheld nothing but sympathetic sensibility, heightened, perhaps, by sympathy of situation.

"Dear Lindorf," said he, when he was a little calm, "you feel too strongly the distress of your friend; and I even fear I have unconsciously torn the bandage from your own wound. Some explanation, some stroke equally afflicting you may have sustained.—I see—I see I ought to have been silent, ought still to have concealed this fatal secret; your own pangs are sufficient, and I did you injustice when I supposed mine might afford you consolation. I perceive, on the contrary, they do but aggravate—Pardon, pardon, dear Lindorf. This proof of thy friendship, this too strong sensibility of what my feelings are, penetrate me to the very heart."

"O Walstein, Walstein," exclaimed Lindorf; and, sinking under the oppressive weight of remorse, hid his face with both his hands—He was going instantly to have discovered the real cause of this his emotion, but he remembered Caroline, and the oath he had made never to reveal what might, to her, have consequences so fatal; this, the first of duties, suddenly was recollected, and this stopped him short.

The Count, seeing him so deeply affected, wished to change the subject. His feelings, ever delicate, were ever averse to give others pain.[25]—"Come, come, my friend," said he, "let us take a walk in your park, and we will speak on these matters another time."[a] Accordingly, they went out together, and the Count discoursed on the country and the Court he had so lately left, and entered into most interesting and curious discussions; for his genius, naturally penetrating and observing, his rank, and the flattering distinctions paid him by the Empress, who highly respected him, gave him the power and the means of seeing and of judging.[26]

This conversation, which Walstein prolonged, and gave all the animation to in his power, purposely that Lindorf might recover himself, had the effect intended; he insensibly became calm, and afterwards highly delighted. No person had the art of captivating the ear and the understanding like the Count of Walstein; his mild and persuasive eloquence, the tone of his voice, which spoke to the heart, and his happy choice of words, rendered his conversation inexpressibly sweet and agreeable: great knowledge, without pedantry or seeming consciousness that he possessed it, happy expressions, perspicuity, and connection in all he said, and that kind of honest insinuation which adapts itself to, and draws forth, the powers of others, rendered him, indeed, a most amiable, as well as a most instructive companion.[b] No person could be in his company without having learnt something, nor without being exceedingly well satisfied with himself. Since his marriage, the Count had lost much of the gaiety of early youth, which even his accident had not before robbed him of; but it was replaced by a strong imagination, an energetic fire, which appertained to him only, and which could only by hearing him be perfectly conceived. While he spoke no person remembered his person,[c] and, more than once, at Petersburg, it was his fault that the ladies did not entirely forget it. Let us add, now we are on the subject, that this person, so ill treated, was so much improved that Lindorf himself was surprised, and Caroline, who had seen him after a two months illness, would have been still more so, had she beheld him now. His hair, which had come off after the fever, had grown again in abundance, was of a fine colour, and well disposed. The scar on his face, greatly filled up, was scarcely apparent; he was no longer meagre, but had an appearance of youth and health, very different from the yellow and livid tints his malady had left, at the time of his marriage: a bit of green silk, and a ribband, properly disposed, removed that disgust which the loss of an eye might, at first sight, have caused;[27] and a little attention to himself had considerably corrected his habit of stooping; so that his shape seemed remarkable only by an easy and negligent attitude, much preferable to upright formality. It is true, he still limped, but he was oftener seated than walking; hence we may well imagine that, with exceeding fine teeth, and infinite expression in his countenance, the Count of Walstein, then little above thirty, was not much an object of aversion. Had he been the same some months sooner, Caroline would not have fled, her letter would not have been written, nor would this history have existed. Every thing therefore is right; let us return to our two friends.

Their walk continued till dusk, and Lindorf, highly pleased with the company of his friend, and fascinated by his conversation, presently recovered himself perfectly. Impatient to know what were the resolutions of Walstein respecting Caroline, he intreated him to finish his history. "It is finished," answered the Count; "things remain just as they were. You know me too well, dear Lindorf, to imagine I should refuse a request made in terms so strong, so affecting, and even so reasonable, as was that of Caroline. I obtained, but not without some trouble, permission for her to return and live at Rindaw, with the friend by whom she had been educated. The King, not very well pleased, I suppose, that a match of his making should have this kind of conclusion, exacted the most profound secrecy."—

"But ought not I to have been an exception?" said Lindorf, suddenly interrupting the Count—"Have I not cause, my friend, to reproach you for this secrecy? What! conceal the most interesting event of your whole life from me!"

"I own it was wrong, dear Lindorf, and often have I reproached myself; but the King had commanded, and both my duties and obligations have given me the habit of paying the most scrupulous attention to his orders: yet, had we met, I should certainly have told you; but the fear of a letter miscarrying, and the conviction that my distress would have grieved you, were additional motives to secrecy; and, in fact, my friend, by your present feelings, I find it is happy you were not acquainted with it sooner."

Lindorf made no reply, though he felt the exact contrary most forcibly; but he did not expect what was coming.

"Yes, my friend," added the Count, smiling, "you have youth and sensibility, and the Countess of Walstein is an angel; you would have asked permission to visit her, nay, I myself should have requested you so to do; you have since been in love, but your heart, then, was free, and might have been put to a trial so severe that I cannot but be happy to think you have escaped it. I own your sufferings from love may be the same; but what, Lindorf, would have been the excess of that wretchedness had the object of that love been the wife of your friend? Nay, even Caroline herself would have been too much exposed to danger. I own, my dear Lindorf," said Walstein, tapping him on the shoulder, "though I love you as a friend, I should fear you as a rival."

Poor Lindorf!—Happily it was twilight, and in a dark room; nay, perhaps, Lindorf had chosen this situation and hour, purposely, to renew the conversation. As soon as he could recover his speech, "I hope," said he, "Walstein does not think, cannot imagine, I ever might be his rival. I hope he will do me the justice to believe that the title of his wife would be pledge sufficient for my faith."

"Yes, if any faith might be kept with youth, grace, wit, and beauty," replied the Count. "But do not understand that seriously, dear Lindorf, which is not seriously meant; and which I should not have said, had there really been any danger.—At present you are but too much out of the power of love; besides, you are not likely to see the Countess; nay, perhaps, even I myself—"

"You yourself!"

"Dear Lindorf, I know not how to act. Perhaps the impediments I have found may heighten sensations which a week's acquaintance ought not to have rendered very passionate: yet do they unceasingly assault me. I more than ever feel my happiness depends on living with Caroline, for Caroline, and by Caroline to be beloved, as much as a man like me may be beloved; yet never had I less hope of attaining these my so ardent desires."

Lindorf listened with downcast eyes. "She still remains at Rindaw," added the Count, "which, since our separation, she has never left; there living in a most profound retreat; unseeing and unseen, and debarred of all the pleasures she has every right to enjoy, and which her short stay at court may, most probably, have taught her to regret. Indeed, I have been told she seemed exceedingly fond of dancing; yet, might it be believed, all these pleasures, these wishes so natural at sixteen, have been less powerful with her than the dreadful antipathy she has conceived to me! This has given her force and fortitude incredible, and Caroline, with pleasure, buries her youth and her charms in solitude, to avoid living with a husband she hates!"

The generous, the philosophic, the capacious heart of Walstein himself scarcely could contain its sorrows. While thus he spoke, the deep and lengthened sigh heaved in his bosom, and the tear was with difficulty detained and repelled.[28] [a]

"Have you heard of her since your return?" said Lindorf, in a low voice. "Are you certain she persists in this unjust separation?"

"Too certain," replied the Count, seeking among the papers of his pocketbook. "Here is a letter from her to her father; he has lately received, and sent it inclosed to me. You there will find she declares her determination to continue at Rindaw, and *that her heart and her reason still revolt at the ties she has formed*"

Lindorf took the letter, read it as he had read the preceding one; but remarked the date, saw it had been written the very day on which he wrote the manuscript, sighed bitterly, and gave it back without speaking.[b]

"The High Chamberlain," continued the Count, "has said, in his letter, that he had written such an answer as became him. The phrase made me tremble; for his answer, no doubt, was harsh and despotic. Caroline, perhaps, at this instant, drowned in tears, accuses me, anew, of tyranny, and her hatred increases. My only happiness is that this her hatred is not caused by a passion for any other man.— Oh, Lindorf! speak, aid, guide me; tell me how I ought to act in a situation so delicate; from you I hope salutary advice."—"Advice," said Lindorf, hesitating. "Walstein ought to take advice only of his own heart."—"I understand thee, my friend," said the Count, "and my heart, already, has dictated what it becomes me to do."

What this was we shall know, hereafter; at present, leave we Lindorf to breathe, who had sufficiently suffered, during this painful conversation; leave we the Count to recover from the fatigues of his journey, and let us return to Caroline.

The terrible answer of her father she had received. Not only did he permit, but he commanded, her to inform the Canoness of her marriage; and prepare, immediately, to quit her, and to return to inhabit Walstein house. "Too long," said he, "has this obliging husband allowed you to indulge a whim which his absence only could make me tolerate; 'tis time it should end. The Count is come back, and does not chuse to be deprived of his wife; he claims his rights, and, for my part, be certain you shall for ever remain deprived of those you have to my affection, and likewise to my wealth, if you make the least difficulty about returning. Expect no one to support you; I speak in the name of a King, a Husband, and a Father, equally angered by your long and obstinate disobedience."[a]

This was not true; the High Chamberlain acted on his own authority, and had neither received the command or the advice of any person for this fulminating letter; but he wished to try if he might not obtain from terror an effect which kindness, reason, and retirement had not produced. He was, besides, outrageous[29] at this unforeseen perseverance of his daughter. A witness of the honours the Count received, at returning from his embassy, of the friendship the King had so openly testified for him, and of the high and unrivalled favour he enjoyed, he impatiently burnt to proclaim Walstein his son, and participate his glory. It was during a fit of this counteracted passion that he had written to his daughter; but Caroline, not suspecting it was possible to alter or disguise the truth, understood all he said literally:[b] the anger of the King afflicted her, and that of her spouse, especially, because she saw not the generous Walstein, whom the manuscript and letters of Lindorf had shewn her in this tyranny; and whom, from being obliged to admire, she began a little to love. But this sensation gave place to fear and dislike, the moment she thought it possible he should abuse his power.

"Alas!" said she, while again she read his letters to Lindorf, and opened the box to look at his picture, which she as suddenly shut again in displeasure, "alas! his character is changed as much as his person. If he be already so much irritated at this my resistance, what will he become when he shall learn the fatal secret of my heart, and that it has yielded wholly to his friend? Of this he cannot long remain ignorant, nor can he but know I love when he shall be told I am acquainted with Lindorf."

Despair redoubled at the thought. The supposition of living with a husband already prejudiced against her, perhaps jealous, and undoubtedly despotic, since he had commanded her to return, was revolting. She no longer felt herself obliged to his condescension for suffering her to depart, and consenting that she should remain at Rindaw all the time he was absent; "he was, no doubt, glad I might there remain shut up while he was at Petersburg; and proves, but too incontrovertibly, delicacy and mild complaisance were not his motives.—Ah! Lindorf, friendship deceives you; the Count of Walstein possesses not those virtues you imagine."

To all this anguish was added that of having to relate her story to the Canoness. As often as she endeavoured to speak expression expired on her lips; never could she determine so to afflict that tender and unfortunate friend, so at once to excite her anger and her grief, by informing her of the secret she so long had kept from her, and of the approaching departure of her dear pupil. The loss of her sight had rendered the company of Caroline her sole consolation; and often did she repeat that the moment she was deprived of that would be the moment of her death; wherefore the idea of being obliged to quit her added increasing pangs to the affectionate Caroline; nor could she resolve to plunge the poignard to her heart by speaking of this dreadful separation, though she thought it inevitable. Yet did she hope it might, for a time, be deferred. Her father had fixed no day; he only had commanded her to hold herself ready against he should come to take her away; accompanied, no doubt, by Walstein, her formidable husband.

To them she left the office of informing the Canoness, and daily waited their coming, in trances of despair; having no other hope but that of dying in the arms of her dear mamma, with grief of being thus torn from her. In this inquietude, this continual agitation, was she, which considerably affected her health, when she one day received a letter. The hand-writing and the arms on the seal were instantly recollected, and caused an emotion, a contraction of the heart which scarcely can be imagined. It was from the Count himself. She trembled as she opened it; and was near fainting when she saw, at the top, it was dated from the castle of Ronebourg, the mansion of Lindorf.—"Merciful God! he is with Lindorf!"— Caroline was obliged to pause awhile, and collect all her fortitude, ere she could read what follows.

From the Count of WALSTEIN to CAROLINE.

> At the Castle of Ronebourg, belonging
> to the Baron of Lindorf, Oct. 17, 17—

"SHOULD I be so unfortunate as that the receipt of this letter might occasion any sensation of apprehension, or dread, let me conjure her to whom it is addressed to dispel all such feelings; kindly to read, and firmly to believe that he who wrote it would rather perish than give her heart the slightest pang.

"Yes, Madam, for, alas! I dare not call you by a name more tender, think me, what I am, your friend; at least what I wish to be; and, as a tender friend, permit me thus, a moment, to converse with you, on that which, of all things in the world, I have most at heart, the happiness of Caroline; nothing is there I will not do may I but hope to contribute to this happiness. Deign to give me your commands; think not of my ease, for willingly will I suffer, and my sufferings shall even become my pleasures, so, Madam, that they may be but for your sake.[30]

"The Baron, your father, no doubt, has written to you. What the contents of his letter may be I know not; but, be they what they may, should they impose the least constraint on Caroline, they belie the heart of Walstein. No, Madam, you are free; absolute mistress of your own destiny and of mine. For me, suffer me here to leave the decision of what I shall hereafter become to yourself; for here I solemnly vow to submit to the sentence you shall pronounce. Yet, how can I entertain the most momentary hope? Have I not, now before my eyes, the letter in which you have declared, to your father, your heart is still the same; that your unfortunate husband is still the object of worse than dislike, and that your sole wish is to live separate from him? Alas!—But be it so, Caroline; you shall be obeyed: your wishes to me are laws; beforetime I was too eager to gratify my own, and thus have fettered you for life. Myself I ought to punish, and endeavour to merit both your esteem and gratitude by absenting myself so long as you shall please so to ordain.

"No, Caroline, you shall not be doomed to live sequestered me to avoid. The Court shall not be deprived of its highest ornament,[a] nor your father of a daughter who of all his honours is the highest. Return to this father, enjoy those innocent pleasures which you so well are formed to enjoy; nor fear to have them empoisoned by my presence. My resolution is fixed. I am here with a friend, whom an unhappy passion obliges to travel, for some years, and I am determined to travel with him; my company will alleviate his sufferings, and my own, will be relieved by the sweet hope that you are more happy, your heart more at ease, and that I am repairing, as far as repair I can, all the wrongs I have done you. To you, Madam, I leave the choice of the name you shall bear; if mine be odious, if you still would wish the world should call you Caroline of Lichtfield, and if you would rather reside with your father, I can easily obtain permission from him, and from the King, that our marriage shall still remain a secret. But if, as it appears by your letter, a secret like this would be too painful a constraint on a mind so frank and ingenuous, if you consent to acknowledge me for your husband, when you come to Berlin, assume the name, the title, and the rank, of the Countess of Walstein.[b] This kind condescension, by satisfying your father and your King, may probably increase your freedom and happiness. You will inhabit Walstein House, you will command my servants; pardon me, Madam, not mine, your's; you will prevail on your tender and respectable friend, whom you wish, and whom, indeed, it is your duty, never to forsake, to come and live with you. As for me, I here engage myself, by promises the most sacred and solemn, never to return to Berlin till you yourself shall please to recal me; happy, too happy, if you but let me perceive a possibility of our future re-union. I rely on your virtues, your principles, your generosity, and will wait, not without impatience, but without fear and without complaint, the day you shall please to fix.—This day will come; yes, I dare hope it will; you will, some time hereafter, feel the want of a sincere and bosom friend; and never, Caroline, no, never, will you find one more sincere, more affectionate, than a husband who adores you, and whose whole happiness will consist in the desire, and the endeavour, to make you happy.

"I wait your answer before I depart. Direct it to Ronebourg, at the Baron of Lindorf's, who is the friend whom I before mentioned, and of whom I shall hereafter often speak, if you will deign to permit me to correspond with you, which will, indeed, be to me a great consolation. Fear neither the King nor your father. I will take care to give a plausible pretext for my travelling and my absence; which, perhaps, may be very, very long; but the real motives of which they never shall know.

"Farewel, Madam; you, most likely, will approve of this my arrangement—Alas! it is very, very different from what I formed when I asked your hand; but, if your felicity be thereby ensured, the end I proposed is still obtained."

EDMUND AUGUSTUS,
Count of Walstein.

The letter was ended; but what were the sensations of Caroline? Surprise, admiration, remorse, affection? Who can answer? All! All mingled and together confounded. She herself knew not what! Long she remained motionless, her eyes rivetted on that paper which had so entirely reversed all her opinions, and the contents of which were so unexpected. Recovering from this kind of annihilation, her first impulse was to rise, open her bureau, assemble all the papers Lindorf had left, run to the chamber of her dear mamma, and there bring her acquainted with this wonderful man! There inform her of the ties by which they were united, and seek, in her friendship, that aid of which her heart at present stood so much in need! This husband, who so lately had been an object of such dread, assumed a form so wholly different, displayed a mind so congenial with her own, that she now could gladly have clasped him to her bosom.[31] Her fetters, so heavy half an hour ago, now scarcely fetters seemed. "Ah! Walstein," said she, "generous Walstein! No; thou shalt not go; thou shalt not make thyself my victim!"

She stopped short, fearing to engage herself too far. Her affections were struggling; her mind was still oppressed, but by ideas far less afflicting. When she came to her friend she had not the pain she before felt in preparing the mind of the Baroness for the secret she was about to disclose; though this preparation was exceedingly necessary, so infinitely far was she from suspecting what she was about to be told.[a]—Caroline, her dear Caroline, so long married, and she never

to suspect it! This was so singular an incident, so surprising, and so little foreseen, that all the tragedies, comedies, novels and romances she had ever read
afforded not one more strange, more astonishing.

After various preparatives, therefore, and many tender caresses, her pupil, at
last, explained all these seeming mysteries in, as well as the reasons for, her conduct. When the good Canoness had exhausted her surprize, anger, and reproach;
after she had, by turns, been vexed and affected; after she had plentifully wept
and murmured; after she had a thousand and a thousand times repeated it was
abominably monstrous they should be afraid of trusting her with the secret, and
still more monstrous that they had sacrificed her poor girl; Caroline begged for,
and obtained, half an hour's silent hearing. This she employed to recapitulate
every circumstance that had passed with Lindorf; this was the most painful part
of her task, but now she was permitted to tell she was resolved to have no reserve,
nothing to conceal from her friend.

"No, dear mamma," said she, affectionately, "your Caroline will have no more
secrets for you; she has suffered too much by those already she was obliged to
keep. Only for these few days have I had the liberty to speak, and but for a few
moments the fortitude; for this I am indebted to the Count. Yes, to him do I owe
the happiness of daring to open my heart to you, and to have nothing painful
to relate. Oh! madam, when you shall know what an angel he is, and how great
have been my wrongs, you will not any longer pity your Caroline; she asks only
a little indulgence, and the patience to hear a long recital; for nothing, hereafter,
mamma, will I hide from you no; nothing, nothing."

Caroline kept her word, nor did she surprise the Canoness by confessing her
love for Lindorf.—"Alas! I saw it well enough," replied the Canoness; "and I,
poor silly woman that I was, congratulated myself on the discovery. I intended—
Yes, yes, I had a great many intentions; had contrived every thing.—See what an
error your fine secret has led me into! Am not I acquainted with the effects of the
passions? Amiable people meet; and, because they are amiable, fall in love. We
are formed for love, and to love eternally; for first impressions are never effaced."

"Ah!" exclaimed Caroline, with enthusiasm, "I hope, mamma, you are mistaken; I hope they sometimes are effaced; at least it shall not be my fault if they
are not. No; it shall not."—"Fault, poor girl, it would be no fault of thine; but
thy struggles will all be in vain.ª What! surely I know! The more you combat love
the more it increases. For how is it possible to cease to love?"

"Very possible, mamma, when love renders us guilty.—Oh! dear, dear
madam, you know not, cannot imagine, how guilty we both were; I for offend-
ing the best of husbands, and Lindorf a friend such as man never had before."

Caroline then began to read her manuscript, and thought she never could
have got through it, so incessantly was she interrupted by the exclamations of the
good kind hearted Canoness. At first she was in raptures with the brave General,

who died to save the life of his King. Then too did the young Count interest her, but still her dear Lindorf lay at her heart. "How charmingly he writes," said she; "how tender, how feeling his stile! Ah! how sorry am I! He would have been the husband for my Caroline." When, however, they came to Louisa, her friendship suffered considerable abatement.—"What praises does he bestow on this girl! Is it for a gentleman, and a Baron, to notice whether or no a village lass be pretty!"—But when she beheld him seriously in love with, and desirous of marrying her, she could contain her anger no longer; nay, so great was it that Caroline felt somewhat sorry for having given it birth.—"Speak not a word in his defence," said the Canoness. "Oh! how has he deceived me! Love a peasant's daughter! Intend to marry her! And, after that, dare to pay his addresses to Miss Lichtfield! 'Tis abominable! and thou oughtest to think thyself most happy for having been married, and not made the successor of this his Louisa. The second love, truly; and the first for a poor villager! How have I been deceived in that man; and who hereafter may one confide in!"

Caroline, more affected than humbled at having been the object of a second passion, made no reply, but sighed, and again continued to read, as soon as the petulant Baroness would permit. In proportion as Lindorf lost ground, in her esteem,[a] did Walstein rise; and he soon became her entire hero. His dignity, energy, and noble mind enchanted her. "You are too happy," repeated she to Caroline, "to be the wife of such a man! What tell you me of his not being handsome? You are wrong; he is as handsome as an Angel, and his sentiments are the sentiments of a God!—How did he speak to that diminutive Lindorf? You do not find him in love with a village girl."

Yet knew she not what to think, for a while, of his behaviour to Louisa; but, afterwards, when she came to the dreadful catastrophe, when she saw the Count wounded, disfigured, and heard to what excess he had carried generosity and friendship,[b] she was suffocated, absolutely unable to restrain herself, her tears, or her exclamations. Lindorf was a monster and Walstein a deity, before whom meer mortals ought to fall prostrate! Her enthusiasm increased in every line, and his letters to his friend made it astonishment! She protested Heaven had created this man, purposely, for her Caroline: his soul was not of this age, he was a Cyrus,[32] an Oroondates,[33] every thing she had heard, read, or could imagine, of sublime. "As to your Lindorf, you see he merely resembles the present race;[34] you will find he still loves Matilda; nay, that he could love a dozen at a time. To be sure, as to this Lady, she is a Countess, but never will I forgive him his Louisa. I make no doubt but he will return to Matilda, now; but I sincerely hope she will act towards him as I did to the High Chamberlain, when he came to offer me his hand after the death of thy mother, and that she, like me, with noble pride, will give her refusal.

"I hope not," cried Caroline, and the hope came from the bottom of her heart; even she herself was surprised at it; never before had she truly felt so anxious a desire that Lindorf again might love Matilda, and that to her he might henceforth be no more than a brother. Walstein, indeed, possessed a soul so superior, so transcendant, one to whom it was so honourable to be allied, that Caroline actually felt her attachment for Lindorf was not, at this moment, the strongest attachment of her heart.[35] It was a moment of enthusiasm, we own; and which the strong and sympathetic feelings of her friend had increased; but we may leave the talk of still increasing them to the care of this friend.

When she came to the last letter, which Caroline had received that day; the letter in which the Count spoke of her, thought of her, and confirmed her in the hope of forever living with her dear Caroline; when she heard the phrase you will prevail on your tender and respectable friend, whom you wish, and whom, indeed, it is your duty, never to forsake, to come and live with you. She no longer could moderate her transports; she kissed Caroline again and again; called her her dear friend, her lovely Countess, and, while the tears trickled down her cheeks, added, "We must not let this angel depart, must we, my child? Must he go?"

"No, certainly," replied Caroline; "I should be the most ungrateful of women, were I to give my consent. Permit me to go and answer his letter, immediately; for the courier returns this evening."

Caroline left the good Baroness all amazement, all rapture at what she had heard; and with matter sufficient to employ her thoughts without dread of dullness from being alone. The very idea of writing to the Count would have petrified Caroline, had it been proposed the evening before; while, at present, nothing seemed more easy; her heart overflowing with gratitude and admiration could not have found an employment more accordant to its feelings; her rapid imagination dictated a thousand things, and, as she entered her apartment, she ran to her bureau. The first object which presented itself, as she opened it, was the box containing the miniature picture of her husband. During her anger against him, to which the letter of her father had given birth, she had concealed the box under the manuscript which she had that day removed; instantly she took it up, opened it, and fixed her eyes on those fine features, that countenance so noble and so mild; and, as she looked, felt a sensation which never till then had she known. She forgot how much his person was altered, imagined she really beheld him, and was astonished how she could have refused her heart to the original of such a portrait. Insensibly did she become affected, tears rose in her eyes, and with great emotion she pressed the picture to her lips.

Thus was she in a most excellent disposition to answer Walstein; and, had she written it at that moment, the answer would have been much more tender than he had dared to hope; but, desirous of confirming these her new sensations, which were the more pleasing because unaccompanied by remorse, she would read once more the letter from the Count. Ah! what ungrateful, what cruel idea then suddenly entered her mind! It was that he, Walstein, required this long, and, perhaps, everlasting separation; he who proposed it, he who seemed to insist on its taking place!—His reasons were evident; he dreaded living with a capricious, unjust woman, who suffered herself to have been so easily prejudiced; a child, obstinate, wilful, and void of reason; for thus, said Caroline, I must appear to him; thus have I deserved to be thought.

The phrase in which he mentioned Lindorf, and which, before, she had scarcely remarked, made also an unfortunate impression. "A friend whom an unhappy passion" obliges to travel. I am determined to "go with him."—How might the Count be ignorant of the object of this passion? Though Lindorf should not have told him, he must, himself, have divined it; it was impossible to be otherwise. Beside, does he not say he is "determined to go with him?"

We are alike easy to suppose what most we wish or most we fear should happen has happened. And now is the active imagination of Caroline busily labouring to paint every object black; and now, the more she reads that letter, which at first appeared so tender, so flattering, the more is she convinced that the generosity of Walstein, only, has dictated his expressions, and that he ardently desires to live from her. For what probability was there, were not such his motives, that he would thus renounce his country, his employments, the Court, and the favour and friendship of his Sovereign? Had he had the least wish to live with her, would he not have made the attempt? Would he not first have seen her, and endeavoured to find what her present thoughts were before he would make so cruel a determination?— [a] "Ah!" said she, mournfully laying down the letter and the picture, "I had a momentary dream of almost happiness, but it is vanished. Happiness is not for me!—How dearly would he have loved me! But how may I now hope that should ever happen since he wishes not to know me, since he despises, nay, perhaps, hates me! And yet, how great is his generosity, his benevolence! But, does it become me to abuse this generosity, and, after having sinned against him so unpardonably, must I likewise banish him his country? No, never; I am determined how to act; I will here pass my life, far from him, far from the world; he shall be at liberty to remain at Court, to benefit his country by his virtues, to make those happy who depend on him, and shall not himself be made miserable by Caroline; he will forget, perhaps, that she exists!"

In the full persuasion that all these suppositions were real, she immediately took pen and paper and, as immediately, wrote what follows.

From CAROLINE *to the Count of* WALSTEIN.

Rindaw.

"No, my lord, I will not delay to write the answer you require; happy if this my promptitude may any way prove how grateful I am, how infinitely obliged to the first, the most generous, of men! I shall not here discuss what the motives were which might induce you to make the proposition your letter contains; yet, believe me, I feel their generous tendency. I hope you will pardon me for refusing my consent to your design of leaving your country and friends; an absence like this might ruin all your future prospects, yet could not change my destiny. Of this you have had the goodness to leave me absolute mistress, and I am determined, happen what will, here to remain. My absence from Berlin injures no one, interests no one; that city has certainly forgotten a young creature whom it scarcely has seen. As for my father, he has ever been accustomed to live without me; the Baroness of Rindaw, my dear friend, or, rather, my tender mother, is the sole being in this world to whom my existence and my presence may be both useful and agreeable. I neither can quit her nor wish her to forsake that retirement in which she has lived so long. Permit me, therefore, to consecrate my life wholly to her, to render her declining years the same kind and continued cares she took of me in early and helpless infancy. Your letter insures your consent; and, provided we are separate, wherefore should this separation be at a distance so immense?

"I wish to live here forgotten,[a] and, if that be possible, in tranquility; but for you, my lord, you owe your talents to your country and your King, nor is there a motive on earth which should sway you to renounce employing them for the good of weaker and less wise mortals.[36] And is it for Caroline to throw the least impediment in the way of purposes so noble? Alas! then should I indeed be guilty, and the bitterness of reproach would make life wretched! But no, I wish to be just, and will submit to my fate; nor ought I to grieve at it since I am permitted to live in the bosom of friendship, and in that peaceful retreat in which I have ever lived. The pleasures of which you speak are effaced from my memory, or, at least, have left a recollection so faint, so shadowy, that I neither wish for nor regret them. Alas! I have no regret but that of not having made the first of mankind happy, and wish have I none but that of hearing in this my retirement that he enjoys the felicity he so infinitely deserves. To this it is my duty to contribute, and this I dare promise I have the fortitude to perform. Solitude has nothing fearful for my imagination; on the contrary, it is the boundary of my wishes, and, since I am convinced it is your desire I should live happy, I do not fear you will give them any opposition —The Count of Walstein at Berlin and Caroline at Rindaw will each be stationed as they ought.

"My friend has this morning been informed of our marriage; and since you consent I should bear your name that shall henceforth be my ambition; therefore, hereafter, to those few persons whom I may see, and those to whom you wish to confide the secret, I shall ever remain

CAROLINE, Countess of Walstein."

Had Caroline refused the title of Countess of Walstein, which she began to have some value for, the Canoness would by no means have acquiesced in this same kind of self-denial. While Caroline had been writing her good mamma had taken care to send for all the servants and inform them that Caroline was Countess of Walstein, with a strict injunction to call her my Lady, in future. She was punctually obeyed, and, in the space of a few minutes, two or three of the maids, and as many footmen, entered, under different pretexts, purposely to repeat my Lady. What will *my Lady* please to have? What are *my Lady's* commands?

No sooner had *my Lady* ended her letter than she ran to read it to her dear friend. "Yes, mamma," said she, when she had done reading, "I have taken a firm resolution to live and die here, and never love any body but you." A few months before, this project would have enchanted the tender Canoness, but she had now far different views. Her imagination was at the highest pitch of enthusiasm in favour of the Count of Walstein, and his re-union with Caroline, the accomplishment of which was now the object of every wish. But, as it was a part of her plan to leave the young Countess ignorant of the manner in which she was determined to act, she pretended to approve her letter. Nay, perhaps, she took no little pleasure in retaliation (for there is no age or character that will not indulge revenge which they believe innocent) and, in her turn, having her secret also. The letter was, therefore, sealed and directed to the Count of Walstein, at the Baron of Lindorf's, and some have pretended that a sigh escaped Caroline as she wrote the direction, though she, at present, protests not; and if there did, we may well believe it was the last.

And now, not only this day, and the next day, and the day after that, but every day, the Count was frequently present to the imagination of Caroline; and the more she thought of him, the more she delighted to think; all his letters were read, and read again; and she every time thought she discovered new proofs, which had not before been remarked, of the superiority of heart and. understanding of this excellent man, whom she had known too late ever to be able now to merit. The picture was taken from its box, tied to a ribbon, and hung round the neck of Caroline, which it no more quitted. Twenty times a day would she take it from her bosom, gaze on it with tenderness, and put it back with a sigh. But the more she was convinced Walstein would have made her a most happy woman, the more did generosity, and, perhaps, vanity, applaud the resolution she had taken, well persuaded he wished not to live with her. There was something, likewise, in her heart, which told her she would much rather have him at Berlin than traversing distant regions with Lindorf. Indeed the supposition of herself being the cause of the exile of these two friends was insupportable. "Let one, at least," said she, "remain happy in his own country." And thus to sacrifice, in part, her own felicity to that of the Count was, in part, to expiate her own wrongs, and to obtain her own pardon.

While Caroline thus meditated the Canoness was not idle. All her reflections tended to find what might be the best means of re-uniting the husband and the wife. Several very natural ones presented themselves to her mind, and which might easily have been put in execution. Such, for example, as to have a letter written to the Count, inviting him to come to Rindaw; or to take Caroline to Berlin, under some feigned pretence, and there contrive Walstein should meet her; or, which might still have been better, to have reasoned with the young Countess, and, by degrees, induced her to a re-union, which she herself was too desirous of long to have refused. But all this was much too simple for the Canoness of Rindaw, too trivial for the end of a romance, in which she was quite in raptures to be one of the *dramatis personæ*. Surprise, gratitude, tears, faintings, if these were wanting the scene must have been insipid.[a] Read, therefore, what her prudent head imagined and brought forth.

One day (it was within a week after the letter of Caroline had been sent) the Canoness said she had long had a desire to visit her chapter, and to pass some time there; "a duty," says she, "I have too long neglected, and which I wish once more to perform before I die. I will therefore set off to-morrow morning, and beg, my dear, you will accompany me." Caroline, surprised at so unexpected a resolution, represented, but in vain, that her age, her infirmities, the permission she had long obtained to live at Rindaw, all made this an unnecessary journey. The Canoness was so positive Caroline could not long contradict her. Beside that she herself really took pleasure in imagining a change of scene; it would retard her interview with her father, remove her for a time from a place which brought too many past incidents to memory, and thus relieve her melancholy. Another motive was added. Long had she desired to form an acquaintance with some young lady, to whom she could reveal her sensations and her thoughts, and who might become her friend. The Baroness of Rindaw, it was true, was a friend; but the respect ever preserved for a person by whom we have been educated, the great difference of age, and the infirmities which made her in continual dread of her death, and thus of being left in solitude, without a friend on earth, all increased an ardent desire to find another, whose soul and sentiments were correspondent to her own, whose age was nearly the same, and with whom she might freely speak, or to whom she might as freely write all she thought and all she felt.

"This," said she, "would give a charm to the retreat in which I am doomed to pass my life. Ah! had I only such a friend as I can imagine, how should I love her, and how would she love me! She should live in my heart, and presently would I forget other and stronger passions;[a] forget that the man to whom, had I known him better, or better known myself, this heart would have been wholly devoted, now wishes to possess no place there!"

When they sent her new books from Berlin, in which she found a correspondence between two friends, she would sigh, and sorrowfully say, "poor Caroline, thou hast no person,[b] no friend to whom thou mayest write all thou thinkest! Thou hast no letter to receive!" This to Caroline was a real grief, and when the Canoness proposed the before-mentioned journey, she imagined she might surely find, in the cloister, young ladies of distinction, some one of whom would be worthy, would be capable of friendship. At length, therefore, she very willingly yielded to the project of the good Canoness, and prepared for her departure on the morrow.

In these her schemes of future confidence and friendship, Caroline did not forget her precious manuscript and the letters, which were become the daily subject of contemplation; and still less her dear little picture, which never quitted her bosom, except to be kissed, and with which she every day grew more and more enamoured. Till the expected friend was found this picture held the place of one, and was become the confidant of her most secret thoughts; to this she confessed all her regret and grief for having lost, past return, the esteem and friendship of its counter part; while the expressive, the comprehensive countenance seemed, though dumb and motionless, to hear, understand, and answer. The happiest moments she enjoyed were those in which this mute conversation passed.

Early the next morning the Canoness, Caroline, and their maids were in the carriage. The former was all chearfulness, she was first ready, and seemed to take excessive pleasure in the journey. As she saw nothing and had, therefore, no outward object to employ her thoughts, she talked much, and wanted a description of every place by which they passed. The first objects, after leaving the court-yard, were the pavilion, the window where Caroline first had seen Lindorf, the door through which he first had entered, and the road along which he had passed when he departed never to see her more. A little further were the turrets of the chateau of Risberg; they had passed the wood in which Caroline had wandered, and come to the park where Lindorf had leaped the barrier to meet her; the difference between her former and her present sensations was very great; her heart did not palpitate now, but it felt a painful contraction. Instead of fixing her imagination on places that might retrace an obliterated passion, or, at least, a passion remembered only with repentance and self-reproach, she turned her thoughts on the wrongs she had done her husband, and mournful was the reflection. We may rest well assured, however, Caroline did not lead the communicative Baroness to speak on such a subject. The journey was performed without any accident, and her friend, infirm as she was, preserved her chearfulness, though she no longer called her dear Caroline, but dear Countess, and that, too, at every instant. She often attempted, likewise, to speak of the Count, but Caroline, more prudent, and restrained by the presence of the maids, equally fearing the Canoness might say too much or too little, took good care to turn the conversation on other subjects.

The place to which they were going was some days journey from Rindaw. Caroline supposed they were almost there, and was wishing to arrive just as she saw the coachman drive down an avenue that led to an antique and large chateau, the weathercocks of which she had perceived at a great distance. Caroline was surprised, and so told the Baroness, who, with significant satisfaction in her countenance, answered, "the servants had obeyed her orders, for that she meant to call and visit a friend who lived there." Caroline had not time to ask questions concerning this friend, of whom before she had never heard mention made, for they were already in the court-yard. The Canoness called the footman, and bade him enquire if the *Count of Walstein* was there, and if two ladies *of his acquaintance* might have the pleasure of speaking with him.

Caroline could not believe her senses! "The Count of Walstein!" echoed she, with a cry scarce articulate. "Great God! Mamma! Did I hear you right! Where are we? Whither have you brought me?"

"We are at the chateau of Ronebourg," replied the Baroness, with infinite satisfaction,[a] "and I have brought thee to thy husband, my dear."

Poor Caroline scarcely hears the end of the phrase; sense and feeling have forsaken her, and she drops,[b] motionless, with her head on the shoulder of her imprudent friend! Her maid raises and sustains her, informs the Canoness of the fearful state into which Caroline is fallen, and calls for salts and hartshorn, which, in their flutter, are not to be found![37] And now the Canoness, in despair, repents, too late, of what she has done. Caroline continues lifeless, moves not, breathes not, betrays not the least sign of existence!

All this passed in the coach, and in the middle of the court, in the front of the chateau, while the footman was gone to deliver his message, and while the servants of the house went in search of the Count, who was walking in the park with Lindorf.— Walstein is found, but cannot imagine who these unknown ladies are; for the Canoness, always in search of surprise, forbade the footman to give in her name, and the Count was very far indeed from imagining it was her, and his wife, from whom he had so lately received a letter. He, therefore, hastens to receive the ladies, and, followed by his friend, arrives. The first object he beholds is Caroline, senseless, with her lace cut, her hair loose, her bosom bare; they are lifting her out of the coach in which the Baroness sits weeping, and raving, and summoning the whole universe to the assistance of Caroline, of whose death she accuses herself, vowing not to survive her.

If a spectacle like this well might affect the Count, inexplicable and strange as it must be, what effect may it be supposed to have had on Lindorf, who, the moment he saw, knew Caroline? Scarcely could he believe his eyes! Scarcely credit the strong emotions of his heart! "God of wonders!" cried he, as he ran up to the carriage, "can this be?" He could not doubt.

The livid paleness of Caroline, her closed eye lids, the cries and groans of the Baroness persuaded him she had just expired, and he himself was presently almost lifeless. Walstein, who comprehended nothing of what he beheld, saw Lindorf reel, and just had time to catch him in his arms. He revives, and beholding Caroline still the same, in all the agonies of despair, exclaims, "It is she! It is Caroline! Your Caroline! My Caroline! Her whom I adored, her who now lies breathless, and whom I will follow to the grave!"

So saying, he tore himself violently from the arms of Walstein, who stood speechless and confounded! The exigencies of the moment recovered him from his stupor: he made way through the croud of servants, whom the cries of the Baroness and the strangeness of the scene had drawn together, and went to the assistance of Caroline. Exposed to the open air, she had begun a little to recover; her half opened eyes endeavoured to move, and her woman, seated on the ground, supported her till an arm chair was brought, in which she might be placed, and carried, more conveniently. The poor distracted Canoness, still in the carriage, paid dear for her imprudence; she wept, exclaimed, called for the Count, and was unappeasable till they told her he was there, and that Caroline was recovering.

Too true it was. Walstein was there; but Walstein knew not whether all he beheld was or was not a dream. Caroline at Ronebourg, and brought thither with violence! For wherefore should she, else, be expiring at her arrival? Lindorf in despair, and fled, uttering words of dreadful import, that still resounded in the ears of Walstein. *It is she! It is Caroline! Your Caroline! My Caroline! Her whom I adored!*—Ay?—Caroline?—Was it Caroline, whom Lindorf loved and by whom he was again beloved?—The Count endeavoured to doubt, to persuade himself that his friend, distracted by grief, by the melancholy turn of his mind, had been deceived; but the Count could not so elude his fears.

Not the change which a year had made in the person of Caroline, nor that her present illness caused, could make Walstein mistake her. He silently fixed his eyes on her for some moments, then, kneeling at her feet, caught her hands, and pressed them with ardour to his lips. The eyes of Caroline moved, but not as they were wont. They had no intelligence; she knew not where she was, or whom that man might be she beheld prostrate before her. Unable to articulate a word, she gently withdrew her hands, joined them together, leaned her face upon them, and shed a torrent of tears. The Count, still kneeling by her, endeavoured to calm and convince her she had nothing to dread, but was disturbed by the repeated cries of the Canoness, who incessantly called for him, as she sat in her coach, and who began to be very impatient that he did not come. At last she called so loud that Walstein was obliged to leave Caroline and go to her. He went with the hope of learning what might be the meaning of this strange adventure; but the poor lady was so affected, so agitated, and said so many things at once that to understand any one of them was impossible. The Count, beside, was himself in a revery. When he came up to the Canoness he perceived she was blind, and this was a new incident of information; he instantly recollected the blind relation of whom Lindorf had spoken, in his letter to Petersburg, and to whom the lady he loved devoted all her cares. Could he have doubted of the fearful meaning of Lindorf's late exclamations, this would have removed his doubts. Alas! they were certainties.

The Count helped the Baroness out of her carriage, and led her to Caroline, whom they had now seated in a chair; nor could she be convinced she was still alive till the dear girl said, with a feeble voice and a gentle mixture of reproach, "Ah! my dear mamma, what have you done?" By little and little Caroline recovered her senses, but she was still so weak, and so ill, as to be wholly unable to walk; the Count, therefore, ordered them to bear her gently into the house, and, giving his arm to the Baroness, followed.

They concluded it was proper to put Caroline to bed; as she herself, indeed, desired they would. The Canoness was determined to remain with her, and Walstein, after having kissed her hand, which she no longer withdrew, retired from her apartment and hastened into that of Lindorf, concerning whom he was become very anxious. He entered, but no Lindorf was there; as he looked round the room, however, he saw a letter, lying sealed, directed to himself. He took it, opened it with emotion, and read what follows, which had been traced by a trembling hand, expressive of the great disorder of the writer,

"A most strange, unexpected, and incomprehensible event has discovered the fatal secret which I meant to have borne with me to the grave. I was not master of myself; to behold Caroline dead, or dying, and to remain silent was beyond human possibility.—Yes, Walstein, it is she, she herself, whom I adored without knowing, without imagining, you had the most distant claim to her. I call Heaven to witness that, the very moment I learnt she was your's, I fled with a determined and unshaken resolution never to see her more. How was it possible I might foresee that here, in this retreat, at my own house—Oh God! this only was wanting to fill up the measure of my crimes; to complete my fatal destiny; this, only, of giving a new and incurable wound to him I had before so irreparably injured!—Yet, let me hope not. Oh, Walstein! Caroline is a miracle! She alone is worthy of you, and you the sole man on earth deserving of her! May you be long happy!— I will deliver you from a wretched friend who seems to exist only for your torment. One favour, only, let me ask; it is the last; suffer your

Lady to remain ignorant that I have seen her, and that you are privy to this my guilty passion. Much am I deceived if she herself do not soon inform you of it; she will not long have any secrets for you. To learn it from her own mouth will be a most pleasing proof of her confidence in you, and she will not suspect I have been despicable enough to betray her secret. Walstein! Caroline! Farewell! Dear possessors of a heart alike torn by love and friendship, for ever, farewell! Forget, but do not hate, the miserable Lindorf!

"P. S. You will command, at Ronebourg, as at your own house; I have left orders for that purpose. When I come to any fixed place of abode, I will write once more, Walstein, that I may be certain you pardon me and are happy; and happy you certainly will be, since Caroline is yours.

"I promise not to attempt my own life; but must live far distant from you both."

This letter had been written with so much haste and emotion that it was scarcely legible. Having once ran it over, the Count immediately went in search of Varner, the valet de chambre[38] of Lindorf. His intention was to send him off, immediately, after his master, to intreat him to return; but he presently found this was impracticable. As soon as Lindorf had found his fears were false, and that Caroline was only in a fit, not dead, he instantly ordered his servants to saddle an excellent English horse, while he wrote the above letter, after which he departed, full speed. He had told Varner to follow, with such baggage as was necessary, and meet him at a place which he himself would take care to indicate; recommended every possible attention and obedience to the commands of the Count, and his guests, and instantly disappeared, forbidding him to follow.

As soon as the Count found there were no hopes of overtaking him, at present, he made Varner promise to inform him, the first intelligence he should receive, where his master was; then again perused the letter, which brought the tears into his eyes. Walstein now became impatient to learn what could have been the motive of this strange visit, and sent to know if he might speak with the Canoness in a private apartment. She came immediately, with the messenger, being as impatient to speak as the Count was to hear. After informing him the Countess was fallen asleep, "though," said she, "the catastrophe has not happened exactly as I could have wished, are not you exceedingly obliged to me, Sir, for having brought you Lady Walstein?"

"Before I can testify my gratitude, madam, I must be certain she was not brought against her will."

"Against her will, my Lord! Surely you cannot suppose it! Against her will! You do not know me. Do you think I would *force* the dear girl to any thing? No, my Lord, she was quite pleased at the journey; nor has she been so chearful for this many a day as she was on the road—Quite impatient to arrive"—

"This is very strange; unaccountably strange," interrupted the Count. "I imagined her fainting, her tears, what she said to you with a tone of reproach, were all"—

"All amazement, at finding herself so unexpectedly here—The agitation of a first meeting—I know not what—Young persons are so timid. I own it would, perhaps, have been better to have prepared her for it; but then, on the other hand, where would have been the surprise? And, if ever your history should be written, this will be the most interesting event in your whole life."

The Count, who knew not the romantic turn of the Canoness, astonished at so strange a remark, gazed with wonder, requested an explanation, and learnt, at last, that, though Caroline was not brought to Ronebourg against her will, it was without her knowledge; which proceeding he was very far from approving, and as frankly told the Canoness so, who excused herself by her ardent desire to see them united, and the fear of not succeeding so well by any other means. "Yet," said she, "had I supposed—But, I confess, I had totally forgotten all that."

"What! what!" replied the Count.

"Oh, nothing—Nothing, nothing—Something I must not mention; though it was certainly the cause of that fearful emotion and fainting—But, a propos, my Lord: I understand we are here at the house of the Baron of Lindorf—that this seat is his—'Tis true, I ought to have known it; but I mistook, or forgot, for my memory is become so weak lately—I believed, though I know not why, that Ronebourg belonged to you."

"No, madam; but it is the same thing; I am at home, here; the Baron of Lindorf is my most intimate friend, and begged me, in his absence, to command his house and servants."

"In his absence! What, is he absent then?" "He is," answered the Count, who, could he have smiled, have smiled he must, at the prudent Canoness, who, with such simple cunning, told all she knew.

"Absent! I am quite happy at that! It is the luckiest circumstance!"

"Why lucky, Madam?"

"I—That is—I—Because—he will not be afflicted—I mean troubled"—

The poor lady knew not what to say; she was sorry to find she had thought aloud, tho' that was by no means a new thing with her, and she trembled lest she had discovered a secret which she supposed it was of the utmost importance carefully to keep. The Count increased her embarrassment.

"You mean to say, Madam, the Baron has avoided the ceremony of receiving strangers; he not having the pleasure of being acquainted with you?"

Notwithstanding she wished to do it, the Canoness could not tell a falsehood with that intrepidity the occasion seemed to require.—"No—Yes—That is—we are not wholly unacquainted; he happened to be one of our country neighbours; his estate of Risberg joins to mine, at Rindaw, and we used to see him every day:

nay, indeed, he is, as I may say, one of our friends; though I think him a little given to change; a—a rover."

Walstein, who thought the Baroness and this conversation very singular, was going to defend Lindorf, when repeated cries from Caroline's bed-chamber alarmed him. She had just awaked in a burning and delirious fever; and every symptom indicated the beginning of a very serious and dangerous illness. Her maid, whom she did not know, unable to hold her, was obliged to call for help. The Count, deeply affected, went up to her bed, out of which she absolutely would get.—"Let them take me back to Rindaw," said she; "I won't see him, he will kill me; I will depart alone, on foot; I will fly, to avoid him, to the world's end."

Her imagination, at other moments, full of Lindorf, made her take the Count for him; and, pushing him from her, she conjured him to fly; reproaching him for being the cause of all her misery. Then, again thinking she spoke to the Count, she exclaimed, with the utmost tenderness, "Oh thou whom, for my happiness, too late I have known, thou whom I love, whom I shall ever love,ª wherefore dost thou fly me? But I will follow, will supplicate, will force thee to see and hear me."

Knowing only so much as Walstein at present knew, it was impossible he could suppose Caroline thought of him while she spoke last, or of Lindorf in what she had said before. But, afflicted as he was for himself, he was still more so for Caroline. He would not leave her, but remained in her chamber all night, after having, with much intreaty, prevailed on the Canoness to sleep in another apartment. Caroline continued in the same agitation and delirium. The Count, mean time, sent to the nearest town for the best physician the place could afford; and, likewise, sent a courier, post, to Berlin, for the first men in the profession. He also thought it prudent to send for the High Chamberlain; but, not wishing to alarm him, he only said, in his letter, he intreated him to come, immediately, to Ronebourg, on an affair of the utmost importance.

The Count never quitted his post, by the bedside of Caroline, except when obliged, and then reluctantly. At day-break the country physician arrived, and Walstein was greatly alarmed at perceiving his ignorance. He pronounced it to be the small-pox, though the Canoness affirmed Caroline had had it in her infancy, at Rindaw, and even told where pock marks remained, which put it out of doubt. Her fever and delirium increased, and on the third day she seemed to be in the utmost danger. Imagine what were the feelings of the Count, thus removed as he was from all efficacious aid; for, let the courier make what haste he could, it was impossible the physician from Berlin should arrive before the seventh or eighth day. These were days of cruel anxiety to Walstein; they were passed in momentary dread of seeing her he adored expire. Her sickness, by increasing his feelings, increased his attachment: the assiduous and tender cares he bestowed on her, the patience and gentleness she discovered at those intervals when she was not delirious, the character her maids gave her, and the real grief they shewed, certain proofs how deservedly she was beloved, all strengthened his affection. To the dread of losing her was added the reproach of being himself the cause of her sufferings. He was convinced the stratagem made use of to bring her thither, which was equivalent to violence, her dread of living with him, her passion for Lindorf, and the natural struggles of love and duty, had thus endangered and might rob her of life. In one of these moments of grief, affection, and remorse, prostrate at her bedside, he took a solemn oath, should Heaven be pleased to preserve her from the grave, be his sufferings what they might, to make her happy.—"God of mercies!" said he, with hands upraised to Heaven, "Save this unfortunate victim of tyranny and love! Deign to hear the vow I make of resigning her to the man who possesses her heart!"

Caroline was incapable of understanding, or, perhaps, she would have intreated him to have been less ready to yield her to another; but she had lain totally senseless during the last four and twenty hours. Happily, the King's first physician arrived that night. He did not dissemble the extreme danger in which he found the patient, and his whole dependance was on her youth. He administered, however, such assistance as had been too long delayed, and said that if she outlived the ninth and thirteenth days he then should have some hope; but till they were past could not pretend to give any.

The Count, though a prey to the most severe affliction, was obliged to dissemble his feelings; for the Canoness suffered so fearfully that her inquietudes were not the least of his distresses. The loss of her sight made it easy for those who had no respect for truth to impose upon her; but not for Walstein. Her questions were incessant, and she was never satisfied unless she heard the most exact and circumstantial account. After he had been carefully attending on Caroline, and, overcome with fatigue, had retired to take a little repose, she never failed either to come to him or send to beg he would come to her. When he was absent it was with the utmost difficulty they could keep her from Caroline, whom she might disturb but could not aid; the Count was the only person who had any power over her, and she was never satisfied unless he was conversing with her. Thus was Walstein often torn from the pillow of Caroline, though he was wretched if he trusted her but for a moment to the care of others. He supported all this with that patience, fortitude, and mildness, of which he alone was capable, and thought himself well rewarded for all his pangs by the melancholy pleasure of watching the most adorable of women. Then it was he felt a real gratitude towards the Canoness for having brought her; for he supposed her present illness had a more remote cause than the agitation her arrival had occasioned: this might have hastened its crisis, but he attributed it wholly to her passion for Lindorf and her affliction at the supposed impossibility of union. In this conjecture every circumstance confirmed him, and her determination to pass her whole life in retirement was not the least. Again and again did he read the letter he had received from her, and in it could perceive nothing but a continued sacrifice of love to duty. *Solitude has nothing fearful for my imagination; on the contrary, it is the boundary of my wishes.*—"No, dear Caroline," said he, "thou deceived thyself; or, rather, virtue deceives thee.[32] I were the most barbarous, worst of men, were I longer to remain an impediment to the happiness of two people to me equally dear, and who, for my sake, are both descending to the tomb. O Caroline! O Lindorf! Wherefore do you not hear me? Wherefore may I not this moment bestow you on each other?"

Neither did he doubt but that her tender exclamation, *Alas! I have no regret but that of not having made the first of mankind happy!* was, at least, as much addressed to Lindorf as to Walstein!—"Happy," said he, "sovereignly happy, ought to be the man whom thou preferest; and happy he shall be.—Can I flatter myself with being this man? Oh! no; too well I know the contrary. But should it be too late, should Caroline be torn from us, should remorseless death prevent the reparation I owe her, ah! what must then become of me!"—The thought was distracting, and yet this thought was every moment renewed.

The High Chamberlain did not arrive till the day after the physician; nor, perhaps would he have been there so soon had not the letter of the Count found him ready to set off for Rindaw; he, therefore, had only to take a different road, and see at once his son and daughter; though this, or the cause of his being sent for, he little suspected. His coming happened to be on one of the days of crisis. Walstein had not left Caroline a moment, and, in his anxiety, had wholly forgotten his father-in-law, when the latter, but half informed by the servants, from whom he had only heard that the Count was with his Lady, entered the chamber precipitately, saying aloud, as he opened the door, "My daughter, the Countess of Walstein, here, and I not know it! Where is she, that I may embrace her?"

"Alas! my Lord, behold where she is;" answered the Count, pointing: "she seemed something better, and we began to hope—But I doubt lest your entrance—

In fact, the patient, disturbed at the noise, opened her astonished eyes, looked round her, saw herself in a strange apartment, her father and her husband both by her bedside, knew them, and, unable to support so many emotions at once, fell into a more alarming delirium than she had ever been in before. The physician came and insisted every body should leave the room, and the Count conducted the High Chamberlain, in the midst of his consternation, to the apartment of the Canoness. Unable to remain long absent from Caroline, he left them together, hoping, at least, that the Baron would release him from the care of attending on the Canoness; but this hope was of short duration. Scarcely were they alone a minute before they mutually began to reproach each other. The lady that she had been so long left ignorant of the marriage of her dear pupil, and the High Chamberlain that she had not informed him of her having undertaken this journey. Thus, proceeding from complaint to complaint, and from one cause of vexation to another, they at last were both so angry, and spoke so loud, that the Count was obliged to go and keep the peace. He found them both highly irritated, and reciprocally saying the most bitter things; though still calling each other, from habit, My dear High Chamberlain! and My dear Baroness!

It is possible that, at some moments, such a scene might have been amusing; but not with Walstein's present temper of mind. He endeavoured to put an end to it, and re-establish harmony, which he could no otherwise effect but by recalling to mind their former passion, at the recollection of which the poor Canoness melted. The High Chamberlain was not quite so soft; but the Count having reminded him of the obligations he had, and *might* still have, to his friend, he was, almost immediately, so moved, that he could not express his feelings; he went up to his dear Baroness, and begged her to excuse his warmth of temper; was sorry, very sorry, exceedingly sorry; while she with dignity and affection gave him her hand to kiss, telling him he abused the power he had over her. After the High Chamberlain had devoutly paid his respects to this once fair hand, peace was restored, and the Count returned to his beloved patient.

Where is the reader who is not by this time acquainted with the character of Walstein? Who will not easily imagine, although it be not circumstantially related, the deep affliction of these his days of incertitude and dread? The more he thought the greater were his terrors; and, during the latter part of this severe illness, he could not leave his Caroline, day nor night; he never quitted his arm chair, which was placed by her bedside; and if, at some moments, over wearied nature exacted a short and painful sleep, he soon waked and started, with the mortal dread of no more finding her who was now become the only object of his thoughts. The thirteenth day at length arrived, which the physician declared was to be the crisis of her fate, and a dreadful day it was. The Count wished singly to support its horrors; he neither told the High Chamberlain nor the Baroness that, perhaps, at midnight, their friend and daughter would be no more. He determined to sit up alone with her; and oh! how ardent were the prayers he sent up to Heaven for her relief! With what agonizing affection did he press that feeble and burning hand to his lips and to his heart! How often did the tears swim in his eyes while fixed on those of Caroline, to which the fever still gave motion, and which, perhaps, ere morning would close eternally.

This last crisis was so violent that the alarmed physician said nothing less than a miracle could make her live over the day. The distracted Count, sunk in grief, unable longer to sustain the sight, or to tear himself from the dying Caroline, had still the farther pang of being obliged to prepare the father and the friend for the fearful catastrophe. He had so continually endeavoured to comfort them and inspire hope, that, far from suspecting, they were lulled into a kind of security which must render the information tenfold horrid. The Count had promised to inform them how Caroline was, but, terrified himself at what he had to communicate, he stopped, for some moments, in the anti-chamber, to calm his own mind and collect all his fortitude. "Ah," thought he, "if this unfortunate father feels, as I do, all the weight of remorse; if to the recollection of having sacrificed his daughter her death be added, how may he support his sorrow!—Oh! my Caroline, thy executioners weep, and thou diest! Yet wilt thou not die unrevenged; for, sure, the torments I suffer are far worse than death."

While he was thus hesitating, the valet de chambre of Lindorf, seeing him, came up hastily, and told him he wished to speak to him; he had received a letter from his master, who was waiting for him at Hamburg, whence he was to embark for England. Varner intended to set off that very night, and only waited the commands of the Count. Instead of giving an answer, Walstein stood silent; absorbed in thought little short of distraction: at length, suddenly starting, he bade him wait, and went into his closet, without himself knowing what he intended.—

"Write to Lindorf! And at a moment like this! What shall I say to him? Shall I take the dagger, reeking from my own heart, and plunge it into my friend's? Shall I desire him to return, only that I may behold him expire on the tomb of her he adores? Yet," said he, with instantaneous recollection, "might not Caroline, might not love work a miracle, which, perhaps, is reserved for love alone?—Were there but time!—If Lindorf were but present!—God of Heaven! who hearest my prayer, grant yet a few days, and Caroline, perhaps, may be restored!"

However vague might be the hope, that, just then, seemed to enlighten his imagination, he listened to it with pleasure, and, snatching up the pen, instantaneously wrote the following words:

"Lindorf, wait not a moment; set off; travel day and night; should you not meet me, come immediately here; and, if meet me you should, I shall have something to communicate.—We shall never return to Ronebourg more."[40]

EDMUND COUNT OF WALSTEIN.

The Count himself took this short letter to Varner, commanded him instantly to set off, never to stop, except to change horses, and, as he hoped for future favour or affection, not to mention a word of the illness and danger of the Countess, fearing lest the dreadful tidings might wholly incapacitate Lindorf for the journey. Should he have the misery to lose Caroline before the arrival of Lindorf, and to survive her death, Walstein was determined to go and meet him, that they might together leave this land of wretchedness and despair, and, in a foreign country, together bear, together endure, their griefs and their regret.

This was destined to be a day of trial to the Count. As he was returning to see how Caroline did, a letter was brought him which had just arrived. At any other time the very sight of the hand writing would have inspired pleasure. It was his sister's, the young Countess Matilda, from whom it was long since he had heard; and, impatient as he would have otherwise been, he was then so wholly lost in sorrow that he opened the letter almost mechanically;[a] yet, having read it, was it possible to remain insensible to its contents?[b]

Dresden, October 14, 17—

"I have been assured my dear brother is returned, yet cannot believe the intelligence true: I know his heart, it would soon have brought him to his poor Matilda, or he certainly would, at least, have written to her, and his letter, and the certainty he was no longer in another country, almost another world, would have been some little consolation. Ah! my dear brother, how many sorrows have I known while you have been in that vile Russia!—What would you have said if you no more had found your poor sister?—For, I assure you, I would rather die a thousand times than ever consent to their wishes. The Baron de Zastrow is a fine young gentleman, an amiable person, polished manners, and adores me.—With such like discourse am I persecuted from morning till night.—And, if it all were true, what would that be to me? The Baron de Zastrow is not the Baron of Lindorf; and, therefore, is nothing—nothing to me.

"Alas! my dear, my tender brother, you see your sister knows how to love, knows how to be constant, and that her levity is not in her heart. But ah! that levity is all vanished; that flighty mirth, concerning which you checked me so much, when you were here, and which made you suspect I had no affection, is all gone. I preserved it as long as I could, because sorrow is no cure for love, and is, beside, very troublesome; and, being determined, certain of the love of Lindorf, of your support, and my own fortitude, I thought I had nothing to fear. I now find my error,[c] and my only hope is in my dear brother. The Baron teizes me, my aunt torments me, and Lindorf writes to me no more; nay, even you, my brother, seem to have abandoned me; but into your arms I throw myself; to you I appeal for succour and support. Come and protect a passion to which you gave birth, and which never, while I have life, can end. Is it not to you that I owe my dear Lindorf? Remember how often you have said to me, my dear sister, love Lindorf, love him as you do me. And oh! how willingly did I obey your injunction! For I love him, not only as I love my brother, but, as the man with whom, of all the men on earth, I would wish to live and die.—I will not believe his silence is any proof either of inconstancy or forgetfulness. You were on your return, and he did not know by what means to send me his letters. No, I will not add to all my other griefs that of suspecting Lindorf; for that is an affliction I certainly could not find strength to support.

"Adieu, my dear, dear brother.—Ah! did you see your poor Matilda, you would not know her; she neither laughs nor sings, but cries all day long, nay, seems as if she would not much longer be pretty; her cheeks are not now as

round as an apple and as red as a rose, as you so often have kissed and called
them.—Ah! return, return, my brother, and give me back all I have lost. If you
come, my chearfulness, my felicity, my love, and the roses of my cheeks will all
come with you.—Ah! would you were married! With what joy should I leave
this place to live with you and your lady! And why are you not? Make haste then
and get married, and make two poor girls happy, your wife and your

MATILDA.

"P. S. Once more let me conjure you to come to Dresden, there to defend and
preserve me for your friend, for the man of your choice and of mine, or I will not
answer for what may happen."

"Merciful providence!" said the Count, as he ended, "must every sensation that
ought to add to my felicity become my torment!"—He deferred answering his
sister's letter, and reflecting on her situation, till he could find a more tranquil
moment, if such he might ever find, and once more entered the chamber of Caroline, where all former ideas were effaced at the sight of what he beheld. The
Canoness, out of patience that the Count returned not, had obliged them to
lead her into the sick chamber, where, unable to see, she had seated herself at the
side of Caroline, had taken one of her hands, and was intreating and conjuring
her to give some sign of life and recollection. But Caroline, feeble, inanimate,
and apparently surrounded by the shades of death, answered not, made not the
least motion, while her unhappy friend yielded to all the dreadful sensations of
horror and despair.

On the other side of the bed stood their two maids, weeping, and, a little farther, the High Chamberlain, sunk silent in an arm chair, with his hands spread
over his face, and overwhelmed with grief. For the first time in his life, he felt
that riches and honours were not sufficient to make his child happy. The physician, in equal consternation, sat by his side, a mournful spectator of this scene of
sorrow, and without apparent hope of ever recalling Caroline to life.

The sight, as the Count entered, the different attitudes and behaviour of the
different persons, made him conclude that all was over, and that the most angelic
of women was no more. All fortitude and philosophy now forsook him, his icy
blood froze in his veins, and seemed to give him hopes he soon should follow; he
flung himself on the bed of death, and fixed his lips on the cold lips of Caroline
without perceiving that she still breathed. "Dear and beloved victim," said he,
rising with distraction, "thou soon wilt be revenged."

The Count was going to quit the room in all the phrenzy of remorse and
despair, which might, perhaps, have induced him to make some rash attempt
upon his own life, had he not been intercepted by the High Chamberlain and
the physician. The latter assured him the Countess was not dead, and that he had

not even lost all hope. "She lies at present," said he, "in a kind of trance, the natural consequence of the fearful struggle she just has had, and she will pass from this state into a sound sleep, which will decide her fate; for, if she awakes, I can then pronounce her recovery more than probable; but, considering her present weakness, I must own I think her awaking very uncertain."

"Oh God of benevolence!" exclaimed the Count, looking with fervour up to Heaven, and afterwards clasping the physician's hands, "is it possible! Sir, is it possible!—May she still live? Can my fortune, can my life suffice?"—

"At present, Sir, my art is useless, and every other human aid; to nature we must leave her, and to that constitution which must have been naturally good, or she would have been dead before this. The cares of the lover and the husband may be more efficacious than mine; to those we will commit her. Come, Sir," said the physician, turning to the High Chamberlain, "go to your apartment, and set your son an example of fortitude."

They were about to quit the room when another strange scene of affliction and death drew their attention. Well might they have been surprised at the silence of the Canoness, while all this passed; but, alas! the poor lady, whether her powers were too weak to resist the terrors of the moment, or whether Heaven had ordained that to be the period of her life and infirmities, a sudden stroke of apoplexy had, unperceived by every person in the room, seized her; she was reclined on one of the pillows of Caroline, weeping, as they had imagined, but most unable to weep, though some signs of life still remained. The servants instantly carried her into her own apartment, and every immediate assistance was given, but ineffectually; she expired in a few minutes, without ever recovering her senses.

An event like this might well draw off attention, for a while, from the first object of their grief. The Count, himself, for a moment, in new astonishment and affliction forgot the old; but, suddenly recovering recollection, he envied the Baroness, whom he thought more happy than himself in not being able to survive the friend she loved.

As for the High Chamberlain he stood wholly astound. To the sorrow of losing his ancient mistress was added the fear of following her; he was the oldest of the two, and her sudden death had so much affected him that he imagined he had only a few moments to live. To behold, in the short space of ten minutes, his daughter expiring, her husband ready to attempt his own life, and his friend actually give up the ghost, might well terrify an old man who was tenacious of life in proportion to his attachment to his great wealth and high dignities. He every moment repeated, "I feel I am very ill!"

Walstein, roused by accumulating terror to recollection, saw the illness of the High Chamberlain was not dangerous, yet recommended him to the physician's care, left the corpse of the Canoness to that of her women, and, after having shed tears of sincere affection to the memory of her who had educated Caroline, and whose friendship for her had apparently brought her to the grave, he again entered the apartment of his dying lady. He sent away the attendants, and approached her bed with feelings that seemed the harbingers of horror. Caroline still continued in that state of stupor or profound trance in which he had left her; the excessive tranquility of her sleep was terrible; a motion of the bosom, almost imperceptible, was the only proof she still was alive, and this motion Walstein imagined he every instant saw diminish. As he sat beside her bed, the tears fell from his eyes, unperceived by himself; incessantly did he place the downy feather on her lips to find whether she still respired; and so doubtful was it that he raised his hands to Heaven, and instinctively exclaimed, "Why, O! why, cannot I die, also!" Sometimes he fixed his eyes on her pale, yet ever charming, face, the features of which still preserved their enchanting form, and felt sensations of love, grief, and regret, so forcible that the most beautiful women in the bloom of health seldom have inspired their equals.

"Angel of bliss," said he, pressing his lips to one of her hands, "pure and celestial spirit, and shalt thou die then, and never know how infinitely thou art adored by the cruel husband who has been thy assassin! Shalt thou die without pardoning him, without knowing that thou thyself mightest still have been happy!—And thou, wretched Lindorf! where, where art thou,[a] now, while thy Caroline is expiring? Thou mightest have restored her to life; and, by yielding her to thee, to thee should I have been indebted for more than mine, also!"

Then would he rise, after meditations like these, so overwhelmed with affliction as to be absolutely without any distinct ideas, and, almost on the verge of distraction, would walk around the chamber with phrenzy in his countenance; till, suddenly recollecting himself, with reproach for having an instant quitted her, fearing lest her last sigh should escape and he not present, again, with impetuosity would he approach. And thus was passed this dreadful night, which, notwithstanding all he suffered, appeared to him very short. The rays of morning were the messengers of terror, the fearful moment approached, and the sentence of the physician was continually present to his imagination; incessantly sounding in his ear, *If she awake I can, then, pronounce her recovery more than probable; but, I must own, I think her awaking very uncertain.* This dreadful incertitude was every moment increased,[b] for her sleep, while it was lengthened, seemed every moment more profound, so that, at last, he no longer had the least hope.

While the Count was standing in this state of dread and despair, he heard her respiration suddenly increase, approached, and saw her breast begin to heave; and, presently, a deep sigh, almost a groan, escaped. —Ah! It is her last!—So fears Walstein. The dreadful moment is arrived! He utters an inarticulate cry, throws himself on the bed, and clasps her in his arms, as if to snatch her from the grasp of Death, or himself die with her.

But Oh! blest surprise! Oh happiness unhoped! It is not an inanimate corpse; it is a living creature! that moves and endeavours to aid itself! The head, that hung helpless, attempts to rise; the extended arms approach each other; the bloodless cheeks and lips once more assume the feeble tints of reviving nature; and her eyes, which he thought for ever closed, now gently roll.—Caroline lives! Caroline breathes, looks around, tries to recollect herself, and fixes her attention on the Count, with somewhat of astonishment, but without the least indication of fear; no, it was with a gentle smile, such as the awakened infant gives it's affectionate mother. She stretches out one hand, which he with rapture receives!—Oh! who may paint his feelings!—In a moment did he pass from the pinnacle of distraction to the heaven of bliss! Bliss he scarcely could conceive real! His whole soul is in his eyes, that, voracious, devour every motion of Caroline; he presses his hand to her heart, kneels at her side, and exclaims, again and again, in a delirium of joy, "*If she awake, her recovery is more than probable*—Oh! God of mercies! Oh! Caroline! Art thou, art thou restored to us? Speak, dear Caroline; speak but a single word; convince me, let me hear thy voice, tell me, is it possible thou canst have recollected that husband—I mean that friend, who would but exist to render thee happy."

"Yes, Sir," said she, faintly, "I recollect you perfectly; there is no other person on earth who is capable of so much kindness, so many cares, and of such unshaken generosity!—But where am I? Where are we?—At whose house?—For that I cannot recollect."

"Dear Caroline, think of your health; think only of your health, for our sakes, and be tranquil; you are at the house of a friend, yes, a friend, Caroline; but let me intreat you not to speak; permit me to call the physician."

He was going to ring the bell, but Caroline stopped him by laying her hand on his arm.—"Only one word, Sir, and I have done. I promise to be docile, but I must ask you—Where is my dear mamma, my friend? Where is the Canoness? Is she well?—How unhappy must she have been on my account!—And my father? I have some confused recollection of having seen him, somewhere, not long since."

"He is here; and you will see him again, as soon as it is proper."

"But my dear mamma?"

"She has left us."

"Then she is at Rindaw, I hope?"

Infinitely as Walstein detested a falsehood, yet, this was no moment to hesitate; the life of Caroline was at stake. "Yes," said he, seizing the clue she had given, "she is at Rindaw, undoubtedly; have no fears for her; she is well, she is happy, she is ignorant of your present danger.—But, dear Caroline, let me conjure you to think only of your own recovery, and how much the safety of all your friends depends on that; I am sure this, to you, will be a sufficient motive."

He rang, a servant came; he gave orders to call the physician, drew the curtains close, sat down by the bedside, and, notwithstanding the excess of his joy, was silent. And now, even at this happy moment, did the tender and preventive Walstein begin to revolve how he best might execute the melancholy task of preparing Caroline for the death of her friend, so as to give her the least affliction possible. The thing first and most necessary was to conceal it from her till she had fully recovered her strength. While he was thus reflecting, the physician entered and confirmed all his hopes. The pulse, though very feeble, was excellent; every unfavourable symptom had disappeared, and recovery was certain, provided proper care was taken. This must be incessant; but could this be wanting while Walstein was present?

"Caroline is so good, so generous," said the Count, "that she herself, I am sure, will be wholly obedient to your injunctions. Duty, friendship, love, all are suppliants; certain of being favourably heard by her sympathetic and affectionate heart."

"Yes," said Caroline, softly, "do not fear, I will do every thing I am bid."—A tear that started to her eye proved how much she was affected by the tenderness of Walstein, and she was going to have added more had not the physician imposed silence. The Count and he went out together, and the physician insisted on the absolute necessity of concealing the death of the Canoness from Caroline; for the least emotion, he said, must indubitably have the most fatal effects. The Count shuddered at the supposition, and, immediately, went with him to the High Chamberlain to consult the means of concealing this event. A long sleep, out of which he had just awaked, had somewhat dispelled his late fears of death, and the resurrection of his daughter gave him still higher hopes; especially when he remembered, which he very expeditiously did, she was certainly left the sole heiress of her friend. The Count, fearing some imprudence on his part, and no way averse to rid himself of a man whose cold and selfish character gave him continual disgust, endeavoured to persuade him that etiquette required he should accompany the corpse of the Baroness to Rindaw, and there see the last duties of humanity performed. This gloomy ceremony was not at all to his taste, but Walstein, desirous of determining him to go, told him that the will of the Baroness was, no doubt, in favour of his family, and that his own interest required him to be present at Rindaw, where this will must be left, to take possession of the lands and wealth bequeathed. This was so unanswerable an argument, to the High Chamberlain, that he never attempted to make another objection; he only required to see lady Walstein, for thus he always called Caroline, before his departure. They therefore concluded to tell her that the High Chamberlain was going to Rindaw, to inform the Baroness of her recovery; and, when he was there, it would be easy to prepare Caroline, by degrees, in his letters, for the melancholy news of her friend's death.

Her father, therefore, was introduced into her chamber, where he told her, after his manner, how happy he was to see her so well; and to leave her with a husband to whom, and for whose cares and attentions, she could not be too grateful: on which occasion he informed her of circumstances she knew not before; and when he told her the Count had neither undressed himself nor once quitted her chamber for several successive nights, the tears swam in Caroline's eyes, and, with tenderness and remorseful recollection, she said, "Oh my Lord! how superior, how noble is your mind! Ah! what would you do for a wife whom"—

She durst not add "*whom you should love*," and the Count gave a very different interpretation to her break; he added "*who could love you.*" And thus did two hearts, naturally so concordant, mistake each other, and prepare themselves new vexations, new torments. Every time that Caroline, uneasy for the health of the Count, conjured him to take rest, and protested she did not want assistance, he, persuaded she desired his absence, imagined that, to a good and feeling heart, the kind attentions of love it could not return, were each a dagger wounding Gratitude: and this painful, this distracting thought, would sometimes make him abruptly leave her, which she, on her part, attributed to indifference. Each, passionately in love and convinced they were not beloved, attributed all those actions to generosity, or to friendship, at the utmost, which sprang from a very different sensation. But let us not anticipate; return we to the High Chamberlain.

We have before time seen he was not scrupulous to excess, concerning telling the whole truth, and nothing but the truth, on certain occasions; he, therefore, so well played his part that his daughter, very unsuspectingly, a thousand times thanked him for his kind attention to her dear mamma, and a thousand times intreated he would make haste to Rindaw. And so many affecting expressions did she use, concerning that dear friend, who no longer existed, that Walstein, unable to suppress his feelings, intreated her to speak no more, but to recollect the severe injunctions of the physician.

"Well, well, I will be silent, only tell her, my dear father, that it is for her, for her alone, and to see her, once again, Caroline wishes to recover. Tell her, also, that the most generous of men"—

He stood by her side, and interrupted her by gently laying his hand upon her lips.—She was prompted to have given that dear hand a kiss; nay, the first movement was made, nor do we know by what fear she was restrained, nor what her feelings precisely were. We only know a slight tremor seized her, and that the Count, perceiving it, was far from imagining it's true cause. He hastened the High Chamberlain away, and saw him get into the post-chaise with pleasure. The corpse of the Canoness was to follow by night, and her women, and the servants she had brought, to which were added others by the Count, were to escort it: Caroline's maid and footman staid at Ronebourg to attend on their mistress.

The physician, whose affairs required he should not long be absent from Berlin, was desirous to return; but the Count, however, by his earnest entreaties, and the liberality of his presents, prevailed on him to stay a few more days, and not to quit his patient, while the most distant possibility of danger or relapse remained. Nor was this a distant period, each new day bestowed new strength; already she began to sit up, and to walk across her room, leaning on the arm of the Count. Her recovery, at length, could no longer be doubted, and the doctor departed for the capital, rewarded, beyond his hopes, for his skill and care.

And now behold the Count, alone, at Ronebourg, with his Caroline.—His Caroline?—Was she his? Alas! he durst not regard her but as the sacred pledge, the deposit of friendship. His last short letter to Lindorf was recollected; the lover must soon arrive, and should he send for this unfortunate lover only to make him a witness of the woman he adored being in the possession of another? And must Caroline, the tender-hearted Caroline, whom the struggles of passion had brought to the brink of the grave, must she see him again, again to lose him? No; Walstein never had so cruel a thought. More and more determined not to violate the oath he so solemnly had pronounced, when he beheld her dying, but to break the arbitrary chains that had bound her his, and unite her to Lindorf, he only waited the arrival of the latter to inform them both of his generous intentions, and the happiness he was preparing for them. Fearing, however, lest the excess of this happiness might, at present, be too much for Caroline, he would not abruptly tell her all he meant to do;[a] neither would he lay that grateful, that affectionate, heart under obligations which would be too oppressive; still less would he suffer her to suspect the pangs his own heart felt in thus renouncing, thus yielding, her to another. "She believes, at present," said he, "she owes her life to me, and, I know, would willingly sacririfice that life to my happiness; but, no, dear Caroline, no, never such sacrifice will I exact; I, I alone wish, I alone ought, to suffer,[b] nor shalt thou ever suspect how infinitely I should be miserable; never shalt thou imagine how ardently I adore; friendship only shalt thou see, even when affection is the strongest; and if I, in return, may obtain thine, if I may make thee and Lindorf happy, shall I be so wretched as I suppose?—Oh! Caroline, Caroline; yes, strange paradox! I feel I may be wretched even while I am virtuous!—To yield thee to another and not to die I must no more behold, no more have intercourse with thee!"

And according to such suppositions did Walstein form a plan of conduct from which he promised never to depart, till the arrival of Lindorf. Not daring to trust the health of Caroline with any other, and unable, himself, to abstain from the pleasure of administering those aids that might restore her to health, he still continued them with all his former assiduity; but he took care seldom to be alone with her; or, if so, by chance, he found himself, he took up a book and read, or played on the flute, of which he was a master, to amuse her. And when he read, and when he played, there was such sensibility, such passion in every tone, in every sound, that the melting soul of Caroline was all rapture. Her mind, more susceptible by her late sufferings and present recovery, which gave a new charm to every object, became each day, each hour, more and more attached to that amiable husband, so kind, so complaisant, so deserving of being beloved. Her inclination for Lindorf had but given latent passions action, had but roused sensibility and dormant love, of which, till now, she had only felt the sorrows and the remorse; but, at present, authorized by duty, it had a charm, a fascination; the words happiness, love, and husband, were united, and she could not but hope he loved her, and had granted her pardon. Never did she tire of making her maid repeat the various proofs of affection he had shewn, during her illness; the nights passed in watching over her; the despair so frequently visible when he supposed her recovery impossible; while each circumstance augmented passion till love seemed unbounded, although she durst not give it an epithet more tender than gratitude.

Attentive to the least actions of Walstein, to every motion, and every word, she was not long before she remarked the uneasy constraint he laboured under, and the care he took to avoid all private and particular conversation, relative to themselves. At the very beginning of her recovery he had told her his friend Lindorf was on the road, that he would not be long before he would arrive, and that he, in the mean while, had his house and servants at his disposal. The best of motives was Walstein's, when he gave Caroline this information; but she, too weak, at that time, to enter into explanations, could not hear the name of Lindorf, and, especially, his intended return, without a painful sensation, an inquietude sufficiently evident, which but confirmed the Count in his suspicions and intents. She, on the contrary, supposed he meant to try her; and, therefore, was the more confused. How often did she, afterwards, reproach herself for not having seized the opportunity of the moment to open her heart; for not confessing her former and her present sentiments! Yet had she a right so to do? When Lindorf fled and sacrificed himself for Caroline, might Caroline be permitted to risk the loss of his friend; to rob him of a protector; who, at last, might tire of an attachment which, to him, had been so fatal?

To these reflections others were added, by which she was restrained. How might she be the first to tell the Count she loved him, while she doubted of his love for her, and while this doubt every day increased? His present conduct was the very reverse of what it had been, during her illness; and she knew not how to account for either the one or the other.—If he love me not, thought she, incessantly, whence that mortal dread of losing me? Whence that despair which had nearly deprived him of life? Or, wherefore, those raptures, so affecting and so dear to memory, on the hopes of my recovery? Still I behold his tears of joy, still I hear those expressions so kind, so affectionate, which love alone could dictate.—But wherefore are those expressions heard no more? Or why, now I am able to hear and answer, is he silent? Wherefore does he avoid me thus? Alas! it was compassion which agitated his capacious and benevolent mind, and which I misinterpreted love, and now, pity gradually decreasing, resentment succeeds—Oh! my Lord, and husband, didst thou but know my heart, my love, my repentance, surely thou wouldst not remain unmoved; surely thou wouldst pardon, nay, perhaps, mightest love and we might still be happy."

Then did she bestow her kisses and her tears on the picture which her woman had taken from her neck, when she fainted, on their first arrival; and which had been carefully concealed. This picture she had asked for at the beginning of her recovery, and it was become to her the most precious thing on earth. At length, unable any longer to support incertitude so distressing, she resolved to oblige the Count to come to some kind of explanation, by testifying her own desire to quit Ronebourg. Nor was this desire feigned; with regret she saw herself in a place she had so many reasons to dislike, and which so continually brought to recollection an error she could not pardon herself. What the Count had said, likewise, concerning the return of his friend, alarmed her. She could not comprehend the motive of this return, but, be it what it might, to be found at Ronebourg would be equally painful to him and her. She knew not how far the Count's knowledge of former transactions extended, for he neither spoke of Lindorf, himself, the letter he had received, the letters he had written, his design to travel, nor of the place where he intended to leave Caroline. In fact, he was wholly silent. Unremittingly employed, by his endeavours to amuse and please her, his attentions were the attentions of love, his language the language of indifference. Sometimes, when he read a passage of sensibility, or played an affecting movement on the flute, the tears of sympathy would stand in both their eyes; but, the moment the Count saw those of Caroline, he would tear himself away, that he might conceal emotions he could not always conquer.

Then would Walstein bury himself in the recluse forest covert, or shut himself up in his cabinet, that he might freely utter his complaints, and vent feelings by which he was oppressed.—"Happy Lindorf!" would he say; "thou knowest not all thy bliss; knowest not my loss.[41] [a] Come, Oh! come, and dry the tears of Caroline, which flow at thy remembrance, that I may behold her happy ere I die!"

Sometimes he would reproach himself for suffering her to remain ignorant of her approaching felicity; for not saying to her, Lindorf, the regretted, the beloved Lindorf, shall be your husband. But how might he say this, unless he were more certain he could fulfil his promise? Lindorf came not, wrote not; and how if death, sparing Caroline, had struck his friend! How, if Lindorf was no longer a living being! His blood froze at the thought—"Merciful God!" said he, "thou heardest my prayers for Caroline; Oh! hear them, also, for my friend! Let him return, let him be happy, and I, only, miserable!"

The situation of his sister was an additional grief. Deceived by her chear-fulness, her levity, which was but the levity of infancy, and mistaken in the perseverance of her character, he had supposed her love for Lindorf very fee-ble, and that the Baron de Zastrow would presently efface the fleeting sensation. But her letter shewed him his error, proved her passion real and lasting, and wounded him to the heart for having given it birth, unable as he was, honoura-bly, to give it consummation. Matilda, like himself, was in love, and, like himself, was wretched; he knew he had but to intimate a wish and Lindorf would marry her, would thus ascertain to him the possession of Caroline; Lindorf would refuse him nothing, and Caroline was too much attached to her duty for him to doubt she would any longer testify her former repugnance. But it was not for Walstein to selfishly take advantage of the generosity of others, and abuse the power gratitude gave. Not his own, no, not his sister's happiness would he thus acquire; nor, indeed, was happiness possible, unless it were mutual. The suppo-sition of her being united to a man whose heart another possessed was not to be borne; he, therefore, resolved, without explaining a secret which not only required too circumstantial a relation for a letter to contain, but, by coming so suddenly might have a fatal effect, to prepare her for the loss of Lindorf, and, therefore, thus he wrote.

Ronebourg, October.

"Yes, dear Matilda, I am returned; your brother and your friend again are yours; and, surely, you know, by sympathy you know, his sentiments are ever the same. They are a part of his being, and fraternal love, the most mild, most durable of all love, is not liable to change; but, on the contrary, a thousand circumstances and considerations ought to continue and increase it. The friend which nature first gave us should have the first place in our affections. I did not think, dear Matilda, it was possible I should love you more than I ever have done; yet your last letter has interested me so much that it seems to have produced this effect. No longer do I love a sweet little girl because she is my sister, and because she is amiable, but I now find a friend, a tender friend, whose feelings I participate, to whom I am obliged for the confidence she reposes in me, and who, in return, merits mine; for I, like her, have need of council and consolation.

"Ah! Matilda, your brother's prospects of happiness are as few as your's. Yet, if I am not deceived, I hope, by affording each other mutual aid, by uniting our reason and our fortitude, we, perhaps, may rise superior to the misfortunes that threaten us, and create a species of happiness for ourselves, founded on self-approbation, and the grateful remembrance of having sacrificed our own felicity to the felicity of our friends.—You understand me not. Well, then, I will explain myself, as far as the bounds of a letter will permit. The circumstances, and they are many, shall be related when we meet, which will be ere long.

"My melancholy story, Matilda, is more similar to your's than you imagine. I, like you, love, and with no less violence; and I am of a sex that has not the habit of holding the impetuous emotions of passion in due subjection. My love is unbounded, and yet—Be you the judge whether it becomes me to renounce it. I need but speak a word, a single word, and the woman I love is for ever mine;[a] but must I seek my own happiness at another's expence? Her heart is not mine. The man she loves is worthy of that distinction, and his passion equals her's. On me, and me only, it depends for ever to separate or unite them.[b] Alas! dear Matilda, how feeble are reason and virtue, where the heart is subject to the imperious mandates of passion! Only imagine that the brother of Matilda is undetermined what to do; yet, I hope, he will not disgrace his sister. But Oh! my dear, my tender friend, I stand in need of your support; to be sustained by your fortitude, nay, perhaps, by your example. Tell me, were you in my place, how would you act? And that you may the better decide, the better feel for me, suppose that you yourself were in the same precise situation; suppose it to be Lindorf you love who is beloved, whose destiny is in my power, and that I may bestow on him, or for ever deprive him of, the object of his passion and mine. Ah! Matilda, already I hear you pronounce sentence; I see my dear and tender sister set me an example of fortitude and generosity; she rejects such partial happiness which to herself must bring remorse, and to the man she loves regret, grief, and, perhaps, detestation.—Regret! my dear Matilda? The happy mortal who possesses thee, ought to have far different sensations; nor will I ever present thee to one who knows not how to esteem thy worth, and who cannot love thee, and thee only.

"And why may not the Baron de Zastrow be this happy man? Why may not he love thee! Thou wilt answer, and I acknowledge, it is equally necessary thou shouldest love likewise. I shall shortly come myself, and, perhaps, shall find thou hast been too severe in thy judgement. Thou seemest to own he is handsome, amiable, and adores thee. These are no common advantages, Matilda; and, remembering how highly thou wilt please thy aunt—Yet be not terrified, I first would know whether he deserves thee; and if thou really canst not love him; for, if so, thou art free. Yes, I promise thee, no earthly power shall force thy affections, while I exist.—Take courage, therefore, my dear girl, if Love should have pangs in store for thee, Friendship, I hope, may alleviate them; for my own part, I will not complain while in my sister I find a friend. Lindorf is in England. Do not expect any letter from him; but I hope he will soon return, and then I shall immediately come to Dresden, shall then open my whole heart, and then shall read thine. Shouldest thou persist in refusing the young Baron I have another proposition to make, which, perhaps, may please thee better. It is to come and live with a brother, who loves thee, till thou shalt have made another choice. But, whatever thy design may be, rest assured thou hast a friend whose affection cannot be expressed.—

Adieu, dear and lovely Matilda, thou, I feel, mayest yet heal the wounds of my heart. Adieu, and think me ever the most affectionate of brothers."

EDMUND, Count of Walstein.

With this letter he sent another to his aunt, Madam de Zastrow, in which he told her that certain reasons obliged him no more to think of the union of his sister and his friend; and that, therefore, he should be happy could she be induced to favour the Baron de Zastrow; but he conjured her not to be precipitate, and by no means to use the least violence. He further said he should soon come to Dresden, and intreated his aunt not finally to dispose of his sister till his arrival.

CAROLINE

OF

LICHTFIELD;

A NOVEL.

TRANSLATED FROM THE FRENCH.

BY THOMAS HOLCROFT.

Idole d'un cœur juste, & passion du Sage,
Amitié, que ton nom soutienne cet ouvrage;
Règne dans mes écrits, ainsi que dans mon cœur,
Tu m'appris à connoître, à sentir le bonheur.

VOLTAIRE

VOL. III.

LONDON:
PRINTED FOR G. G. J. AND J. ROBINSON,
PATERNOSTER-ROW.
MDCCLXXXVI

CAROLINE

OF

LICHTFIELD.

THESE two letters being sent, and thus being more tranquil, relative to the fate of Matilda, the Count applied himself wholly to the plan he had formed, in order to ascertain the happiness of Caroline. He had desired the High Chamberlain to come to Ronebourg, so soon as his daughter should be informed of the death of the Baroness. It could not be long before Lindorf must arrive,[a] and the Count was determined to set off for Berlin the moment he came; pretending to have received an order from the king, and to leave Lindorf at Ronebourg, with the High Chamberlain, that he might obtain a divorce from his Majesty, and his consent, also, for the marriage of Lindorf and Caroline. He then intended to write and inform them of their happiness; and, without seeing them, to depart for Dresden. From Dresden, he meant to go to England with Matilda; or without her, if she determined to marry the young Baron de Zastrow; and to reside there with his mother's relations. He felt sufficient fortitude to make Caroline and his friend happy, but not to be a daily witness of their loves; and this plan, once fixed, he held to be unalterable.

Alas! he knew not yet all the power of love; had yet not felt all its vengeful effects. The more he struggled with passion the deeper was it rooted in his heart. How often, when beside Caroline, unable to restrain his feelings, was he ready to kneel at her feet, confess his affection, his internal struggles, his despair; appeal to her generosity, recal to mind the sacred bond by which they were united, the vows they had mutually made, and employ every resource, of pity and of passion, to supplicate her consent to live and die with the husband by whom she was adored. By flight only could he obtain a victory over himself, on these occasions. Once out of her sight, and virtue, delicacy, and friendship, again were ascendant. Love ceded to duty; and he had the fortitude to imagine Caroline in the arms of another, and not expire at the thought![1] Then would he remember Lindorf, banished from his country, dragging an unhappy being through foreign climates, deprived of his mistress and his friend, without consolation and without hope; and, remembering, shudder and detest his weakness: again renew his oaths to subdue it, and, fearing to expose himself to future dangers, deprive himself of the pleasure of seeing Caroline; who, ill interpreting the cause of his absence, would, on her part, weep and afflict herself at conduct which she supposed to be the most unequivocal proof of indifference.

In her moments of vexation and despair, she strengthened herself in the resolution of returning to Rindaw, and of entreating, nay, of absolutely requiring his consent, should he offer any opposition. "Alas!" would she reply to this doubt, "far from opposing, he will gladly seize the means of living separate from Caroline.— Separate!—What! am I no more to see him, to hear him no more? And, when I quit this place, must a lasting separation ensue? And must I ask it; must I myself pronounce the fatal sentence? No! never shall I acquire force adequate to a task like this! When he shall have the cruelty to command, submission will surely be sufficient punishment."

Yet did her friendship for the Baroness, at some moments, make her even desire this separation, and vanquish her fears of quitting Walstein. The High Chamberlain, as had been concerted with the Count, endeavoured to prepare her to support the death of her friend. In his first letters, he spoke of remedies she had taken, to recover her sight, which were powerful and somewhat dangerous. He afterwards wrote word her blindness was past cure, and that it afflicted her so much she had fallen ill. Caroline no sooner heard this than she wished to fly to attend and console her; but she herself was yet too feeble for the fatigues of such a journey. She wrote the most affecting letters, both to her friend and her father; and, every returning courier, hoped to hear of her recovery. At length the letters of the High Chamberlain became so alarming, and affirmed so positively the Baroness of Rindaw was in the utmost danger, that Caroline immediately determined to set off; and sent to beg the Count would come and speak with her.

He found her with her eyes swimming in tears, and well divined their cause.— "O! Sir," said she, the moment he entered, "read here what my father has written! My dear mamma is very, very ill; nay, perhaps, worse than he says. Let me intreat you to give immediate orders for my departure; for I will instantly be gone to Rindaw. Never shall I forgive myself for having delayed so long. Should I be too late, should I never more behold the tenderest, dearest of friends–"

The Count, finding this idea had presented itself to her mind, and that the apprehension had had half its effect, thought this the time to inform her of the truth: beside that her resolution to depart, immediately, made secrecy any longer impossible– "Dear Caroline," said he, seating himself beside her, and taking one of her hands, "let me intreat you, in the name of Heaven, to be calm; think of the injury you may do yourself! Scarcely recovered from a most dangerous illness, can you sustain–"

"Yes, any thing, every thing! It is my duty to devote my returning strength to the service of the friend who has been, to me, the best and tenderest of mothers. I feel how much I have neglected this duty, and shall, indeed, be most happy, may I but have the means to repair my wrongs."

She was going to rise and make preparations, but the Count again detained her. "A moment, dear Caroline, be appeased for a moment, I conjure you, and listen to me—I have also received a letter from your father."

"Merciful God!" cried she, turning pale, and presaging what was coming; "a letter to you! Tell me! I beg you, instantly, tell me its contents. Has my father concealed any thing?—Oh! Sir,—–" Her oppressed heart could no longer resist the violence of agitation, and her sobs interrupted speech. The silence of the Count, his downcast eyes, the timid compassion of his countenance, and the vague answers he returned, confirmed her fears, and her despair became excessive. "Oh God! Oh God!" exclaimed she, "I perceive, I perceive I no longer have a friend, no longer have any thing in this world! My dear mamma no longer exists, and I have lost my all!"

"Not so, dear Caroline; there still is a friend in the world, who hopes to prove how dear you are to him, and how much he is interested in your happiness."

Caroline loved this friend too well herself to be wholly insensible of that consolation he wished to impart; and to those new proofs of tenderness which she no longer had dared to hope. Her tears still flowed, abundantly flowed, but less bitterly. In the assaults of violent grief, the feeling and impassioned mind experiences relief by the company of a beloved object, and in the alleviations of love. She grieved, but the Count grieved with her, felt as she felt, and partook of her affliction. In these their moments of melancholy, their souls were in unison. Caroline had lost the tenderest of friends, but the very moment in which she was informed of this misfortune was that which gave her the sweet hope of being beloved, by the husband she adored; for, in this first transport of despair, which softened fortitude and shewed Caroline still more lovely, the Count was not able wholly to repress his passion. The sorrow of Caroline demanded every care and consolation friendship could afford; and Walstein, while he endeavoured to assume the form of friendship, had all the tenderest actions and looks of love. Caroline, thus, in the midst of affliction, had a glimpse of a happy futurity, and mourned that her friend was not to be a witness of her bliss.

She desired to be informed, circumstantially, of her illness and death; but the Count, who understood nothing so ill as dissimulation, referred her to the High Chamberlain, who would soon return; yet, to quiet her remorse for having too long delayed going to the aid of her friend, he told her she had died some time since, and when it was impossible for Caroline to have gone to her assistance. No sooner was the High Chamberlain informed that his daughter knew the truth than he returned to Ronebourg, and told her, himself, she was left sole heiress to the Canoness. She had made her will anew, after she had been informed of her marriage, and it was to the Countess of Walstein she had bequeathed all her possessions: she had indeed left a legacy to the Count, purposely, as she herself had worded it, to prove how highly she was satisfied at his union with Caroline. She recommended, in most affecting terms, the happiness of this her beloved pupil, to Walstein; and to Caroline that of the best and most sublime of men.

The reading of the will drew many tears from Caroline; nor was the Count less affected. The High Chamberlain, alone, read it with perfect satisfaction, and comprehended not how an augmentation of fortune could become the subject of sorrow. Caroline, alas! found only new motives, in these benefactions, to regret a friend so tender and so generous. Walstein, distracted by a thousand contrary sensations, could not hear of union and happiness, which he so soon was to renounce,[a] without extreme emotion. When the Baron came to that article, he suddenly kneeled to Caroline; "yes," said he, with vehement transport, "yes, by honour, by love, by every thing sacred I swear, you shall be happy, Caroline"— He could not continue; and Caroline, affected to excess, tenderly stretched out her hand to raise him, while she felt, more powerfully than ever, that on him only, of all the world, this her promised happiness depended, and on the sentiments he should entertain for her.

Had they been alone, perhaps she might then have told him what her's really were; perhaps this might have been the happy moment of an explanation too long delayed; but the presence of the placid High Chamberlain checked such effusions of the heart. He, with wonderful tranquillity, continued to read his will; which contained nothing farther, except legacies to servants and vassals. The Count, unable to support the continuance of his present emotion and the tears of the compassionate Caroline, left the room and walked into the park, whither all his feelings went with him. He began no longer to understand his own proceedings; and, sometimes, asked himself wherefore he thus should wilfully be forever miserable. Wherefore should he yield the possession of her on whom he had so many claims, and without whom it was impossible to live? "She begins," thought he, "to be accustomed to me; nay, I even think I behold expressions of affection in her eyes. Alas! I know it can be but friendship, esteem, gratitude; yet may not these sensations, in a mind like hers, well supply the place of love? Or may I ever hope to inspire others? Does she not already grant more than I could ever expect? But, while I know, past doubt, her heart wholly appertains to another, to Lindorf!—Lindorf? Alas! perhaps he no longer is in existence; perhaps he has fallen a victim to a passion the effects of which I have every cause to fear; perhaps he has sunk under his grief, under the grief of Caroline, by which my own heart has been so often wounded, and which must be renewed, with such excess, should she hear tidings so fatal!

The Count shuddered while he imagined he himself might be the messenger to inform Caroline of the death of the man she loved; that he himself must then be considered as the cause of his death. The silence of Lindorf, after the short letter he could not but have received, appeared to him a certain proof his fears were but too well founded; and so much did this and such like fears torment him that scarcely could reason sustain the conflicts of the heart.[a] At one moment he would passionately wish the return of Lindorf, and dread it worse than death the next; equally fearing to see him arrive, or to hear he was no longer in existence. Thus did a man so philosophic, so sage, so wholly till then master of himself, at length, feel the empire of passion and its tyrannic power; and, while thus he felt, terrified at its effects, again swore to vanquish it, to devote himself, if it were not too late, to the felicity of those he loved.

From one of these tormenting terrors he was, at last, relieved. He received a letter from Varner, the valet de chambre of Lindorf, to whom he had given his short and pressing letter, written to conjure his friend to return.[b] "The good Varner entreated his Excellency not to be uneasy at not having yet received an answer to this letter, for that, when he came to Hamburg, his master was not there; he had embarked, a few days before, for England, with a Saxon gentleman; and he, Varner, detained three weeks at Hamburg by contrary winds, had neither been able to join his master, who expected him at London, nor, consequently, to remit him the letter his Excellency had confided to his care."

The first pleasure of the Count was to learn that Lindorf still lived, and, by being able to travel, was in good health. Nor was this pleasure single; Lindorf had not received his letter, his return was therefore deferred, and this short delay, which likewise deferred the moment when Walstein should be obliged to quit Caroline, cede her to another, and live for ever from her, was to him an age of happiness. He hastened therefore to her chamber, that he might not lose moments so precious. Her father was with her. "My dear Count," said the High Chamberlain, as Walstein entered, "my daughter, here, is exceedingly desirous of quitting Ronebourg, but dares not speak to you on the subject. For my part, I can see no reason in the world why you should remain longer here; for, at present, the Countess is sufficiently recovered to undertake the journey. The King may complain of your long absence; he commanded me to hasten your return to Berlin, and in a tone that will not admit of longer delay; and I must certainly be gone; for my presence is absolutely necessary at court. If, therefore, your Excellency shall think proper to give orders, we will incontinently[2] depart together."

The Count made no reply, but fixed his eyes on Caroline; in order to enquire of her countenance what was passing in her heart, and whether she really wished to leave Ronebourg.[c] Caroline blushed, looked down, and, by her silence, seemed to approve. Yet was the embarrassment of the Count beyond description great. He could not be ignorant how much the King desired his return; for, since his arrival from Russia, he had only remained four and twenty hours at Berlin; and had had but one short interview with his Majesty. To the friendship of the Sovereign, only, was he indebted for his present long absence; and frequent couriers brought him pressing letters from the King; or rather from a man who reclaimed his friend. Walstein knew, likewise, that his marriage with Caroline was then become public. The High Chamberlain, who so long had laboured with this secret, had told it the whole world, as soon as his daughter was gone to Ronebourg. The King himself, knowing the Count and Countess were together, had openly spoken of their union; wherefore longer mystery was impossible. Yet how might the Count, with his present intentions, take Caroline to Berlin as the Countess of Walstein, and there present her at court, and to every body, by a name she so soon was to quit?

He then felt how much the delay of his letter to Lindorf deranged all his projects. He no longer could refuse the request of the King, which might every moment be changed to a command: he could not think of leaving Caroline, alone, at Ronebourg; and still less of taking her to Rindaw, where every thing must tend to nourish and increase affliction. While reflecting, in this dilemma, how he must act, Caroline, pressed by her father to confirm her desire to depart immediately, said, "she should, with pleasure, accompany my lord the Count to Berlin; but that she hoped, both he and the king would have the goodness, for some time, to dispense with her seeing company; and that, while she remained in mourning, she might be permitted to live retired."

Walstein eagerly caught the idea; and the health of Caroline, not yet sufficiently re-established, together with her deep mourning for a friend whom she had loved as a mother, were, in reality, excellent pretexts for complying with her request, and neither receiving nor paying visits, at Berlin, for some months. In less time than that Walstein well might hope his future fate would be decided. Caroline, mean while, would live almost unknown, at Walstein-house, where she would see only her father, and himself; which, to him, was a most pleasing reflection. It was some alleviation to despair not to be obliged to quit her before the dreaded hour of final separation should arrive. The sage in love is but a man. The Count no longer saw impediments. Caroline living in his house, and in his sight, was perfection of bliss; and, though he still destined her for a man he supposed she loved, though still determined carefully to conceal his own passion, he could not refuse himself this intermediate enjoyment of happiness; which, beside, would remove every difficulty, relative to where Caroline should remain.[a]

The day of departure was, therefore, fixed; and the tender Caroline beheld it arrive with rapture. She should no longer live in the mansion of Lindorf: it was now determined she should for ever pass her life with the husband she adored, and she thought herself certain of soon effacing from his memory, by offices of tender affection, the capricious and erroneous conduct which her heart, at present, disclaimed; and which she herself could never pardon. Walstein, attentive to every action and look of Caroline, perceived she went with pleasure; but this pleasure he ascribed to virtue, and to the desire she had, henceforth, of avoiding every thing that might bring Lindorf to memory.[a] His esteem, consequently, his affection, were redoubled; but, thinking thus, he was but the more strongly confirmed in his determination of rewarding the virtue he so much admired.

Behold them, then, at Berlin, and alighting at Walstein-house; a place of so much former terror to Caroline. She entered it with all those gentle sensations, those mild hopes, so sweet to the soul, and which seemed a prelude of the felicity she was about to enjoy. To these succeeded the recollection of her bridal day, her behaviour to the man she now adored, the mixture of hope and fear concerning the real sentiments of the Count, and the melancholy reflection on the death of her dear friend, whom she wished a witness of her present happiness. These, all conspiring, contributed but to augment that emotion which she no longer could conceal,[b] and which brought the tears into her eyes. The Count saw those tears; his heart melted at the sight; he attributed them to a very different cause, and would instantly have given her every assurance that cause should be removed; but we have before seen the motives by which he was withheld.[c] He would not give her a prospect of bliss as yet uncertain; nor would he have to combat with her delicacy and generosity. Neither, indeed, had he the power to pronounce *I yield Caroline to another.* No, he might have acted; but, on such a subject, he could not have spoken!

The High Chamberlain supped with them, and retired inflate with joy at beholding his daughter now established Lady of Walstein-house. When he was gone, the Count led Caroline to the apartment which long had been destined to receive her; at the time of his marriage, and while he was far from presaging the events that were to succeed. He had furnished it with all possible taste and magnificence, in the dear expectation that his young and beauteous bride was soon to become its inhabitant. This expectation, at last, was realized. But how? In what manner? And at what moment? How much might he well regret past suspence, and the hope which, during uncertainty, he had cherished!

"This, dear Caroline," said he, as they entered, "is the apartment which has long been reserved for you." Caroline, who supposed a latent reproach was lurking in these few words, looked down, and alternately blushed and turned pale. Walstein saw this, but saw not the true motive. Eager to deprive her of her fears, "you," said he, respectfully kissing her hand, "are absolute here; queen of this apartment, neither I nor any one else shall enter it, without your free permission."

Hastily the Count retired; had he remained a moment longer, he, perhaps, had forgotten Lindorf and all his oaths—"Ye powers of friendship!" cried he, as he entered his own chamber, "sustain my fortitude. Caroline, dear adored

Caroline, Lindorf, my friend, appear, be ever present to my imagination, there incessantly repeat you cannot be happy asunder!"

Thus did the whole night pass in mourning over and lamenting his destiny, and the rigid sacrifice which virtue, principle, friendship, and even love itself, loudly demanded. Caroline, though more tranquil, yet slept but little and reflected much. Though her chaste simplicity felt not all the singularity of Walstein's conduct, yet could she not be wholly ignorant that her spouse had a right to partake of her apartment; and she thought her own wrongs too many, and too great, not to attribute his leaving her thus to well-founded resentment. Succeeding evenings but confirmed the idea; Walstein, fearing again to encounter dangers he found himself so near sinking under before, not only forbore to accompany Caroline to her apartment but began, as he had done at Ronebourg, before she knew the death of the Baroness, to absent himself as much as possible, and never be with her, except in the presence of her father, or her women; and even then he had an air of constraint, of anxiety, so visible, he feared so much to meet her eyes, or to approach her touch, that she no longer doubted of his indifference; nay she even dreaded it was aversion. This conduct, far from irritating, sensibly affected Caroline. Herself, alone, and her former caprice did she accuse. Perhaps he sought to punish them, and he had good right; or, rather, her unjust slight, and the dislike she so long had testified, had at length, wholly incurred his hatred. Yet his tender and continued cares, his mild and gentle attentions during her illness, and her grief, what were they?—Generosity, natural benevolence, sympathy, compassion; which ever are inherent in the noble mind. But she too plainly saw, at present, the chains by which he was restrained were become detestable; yes, he groaned over that fatality by which they had been united. She recollected his travelling design, and doubted not but he still intended it should take place; she even, for a moment, thought to prevent his being again at the pain of proposing her return to Rindaw; and thus, by voluntarily absenting herself from the Count and the court, restore him the liberty of which she thought him so ardently desirous. But this proposal was become much more difficult to execute than when she wrote her letter at Rindaw. At present she loved him, passionately loved him; and never could she collect the fortitude to abandon the object of this her most tender affection. Therefore, her design was no sooner formed than forsaken; and to that succeeded the resolution to try all possible means of regaining the heart of her husband, and, by love, obliterating the remembrance of former wrongs. While she meditated she hoped. "He is so benevolent, has so much sensibility, is so little inclined to revenge injuries," said she, "that, when he shall behold how infinitely I love him, will he refuse to return my love; or will he not, at least, grant me his friendship?"

Thus did the noble and sympathetic heart of Caroline cling to her Walstein; thus teach her how to estimate his worth;[3] and thus did hope, with mild and benignant impulse, bid her seek his society with greater assiduity than even he sought to avoid hers. Observant of this new ardor, the Count, far from imagining himself beloved, attributed all the attentions, all the thousand kindnesses of Caroline to systematic gratitude, and duty; which a soul so feeling, and so virtuous, as hers, had imposed upon itself. Momentary appearances confirmed the suspicion. Caroline, young and timid, feeling sensations she thought she had not the power to communicate, reproaching herself for, and even exaggerating former errors, fearing by officiousness to displease a husband prejudiced against her, often had an air of reserve and constraint, which persuaded Walstein her heart was acting contrary to its most ardent desires. Sorrowful at the ill success of her endeavours to inspire affection, often would she suffer melancholy to invade her mind; often would retire to her chamber, and on her lovely cheeks leave traces of tears which the Count imagined to be the bitter tears of duty; shed in lamenting the severity of fate, that separated her from the man she loved.

Him, day after day did Walstein wait for. Him, the lover and the friend, for whom felicity so supreme was held in reserve; nor could he comprehend wherefore he did not return. Beside the letter he had sent by Varner, he had also written after his arrival at Berlin; and his letter, under cover to, and recommended to the care of Lindorf's banker, at Hamburg, by him to be forwarded to England, must have reached him if he were not already on the road, coming back. This letter was more pressing than the former. Without fully expressing all he meant, he used every argument to hasten his return. "On this his own happiness, and the happiness of those he most loved depended; if prayers and entreaties were not sufficient, he absolutely exacted a compliance.—Recollect, dear Lindorf, how often you have given me the right of disposing of your future destiny. This right, which I hold from friendship, and, perhaps, from gratitude somewhat too enthusiastic, I now claim. Yes, I now recal to memory every circumstance which may make you hold yourself my debtor to tell you the hour is come when it depends on you to cancel them all, and, by one single act, place all obligation to my account. I can only add, if in a month, at farthest, I have not the pleasure to embrace you, at Walstein-house, you will give me reason to doubt of an attachment which I think I deserve, and to suppose I no longer have a friend!"

This letter, so strong, so pressing, remaining unanswered, gave room to imagine, and even to believe that, in fact, Lindorf had set out for Berlin before it arrived at England; and that consequently he must soon be there. Dreadful as this moment was, in which a separation from her he adored was to take place, still Walstein waited for it with a kind of impatience, arising from a conviction it would ascertain the happiness of Caroline, and from a wish of being himself freed from that incertitude which suffers the soul to wander among illusive chimeras, which an instant might destroy, and to which misery itself is sometimes preferable.

How, indeed, was he to defend himself against the phantoms of hope, seductive and dear as they are to the heart, and whose spells each day became more potent, more irresistible? Nothing, indeed, but the modesty and present error of Walstein could have prevented him from perceiving they were not phantoms, were not illusive. Far from desisting, Caroline was still more affectionate, more attentive, mild and tender. The happiness of her existence was the prize for which she contended. And how might she perform too much for a husband like Walstein, whom she so long had offended, by aversion most unjust; to whom her heart had been unfaithful, and which had so many errors, nay, to Caroline, crimes to obliterate? Repulsing diffidence, therefore, and hoping every thing from perseverance and affection, a thousand kind arts were employed to draw and attach him to her, of which love alone is susceptible, and to which love alone can give such wondrous force.

The Count was exceedingly fond of music, and Caroline was incessant in her endeavours to arrive at excellence. Often did she entreat him to accompany her on the flute or violoncello, which he played equally well; often did she sing, with all the charms of sensibility, the most expressive and melting airs, and such as most were likely to make impression on a soul like Walstein's. The Count had a taste and talents for drawing, but other occupations had prevented him from making any great progress in the art. Caroline, on the contrary, educated in retirement, had applied herself with infinite success to that delightful art, which can people solitude, and, in despite of wintry frost, retrace nature's beauties, create meads, rivers, mountains, and forests, and make permanent the fleeting and perishing beauties of Flora.[4] Caroline was particularly successful in flowers and landscapes; which also was the species of painting the Count most preferred. She offered to instruct him, direct his essays, and correct his errors; in return for which, she entreated him to select books, and superintend studies which she was desirous to engage in, but which are too generally neglected in the education of women. While he was drawing by her side, sometimes would she read, and her former custom of reading aloud to her dear mamma, added to the native intelligence and feeling she possessed, rendered her indeed a most excellent reader. Walstein, when he saw her fatigued, would read in his turn; and while her countenance, obedient to the powers of genius, assumed the passion or imbibed the wisdom of the writer, her skilful and delicate fingers would knit, or knot, or embroider, the garter, the purse, or the waistcoat; all of which were destined pledges of affection for her Walstein. Ever desirous of finding new sources to give him pleasure, every action had that for its object. For him only did she exist, and continually would she invent pretexts either to go into his apartment, or invite him into hers. Though she saw no person but him and the High Chamberlain, who supped with them almost every evening, never was she dull for want of company. Far from that, she continually refused the solicitations of the Baron to present her at court, seemed most desirous of prolonging her retreat, and, with mild and timid eyes turned to Walstein, said "never before had she been so happy!" Yet, notwithstanding all the thousand hourly repeated proofs of love which Caroline no longer sought to hide, still did the Count, fascinated by fear, and dreading to yield to the sensations by which he was continually assaulted,[a] repel truth, and retain foregone and chimerical conclusions.

"Not for me," would he say, "is it to be beloved. No, the affectionate, the tender, the adorable Caroline has the art of giving to friendship—alas! what did I say? Not even to friendship, but, to simple gratitude, all the appearance and expression of love. It is not the presence of Walstein, but the remembrance of Lindorf, by which she thus is animated; and to him, doubtless, doth she secretly address all those affecting attentions, those tender speeches, and those sweet looks, which may not have me for their true object—What! know I not that she loves Lindorf! Nay, that him she ought to love!—Yet, should it be true!—Should it be me!—Should my present intents, which distract and rend my heart, make me the most ungrateful of men! Should that bliss of angels, which I am reserving for another, be destined by Caroline for me!—Alas, it cannot be.—Oh! Caroline! Caroline!—Yet, how may I know what passes in her heart, without acquainting her with the secrets of my own; without discovering the passion by which I am consumed? And yet how may I make this known, certain, as I am, that duty, generosity, and compassion would dictate her answer? Though she love me not, her present actions and manner prove she would not an instant hesitate to sacrifice her heart and her happiness to me."

Thus tormented, thus agitated, by hope and fear, did the Count make both himself and the tender Caroline miserable. But sensations so violent cannot long endure: Lindorf comes not, nor will the Count find, either in delicacy or friendship, the power to resist love that thus is industrious to convince him it is mutual.

One evening, when the High Chamberlain was detained at court, the Count supped alone with Caroline, who was more tender, more endearing, more enchanting than usual. If she *said* not I love, it was almost impossible to misunderstand her *actions*. The emotion, the agitation of Walstein augmented every moment, and he must either betray his feelings or fly the danger. He just had strength sufficient to perform this painful task, but it was the last effort of reason. Shut up in his own apartment, he reflected on his present state, his love, his claims, and the conduct of Caroline.

"No," said he, "it is not, it cannot be, illusive. I am beloved. I no longer have cause to doubt. If I touch her hand I feel it tremulous; or if she takes mine she gently holds and presses it, unwilling it should be withdrawn; if I quit her with mournful looks her eyes follow me; and, this very evening, I beheld them moistened with her tears. All the animation, all the tenderness of affection, were painted in her countenance; and yet I left her; yet I forbore to kneel at her feet; yet I forbear to tell her how infinitely I adore her; neglect to supplicate a confirmation of my happiness, and of that love which every incident tends but to confirm."

Never had the idea presented itself to him with so much force and certainty: it enrapt him so far that, no longer listening to ought but sweet hope, he determined to return, confess his passion, and obtain from Caroline an avowal of hers, of which he no longer doubted. All his oaths, resolutions, and projects disappeared; all were annihilate; he forgot that Lindorf had existence: Caroline, only, he beheld! His Caroline! To him united, by him beloved, and him loving; nor was there longer mortal man who should bear away this treasure of his soul!—In an instant, Walstein, again, is in her apartment. He sees her not, but he hears her guittar, hears the melody of sounds that vibrate to his heart; he approaches, softly, a door, half open, that leads to a small chamber, whither Caroline has retired. It was her favorite apartment; there she passed an hour, every evening, before she went to bed, reading, singing, or playing. Caroline was half undressed, reclining in an arm chair, and gently touching her guittar as she sang. The air was melancholy, and she seemed deeply affected; stopped occasionally, and put her handkerchief up to her eyes; then again continued, with less power, but more passion, in her voice. Walstein thought he had known all her favorite songs, yet this was new to him. He listened with mute attention, earnest to hear the words.[a] Caroline sang so low that he could only catch now and then a line, one of which, however, struck him, and he listened still more eagerly. At last he distinctly heard the following part of a stanza:

> Ah! wherefore, Love, or whither fly,
> In search of bliss I'd fain impart?
> If thou forsak'st me, how may I
> Hope cherish in this bleeding heart?

The expression, the marked tenderness, with which she sang, were sufficient proofs Caroline's complaint had reference to a real, not an imaginary lover. But who was this lover? Was it Lindorf? Was it Walstein? Diffidence and doubt again possessed his heart; he looks, he listens, and presently the shadowy pleasure of doubt itself vanishes.[b] Caroline laid her guittar in her lap, and untied a black ribband which she always wore around her neck. Till then the Count had supposed it was only an ornament, but he saw with surprise a miniature picture was pendent to it, and which Caroline had always carried concealed in her bosom.[c] Too far off to distinguish the features, he yet could see,[d] as she put it to the candle, that it was the uniform of an officer in the Prussian guards; it was, therefore, the uniform and the portrait of Lindorf! Caroline, at first, fixed her eyes upon it, then pressed it to her heart, and next to her lips, with extreme passion. The tears ran down her cheeks,[e] and fell upon the picture; she carefully wiped them off, again looked and sighed, laid it on the table, took up her guittar and sang another stanza of the same song, which the Count distinctly heard.

> The sole, the sovereign, balm I find,
> Dear emblem of my Love is thee;
> Thou bear'st his features, but his mind,
> Ah! who shall paint it's energy?
> Then wherefore, Love, or whither fly,
> In search of bliss I'd fain impart?
> If thou forsak'st me, how may I
> Hope cherish in this bleeding heart?

When she had ended, she once more took up her picture, gave it another kiss, tied it round her neck again, and, as she put it down her bosom, said, with a mixture of tenderness and chagrin, "thou, however, shalt never forsake me;" then, taking up her candle, passed into her bedchamber, after having rung for her attendants, without so much as looking towards the half open door. The action of rising, the removal of Caroline, and the darkness, in which Walstein was left, awakened him from a kind of stupor into which he had sunk; from a dream of terror, which, as he awoke, instead of vanishing was confirmed! All his imagined happiness was fled, and again he was ingulphed in wretchedness at the very instant imagination had conducted him to the ultimate of bliss! Yet, ever generous, even in the horrors of despair, his first intention was, when he had somewhat recovered himself, to go immediately to Caroline, not to intercede for himself, but to assure her Lindorf, her fugitive, her beloved, should return, should be hers. The arrival of the maids, however, prevented him from executing this his design, and he presently afterwards felt he no longer had the fortitude, personally, to tell her he would for ever yield her to another. His heart palpitated with such violence that such a declaration seemed as if it must have cost him his life, and he even shuddered lest, had he seen her at that moment, instead of acting as friendship and justice required, he, in his delirium, should suffer passion to invade the rights of love.

No, he would see her no more! He might not, could not, durst not, see her more! He still found sufficient virtue to fly, to restore her to liberty, but never to bid her an eternal adieu; or again to gaze on those impassioned eyes, the danger of which he had so recently proved. He returned therefore to his chamber, where he passed some hours in a state of undescribable anguish; incapable of determination, of all certitude whether love or generosity, Lindorf or Walstein, should prevail. He wrote letter after letter to Caroline: in one he claimed his rights, and endeavoured to move her compassion; detesting his tyranny, and tearing this, he began another, in which he bad her for ever farewell, without the least mention of his own excruciating pangs. "What," said he, again, with increasing agitation, tearing the paper, "shall she even remain ignorant of the adoration in which I hold her? Shall I die without so much as exciting her compassion?" He began once more; once more painted his love in all its enthusiasm, and the sacrifice he was about to make in all its horrors. Still less satisfied than ever, he tried anew to write with more moderation; and again and again he tried, and was each time alike unsuccessful.

At length, however, the fatigued and exhausted spirit sank into a gloomy calm, and Walstein came to a firm and irrevocable determination.—This was to go betimes in the morning to the King, who never was in bed long after day-break, and to whom he was never denied admittance, to obtain, immediately, without further let or delay, a divorce; to send it instantly to Caroline, and as instantly to leave Potsdam, retire to his estate, at Walstein, and there make proper prepara-tions for travels which he knew not when he should end. The more he reflected on present circumstances, and the contrary passions by which he supposed himself and Caroline tormented, the more did he persist in this project, and deeply regret-ted not having put it in execution immediately after his arrival at Berlin; instead of suffering himself to be thus seduced by the fascinating pleasure of living with Caroline. "Long since," said he, "would she then have been easy, and I myself per-haps less wretched; I then should not have known the enchantment of her smiles, the irresistible allurement of her friendship, and the bewitching influence of her attentions: or, at least, I should have known them but in part; attentions which I interpreted into love, and which might have supplied its absence, had I remained ignorant that she loves another, over whose memory she in secret mourns.— Mourn! Does Caroline mourn? Caroline! For whom I would sacrifice a thousand lives! And shall I hesitate then to yield up my happiness?"

The thought was most natural and appealing to the noble heart of Walstein. He wrote, or rather began to write a letter to send Caroline when he should have obtained a divorce. He afterwards wrote also to the High Chamberlain, to give this transaction such a colouring as that he might not impute it to his daughter, or Lin-dorf. These letters he put in his pocket, and, aided by his valet de chambre, made every necessary preparation for his travels. As he supposed he was no more to visit Berlin, he passed the rest of the night in putting his papers in order, and collecting certain of them, which he meant to take with him. As soon as day appeared, he set off for Potsdam, where the King then was, and entreated a secret audience.

How, in the mean time, was poor Caroline employed?—She awoke from a sweet sleep, which had calmed her inquietude, and already began to be impa-tient again to see that dear and cruel husband who thus fled her embraces, and whom she yet had hoped to win by affection and perseverance. Nay, indeed, she had lately flattered herself with success, and that there was very little of the extraordinary in his conduct. He seemed pleased to be with her, seldom left her during the day, and had all those little preventive cares which are so peculiar to love; she often caught him looking passionately at her, and, once, surprised him ardently kissing a ringlet of her hair. What more was necessary to Caroline? Educated in the utmost innocence, without friendship or other conversation than that of the chaste Canoness, never having read other books than what she recommended, she was most happy when in the sight and hearing of her husband.—To suppose herself beloved, to pass her life in his company, was bliss supreme; and when he quitted her, at night, her only chagrin was that of being separated from him till the morrow. These, likewise, were the only moments in which she longer doubted of his love; "for," said she, "he might stay, if he pleased; we still could converse a little longer; or read, or sing, and then, when I awoke in the morning, I should have the dear pleasure of seeing him immediately. For why might he not as well sleep in my chamber as in his own? Oh! that I durst but tell him so!—But he does not love so much to be with me as I do to be with him; he pines not as I do when we are asunder."

Then would Caroline weep without knowing why; then would she gaze on her little picture, kiss it, repeat those tender things she durst not say to the original, commit it again to her bosom, go to sleep with it, and, on the morrow, when she met the Count, no more remember any thing but the pleasure of being in his presence.

This was nearly her diurnal history; though, on the evening we have been describing, she was more than usually moved by the emotion of the Count; and, particularly, by his sudden retreat, which came so unexpected, and which, by the manner of it, had produced this effect. She, then, began to reflect there was something extremely singular in the conduct of her husband; such frequent inequality of behaviour, so many contradictions, and circumstances she knew not how to explain, raised her attention. Was she beloved, or was she not? To answer this question she endeavoured to recollect every incident that had any relation to Walstein, from the moment after their arrival at Ronebourg. While thus ruminating, a song she had composed, at the time the Count endeavoured to avoid her, and when she imagined herself hated by him, was recollected, and the recollection affected her; she sung it, and her tenderness was redoubled. Then it was that the Count had overheard her, unfortunately, as she was ending the song, which was as follows.

When now no longer starting fears,
With boding ills, disturb my peace;
Now love and duty dry my tears,
And bid my former terrors cease;
All! where, my Love, or whither fly,
In search of bliss I'd fain impart?
If thou forsak'st me, how may I
Hope cherish in this bleeding heart?

Thy daily sorrow, nightly care,
Each word, each look, to love I gave;
Love drove away the fiend despair,
And flew to snatch me from the grave.
Then wherefore, now, or whither fly,
In search of bliss I'd fain impart?
If love forsakes me, how may I
Hope cherish in this bleeding heart?

But if, deceiv'd, not love had ought
In what so well with love agrees,
To life, ah! wherefore am I brought,
To perish by a worse disease?
Ah! wherefore, Love, or whither fly,
In search of bliss I'd fain impart?
If thou forsak'st me, how may I
Hope cherish in this bleeding heart?

The sole, the sovereign balm I find,
Dear emblem of my love, is thee;
Thou bear'st his features, but his mind,
Ah! who shall paint its energy?
Then wherefore, Love, or whither fly,
In search of bliss I'd fain impart?
If thou forsak'st me, how may I
Hope cherish in this bleeding heart?[5]

Had the Count heard the first stanzas he must have known they related to him; but the latter, and, especially, the address to the picture, wholly led him into error. His portrait it could not be; and the energy was the energy of Lindorf, who, flying, thus sacrificed his happiness to his friend.

As to Caroline, having sung, wept, and kissed her picture, she went to bed much relieved and more tranquil. "He loves me," thought she; "I am sure he loves me; but he believes he is not beloved. He remembers the repugnance which I so unjustly, so unkindly, shewed on the day of our marriage. And can he suppose I still am unjust and unkind? But I will undeceive him, will forget my fears, will commit all the secrets of my heart to the bosom of my husband, and prove how totally this froward[6] heart is changed. To-morrow, yes, to-morrow I am determined I will tell him all; tell him every day, and every moment that I adore him, and we then shall see whether he will fly from me thus each evening after supper."

This resolution made her perfectly calm; she slept in peace, had delightful dreams, awaked with the purest sensations of pleasure, and was more than ever determined to execute the project she had conceived on the over night. No more she felt the same fears, the same diffidence of herself. Walstein loves her; she is convinced he loves her. Doubts and recollections of the past are the occasion of his continued reserve. Unable any longer to support these, she, with a word, will expel them all. Yes, she will, will prove to him, by a thousand incidents, that he is the sole object of her affection; that he lives and reigns singly and wholly in her heart. Poor Caroline! That heart, of thine, so innocent, so tender, may not contain its transports, while, in this delirium of bliss, thou rememberest it shall no longer have a thought concealed from thy beloved Walstein; from that noble husband to whom thou art indebted for thy life, and to whose happiness this life thou meanest to consecrate. But, ah! that heart not yet knows half it has to suffer!

Timidity is natural to youth, and especially to youth educated as Caroline had been. The superior virtues and wisdom of Walstein commanded a respect which not even the most mild benevolence could wholly obliterate. It was therefore that Caroline had been silent so long;[a] and even now, determined as she is, she knows not what means are best, how to behave, or what to say; and the more the moment approaches, the more her embarrassment is increased. Oh! how does she regret her dear mamma, who, had she lived, would, long since, have been her faithful interpreter; the voluntary pledge of her truth and tenderness! But how might she herself explain them? Should she write?—She began, but her emotion was too great, her hand trembled, she could find no expressions that could convey her feelings; no words were adequate to her ideas; she could not frame a single phrase—"No," said she, "it will be better to go, to run to him, to throw myself into his arms, to say—Perhaps, I may not say a word, but surely he will understand my silence; surely he will not be able to look at me without imagining what I wish to say; he will pardon me, will dispel my fears;[b] reserve, diffidence, and doubt, shall vanish all; he shall be wholly mine, and I wholly his; the happiest of wives and of women!"

The thought inflames her ardour, she kisses her little portrait to increase her courage, and flies to the apartment of the most beloved of husbands! She enters— But no husband is there! He seems not even there to have slept!—A large trunk, in the midst of the chamber, in which are various other packets, seems to announce a removal, or a journey.—Caroline shakes from head to foot! Scarcely has she strength to ring the bell! A footman appears; tremblingly she asks— "Where is my Lord the Count?"

The footman, surprised at the question, answers, "I thought my Lady had known"—

"Known, what?"

'That my Lord set off betimes this morning.'

"Set off!—God!—"

"William, his valet de chambre, has been up all night, making ready. He has left orders that this trunk and these packets should follow. He does not know where my Lord is going, but he believes, to England.'

"England!—Leave me!"

The footman goes, and Caroline sinks in the first chair she can stagger to; where, for the second time in her life, she feels all the affliction, all the torture of despairing love. A second time sees the man she loves neglect, abandon, fly from her!— But what a difference between the present and the former flight! When, at Rindaw, Lindorf left her, it was necessity, it was virtue, it was her own wish; the separation was a cruel one, but the reflection that she had done her duty was, indeed, the most effective consolation! Beside, she knew she was beloved, and that he who fled partook of all her affliction. Far different are her present pangs, which every circumstance but augments. Not a clandestine lover but a beloved husband flies, in whom every hope of future felicity centers. A husband that hates her; or could he abandon her in a manner like this?—At what a moment too!

"Oh God! Then when I flew to him with open arms, when I imagined how unspeakable his joy would be; then to depart, without mentioning the least word of his intent, without seeing me once again! This must be hatred, or a most cruel, most unconquerable indifference! Yet, yesterday evening, how did he look at me! With what tenderness did he take my hand, and press it to his heart!— It is true, he repulsed it again with terror, and instantly left me!—For ever left me!—No, no; it cannot, it shall not be. He is no dissembler. Walstein is not the most barbarous of all human beings.—It is error—The servant is mistaken; he will return; yes, he will, he must; and here will I wait his return."

Scarcely had the poor distressed Caroline indulged this momentary glimpse of hope, which somewhat recovered her sunk spirits, before the footman re-entered, and brought her a packet of papers, sealed up. —"It comes from my Lord, the Count; the courier is this moment arrived from Potsdam"

Caroline had just sufficient strength to receive it, and, by a sign, bid him retire. And now behold her alone, holding the packet she dares not open, Life or death lies there sealed up. It was large, and addressed *to the Countess Caroline, Baroness of Lichtfield, in her Hotel*[z] —It was strange, this; most strange!—"What! will he not call me by his name?[a] God of Heaven! Is it possible?" Her trembling fingers break the seals; and, as the cover is torn, she finds, first, a parchment deed, next, three letters, and, last, an unsealed open paper, on which her eyes are rivetted.

Souls of sympathy, that now with Caroline remain in fearful suspense, imagine a paper,[b] a fatal paper, signed by the king, sealed by the king; imagine a deed, or rather a declaration of divorce, by which *the King consented to the dissolution of the marriage of Edmund Augustus Walstein and Caroline of Lichtfield, decreed it null and void, and the parties free to contract elsewhere!*

Yes, the eyes of Caroline were rivetted, wild, yet shed not a single tear! Thus, a while, she stood: at length, the writings dropped from her hands, a dark cloud enveloped her, a cold sweat overspread her pale face; she sees no more, breathes no more, a universal palpitation seizes her; her last thought is a hope that the hand of death is upon her,[c] and she sinks into insensibility!

Thus did she some time remain; and, when nature began somewhat to revive, she imagined she had been in a fearful dream; but not long did this deception continue: the chamber, the trunks, the letters, the paper were there, witnesses of the reality of her wretchedness. She looks at the direction of those letters.[a] The first is to her father, the second to Caroline, and is rejected with horror—"What can he say, while thus he murders me, while thus he himself dissolves our union?"

She examines the third and what is her surprise! It is directed to the Baron of Lindorf, at Walstein-house, Berlin; and at the bottom of the direction is written, *I conjure Caroline to give this letter with her own hand, to my friend, the very moment he arrives, which must be soon*—"To Lindorf!" exclaimed she: "and at his own house! And to me the letter entrusted! Oh God! Oh God! what can be the meaning of this! Lindorf here!—Could he be capable!—Is he the cause of?—Oh! would to God it may be jealousy! How easily shall I be able to prove it groundless!"

Caroline eagerly takes up the rejected letter, addressed to her, opens it, begins to read, and hope revives in her heart. —No! not jealousy, not hatred, not indifference, not resentment are there; but generosity, delicacy, love; passionate love, tender, excessive, heroic love; and in an instant Caroline passes from the depths of misery to the purest heaven of bliss. "He loves me! He loves me!" said she, "he loves me! and our marriage is not dissolved! Soon shall he know Caroline loves him also; will be his, and his only; will exist for him, with him, by him, and never, while life endures, will leave him more!"[b] Blessed as this letter was, scarcely could she end it, so eager was she to give orders, instantly to prepare the post chariot; but, while it is preparing, again she reads, again she devours its contents. The words are hosts of angels, and the small paper the infinite regions of bliss.[8]

"Dear and tender Caroline, cease to grieve, cease to subdue your feelings; not to a tyrant has the care of your happiness been committed. The tears I have so lately seen shed, on the picture of a regretted lover, shall be the last which for this reason you shall shed—Oh! may my prayers be heard, and may the God of goodness grant, as an ample reward for my own sufferings, that her whom I adore may be henceforth, and for ever, happy; then shall I, though separate and far, far from her, though knowing her another's, still be able to support existence. Yes, angel of my soul, be happy; be his whom your heart hath selected, and who merits, at least as much as mortal may, a blessing so supreme. No longer shall your sensibility, by virtue tortured, lament a union which your soul abhors; no longer shall you shed those secret and corroding tears, which I would rather perish than be the cause of. Love and duty shall be allied.

"Oh Caroline! still do I hear those moving, those passionate sounds, dictated by grief, and addressed to the object of your tenderness. But complain no more; no more reproach him with an involuntary absence which he to friendship thought he owed. He shall be restored to your arms, Caroline; you shall see him, kneeling at your feet, and presently shall you both forget your former pains.

"Pardon, Oh! pardon, Caroline, that I so long have neglected to give you happiness and joy. From the moment that first I learned your secret, that fatal moment when I saw you expiring, when I felt there was a degree of misery superior even to that of resigning you, I then swore to unite you to each other. Caroline, thou thyself canst witness how sacred I have held the wife of my friend, the beloved of Lindorf—yet will I own, blinded by my passion, I have had momentary illusions, have thought it possible I myself might be ineffably blessed, have misinterpreted the efforts of duty and virtue into softer sensations, and had almost prepared the iron scourge of never ending regret for myself, and pining grief and melancholy for thee. But it is past, the charm is broken, and I feel it is time to fly. Yes, in a delirium of hope was I almost lost; but, with the first rays of returning day, I will depart to obtain what shall for ever banish all such future rash hopes, to which I have too, too, weakly yielded. I go to restore you to yourself; or, rather, to the original of that picture you hold so dear. Farewell, Caroline; I perceive I say what I ought not; I shall give a pang to your generous and tender heart, by exposing the weakness of my own. At length, however, dear Caroline, know me for what I am. Know that, be my misery what it may in quitting you, in renouncing you thus eternally, it still would be infinitely greater were I to remain and usurp those rights which are due to love alone. To possess the person of Caroline and to know that another possesses her heart, to be equally an impediment to her happiness and the happiness of a dear and respected friend, this were impossible to support! But to be a spectator of, or, at least, to imagine, your mutual felicity, will spread a gleam of comfort over desponding life. Caroline will owe that felicity to me, will think of me with tenderness and gratitude, and thus, while I live, I shall live certain of her friendship, and when I die she will shed a tear over my tomb.[2] —Farewell!—Caroline, farewell! I fly to merit the friendship I so earnestly covet.

"*Berlin, five o'clock in the morning.*

"*P. S. Dated at Potsdam, ten o'clock, and after having had an audience with the King.*

"All is over, the chains which have ever hung so heavy on Caroline are broken. She is free, and shall soon be Lindorf's. Oh! tell me, tell me, Caroline, that you are happy. Let me have this consolation—My friend is ignorant of the bliss that awaits him. I know his generous friendship, and the same feelings that drove him from Rindaw and his country, may, perhaps, still make him refuse this felicity. This must not be: for this reason I have written a letter, addressed to him, which will end all his scruples, and prove that he only can contribute to the small degree of happiness of which Walstein is now capable by making himself and Caroline happy.

"I still have a favour to ask, and, surely, Caroline, in a moment like this, will not, by refusal, increase my griefs. No, I know her heart too well.—It is to accept the house she at present inhabits. You like its situation, Caroline; your apartments please you; they were designed for you, furnished for you, and never shall any one but you inhabit them—You will not, surely you will not, by a cruel denial, make your wretched friend still more wretched.

"Again and again, farewell! Dear and adored Caroline, farewell!—And is it true, then, that you are no longer mine, that I no longer have the least right?—What talk I of rights, I never had any; those the heart only can accord, and, at present, I shall be certain of your pity and esteem. Ah would you but sometimes write to me, would you but describe your happiness—But no, it cannot be: never must I write to the wife of Lindorf. If Caroline of Lichtfield will for once deign to answer me, only once, before she bears another name, her letter will reach me at Walstein, where I shall remain eight days, before I set off to Dresden, to visit my sister.

"I am going to depart!—And shall I never see you more? Shall those heavenly hours which, by your side, I have passed never return? Shall I never more listen to your sweet voice?—Caroline, I rave, for never, while thought remains, will you be absent from my imagination. Whatever hospitable, or inhospitable, land may contain my body, my soul will be ever present with you.

"Herewith I send the King's confirmation of your liberty, a letter to your father, one to—to your husband, and the deed of conveyance of Walstein-house. Let me know, at least, that you have received those papers; let me, once again, entreat you to tell me you are happy, and all the purposes of this world are ended with

EDMUND AUGUSTUS WALSTEIN."

Again this dear letter is read till the chariot is ready, except just for a moment that Caroline runs into her own apartment to fetch the manuscript of Lindorf; the picture, that principal cause of mistake, is warm in her bosom. And now she departs, entreating, conjuring the postillions to be expeditious, and, notwithstanding all their endeavours to oblige so sweet a petitioner, still she finds they go but slowly. The Count was some hours before her, and yet, so great was the diligence she used, he had not been very long at Walstein before she arrived. Shut up in his closet, a prey to the most violent grief, insensible of every thing but the loss of Caroline, whom he never was more to behold, dead even to the consolations of virtue, he there had retired from the world, and the sight of human being. A momentary gleam of comfort had come over him when he first was met by his vassals and servants. Louisa, Justin, and the aged Josselin, had been at the head of them, had fallen and clasped the knees of their benefactor, had presented their two little boys, and, with blessings and prayers, and smiles, and tears, had given him salutation. Louisa was pregnant again, "Oh! my Lord," said she, "your arrival is the forerunner of happiness. I shall have a little girl, for which so often

I have prayed; and now my Lord is married, if my Lady the Countess will but have the goodness to stand Godmother, and let my child be christened after her, I shall never be thankful enough for the favor."

The grateful Louisa spoke daggers! The Count could not support it.—"Alas! child, I am—I am no longer"—Walstein was obliged to break off abruptly and fly to conceal the bursting efforts of nature.

These good people still were assembled in the court, and with them some of the villagers, who all were lamenting the grief in which they had seen their good lord, when Caroline arrived. She opened the door, sprang from her chariot, and, without seeing or hearing person or object that surrounded her, exclaimed, "Where is he?—Where is the Count?"

William flew!—"Here is my Lady the Countess!"—

"Yes, dear William, here am I! Where is he? Lead me to him instantly!"

William ran before her, pointed to his master's closet door, and retired. Caroline opens it, runs, falls into his arms, and in a broken voice exclaims, "My Lord! My Husband!—Wherefore hast thou quitted thus thy Caroline, who adores thee, who loves thee and thee only in all the world, and whom thou wilt kill shouldest thou abandon her?"

The haste with which she ran, her eagerness, her sobs, all cut speech short and interrupted respiration; her head reclined on the shoulder of the Count, her arms hung round his neck, and her tears fell into his bosom. Walstein was not less agitated than herself; at last, taking her in his arms and placing her on a sopha, he falls at her feet.

"Caroline!—Caroline!—Is it you Caroline!—Is it, or is it some pitying angel who has assumed your form? Can what I have heard be possible!"

"Doubt it not, doubt it not! Here, here (Caroline untied the ribband and took the portrait from her bosom) look, behold the picture I love; nay, look at it well; say whose likeness it is; behold who thus entirely possesses my heart, and for whom alone I would live and die!"

Walstein looked!—With astonishment looked!—It was he!—Good God! he himself! At least such as he himself had been; and Caroline proved she still beheld him as he had been, and that, to her, he had undergone no change. True it was, indeed, that he every day became more like his portrait, and that, at present, the likeness even could not be mistaken. But by what magic, what miracle could this portrait, of the existence of which the Count himself was ignorant, fall into the hands of Caroline, be worn next her heart, and become the object of her dearest her tenderest caresses? He looks, he faulters, he is ready to sink under the excess, and yet cannot he believe it real! It is a heavenly dream out of which he fears to awake! Few are his words but those few all are expressive of rapture, astonishment, and remaining doubt. As soon as passion would permit, Caroline, blushing, drew from her pocket all the letters and the manuscript which Lindorf had left her— "Take these," said she, "read, and you will know all. No more will I have any secrets for my Walstein; they have already made me too wretched.— Yes, I loved Lindorf; at least, I had sensations that bore some resemblance to those I feel at present. What the difference is you yourself shall judge. When Lindorf left me, at Rindaw, I wept; yes, wept; and not a little; but my grief soon found alleviation, soon subsided, and soon did this small picture become dearer to my heart than Lindorf. This morning, on the contrary, I wept not, when I received the fearful sentence of separation. Not a tear escaped: but I thought either death or distraction must have been the instantaneous effect, and should you persist in that your dreadful design it would be as though you were to say to me *Caroline I wish thee dead*—But, Oh! rather say Caro I wish thee mine, and mine thou ever shalt be—Here—here is the paper! The— the Divorce! Look how insignificant it is at present!"

It was torn in a thousand pieces, and Caroline cast it with indignation into the fire—Walstein could not utter a word! He gazed, he wept, he took her hand, pressed it to his lips, to his heart—He gazed again, and exclamations, without connection, without meaning, succeeded each other. He took up his own picture, and, in his delirium, kissed it with transport! It was the sacred proof of the affection of his dear Caroline!

Caroline pressed him, once more, to read the manuscript, but this he could not, this would have been to have taken his eyes off her, and have robbed himself of moments the most precious, the most extatic the human heart knows.—"No, dear Caroline, do not, do not ask me to read now. I do read, I read your heart, I there find I am beloved; and what farther knowledge can I want?"

"But you know not the history of the portrait." "No matter; I know it dear to you, and that is all I wish to know."

"Nay, but hear, at least, that it was Lindorf who taught me to estimate the worth of Walstein; who first inspired admiration, which was afterward productive of love."

"Lindorf!"

"Yes, let me do him justice; to Lindorf you are indebted for the heart of your Caroline."

"To Lindorf!—Generous Friend!"

"To you he owes every thing."

"No, no, I am indebted to him for more than life."

Walstein then took the manuscript and read, and Caroline presently saw the struggling efforts of sensibility; often was he obliged to stop, and endeavoured to stifle his tears, and as often did he tell Caroline, with a broken and passionate voice, that Lindorf most merited her affection. Caroline, with her angel hand, stopped his mouth, and obliged him to continue his reading. He passed rapidly over events which were already familiar to his memory, but when he came to the epocha of the first meeting of Lindorf and Caroline, his very soul seemed a part of the paper, each syllable, each phrase was devoured, and he read with his eyes only, for circumstances like these might not be read aloud. Caroline, with fixed looks, continually endeavoured to discover the different sensations by which he was agitated.

When he had ended, he gave her back the manuscript in a manner that shewed how much he had been moved.—"I see," said he, "I have a wife and a friend such as never man had, and that they both have sacrificed their own felicity to mine —Ah! wherefore, Caroline, did you oblige me to read this manuscript? Why not leave me in that blessed dream into which I so lately had been lulled?"

"A dream? Unkind Walstein! Is that an epithet for feelings such as mine? Do you forget that this is your picture?"—The word picture, pronounced with the utmost affection, was convincing, and restored the Count all his confidence and bliss.—"And now," said she, "that you have read your own story, and that of Lindorf, listen to the history of my heart."

Caroline, then, circumstantially, related all that had passed from the moment of their marriage: the innocence with which she supposed she loved Lindorf as a brother, and her terror at first imagining a lover; the scene of the garden, of the pavilion, her grief, her tears, her regret, her struggles, all were told. She next informed him how, induced by esteem and admiration at reading his letters to Lindorf, she had begun to think of him, to look at and love his portrait; spoke of what she felt on receiving the letter in which he proposed to leave his country, and of the delicacy, the sensations, and the mixture of chagrin that had occasioned her answer. When she came to the court yard of Ronebourg, "I protest, I vow," said she, "it was agitation only at finding myself so unexpectedly in the presence of a husband whom I had so cruelly wronged, and by whom I had so much cause to be hated; it was not Lindorf. No, you long had utterly effaced every impression he had made upon my heart."

The Count listened in rapture. He was enchanted, and took care not to give her the least interruption. With what enthusiasm, what truth, what eloquence, what affection, did she speak! How did she dwell on every circumstance of her recovery at Ronebourg, of her hopes and fears since their arrival at Berlin, and her continual intention of explaining her feelings; of the timidity by which she was restrained;[a] of her desire to please him, to win his affection, to attach him wholly to herself, and make him happy; of her grief at her ill success, her resolution, that very morning, of speaking, and her extreme affliction at finding him gone; of her despair at receiving the fatal packet, and of the joy that succeeded when she was so fully convinced, from his letter, how dearly she was beloved by her husband. All was expressed with that rapidity, that persuasion, that passion, which so entirely remove doubt—"At present," added she, "you are as perfectly acquainted with Caroline as she is with herself; I have nothing more to relate, except to paint how happy I am. Oh! but how? It is wholly impossible! I love, am beloved, and may, without a blush, receive and return all the most endearing proofs of love! Yes, my dear Lord, our hearts are now acquainted with each other, and estimate mine by your own."

Walstein would have replied, would have entered into explanations concerning his own conduct, but he was interrupted by the arrival of William. He entered, saying that the villagers, having heard the beauteous lady they had seen was the Countess, were very unwilling to go without being permitted to see her again, and very earnestly entreated she would let them pay their duty to her, if it were but for a moment. Caroline, led by Walstein, descended into the court, and was received with redoubled cries of *"Life! Happiness and long life, to my Lord and my Lady!"* The Count ordered wine and money to be distributed, and Caroline, clasping his hand most affectionately, whispered, "these good people, my Walstein, know not that they really celebrate our bridal day, the epocha of happiness confirmed!—Would you but permit—"

"Permit, Caroline!—Speak, command."

"See what a number of young people here are. Do you not think there are some lovers, among them, who wish to marry, but whom poverty keeps asunder? Ah! let us make them as happy as we are ourselves!"

The Count kissed her hand with transport.—"Dear, adorable Caroline!— Let us do still more; let us perpetuate the memory of this fortunate day, since it is the day when Caroline is given to my arms. Let us, here, in this scene of bliss, annually, bestow six marriage portions, and do thou, my Caroline, inform the good peasants of the institution."

Caroline again pressed the hand of Walstein, spoke to the people, and new acclamations, new benedictions were uttered with redoubled fervency; in the midst of these tumultuous transports, the voices of young lovers were still louder and more ardent than the others, and their prayers that God might for ever bless their good Lord and Lady reached the skies!

Walstein, perceiving Louisa and Justin in one corner of the court, with their little family, called, and presented them to Caroline. "Here, my love," said he, "are some good people with whom you are already acquainted." "Ah!" said Caroline, "this is the beauteous Louisa."—Louisa blushed and became more beautiful; for, though childbearing and the duties of her station had somewhat faded the roses on her cheeks, she still was exceedingly handsome.

"Oh! yes, my Lady," said Justin, with his open expressive countenance, which at once bespoke the capacity of his mind and the honesty of his heart: "You are very right; this is my beauteous Louisa, there's not a man in the world, it's my opinion, has so handsome a wife, except my Lord the Count; and that is but just. It is the recompence of heaven for having bestowed Louisa on the poor Justin."

It was now Caroline's turn to blush! She caressed the two boys who were fine little fellows, and, perceiving the pregnancy of Louisa, prevented her petition, by offering, of her own accord, to stand godmother to the child. Louisa would have knelt at her feet, if Caroline would have suffered her; but Justin nothing could restrain; he kissed the hem of her robe, and, rising, said, "Surely God loves me, for he hears and grants me all my prayers! No sooner did I ask him to give me Louisa than he put it into the heart of my Lord to make her mine; and then I again begged a Louisa for my Lord, and behold he has found one! Well then, I next will pray him to grant my Lady two little boys, as handsome as ours; nay and I have no doubt but they will soon be here."

Caroline turned away, stooped to the children, and gave each of them a kiss and a ducat, while Walstein, affected, shook Justin by the hand, and threw his purse into his hat. To escape thanks and prevent the efforts of gratitude, which, when beyond expression, are always painful, he asked Caroline to walk in the garden, to which she instantly agreed. It was then the month of December, the air was piercing, the earth covered with snow, and the waters with frost, yet neither frost nor snow were seen, nor was the sharp air felt by Caroline and Walstein. Never did walk in spring appear to them so delicious. Long has it been known that love can embellish all things, and that, where the beloved object is present, there is neither winter nor summer, spring nor fall. Indeed, the gardens were remarkable for their beauty, extent, and the taste with which they were disposed; and, as such, were visited by travellers. Caroline had seen something of them, on her other bridal day, and perhaps more than she saw at present, though she now walked all over them. At length, the Count, fearing the effect of the cold, brought her back to the Chateau. Here they found a collation such as the rustic hoards of Louisa could afford. She had been busy in providing cream, new cheese, chesnuts, honeycombs, and a part of the kid that Justin had killed. "How fortunate it was," said Louisa, "that I had it ready dressed to regale our good old father."

"What Josselin!" cried Caroline; "nay then, Louisa, you must go and bring him to eat with us." Louisa ran to seek him, and in the Sire came, supported by Justin, and tremulous still more with joy than old age. The Count and Caroline rose, both went to him, and each taking him by an arm placed him in a great chair; after which the Count, filling him a bumper, said, "Drink this, my brave Josselin, to the health of the happiest of mortals!"

"And this," said Justin, "to him who well deserves to be the happiest!"

Josselin would have spoken, but he was so much affected he could only utter parts of sentences, and raise his hands and eyes to heaven. After, however, having drank a third glass to the health of my lady the Countess,[10] and after a long look at her, he suddenly exclaimed—"Blessed be God for having made so beauteous a Lady purposely for our good Lord! Oh yes! you are beautiful, madam, and very,

very good! I can see, I am sure you are; but you have an angel for a husband! Did you know what he has done for us, how he preserved, how he provided for, my Louisa!"

And now the good Josselin, animated by wine, and having once begun to speak, was not willing to be silent. He recounted the whole history, to Caroline, of the marriage of his daughter; and how he would not hear of Justin, and how my Lord the Count came round him, and how he gave them a good farm, and fifty ducats down, and how he had the misfortune to wound himself as he went from their house, and how they carried him on hurdles to the Chateau of Ronebourg; and a thousand other *hows* which Caroline knew as well as he, yet would she not interrupt him; the pleasure the old man felt in talking was a pleasure to Caroline; nay, she even listened with delight to this simple but natural village eloquence;[11] it flowed pure from the heart and never thought of well-placed words or studied expressions; and particularly to the praise of Walstein which was incessantly repeated, and which drew the sweetest tears of sensibility to her eyes. She looked up to this dear, this beloved husband, and saw his heart in sympathy with hers; she stretched out her hand to him with a soft smile, an expression which no words can convey. Love, virtue, and happiness were united, and this single moment would have been a large compensation for an age of pain.

Josselin drank, talked, and became more and more animated. He spoke of his house, his family, the care his children took of him, of his dear Justin, who was the best of sons, of husbands, and of fathers. "An it were to do again," said he, "I would give him my Louisa if he were not worth a groat. Not, my Lord, that your bounty has done any harm. And then when I see these little urchins, playful, capering round me—Ah! how does it rejoice my very heart! It makes me young again; and, if my dear Cicely were still living, I should be happier now than ever—But, pray, my Lord, what is become of our master's son, the young Baron of Lindorf? I can remember him less than either of these. Many a time have I had him in my arms: nay, I am his nurse father, and shall always love him. I was told he was going to marry the sister of my Lord, and right glad we were to hear it; for such honourable noble souls ought to marry. Is it true my Lord? Is he your brother?"

"Not yet," said Caroline, rising, and returning Louisa's youngest boy to his mother, whom, till then, she had held in her lap. Justin and Louisa understood by this it was time to retire, and Louisa hinted as much to her father; but the old man was so happy, in his arm chair, with the Count, the Countess and the bottle, that he could by no means resolve to leave them. "Let me alone, my child," said he; "it is the happiest day I ever beheld, and, at my time of life, one has not much happiness to lose."—"But we are troublesome, father," said Louisa, "to my Lord the Count." "Not in the least, I tell thee; thou art a foolish girl; I know him better than thou dost; why it is his delight to see others happy; is it not my lord?

Am not I right and is not she wrong? But our children, now a days, will be wiser than their fathers."

Walstein smiled, and Caroline again sat down, and made a sign to Louisa; while the old man, more happy than a monarch, began to sing. He could not finish his song. "So it is," said he, "I am good for nothing now; but I have a heart for all that. Ah! madam, if you had but heard me give the word of command! But come, son Justin, it is now thy turn. Where is thy flageolet? Play madam a tune. Louisa shall sing, and the little apes here shall dance. Pshaw, what simpletons you are, you think of nothing: an it were not for me, here would you leave my Lord and Lady to yawn themselves to sleep."

Caroline having signified she really should be glad to hear Justin play, he took out his flageolet and played some allemandes,[12] to which the little ones danced with much more grace and meaning than could have been expected, while their mother watched every motion, and the old man chuckled as he looked at the Count and Countess. "Did not I tell you," said he, "it was worth your seeing? and now, Louisa, do thou sing the song thy husband made a few days ago."

"How!" cried Caroline; "is Justin a Poet too!"

"No, Madam, no poet," said Justin: "I only write a couplet now and then for my Louisa." He then played a wild pleasing melody, by way of symphony, on his flageolet, and Louisa, with the timid simplicity and sweetness of the village voice, sung as follows.

> The marriage honey moon, they say,
> Grown languid on the marriage day,
>   Now scarce, alas! that day outlives;
> But, ah! Louisa, thou dost prove
> How little such folks know of love,
>   Who thus describe the joys it gives!
>
> Poor silly people! Wherefore tire
> Of bliss which I so much admire,
>   Taste each returning day so pure;
> And, feeling how I still adore,
> Still each returning day am more
>   Convinced it ever shall endure?
>
> I hear of kings and mighty men,
> I know no kings, and, therefore, can
>   No fancies form of kingly joys;
> But this I know, not lands or towns,
> No, I'd not give for globes or crowns
>   My dear Louisa and my boys.[13]

Louisa ended, and Justin laid down his flageolet. He had supposed it possible that, as he himself loved so much to hear his Louisa sing,[a] others might wish to hear her sing likewise; foreseeing therefore this occasion, and overflowing with gratitude at the return of his Lord, while the Count and Caroline had walked into the garden, Justin, anxious to make this gratitude known, had composed the following stanza, which, modestly advancing a few steps, he himself now sung.[14]

> Ah! might my artless song but show
> How much to my kind Lord I owe;
>   Might I but half I feel impart;
> I then, to all my former store,
> Should add one grateful pleasure more,
>   And ease my now half bursting heart.

Justin sung with as much feeling as he wrote, and the Count and Caroline, affected and astonished at his talents, gave him all the praise he merited. The modest and the simple Justin said it was Louisa who had taught him every thing, for had it not been for the pleasure he took in pleasing her he should have known nothing. "But," said Caroline, "have you composed this last stanza instantly, and without having thought on it before."—"Not entirely," replied Justin; "though I do think, my Lady, I could undertake, ay and perform too, a more difficult thing for my Lord the Count."

The heart of Caroline was full, or rather overflowing. During the song, the good Josselin had fallen asleep, but his children awaked him sufficiently to get him away, and as soon as Caroline was alone with the Count she gave vent to the sweetest tears she had ever shed. The old man, the happy couple, the veneration and love they all had for the Count, which extended itself to her, had all together such an effect upon her feelings, and imagination, that her husband appeared a supernatural being, a benevolent Deity,[a] whom it was her duty to adore, and whom, in reality, adore she did. As soon as her mind was a little calm, "permit me, my dear Lord," said she, "to ask you the same question that Josselin asked some time since. Will not Lindorf become our brother?"

"Would to Heaven he might" answered the Count; "but you forget, my love"—

"What?"

"That it is not Matilda, now, who could make Lindorf happy."

"And why not?"

"Because, for some months, he was in love with Caroline of Lichtfield."

"But that Caroline no longer exists; he will never see her more; in her stead he will find Caroline of Walstein, who never can inspire any thing but fraternal friendship, which cannot any way impede his love for Matilda. Let him but see her, once again, and he himself will not be able to comprehend how he might, for a moment, forget her. I wish I were certain that Matilda's affections have undergone no change; there is a word in one of your letters which gave me a little uneasiness. Do you suspect she does not love Lindorf, and that the Baron de Zastrow"—Walstein smiled, pressed the hand of Caroline, and interrupted her by taking out his pocket book and giving Caroline the last letter he had received from Matilda to read— And, Oh! how much affected was she as she read! How often did she repeat, "Dear girl! Charming Matilda! Lovely Sister! Yes, thou shalt live with us, shalt regain thy lover, thy brother, and the tenderest of friends. But why," added she, as she returned the letter to the Count, "did not you, my Lord, immediately fly to Dresden, to give aid and ease to this dear Sister?"

"I will tell you why, my love—My Caroline was dying, and while she was in danger could I leave her?"

"Well, but you answered Matilda's letter?"

"I did; though, at present, I wish I had not; and confess I begin to be uneasy at her silence."

"Good Heaven! How you must have grieved her! Dear Matilda!"—Then, suddenly rising, Caroline, with clasped hands and ardent impetuosity, went up to the Count, and, with a tone of most earnest supplication, added, "My dear, dear Lord, let me beg, let me conjure you, not to refuse me the favour I am about to ask. Let us depart to-morrow morning for Dresden, to relieve Matilda; I burn to be acquainted, to live with her, to give her consolation, and I hope happiness. Only read her letter again, and you cannot have the least hesitation. She is now, perhaps, in tears, is this moment in distress, when I am so happy; and I myself am the cause of her affliction!ᵃ And have I, then, dear Matilda, have I robbed thee of thy lover, and deprived thee of thy brother? Oh! how many wrongs have I done thee! No, no, never, never shall I be truly at ease, till I see thee as blest as I myself am." Caroline spoke with so much energy, her eyes and features expressed so well her sensations, and she herself was so beautiful, that Walstein fell involuntarily on his knee before her, where he long remained with his lips fixed on her hand, without the power to answer a word—"Tell me, my Lord," added she, with earnestness,ᵇ "shall we, are we to depart to-morrow?"

"Lovely, adorable Caroline!" cried the Count, "how well thou knowest my heart! My absence from my sister, and the apprehension that she may be unhappy, were the only things that could possibly interrupt my present felicity; but to leave you, Caroline, or to propose a journey in the depth of winter, and during such severe weather, was more than I could undertake."

"Nay, my Lord, now you surely joke. I thought it was always fine weather when one went in search of a friend in the company of a lover. We shall pass through Potsdam: shall you see the King?"

"By all means, my love; it is a duty I cannot neglect; and, if I might venture, I would ask, in my turn, whether Caroline would—." Caroline perfectly understood the Count, and blushed; she had not seen the King since the day of her nuptials, which was now above a year;[15]ᶜ and, feeling how much cause he had to be dissatisfied with her conduct, she trembled at the thought of being presented. While she was last at Berlin,[a] her mourning and her health were sufficient pretexts to obtain delay, and the Count, we have seen, had his reasons for wishing to indulge her in this delay. At present, he perceived her inquietude, and stopped short; but she, immediately recovering herself, answered, with an enchanting smile, "It is high time, my Lord, is it not, I should no longer remain so childish?[b] —Well, lead me, take me to him; I will kneel at his feet; I suppose he will scold me; he will do very right; for I have well deserved his anger; but, when he has ended, I, however, will scold him in my turn."

"You! my angel."

"Yes, I; and very severely, too, for having signed that dreadful paper, this morning."

Each word Caroline uttered transported the Count with happiness and love, even to intoxication, dispelling every shadow of remaining doubt, if doubt might remain after the frank and natural manner in which she had spoken of Lindorf, and her desire to see him and Matilda united. But, no, Walstein had no doubts; the ingenuous and affectionate Caroline knew not dissimulation; she expressed her feelings too forcibly, and with a conviction that deceit cannot assume. Had she been silent, indeed, her eyes, her smiles, the pleasure painted in her countenance, would all have spoken: her lips knew not falsehood, and her features were the organs of a pure and angelic soul. When Caroline said I love no protestations, no vows, were wanting; and this she had said so often, during the course of that fortunate, that blissful day, that the Count might well remain persuaded of her truth.— They supped on the kid that Justin had killed so a-propos; for the Count, when he set off for this estate, was too deeply afflicted to think of food; and this simple repast was the most delicious either of them had ever made. Our history does not inform us whether long habit made the Count, as usual, leave Caroline's apartment after supper; the reader must, therefore, suppose what he pleases on that subject: but, in the morning, Caroline made the Count promise they should soon return to this charming estate; "for," added she, with a softened voice and downcast eyes, "I shall love it as long as I live!"

In proportion as they drew near to Potsdam, the fears of Caroline augmented; this the Count perceived, and endeavoured to inspire her with fortitude. He related a thousand traits of the King's goodness to him, who, said he, "is more than my King, he is my friend.[16] Yes, dear Caroline, it is to my friend I am going to present one who will make life a continued dream of felicity, and one whom I received from himself. Had you heard him yesterday morning, how long he persisted to refuse the cruel favor I came to beg, and when, at last, he yielded to my persecutions and signed that fatal paper, had you seen him return it to me, you would have no fears. 'Reflect, think again, dear Walstein,' said he. 'I am truly grieved at your determination. I wished to make you happy, and still I think you might be so; it is with infinite regret I have signed the paper, and I sincerely hope you will make no use of it.' Such Caroline is the monarch who soon is to be a witness of the felicity of his friend."

By this time they were in the court of the palace, and the Count, alighting, left Caroline in the carriage. The King, according to his custom, was mounting his horse to ride round the fort and exercise his troops. He perceived Walstein and stopped—"Ah! are you there, Count?" said he; "I am glad to see you; I thought of you all day yesterday, and, though I saw the High Chamberlain, did not mention a word of what has passed. Do not be rash, let me, myself, speak to Caroline. I scarcely can consent—"

"My gracious Sovereign, she is here!"

"Who?"

"Caroline! My wife! My lovely, my adored wife! The wife your Majesty bestowed on me, and who is now more beloved, more dear than ever!"

"Are you in your senses, Walstein?"

"Perfectly, Sir; it was yesterday morning that I was frantic; but Caroline has restored me to reason, life, and bliss! She loves me, wishes to be mine, and once more I throw myself at your Majesty's feet to beg her as the greatest of all blessings your royal bounty could grant!"

Yes, the Count was kneeling to the King; who, himself, not perfectly understanding how a woman might be the cause of all this delirium,[17] laughed, bade him "rise and explain." The Count obeyed; related the despair of Caroline, her arrival at Walstein, their present intended journey to Dresden, for which he now asked the King's permission, and, afterwards, earnestly entreated his Majesty's confirmation of their union before their departure. Both were willingly granted, and the Monarch himself went up to Caroline, who was still waiting in her carriage till the Count's return. She was a great deal affected at seeing the King approach, and would have descended from the coach, but the King said to her, "Stay where you are, Lady Walstein, stay where you are; all is well; forget what is past. I am satisfied, live happy, and let me have as many subjects as possible like yourselves. Walstein, make no delay, depart, return as soon as you can, and bring with you the lovely Matilda." His Majesty then took the Count by the hand, saluted Caroline, and left them both exceedingly moved by this benevolent condescension, which Kings are so seldom disposed to bestow. They set off, immediately, for Berlin, made preparations for their journey, and were soon on their road to Dresden, anticipating the mutual pleasure the meeting with Matilda would occasion. The Count foresaw many difficulties which might arise from his aunt and young De Zastrow, but was determined to overcome them all, and bring Matilda to Berlin. He concealed his fears from Caroline, whose hopes ran high and happiness was great, in thinking she should gain a sister and a friend. We have before related how desirous she was of a blessing so necessary and so precious; and to have the sister of Walstein for this friend, with whom she might converse, while he was absent, of all her past and present feelings, certain of being heard with an interest almost equal to her own, was to double this blessing.

To love is not sufficient; friendship, to whom love may unbosom itself, is also necessary; and Caroline, already, felt the delicious transports of telling Matilda how dearly she loved her brother. In this their impatience, for the Count was as desirous as Caroline of being at Dresden, they travelled the two first days with all possible speed, making no stay, by day, except to change horses, and at night only taking two or three hours repose. But the strength of Caroline by no means equalled her wishes, and the second evening she found herself so fatigued she was obliged, when they came to a small village, to entreat the Count would go no farther that night. Walstein, it may well be supposed, readily consented; but, suspecting the accommodations would not be very good, he sent a servant before to procure a bed. At last, they were met, at the end of the village, by the servant, with the landlord of a small, indifferent inn. Our host, judging, by the attendants, his guests were great people, and fearing to lose the promised harvest, came himself, to make it the more secure. He had only two bedchambers, each with two beds, and both these were in the possession of a young gentleman and his lady, who had arrived the evening before. The husband had a wound in his arm, which, by the motion of the carriage, had been opened; and this was likely to detain him some days longer; for which reason, to make certain of the two chambers, he had paid for them beforehand. This, however, did not much embarrass our host, who was a merry, unpolished, country fellow.[a]

"I warrant me" said he "they will let you have one of the chambers, for what occasion have they for two? They are so loving, and so handsome, that they are never asunder all day; and why may they not as well be together all night? No, no; they will not be vexed at that."

The host kept talking till they came to the inn, but the Count, however, thought it necessary to go himself, and entreat the strangers to suffer the Countess to lie in one of the beds. Meanwhile the hostess shewed Caroline into her own chamber. The Count went up a dark stair case and wanted the landlord to introduce him; but he, little used to the forms of good breeding, led him into a kind of entry, at the far end of which was a door open, and, telling the Count he would find them there, left him to introduce himself.

Walstein advanced, and saw a young lady at the farther part of the chamber, elegantly dressed, and tying a black scarf round the neck of a young gentleman, so as to support his arm. As her white and charming hand passed his cheek he employed his other arm to seize and kiss it with rapture. The picture was interesting, and the Count durst not disturb the young couple, whom he silently beheld, remembering his own happiness. Fearing to be thought rude, after standing a moment, he was going to retire; but the young lady, happening to look towards the door, saw him, gazed for a moment, flew to him with open arms, and, with astonishment in her countenance, exclaimed, "It is my brother! my dear dear brother!"

Lindorf (Yes! it was Lindorf himself!) forgot his wound, and instantly rose—"Heavens! Is it possible! Can it be Walstein?"—Walstein it was, and Lindorf pressed him to his bosom; while Matilda, hanging round his neck, kissed and kissed, and knew not whether to weep or dance for joy.

Need we say the Count was astonished?—Matilda and Lindorf! His sister and his friend both in his arms! Had his senses refused belief his heart would have convinced him it was truth; and, though unable to comprehend by what miracle he might find two such people in such a place, he, nevertheless, yielded to all the transport the prodigy[18] inspired. For some time, Lindorf! Matilda! Brother! Sister! Friend! Interjections, and exclamations only were uttered, only were heard—The Count added the name of Caroline, and, at length, said, "she is here, dear Matilda, here, with me, let us go to her."

"Here! Caroline here! My sister here!" cried Matilda.

Light and swift as the young greyhound at his returning master's voice, Matilda flies down stairs and already is in the arms of Caroline, who, presently, knew her; more indeed, from her affectionate caresses, and the repeated epithet of "dear dear sister," than from the portrait of Lindorf. The gentlemen followed, and the surprize of Caroline increased; but surprize and pleasure of the purest nature were her only sensations. Lindorf is her brother, and her friend, and she hesitates not to kiss him with that frank and natural tenderness by which true and simple friendship so well is characterized. "And may I, then, call you brother," said she; "may I tell you I love you! Oh! yes, I know not how much I shall love the husband of my dear Matilda, and the friend of my dear, dear, dear Walstein!"

This open ingenuous manner would have taught Lindorf, had he himself been insensible of, his duty. He certainly feared to meet Caroline: the scenes that had so lately passed could not be totally obliterated from his imagination;[19] but the manner in which she received him, the tone of voice in which she uttered those few words, in the presence of Walstein and Matilda, wholly deprived him of all dread, either of himself or her. He was surprized to find that the redoubted Caroline was no more than the wife of his friend and the sister of Matilda; and for whom he felt no sensations beyond these tranquil and legitimate bounds—"Yes," answered he, with fortitude and enthusiasm, "yes Caroline, I am your brother, your friend, the friend of Walstein, and I feel myself worthy of these titles, which are become so dear, so inestimable!" Then, seizing the hand of Matilda—"Dear Count," said he, "you invited me to return, and promised me happiness. Here, as the ultimate happiness to which I aspire, let me receive this hand, which once was promised me from my Walstein, I think my future life will prove I know its value."

The Count was not long in considering an answer, and his reply was accompanied with an earnest wish to hear what strange circumstances had united them; if they were yet married; what had occasioned the wound of Lindorf; where they were going, whence they came; and, in fine, the full explanation of what, at present, seemed so wholly enigmatical. We are not without our hopes that the reader, in some degree, participates the Count's curiosity; and that he now imagines himself in the rustic chamber of a rustic inn, in company with four persons, the most happy the earth contained, feeling all that love and sweet friendship can feel, seated round an antique chimney, speaking all at once, and each asking a thousand questions without yet waiting for a single reply.

And now behold the lovely Matilda weeping and laughing both at once, kissing her brother, embracing Caroline, holding out one hand to her dear Lindorf, and then, suddenly, with a mighty grave face, and serious tone, commanding silence! "Yes, silence! For one full quarter of an hour, I impose silence on you all," said she, seating herself erect; "for, I assure you, I am not a little vain of having a story to relate. It is almost as singular," said she, to her brother, "as the fine tales you used to tell me when I was a very little, little girl"—Silence being thus obtained, and the eyes of the rest fixed on Matilda, she, addressing herself to the Count, thus began.

"There was a bird-catcher—"

"A bird-catcher!" exclaimed they all at once.

"Yes, a bird-catcher," replied she, with great gravity. "Before I begin my history I first intend to relate a little fable and put a question to my brother. Do not be impatient, I shall soon have done—There was once a bird catcher who, by his tricks and artifices, enticed a poor little bird into his nets. Ah! how wretched was that poor little bird! How did it beat its wings in its confinement, and call all its friends to its assistance! But the bird-catcher took care not one of them should hear its cries. At last came a linnet, and flew round the net in which it was entangled. 'Poor little bird,' said the linnet, 'thou wouldest lament still louder if thou knewest all the mischief that awaits thee. To-morrow they will clip thy wings, forever deprive thee of thy liberty, shut thee up in a cage with a bird thou dost not love, and forever prevent thy meeting the mate thou hast left at freedom in the groves.' Then did the little bird, at hearing this, cry still louder; and the linnet was so moved that it said, 'Let us try if there are no means to save thee.' Whereupon they both began to peck at the threads of the net, and, crack, by and by, one of them was broken; so that the little bird got first its head out, next one of its wings, at last both, spread them, vaulted aloft in air, and flew, right joyous, again to find its friends and former happiness.

"And now tell me, dear brother, whether was the bird-catcher, who thus tried to deprive the poor little bird of its liberty, or the poor little bird, that endeavoured to regain this liberty, wrong?"

"The bird-catcher, my dear girl," cried the Count, enchanted at the art, simplicity, and grace she had mingled in her apologue. "The charming little bird will never be wrong if it appeals to me; for I am certain my heart will approve what even my reason may condemn."

Matilda, instantly, clasped the neck of Walstein, and with tears of joy, exclaimed, "I have found my brother; he is still the same, ever benevolent and ever good, and I no longer dread either his reproaches or my own. Surely, I did right in quitting those malicious people who made me doubt his friendship."

"Doubt my friendship! Dear Matilda, let me beg you to explain your meaning."

"Yes," continued she, with vivacity, "they have had the cruelty to say, nay even to prove, you no longer loved me, wrote to me no longer, and would see me no more: that you forbad me to think of Lindorf, commanded me to marry the Baron De Zastrow, had departed for Russia, and, in fact, that I had no longer any brother, for it was the same thing."

Matilda could not proceed, and the tears ran down her lovely rosy cheeks; yet, while she wept she smiled: it was a summer shower which refreshens nature and inspires new pleasure.

"What a child am I!" said she; "I knew it was all false; I enjoy your company, here you are, you love me, and yet you see the supposition makes me weep; but no, I will laugh; and now—there, now will I relate the full and whole history of the poor little bird."

Before she began, the Count asked several questions concerning what they had told her against him, and found his aunt had intercepted and concealed the letter in which he had promised his sister soon to come to Dresden, and set her free. She managed so as to make Matilda believe the Count had written to her, his aunt. His wish that she might marry the Baron De Zastrow was changed into a positive command, and the voyage of Lindorf into England was a love affair, and a project of marriage with an English lady. The letter of the Count, instead of Ronebourg, was dated at Petersburg; and the innocent Matilda, being shewn her brother's handwriting, was the dupe of all these artifices. The arrival of the Count, it is true, would soon undeceive her; but they hoped to have Matilda married before that happened, and since the Count had wished, he certainly would easily be brought to pardon, the marriage.

Had Matilda been of a less determined character her aunt would, no doubt, have obtained her end; but she found an opposition, a fortitude which nothing could shake. It seemed inconceivable to young De Zastrow; for never, till then, had he supposed it possible to resist the elegance, the graces, and the charms he had acquired in his travels. A year's residence at Paris, his acquaintance with certain noble and fashionable gamesters there, and his success with actresses, who had made most heavy demands on his purse, had so fully convinced him of his irresistible merit, that he had imagined nothing more was necessary, in order to conquer, than to appear. To his aunt he left the care of courtship, and thought Matilda had every right to yield when he had declared, upon his honor, she was as handsome as an angel; that her shape was quite charming; that there was something of a French cast in her countenance; that she was almost as desireable as Mademoiselle du Thé, of the Opera house;[20] that she sung nearly as well as Mademoiselle du Gazon, of the *Theâtre Italien*;[21] and that, when she was his wife, he would incontinently take her to Paris, where there was no doubt but she would *strike*.[22] All which he said looking at himself in the glass, admiring his leg, displaying the brilliant on his finger, and, occasionally, interrupting himself to expatiate on the merits of certain fashionable baubles he had brought from France.

"Such," said Matilda, "is the being with whom my aunt is so enraptured; to whom she was determined to marry me; and of whose person, wit, and passion, she was continually vaunting. I own that, for my part, I could see nothing but a very fair complexioned, very mincing, very delicate, very vain, very self-sufficient young gentleman; who loved only one person in the whole world, himself, and who only did me the honor to think of me because I was the sister of the King's favorite, and the heiress of Madam de Zastrow. I by no means endeavoured to conceal my thoughts, concerning either him or Lindorf, from my aunt; she well knew I disliked the one as much as I loved the other, and her whole endeavour was to make me reverse this manner of thinking.—'You see,' said she, 'your brother has changed his opinion.'—'Yes, madam,' answered I, 'but his opinion has not changed my heart.'—'Your Lindorf no longer loves you'—'And must I punish myself for his infidelity?'—'You will never see him again.'—'I may love him, nevertheless, and keep my promise.'—'But his inconstancy releases you'—'Not in the least; his inconstancy releases himself, but if I am not inconstant is that my fault? Or can he, or you, or I myself, or any other being in the world, make me forget to love him and teach me to love another?' (What did Lindorf feel as thus Matilda spoke?)[23]

"These conversations usually ended in ill-humour. I was, by turns, scolded, caressed, flattered and menaced; and, notwithstanding all my firmness, was almost driven to despair. At length, I determined to write; not to you, brother, for I supposed you still in Russia, and they might have married me again and again before I could receive your answer; beside I was somewhat piqued at your neglect and silence; therefore, I say, once more, not to you, but—to Lindorf I wrote."

"To Lindorf! In England! How did you know his address?"

"Know? I knew not, perfectly, if he were there; for I sometimes would flatter myself they had been telling me falsehoods; though many circumstances led me to think he was, and I wrote. Writing was a momentary ease and consolation, and, though my letter remained in my pocket-book after it was written, I still imagined myself less unhappy. I had some small hopes of discovering if Lindorf really were in England, and, perhaps, of remitting him this letter, and you shall hear on what these hopes were founded.

"When I arrived at Dresden, Mademoiselle de Manteul, an amiable girl, but somewhat older than I, had been exceedingly polite to me, and the intimacy of the family at my aunt's occasioned me to see her often. She long had lost her mother, and lived with an old gouty father and younger brother; therefore, enjoyed a liberty which rendered her house and acquaintance exceedingly agreeable, and she was, continually, either with me or inviting me to visit her.

"Flattered by the friendship of a young lady of five and twenty, I returned her politeness, and we became as familiar as circumstances would permit. Somewhat timid, on account of the difference of our age, which she, however, endeavoured to make me forget, I, though most desirous of a confidante, durst not tell her the secret of my heart. She had a kind of—of forwardness in her manner, owing to her education, and was, likewise, most intimate with my aunt, to whom she assiduously paid her court; beside which she had an evident partiality in favor of the Baron de Zastrow, so that I feared making an additional enemy, instead of a friend. I could with much greater ease have confided my thoughts to her brother, whose age was nearer my own, and whose mild and manly character might render him more indulgent; but he, also, was the friend of the young Baron, and, indeed, rather seemed to avoid than to seek being alone with me, and it was not long before he informed us he was going to travel for some years.

Oh! how did my heart palpitate when I heard England was to be the first country he visited! How then did I wish to tell him my secret, entreat him to seek out Lindorf, and conjure him to take charge of my letter! But no opportunity could I find. He was too busy in preparing for his departure, and seemed sorrowful at being obliged to leave Dresden and his family. I seldom saw him, and, when I did, found myself abashed. If ever I approached, with intent to speak of his voyage to England, and to add a word relative to what lay nearest to my heart, I trembled, knew not what to say, and remained silent; blushing as if I had spoken, or as if the whole world had read my thoughts. Mademoiselle de Manteul was generally a third person, and, seeing my embarrassment, increased it by her pleasantries.

"At length, this brother departed, while I still was seeking the means to induce him to take my letter and give it to Lindorf; and I was left in the utmost despair at having missed so favourable an opportunity.

"One resource still remained; my friend might send it to her brother. But then it was necessary to make a full confession, and interest her in the success of my passion. The better to lead to this I continually spoke of England, her brother, the letters she would receive from him, and the dear pleasure of having a correspondence with a person one loves, though I yet had not dared to pronounce the name of Lindorf. She came to me one morning, and threw a letter into my lap. 'There,' said she; 'you who think it so sweet a pleasure to receive letters; I make you a present of that, which, indeed, ought to have been addressed to you; for my brother, though he has written to me, has spoken only of you.'

"'Of me!'

"'Yes, of you, little witch. You are the cause of his absence, you have robbed me of my brother; read, read, and return it quickly.'

"Nothing of what this meant could I comprehend; but, beginning to read, was soon better instructed. The poor youth had spoken to his sister of sentiments which I neither suspected nor could return, and for which I was much afflicted, and, therefore, would not have read beyond the first page. But, Oh! what a pleasure was I about to deprive myself of! My friend obliged me to go on, and I turned over with vexation and sorrow. Scarcely had I cast my eyes on this second page before I saw, at the bottom, a name!—a name!—Oh! how instantly did grief give way to pleasure, to joys the most extatic! It was the name so dear to my heart, so ever present to my thoughts; yes, it was the name of Lindorf; *the Baron of Lindorf, Captain of the Guards.*

"No deception is there; it is he, he himself,[a] and already have I read every syllable, have uttered a hundred exclamations, have pressed the letter to my lips, to my bosom, and have wept and laughed as if I had had no witness of my raptures, folly, and frenzy. Looking up, however, and seeing the astonished air of Mademoiselle de Manteul, I ran into her arms, and hid my emotion in her bosom. Gently raising, she asked me what it meant. 'Matilda!' said she; 'my dear Matilda! Why are you thus overjoyed? What is it that thus can agitate you?'

"'Ah! read, read—read yourself,' said I, pointing to a certain passage in the letter; 'this will be my explanation;' and while she read, again I hid my face in her bosom.

"'I have had the happiness,' said M. de Manteul to his sister, 'to meet with the Baron of Lindorf, at Hamburg, a captain of the Prussian guards, and hope we shall become intimate friends. We have been shipmates together, and lodge in the same house. We are seldom asunder, our tempers and dispositions accord wonderfully, for he, like me, is melancholy, apt to be absent, and regrets his country. Without being his confidant, I dare pronounce his heart is not more free than mine.'

"'Ah!' exclaimed I, raising my head and joining my hands, 'it is not true, then, that he loves an English lady, or that he has been six months married! My heart told me it was not!'

"'But who, who are you speaking of? Do you know this Baron of Lindorf?'

"'Do I know him!'

"'Ay, do you know him? Do you love him?'

"'Love him! Better than life! Beyond all thought!'[24]

"And thus, from question to question, Mademoiselle de Manteul became the confidante of all my secrets, and fully informed of my situation. I related your friendship, my dear brother, with Lindorf, and your desire to see us united, but, as one must always reserve a little of one's wealth for one's self, I did not tell her that you had changed your opinion; though I let her know my doubts and fears concerning Lindorf, which her silence seemed to confirm. Yet was it possible, and I endeavoured to persuade myself it was true, that the difficulty of conveying his letters to me was the reason why I received none. My brother was no longer in his interest; he, no doubt, knew it, and that *melancholy*, that *absent air*, his *regrets for his country*, and his *enslaved heart*, had each made its impression, and reanimated all my hopes.

"My friend had listened with an evident concern, and, when I had ended, affectionately kissing me, said, 'My poor, dear Matilda, why did you not tell me all this sooner? How great would have been the pleasure of the confidence you have refused me!'

"'I feared lest you should take the part of young de Zastrow.'

"'Me! Oh, no!—So far from that I perfectly approve your resistance, and am only afraid lest you should yield at last.'

"'Never! Never!—While I live, never will I love man but Lindorf!'

"'Add, also, none other you ought to love; for, in reality, you are as much betrothed as if actually married, and to espouse another would be guilt, perjury.'

"'It would, it would!'

"'But what is Lindorf doing in England?'

"'Alas! I know not; cannot comprehend. I have not heard from him these six months!'

"'And why do you not write?'

"'I have written.'

"'And where is your letter?'

"'In my pocket-book.'

"Mademoiselle de Manteul burst into a laugh. 'It must produce wonderful effects,' said she, 'while it remains there. Oh! what a child you are! Give me your letter, and your lover shall have it in a week.'—How did I kiss Mademoiselle de Manteul!—And yet her brother's love of me somewhat damped my joy; though I admired his sister's goodness, thus to sacrifice his interests to mine. I was even fearful of abusing it, and shewed some hesitation. — 'The task,' said she, 'I own, is a little cruel; but we must cure him, and this I think will be an infallible means. Give me the letter.'—And soon the letter was taken from my pocket-book and in her hand: It was sealed.—'You positively promise, my friend,' said she, as she received it, 'to be only Lindorf's; never to marry de Zastrow.'

"'Positively! Positively!'

"'Very well, that will set my conscience at ease; for I now shall be serving a persecuted, married pair. Leave the management of every thing to me. We must gain time till you can receive an answer, and take care to leave me with the young Baron, as often as possible. I will flatter and coax him, and thus relieve you from the pain of practising deceit.'

"'Oh! I cannot deceive. I have always told him, and always shall tell him, I will love none but Lindorf.'[a]

"'And what is his answer?'

"'That he has no faith in eternal constancy.'

"'He has not! I understand him. But we will prove what women are capable of; shall we not, my dear Matilda?'

"I most sincerely promised we would, and left her, more than ever determined on unshaken constancy and resistance."

Walstein, here, smiled; and whispered something to Lindorf, which the latter returned with like significance. The ladies, and especially Matilda, desired to know what they said.—"Oh! I promise you, you shall know by and by; but go on, my dear girl, with your story. You were telling us of the tender friendship of Mademoiselle de Manteul."—"I was," replied Matilda, with ardour; "and never, perhaps, was friendship like hers; as you would have said, had you heard her speak, seen her eagerness, and her zeal. You would have supposed the secret hers, and that her happiness, not mine, was at stake. Every means did she take to increase my fortitude. I might, perhaps, have suspected myself; but my friend was five and twenty, was therefore prudent, and, certainly, would not give me ill counsel. Determined, therefore, with all possible obstinacy, not to yield, I waited, but not with dread, for the answer of Lindorf; persuaded he would tell me truth, and, if I found I was no longer beloved, my resolution was taken."

"Why, what would you have done?" said Caroline, with vivacity.

"Every thing I could to have forgotten him; but, at the same time, have kept the vow I made, never to marry, never to trust a perfidious sex, capable of loving twice."

This was very innocently said, but it was a dagger to the feeling heart of Caroline. She blushed excessively, cast her fine eyes on the ground, half looked up at Walstein, and, as instantly, again, looked down. He saw her charming confusion, enjoyed it for a moment, tenderly kissed her hand, then, addressing himself to Lindorf, said, "You, my friend, no doubt, approve Matilda's mode of thinking, and, perhaps, you are right; but each person has his opinion. I think nothing can be more flattering than to be the second object of the attachment of a delicate and tender heart; and I should think this attachment more durable, and more certain, than that of a heart that never had occasion to suspect and be aware of itself."

"How!" exclaimed Matilda; "does my brother Walstein preach inconstancy?"

"I do not think a second passion deserves the name, and I only admit of being twice in love."

"Aha! No oftener?"

"No, certainly; no oftener," said Caroline, faintly, and pressing the hand of Walstein to her bosom.

"Well, for my part," replied Matilda, "I find the first time once too often, and that women are very silly creatures ever to love, since love has so many pangs for them and so few for the men. Here was this good gentleman amusing himself, in all tranquillity, at London, while I was scolded, persecuted, and despairing from morning till night"—(Lindorf with a look petitioned mercy; Matilda smiled and continued.)[25] —"I found myself, however, much less unhappy since I had gained a friend, to whom I might tell all my griefs; and this friend was so kind, understood so well all my feelings, approved so highly of my love and constancy, and spoke so well of Lindorf, and so ill of de Zastrow, that my obligations were infinite. Nay she was even complaisant enough to admit his visits and endure his conversations, for whole hours, to serve me, and advised me to invite him to come on those evenings I was to visit her. 'That will be the means of amusing him and not exposing yourself,' said she; 'and, likewise, of pleasing your aunt. I promise never to leave you; for, indeed, there is nothing I would not do to serve you.'

"My aunt now became very good humored, teized me no more, and I hoped, thus, to gain time; but it is now three days since she brought me two large sheets of paper, commanded me to read them, sign which I pleased, and left me in utter astonishment. They seemed like two large contracts! And was I then permitted to chuse between Lindorf and de Zastrow? Such for a moment were my hopes; but I soon saw they both related to the odious de Zastrow, whom I hated more and more. One of them was what I had suspected, a marriage contract with him, to which nothing was wanting but my signature, and by which I was made heiress to my aunt. The other was a deed of conveyance of this inheritance to the Baron de Zastrow, should I refuse to sign the first. Oh! how happy was I thus to be left to my choice! How instantly did I sign the conveyance, and run with it, joyously skipping, into my aunt's apartment! Her nephew was with her. 'There, there, there!' said I; 'it is done; I have signed it, most willingly.' Young de Zastrow, as vain and self-sufficient as ever, had not the least doubt but it was the marriage contract, and, kneeling, returned me a thousand thanks for my condescension. 'I am quite delighted, Sir,' said I, laughing, 'to see you so pleased, though, really, you owe me no thanks, I not having the least merit, for I have only followed my own inclinations.'

"His transports now redoubled, and I was malicious enough to repeat, with great solemnity, 'Yes sir, I assure you I have wholly followed my inclination—to remain free—beside, my aunt has a right to bestow her benefactions where she pleases; nor have I ever wished to enjoy wealth which seems to be put in competition with the greatest of earthly blessings, the right of bestowing my heart and hand.'

"Imagine the look and manner of de Zastrow as he rose—My aunt saw which paper it was I had signed, and her eyes spoke her feelings; but, before she had time to give them utterance, I fell, and, kissing her hands again and again, said, 'My dear, dear aunt, do not be angry; every thing is well as it is; neither mention marriage nor an inheritance which I never desired, nor ever once thought of; only let this contract be destroyed;' (as I said this I tore it in a thousand pieces) 'leave the deed of gift in the possession of my cousin de Zastrow; men have more occasion for riches than we have, and I covet nothing but your friendship, the friendship of my brother, and the love of Lindorf, or, at least, the liberty of loving him all my life. The Baron de Zastrow will find many women who will be proud to be distinguished by him, and who will not be in love with Lindorf; who, therefore, might afford him that happiness I cannot; and, when you should see your poor Matilda lying dead of a broken heart, who, then, could restore her to you?'

"I thought my aunt seemed affected and was about to yield to my entreaties for she tenderly raised me, pressed my hand, and, turning towards de Zastrow said, 'you hear her, nephew, what do you think?'—De Zastrow was striding furiously about the chamber. 'Think, madam,' answered he, with a tragic terror in his voice and features, 'I cannot think. Death or Matilda must be mine!' At the same moment he drew his sword; yes, I assure you, he drew his sword, and seemed determined to kill himself. I sprang to him and seized his arm; my aunt cried out like a person expiring, and said she was *very very ill!* I knew not which of them to attend, nor could I calm either, till I promised to do every thing they pleased; while I myself was so much agitated, and terrified, that I scarcely could utter these few words, which, however, produced an astonishing effect. The sword was in its scabbard again, my aunt came to herself, kissed me, caressed me, and earnestly begged me immediately to sign.

"Luckily for me, however, I had prevented all signing for that night; as the torn contract, scattered about the floor, informed them. It was, therefore, deferred till the morrow; but they required me to renew my promise. The moment my terror was gone, I shuddered at what had passed, and at the engagement I had entered into without knowing what I did; and when I was desired to confirm this engagement I was so much affected that I fainted away. They were obliged to carry me into my chamber, and lay me on a bed; the motion somewhat brought me to myself, for, though I could not speak, I heard what they were saying. They thought me still in a fit, and my aunt said to the Baron, 'Do not be alarmed, nephew, this will soon be over; we have terrified her a little too much, but the greatest difficulty is conquered, she has promised; to-morrow she shall sign, the next day you shall marry her, and her brother may then say what he pleases. At present we must leave her undisturbed'—After which they quitted the chamber, recommending me to the care of my woman.

"Oh! what infinite matter was here for reflection, when I came perfectly to myself; which this contributed to effect! I considered and re-considered every word, nor was there one that did not give either surprise, anger, fear, grief, and even joy. I presently dismissed my attendant—*We have terrified her a little too much!* repeated I. And so they have been playing a scene, in which I have been the dupe of the comedy! A trick, concerted between my aunt and this self-killing cousin, to obtain my consent!—I despised the artifice, and, from that moment, held myself free; yet I shrunk back with horror when I recollected *She has promised; to-morrow she shall sign, and the next day you shall marry her*—'No; I will die, first,' repeated I. What followed gave me a ray of hope. *Her brother may then say what he pleases—We shall no longer fear him.* 'So they stand in awe of this dear brother, then, whom I thought in the interest of my persecutors, but he is not! They have deceived me in that too; and I still have a protector, a friend, who will not forsake me.'—Alas! in my joy of having again this friend, this good brother, I forgot how far distant we were, and that the next day my fate was to be determined.

"I remained thus, agitated by a thousand different thoughts, when Mademoiselle de Manteul entered. The moment I saw her, I held out my arms, and, weeping, exclaimed, 'Oh! come, come to the assistance of your wretched friend!' Yet little did I imagine all her friendship was capable of performing! She was as pale, trembling, and affected as I myself—'I know every thing,' said she; 'I have just left your aunt. What have you done, Matilda? You have promised to marry de Zastrow.'

"'He was going to kill himself.'

"'Kill himself, silly girl, men are not so ready to kill themselves. But what do you mean? Do you intend to keep this fatal promise? Do you recollect all those you have made to Lindorf?'

"'Ah! can you think I have forgot them?' passionately, answered I. 'No; they are all engraved on my heart, and ere they are effaced they shall tear that heart from my bosom! Yet, what am I to do? How may I free myself from this detested marriage? Speak, tell me, dear friend; can you imagine any means of delay till I write to my brother, till he can return and protect me? For, from what I have just heard, that I now am sure he will. Oh! if he were not in Russia, I know what I would do.'

"'Why, what would you do?' said Mademoiselle de Manteul, who seemed deep in thought; 'what would you do?'

"'I would escape; fly to him for safety.'

"'And have you the courage?' said she. 'How I admire you, my young friend! This is, in reality, the sole means left. I myself thought of it, but durst not make the proposition.'

"'Alas!' answered I, 'the thing is impossible; my brother is in Russia. I never shall find the means of going thither.'

"'I own it is difficult; but have not you a maternal uncle in London?'

"'I have; my Lord Seymour.'

"'Suppose you were to put yourself under his protection?'

"'What! fly to England and Lindorf there! Can you imagine—'

"'No; I should not have imagined that would have been a reason to avoid England.'

"'Ah! my dear friend,' said I, shaking my head, 'if you have no other proposal but this to offer I am undone. Rather would I go to Russia, impossible as it is, and seek an asylum from my brother, than to act with such imprudence.' I spoke this with so firm a tone that she offered no reply, but asked me what it was *I just had heard*. I then repeated my aunt's conversation, and, suddenly interrupting me, she exclaimed, 'If they have deceived you in one respect they may have in another, and, it is my firm opinion, your brother is not in Russia, for I recollect to have heard something as well as you—I will go immediately to your aunt, and, if I am not mistaken, presently discover the truth. We then shall know what we have to do.'

"She went, and it was not long before she returned. Pleasure sparkled in her eyes. 'I was right in my conjecture,' said she, as she entered; 'they have imposed upon you; your brother is at Berlin, married to a lovely lady; his letters have been intercepted, he is soon coming to Dresden, but they are determined to marry you, with or without your consent, before his arrival. To-morrow you will be forced to sign the contract: nay, they will even guide your hand, if you will not sign it willingly, and the day following you are to be married. All this has your aunt told me in secrecy. *My niece has promised*, said she, *and she shall keep her promise.*'

"'Oh! my God! my God!' cried I, 'what shall I do? And you tell me these things with apparent pleasure.'

"'Why, I really thought it would please you to hear your brother is at Berlin, and that you may, if you please, free yourself from their tyranny.'

"'Perhaps I might—but—'

"'But—What, and is all your courage gone so suddenly?—Ah! poor Matilda; I perceive you never will have the resolution to remain firm. Lindorf has got your letter, is returning, or, perhaps, returned; and what will he say when he shall find you are married?'

"'Cruel friend!' replied I, with chagrin; 'is this your consolation?'

"'What would you have me say to a feeble and timid child, who does not know her own mind? Those evils we want the fortitude to rid ourselves of we must endure; and I can assure you that, in two days, if you are at Dresden, you will be the Baroness de Zastrow.'

"'Never, never,' answered I, with enthusiasm—'Never shall that hated name be mine, I will prove that this feeble and timid child has more resolution than you suspect; nay, has enough to face even death itself.'

"'Die! pshaw! Who would die, when they may live, and live happily?'

"'I see no means; it is impossible. I cannot go by myself to Berlin. I should lose myself a thousand times; neither should I ever have the strength to get thither.'

"Mademoiselle de Manteul could not forbear laughing—'Poor girl! And so you thought I meant to send you to Berlin alone, and on foot, a fugitive heroine, in disguise, no doubt, with a bundle in your hand, and a large straw hat tied under your chin, beneath which should be discovered a certain dignified and noble air, which some piteous[26] stage-coachman perceiving should give you a place on the box.[27] This, no doubt, would be vastly clever and interesting, but the way I mean to propose is much less dangerous and more simple. One of my former maids is married to the post-master of the city. She is entirely devoted to me, and her husband will not only furnish a chaise and horses but drive you himself; will accompany you till you get safe to your brother, and, if you please, you may now escape, and wait at their house till you set off. You have your choice to do this or marry de Zastrow; for there is no alternative; you must determine for the marriage or the elopement; and, if you let the moment slip, it will be impossible for me to serve you.'

"'My choice is made,' said I, instantly; 'and, sure, I am most fortunate in a friend. I will fly to my brother, who will protect me for my Lindorf—And yet it is a great crime to deceive my aunt.'

"'Your aunt thinks it none to deceive you, most unworthily.'

"'But suppose I were to try, once more, to move her'—

"'Your trial would be vain. Tears, prayers, persecutions, and even faintings, are expected, which, far from being moved at, they perhaps will profit by.'

"'I will be gone,' cried I; 'neither scruples nor remorse shall stay me. I am shamefully treated, and I have no longer any other inquietude than that which the fear of escaping in safety gives.'

"'Nothing is easier. Take my gown, cloak, and veil; they will suppose it me, and leave me to follow you. Wait for me at our house, I will presently be with you.'"

"Mademoiselle de Manteul is not very scrupulous," said the Count, smiling. "You cannot imagine half her zeal," continued Matilda. "I myself was incapable of either acting or thinking; but she, in a moment, got every thing ready, helped me to put on my disguise, opened the door, kissed me, pushed me forwards, and said, 'Go, go, dear Matilda; you have not a moment to lose: they may be coming here the next minute, perhaps; fly, or farewell all hope.' Fear gave me courage, and I had got to the bottom of the staircase when I recollected I ought to write a note, and leave it on my table, for my aunt; that she might be certain, at least, I was not dead. I returned, and Mademoiselle de Manteul, terrified at seeing me, thought I had met some one on the stairs. Scarcely had I begun to tell her what brought me back before she interrupted me. 'You are mad,' said she! 'Write a letter! Give your aunt time to come and catch you! She told me she was coming up presently—Begone, begone! They are not so easily to be persuaded people are going to kill themselves as you are!'

"The fear of being caught made me compliant, and I got out without being perceived. I had not far to go, nor was long before my friend came to me. 'We have a whole hour to take our measure in,' said she; 'they think you are asleep and I advised them to leave you in peace at present. The first thing you have to do, therefore, is to go to the post-house; for, should they find you absent, they will come to seek you here immediately. You will there remain in safety. If you want any money I can assist you.'

"Thanks to your goodness, my brother I did not want this kind of assistance. My friend, therefore, went with me to the mistress of the post-house, who consented to every thing she proposed, and with whom she left me. It was very probable they would come to seek me at the house of Mademoiselle de Manteul, and, therefore, necessary she should be at home to avoid suspicion.

"No sooner was I alone than I began to be deeply affected at the terror of my aunt, when she found me gone, and was wholly ignorant what was become of me. Disobedience and flight were sufficient offences, and needed not aggravation. I, therefore, resolved to repair them, as far as was in my power, and, having called for pen, ink, and paper, wrote nearly thus.

"'I have just been informed, my dear aunt, my brother is at Berlin, and am so impatient to see him that I have gone without asking a permission which, in all probability, would have been refused, and have thus spared myself the regret of a denial and again being disobedient. I am already sufficiently afflicted for having displeased you by my resistance to your will. Ah! why, my dear aunt, have you forced me thus to displease, thus to refuse compliance, thus to fly from you? How happy should I have been could I have contributed to your felicity! The Baron de Zastrow must have sufficient delicacy to feel that a promise, extorted by terror and disowned by the heart, is not binding. I hope he will no more think of killing himself, for I am no longer there to catch his arm; I would earnestly advise him to live, and, above all, to live happy without Matilda.'

"I gave this note in charge to one of the landlady's children, and bade him deliver it to the porter, without saying who it came from. More at ease, now I thought my aunt would be so too, I waited with tolerable patience for Mademoiselle de Manteul, who had promised to see me again before I set off, and who, at length, came.

"'You have not a moment to lose,' said she, 'you must depart at day-break; the Baron is searching you through every house in town; he has just left ours, and I encouraged him to continue this search, which will give you time to get the start. It was exceedingly lucky you did not write, as your silly whim would have made you.'—I durst not confess I just had wrote, but now felt my imprudence, and the fear of being pursued was so strong that I was unwilling to go.

My friend employed all her eloquence to encourage me; she described the anger of my aunt, the necessity I should be under of confessing where I had been, and who had assisted me, the ascendant which my elopement and return would give her over me; told me there would be no possibility of appeasing but by obeying her, and that, if ever I entered her house again, she was certain I should be married within two hours—'I will go,' said I; 'I will go instantly; the die is cast, and, be the event what it will, I will go;' and accordingly orders to get the chaise and horses ready were immediately given. Mademoiselle de Manteul, fearing I again should relapse, would not leave me. She was under no apprehensions about her father, whose gout kept him at home; she sent him word that she should sup out, and remained with me till the moment of departure. Of de Zastrow, of my brother, of Lindorf, of every thing that might encourage me to keep my resolution, she spoke. 'Depend on me,' said she; 'I will go, in the morning, to de Zastrow, and lead him to suspect you are flown to England. He shall not easily get away from me, and by that time you will be so far on the way to Berlin that all pursuit will be in vain.' This gave me a little confidence; or, rather, it was now too late to listen to fear. To recede was no longer possible, and I beheld the moment of departure arrive with pleasure. Unable to express my gratitude, except by my kisses and tears, while my friend was enraptured to see me, as she said, escape so many dangers, I got into the chaise and—"

"Alone!" interrupted the Count.

"No; the mistress of the house, who is now with me, and who, formerly, as I said, had served Mademoiselle de Manteul, whose husband conducted us"—

"But where is Lindorf?" replied the Count, again stopping her short. "It seems that Mademoiselle de Manteul, not he, has carried you off."

"And did you think it was Lindorf?"

"I own, I am glad to find it was not; though there seems something incomprehensible in all this!"

"A little patience, brother, and you will not hereafter judge of your Matilda from appearances.

"And now, behold me in the post-chaise, with the good Marianne, for that is her name; escorted by her husband, on horse-back, stopping only to change horses, tossing ducats[28] into the postillions hats, and taking each bush for the Baron de Zastrow. My companion did all she could to inspire courage. Mademoiselle de Manteul was her oracle, and she, every minute, repeated 'there was nothing to fear, for Mademoiselle had told her so.' These assurances made me more tranquil; and, having travelled the first day without interruption, I thought myself in perfect safety. Just, however, as we came yesterday to the post-house I, very imprudently, put my head out of the carriage, and presently heard a voice, I thought I knew, cry, 'It is she! It is she herself! Postillion! Stop! On your life stop!' And I presently saw young de Zastrow, at the side of the chaise, with a thousand menaces in his countenance."

"De Zastrow!" cried the Count and Caroline.

"Yes; De Zastrow, and without the help of witchcraft. What you suppose some malicious fairy has winged him through the air. Nay, to say the truth, I supposed so myself, at first; but alas! I soon found this good for nothing fairy was neither more nor less than my own imprudence. The note I had written had indicated the road I should take, and the Baron had not lost his time in further search at Dresden. He supposed I had, no doubt, written it in the carriage, and that, by setting off immediately, he should easily overtake and bring me back; and this supposition made him depart two or three hours before me. I imagined myself pursued while, on the contrary, I was full speed pursuing, and, unfortunately enough, overtook him at this post-house, where he was waiting for horses. How great must have been the surprise of my dear friend, Mademoiselle de Manteul, when she found, in the morning, he was gone! And how excessive her inquietude and fears for me! At present, however, I hope she is easier."

"Yes, yes," said the Count, smiling, "she is easy enough, never fear. But go on with your story, it is quite romantic."

"Romantic, indeed! I assure you, I think it a very extraordinary story! But we are not half at the end of it yet—Let me see—The terror, fright and consternation, at the sight of de Zastrow. Yes; yes; I was there—Well, then, I shrieked, and hid myself in a corner of the chaise, while Marianne screamed to the postillion to go on; de Zastrow threatened and bad him stop, his servants came up, and the croud increased. Something must be done, and I thought it best to speak to the Baron, to ask him by what right he interrupted me, or pretended to deprive me of my liberty, and to tell him, openly, I would rather die than either marry him or return to Dresden. Accordingly I again looked out of the chaise, and there I saw—!

"Now, if you please, you may talk of witchcraft, fairies, and romances; any thing, or every thing, you can suppose miraculous and inconceivable; for there did I see—Lindorf! Yes, Lindorf himself; who, instead of in England,[a] was there, beside the chaise, as much astonished as myself—'Matilda!'—'Lindorf!'—These exclamations were mutual and instantaneous, and I really believed heaven had sent him to my succour; therefore, leaping out of the chaise—

"I cannot go on," said Matilda, "you must finish the story, Lindorf; you know the remainder better than I do." Then, with her head reclined on the shoulder of Caroline, she whispered, "I hope he will not tell how I sprang into his arms and clasped him in mine with all my strength."

"Aye, aye, let me conjure thee, dear Lindorf, to go on," said the Count, impatiently; "prithee, explain by what strange chance thou camest, just at that precise moment, on the Dresden road, and in company with the Baron de Zastrow."

"I had returned," said Lindorf, "to answer, in person, the charming, the tender letter I had received at London. My being there at this moment was accidental, but I was not in company with the Baron de Zastrow. It was chance, or, rather, my guardian genius[29] that brought me to the post-house just then. I was unacquainted with the Baron, but I saw a young man of quality, impatient to obtain horses, and quite furious because none were to be found. He enquired, at the same time, if a young lady, whom he endeavoured to describe, had not lately passed that road. They answered, no, and he again began to swear it was false, she must have passed; and again to bestow his curses on the postillions and the postmaster. As soon as I alighted from my chaise, for I was going to Dresden, he came up, and said, 'you, certainly, Sir, must have met a young lady, alone, very handsome, driving full speed!'[a]

"'No, Sir, I assure you, I met no such lady; nor, indeed, any lady that I remember.'

"'This is very extraordinary!' said he, stamping—'Perhaps the note was a new trick!—Excuse me, Sir, for questioning you so abruptly. I am pursuing a woman I adore, who promised me her hand yesterday, was to have married me to-day, and who eloped last night!'

"'The misfortune is the greater,' answered I, 'Sir, because you do not seem that kind of person the ladies would fly.' My compliment seemed to please him, and acquired me his entire confidence. He bowed, and with much self-sufficiency, which he endeavoured to render modest, replied, 'I own, Sir, it is not the first time I have been told so; and there have been ladies who have gone farther than telling; but you see how different tastes are; and, certainly, that of women is very often very capricious. Is it not quite extraordinary that her I am pursuing is yet not eighteen;[30] and that, notwithstanding, she has a whim of romantic fidelity for a lover who has forsaken her, and whom she will never see again? I am unacquainted with him, but should suppose personal accomplishments not infinitely in his favor; and, as to birth and fortune, in these I yield to no man.'

"'All this, Sir, I make no doubt, is true; but if your rival has the advantage of being beloved'—

"'Beloved or not beloved,' said he, 'it is equal to me; he is absent, will see her no more; if I can overtake her she is mine, and shall be obliged to adore me.'

"This conversation past before the post-house, and I was amazed at the facility with which this indiscreet and vain young man spoke to a stranger, as well as at his total want of delicacy, and silently approved the fugitive lady. Just then a chaise came up, full gallop, from Dresden, and interrupted us. He did not seem to have the least suspicion, and looked towards it from mere curiosity, till, the chaise stopping, a lady looked out. I had but a glimpse, and did not know it was Matilda, but my gentleman, instantly, exclaimed, 'It is she! It is she!' While the lady drew back, exclaiming, in her turn, 'It is he!' The maid bid the postillion drive on, while de Zastrow, with uplifted cane, threatened to knock him off his horse if he moved a step. I hesitated, for a moment, what part I should take. The frankness of the youth had, in some measure, laid me under an obligation; and yet I felt myself affected for the unfortunate lady, whom they were going to marry against her consent. My first intention was to become a mediator, if possible, and to inspire the terrified lady with fortitude, for which purpose I approached the chaise, far from imagining how deeply I myself was interested in this adventure. As I came up I heard my own name repeated in an accent of amazement! The door opened, and out flew Matilda, whom I instantly knew, notwithstanding the finished beauty, alteration, and growth, of her person! The charming Matilda placed herself by my side, took me by the hand, and said, in a voice which terror and joy had rendered faint, 'Dear, dear Lindorf! God has surely sent you to the assistance and defence of your Matilda! They want to rob you of her, but they never never shall! She will be yours, and yours only!'

"No sooner did the Baron hear my name than, throwing away his cane, drawing his sword, and arrogantly advancing, he exclaimed, 'Lindorf! What treachery is this?' Then, addressing himself to Matilda, said, 'I entreat, Mademoiselle, you will go into my post-chaise. I have the positive commands of your aunt to bring you back to Dresden, and I dare say the Baron of Lindorf will not think proper to oppose those commands.'

"'That we shall presently see, Sir,' answered I coldly, while I supported Matilda, whom so many contending passions had occasioned to faint in my arms. I gently carried her into the post-house and laid her on the first bed I found; then, recommending her to the persons present, telling them they should be answerable for her forthcoming, I immediately left her, and went in search of the Baron de Zastrow. I found him demanding entrance, and forcibly withheld by two or three men, who let him go the moment I appeared. We walked together to some distance, and went into an enclosed garden. 'You have accused me of treachery, sir,' said I, 'and appearances may give some small justification to the suspicion; but I assure you, on my honour, that chance, only, a most lucky one it is true, has brought me here. When I spoke to you, I was ignorant both that you were my rival and that Matilda had fled. If you think this sufficient satisfaction, and will leave the young Countess of Walstein absolute mistress of herself, I promise you to abide by her decision, and here offer you my future friendship and esteem; if not, I will defend my own pretensions and her liberty at the hazard of my life.'

"'Defend them, then, traitor,' replied he, attacking me with so much impetuosity that, being off my guard, I received a wound in the left arm. It was not dangerous, and only roused my anger; and the Baron took so little care, thinking himself certain of victory, when he saw me wounded, that I easily disarmed him. His sword flew out of his hand and, as it fell, I set my foot on it—'Your life,' said I, 'is now in my power; I am wounded and you are not; but, disregarding this small disadvantage, I am ready to restore your sword, and, again, put it to the chance of victory, if you do not renounce your pretensions to Matilda, and promise to depart for Dresden, immediately, without seeing her.'

"He hesitated, and I saw, by the change of his countenance, my manner of acting had made some impression. Pride still struggled, but honour, at last, was conqueror, and he presented his hand. 'Recollect,' said he, 'sir, you have, on these conditions, offered your esteem and friendship. I feel, at present, I shall be proud of and will, therefore, endeavour to merit them, by prevailing on my aunt to confirm that happiness which is justly your due. Forget the past, and make my peace with Matilda. I pretend only to her friendship; though,' added he, with a mixture of former self sufficiency, 'I am not accustomed to disdain; nor do I know by what fascination I so long have supported hers.' I embraced him, said she would certainly be the last cruel beauty he would find, and that, had not her heart been pre-engaged she could not possibly have resisted so many accomplishments and so much merit; after which we parted the best friends in the world.

"As soon as I saw him get into his chaise, I hastened to Matilda, concerning whom I was very uneasy. Her fainting, however, was most happily timed, since it deprived her of the knowledge of a transaction that might have occasioned dreadful terrors. She began to recover and, looking round her, asked where she was, as I entered; then, resuming all her accustomed grace, 'Dear Lindorf,' said she, 'and is it not a dream? Is it true that I have once more found thee, and that we never shall forsake each other again?'"

Scarcely had Lindorf finished his phrase e'er he felt the white hand of Matilda upon his mouth.—"Fie, fie, young gentleman," said she, "I see no occasion to repeat all that passed so literally. My dear brother, and my dear, dear sister, do not believe a word he says. For, what if I had thought all that, can you suppose I would have spoken my thoughts? And, even, if I did, you know I was fainting. Who can tell what they do after so strange a meeting, pressed by one lover, protected by another, and amongst rencounters and battles, and all this hurly burly? One may be allowed to be a little extravagant and silly, on such occasions; but, at present, I assure you, I am as prudent as"—Matilda smiled, with malicious pleasure, on Lindorf; then, suddenly clasping his hand, added, "Well then, I say again and again, every thing I said yesterday! And I hope we shall never forsake each other more!"

Matilda was so charming, as she said this, and there was such a mixture of rapture, pleasantry, and confusion in her countenance, that Lindorf imagined he loved her dearer than ever he had loved woman, and expressed himself with so much enthusiasm and fire that every body thought the same. Caroline was transported, she kissed the Count, and said, "Was I wrong when I told you how dearly he would love her?" Walstein beheld Lindorf with astonishment, nor yet could comprehend, perfectly, all he heard and saw. To reason and friendship he had attributed the attachment of Lindorf to Matilda; for well he recollected to

what excess he had adored Caroline; nor could imagine how a passion so energetic might so soon change its object. Yet was there every appearance of sincerity
in his manner, and words; and Lindorf was no hypocrite. Beside, the Count was
so accustomed to read his thoughts that, had he been under any real constraint,
it could not have escaped him, and he could observe nothing but sincerity.
Lindorf, on his part, guessed what was passing in the mind of the Count, and
whispered, "when we are alone, dear Walstein, you shall hear my story, and your
surprise will then not be so great. In the mean time, do not imagine your friend
has acquired a facility at feigning; or that he does not feel all he expresses." The
Count clasped his hand, and entreated Matilda to finish her story. There was
not much to say, but the least circumstance was interesting to the Count and
Caroline. Matilda replied, "You forget, brother, that Lindorf is the historian, at
present"—Lindorf thus continued.

"I found a village surgeon to dress my wound,[31] and hoped I might have
concealed it from Matilda, as well as my contest with the Baron. I, therefore,
only told her he had listened to reason, departed for Dresden, and promised
to appease his aunt. She was most happy at the intelligence, and, being equally
impatient to see our friend and brother, we presently departed. The motion of
the carriage, and, perhaps, the emotion of my heart, soon disturbed my wound,
and Matilda was greatly agitated when she saw the blood. It was impossible any
longer to conceal the cause, and we were obliged to stop here to dress it again. It
was found deeper than had been imagined, and I was condemned to take four
and twenty hours repose. In vain did I solicit my lovely partner to continue her
journey, and leave me in this wretched inn; no entreaties could gain her consent."

"No, to be sure," interrupted Matilda, with vivacity. "I know my duty better. Who ever heard of a heroine of romance abandoning her wounded knight,
who had defended her against a ferocious ravisher? I even thought it necessary,
according to custom, to dress that wound myself, and bathe it with my tears. Did
not I Lindorf? And I hope you will own I tied the scarf with tolerable grace. Was
not my attitude and manner affecting, brother?"

"The very picture of a princess of the age of Amadis."[32]

"No; one of the mistresses of the famous Galaor," said she, glancing at Lindorf.[33]

"It was the mistress, then, that fixed the rover," replied he, kissing her hand.

"So said Galaor to every mistress, and they believed him; but I," continued
Matilda, "am not so credulous, and mean to put your sincerity to the proof—In
those times, a woman, with vast *sang froid,* commanded her lover not to pronounce a single word for two years, and he obeyed.[34] Oh! happy age! I, though
I only shall impose rest and silence on my wounded hero till to-morrow, am
certain to find him disobedient!"

"Never, never," said Lindorf kneeling; "and there will be some merit in my
submission, for I have many things to tell my Walstein."

"And so you would have passed a whole night in chattering, mean while the fever and the wound—I reiterate my absolute command!—Silence and rest till to-morrow!"

Exact obedience was promised, though not without reluctance. The friends were both impatient to communicate their sentiments; and, particularly, the Count, who was doubly interested to find the heart of Lindorf cured of passion for Caroline, and capable of making Matilda happy. It was, therefore, agreed that, in recompense for this their silence, they should travel, on the morrow, in the chaise of Lindorf, and leave the coach of the Count to the ladies. This arrangement was equally acceptable to Caroline, who was herself most desirous the friends should mutually explain their feelings, that Walstein might be convinced of the exact truth of all she had told him, and inform Lindorf of her present love for her husband. Matilda, perhaps, might have preferred the care of her wounded knight; but Matilda dared not say so; and her brother having mentioned sending his servant to Dresden, with letters for his aunt, she also retired to write, both to her and Mademoiselle de Manteul, to whom she sent back the servants and chaise.

She presently returned with her two letters. The Count read that to Madam de Zastrow, approved it, added a few lines from himself, and, perceiving Matilda concealed the one she had written to Mademoiselle de Manteul, said, smiling, "I suppose you express your gratitude in strong terms to your zealous friend."

"I express it as I feel it; and, I think, that is saying a great deal. You, who are one of the heroes of friendship, ought, certainly, to be delighted to find such an instance of its effects; especially in a woman."—The Count continued to smile.—"And pray now, what is the meaning of that ironic air? What, you are incredulous?—Sister Caroline, I hope you will take the part of the sex."

"We will both take its part," answered Caroline, "and prove how capable women are of friendship."

"I never doubted it," replied Walstein; "nay, I even believe that pure disinterested friendship is less rare among women than it is supposed. It is a sensation wholly accordant to their gentle and tender nature; but you will forgive me for not imagining Mademoiselle de Manteul one of its models."

"Brother!—After so many proofs!"

"I am almost sorry, dear Matilda, to rob you of that happy credulity which so well proves the innocence of your heart; but, I must own, I have very strong doubts concerning those proofs.ª Mademoiselle de Manteul appeared greatly affected; but was it for you or for herself? Was it to serve a friend or to get rid of a rival? Every circumstance, I think, bespeaks the latter."

Matilda was confounded. A thousand little incidents were recollected, and a thousand others rushed forward to prove her brother was right; yet could she not instantly give her up, and replied, with vivacity, "Surely you must be deceived, she dislikes, nay, detests the Baron; she was always speaking ill of and turning him to ridicule."

"Right, right; to augment your repugnance. This is the very cause why I say she is not a true friend. Had Mademoiselle de Manteul, the victim of an involuntary passion, opened her heart to you, and given you secret for secret; had you together concerted the means of avoiding a marriage that must render you both unhappy, I should have faith in her friendship, and even be far from blaming her; but all this artifice at her age is odious: she only had herself in view by prompting you to an imprudent step, which the event has justified, but which might have been your destruction."

Lindorf, here, took up the subject. "You are too severe, dear Walstein; be the motives of Mademoiselle de Manteul what they may, she has served me so essentially that it becomes me to undertake her justification, and I see nothing in all this but artifice which may well be permitted to love; besides, while she was serving herself, she was, also, saving her friend from inevitable misfortune."

"No doubt," said Matilda, who took courage at seeing herself supported; "for, one day longer, and I had been forced to marry that odious Baron."

"And do you not perceive, my dear girl, that, I being on the road, one day longer and you had been for ever freed from tyranny, without that violence which is ever prejudicial to a young lady's reputation, and without offence to an aunt to whose cares you are certainly much indebted? Your only error, dear Matilda, was that of suspecting my friendship; of supposing, for an instant, I could abandon you; and of blindly confiding in an imprudent young lady, though, I own, she is rather to blame than you."

"Dear, dear brother," cried Matilda, all in tears, and running into his arms; "pardon us both. Ah! how do I reproach myself for having mentioned, for having given you an ill opinion of her! But so far was I from suspecting it, that I supposed you would admire her conduct and her zeal."

Lindorf joined Matilda, and chid his friend for his severity. Caroline clasped Matilda to her bosom, and, while she dried her tears, wept in concert—"Think not I wish ill to Mademoiselle de Manteul," said the Count, exceedingly affected. "No, to her I owe the happiness of beholding those I love united. So freely do I pardon her, that I sincerely hope she may marry de Zastrow, and will even speak in her behalf to my aunt. And now, Matilda, do thou pardon me for having afflicted thee, and undeceived thee. It will be a lesson to thee, my dear, and the last I shall ever give thee; for, from this moment, I commit thy conduct, and thy felicity to Lindorf. Thou knowest how ardently I have desired to see thee his. Oh! Caroline, Oh! my sister, Oh! my friend, scarcely can my heart contain its joys, the sweet sensations this happy moment brings!"

Matilda a thousand times thanked her brother for his sincerity, and for the instruction it contained; "though," said she, "I scarcely can repent my imprudence, since it has made us all happy a day sooner;" and added that she would, in a postscript, let Mademoiselle de Manteul pleasantly understand that, at present, she was acquainted with her motives.— The Count was not at all deceived in his conjectures, for Mademoiselle de Manteul had been solely prompted by her passion for the young Baron de Zastrow, who had paid her some attentions before he went on his travels, and who, she hoped, would have married her on his return. The arrival of Matilda at Dresden, the wishes of her aunt, the attachment of the young Baron to the amiable spouse destined him, all repelled hopes which the confidence of Matilda once more animated. She had only sought her friendship to have an opportunity of seeing the Baron revive his former sentiments, discover those of Matilda, and, if possible, turn them towards some other object. At first she had had her brother in view, and, therefore, had shewn Matilda his letter; but her joy was excessive when she learned this lover already existed, and that her young rival was determined on the most peremptory resistance. This it was her advantage to encourage all in her power; but this alone was not sufficient; the best means of obtaining her own end, she supposed, would be to remove Matilda from Dresden. This might best be done by engaging her to take some step which should absolutely break off the intended match. She it was who persuaded Madam de Zastrow, and her nephew, that, by terrifying Matilda, they might obtain her consent; and what the consequence of this terror and the success of her schemes were has already been seen. Yet was she but little benefited by her artifice, for the young Baron, recognizing, in the post-chaise, the former maid of Mademoiselle de Manteul, and being convinced she had favored Matilda's flight, was irritated at the perfidious trick that had been played him. But this perfidy was the consequence of affection; and when the vanity of man is flattered he is generally indulgent.

Return we to our happy travellers. The wound of Lindorf healed apace, so excellent a balsamic[35] is happiness, and they set off for Berlin; Caroline and Matilda in one of the carriages, and the two friends in the other. Leave we these lovely ladies to speak of those they held most dear, to congratulate each other, to form plans of future delight, and to vow eternal friendship. Leave we them frequently to look out of the carriage after the post-chaise that followed, wishing impatiently to arrive, and let us examine how Walstein and Lindorf passed their time.

They partook of the impatience we have mentioned; but man feels not so sensibly those short privations which are subjects of such real uneasiness to the tender heart of woman. Perhaps, on great occasions, the former may be more ardent, more passionate, more capable of risking every thing for the object of their love; but the daily proofs, the intervening fears, and all the shades of a delicate and constant passion, are much more peculiar to women; few men are susceptible of them, nay, few know their value. Our travellers, indeed, had not time to think of them; yet had they been in the chaise some time without entering into any conversation. They sat silent, for Lindorf knew not where to begin, or what to say to the husband of Caroline, and the Count feared lest the most trifling question might bear the aspect of reproach: he, however, was the first to speak, and told his friend how much he had been afflicted by reading the manuscript he had left with Caroline. "I have not the least fear or scruple," said he, "in confiding the happiness of a sister to the man to whom I am so infinitely indebted, and who, loving and beloved by the most angelic woman the world contains, could not only sacrifice his own passion, but endeavoured to inspire her with the love of another. Ah! dear Lindorf," said he, "while to you I owe the heart of Caroline and the felicity of Matilda, is it possible I ever can acquit myself of the wondrous debt? Yet, speak, explain how this sudden revolution in your affections, which yet I understand not, has happened. Is not all you testify for my sister another sacrifice of generous friendship? Endeavour not to impose upon yourself. Can Caroline—"

"Dear Walstein," interrupted Lindorf, instantly, "I would utter oaths if I did not know the word of your friend were sufficient. Believe that friend, then, when he assures you he is worthy of becoming your brother; and that nothing has he expressed that he has not felt. I love Caroline, no doubt, but it is as I love her husband, with friendship as pure and strong as it is durable; but I love my dear Matilda as the sole woman on earth who now can make me happy—You are surprised, but hear what I have to say. Learn what has passed in the heart you yourself have formed since last we parted."

The Count was most desirous to hear, and sat attentive while Lindorf thus continued.

"Since you have read my manuscript, Walstein, you are informed of my first acquaintance with Caroline, and what were the sentiments she inspired. I shall attempt no justification of myself. You can judge whether it be possible to see her with indifference. I protest, however, before heaven, that notwithstanding all her beauty, all her charms, she would have been totally indifferent to me had I had the least suspicion she was your wife. But this how might I have? You were silent; Caroline, then so young, bore not your name, and the good Canoness gave evident marks of wishing to see us united. Every circumstance told me she was free and that I might dare to love her—Oh! wherefore, my friend, that fatal reserve?—Yet let us pass this over. Ignorant in my guilt, I offended the man for whom I would willingly have sacrificed my life; he has seen some faint picture of my grief, my remorse and the resolution I took, the instant I discovered my crime, to fly. I thought I might, in some measure, repair the involuntary wrong I had done by shewing Caroline who and what the husband was she fled. I knew her soul congenial to yours, capable of estimating its worth, and that you were formed to admire and adore each other."

"It was thy noble friendship," exclaimed the Count, "which alone could draw me with such features and such colours as could affect the heart of Caroline.[a] Yes, dear Lindorf, to thee alone I owe that heart and all the exquisite felicity I enjoy. No, had it not been for that passion with which thou so continually reproachest thyself, Caroline, perhaps, never had loved me. But go on, dear friend, I long to be convinced thou art equally happy, and that thou thinkest Matilda a proper recompense for the sublime efforts thou hast made to conquer a passion which could dictate the manuscript thou leftest at Rindaw and banish thee from Caroline."

"I left her," replied Lindorf, "determined never to see her more, till, by wholly subduing my fatal passion, I were worthy her and you; and far was I from foreseeing this blissful moment was so near. The solitude of Ronebourg augmented my love and gloomy melancholy; incessantly did fancy transport me to the pavilion of Rindaw, incessantly was Caroline present. I saw her, heard her, conversed with her, and when the sweet illusion vanished, despair and remorse acquired additional strength, and they were tried to the utmost by your arrival and conversation. You loved Caroline, your happiness depended on being beloved by her, and again I renewed my vow of surmounting my passion; or, rather, of forsaking my country, and carefully concealing from you I had been your rival. This vow had been held sacred; never had the name of Caroline escaped my lips had not she, like an apparition, appeared at Ronebourg, the occasion of which I yet understand not, and deprived me of reason. Excuse me from describing all I felt while I thought I beheld her dying, but imagine what it must be when it could make me betray the secret of my heart, and inform you that a friend, towards whom you had acted with such magnanimity, was the guilty lover of your wife!

"My determination was to take vengeance on myself, and follow her whom I thought dead; but signs of returning life prevented me: she was restored to you, and I wished not to interrupt your happiness by the horrid spectacle of suicide. I went into my room, wrote the letter you found, mounted my horse, and rode full speed, without knowing whither I went, or taking so much as a single servant with me. The first day I suffered my horse to take which road he pleased, and, at night, stopped at a wretched inn; I endeavoured, however, to collect my ideas, and resolved to follow my first intention, which was to go to England. I had written to court and obtained permission for that purpose, my servant and baggage might soon follow, and I immediately took the road to Hamburg[36] where I meant to embark. I rode post day and night, and this continual change of scene corresponded with the agitation of my soul to which repose was insupportable. I wished to find a vessel ready to sail from Hamburg, and to step into it as I got out of my chaise; but, happily, there were none ready. Some hours after my arrival, I was seized with a burning fever, which lasted several days; the physician, whom my host called in, had me bled so abundantly that excessive weakness was the consequence,[37] and retarded my departure. Obliged to remain at Hamburg till I gathered strength, I wrote to my valet de chambre to come to me there. My sickness was the natural consequence of my feelings, and the fatigues of my journey, and was certainly a fortunate one. It calmed the violence of my transports, and obliged me to follow the plan I myself had laid down, as soon as I knew you to be the husband of Caroline.

"At present, when I no longer feel this weakness, I may own that more than twenty times on the road was I tempted to return to Ronebourg, and from your hand demand Caroline or death. Had I been obliged to remain at Hamburg without falling ill, perhaps, I should have been overcome, and for ever have rendered myself unworthy your esteem and friendship. My fever, and its consequent weakness, shewed me objects under a different point of view; and, whether the organization of the body influences the mind, whether it was the result of reflections incessantly made, or whether friendship really triumphed over love, certain it is my passion, each day, became feebler; or, rather, reason became stronger. I still adored Caroline, but I adored her as a deity, without daring to suppose I again might see her. I shuddered even at the idea, and, far from wishing to return, I wished to remove farther off, and therefore waited impatiently for Varner.

"Such was the temper of my mind when the young Baron de Manteul arrived at Hamburg, and came to lodge in the same hotel; my host immediately informed him of my illness, exaggerated the danger I had been in, the care he had taken of me, the slow recovery of my strength, and inspired him with a wish to become acquainted with me. He sent up his compliments, and, as his was a Saxon family well known, I received him with pleasure. His appearance gave me a favorable impression, which was confirmed by his conversation. He was equally pleased with me, and in a few hours we were old friends. He, likewise, was going to England, but could not stop more than three days at Hamburg: hearing I intended to cross the sea he earnestly entreated me to embark on board the same ship. My health, which daily grew stronger, permitted me to depart, and I willingly consented to a request by which I should gain such an agreeable companion. I left a letter of instructions for my valet with the host, and in two days we left Hamburg, mutually congratulating each other on this lucky rencontre: we further agreed to live together, at London, and take lodgings in the same house.

"This young gentleman was the more agreeable to me for being almost as melancholy as myself, and we often sighed in sympathy: he first made the remark. During the voyage we were alone on the deck, each absorbed in his own ideas, and each preserving the most profound silence. Manteul at length spoke; 'I think,' said he, 'I have discovered another conformity between us. Is it not true, dear Lindorf, that your heart is engaged, and that you deeply regret some person whom you have left in your own country?' I not choosing to give a direct answer, retorted the question on himself, and told him he had made the confession.

"'I own it,' replied he; 'and, did you know the person I regret, you, then, would have some knowledge of what my feelings are. When I quitted Saxony, I imagined I fled from the danger of loving the most charming woman in the world; but, now I see her no more, I feel the mischief is done, and that I fled too late.'

"I owned my heart was as much enslaved as his, but added nothing farther; I rather endeavoured to turn the conversation, by making reflections on the pangs and effects of love.

"We had a good voyage and arrived safe at London. The novelty of this vast city, its riches, the multitude of its inhabitants, and that peculiarity of manners which distance and a government so different produce,[38] greatly relieved my melancholy; and, as I most sincerely desired to be wholly cured of it, I myself ardently sought amusement. I recovered health and strength apace, and even a part of my natural chearfulness, yet did Caroline occupy my heart and thoughts, and, whenever I was alone, I found they turned wholly on her; but, as I dreaded the dangerous recollection, I took every possible means to remove it, and remained alone as seldom as possible. Manteul seldom left me; he found, each day, his attachment increase, and seemed to fear we should part too soon. He told me he had received letters from Dresden, which had lain at his banker's, waiting his arrival at London, that gave him vast pleasure. 'My return,' said he, 'may be much sooner than I supposed; but the event that will then call me back will be so happy a one I shall only have my friend to regret.' I could easily perceive he wished to open his heart to me, but that would have required a reciprocal confidence, and I was determined never to reveal my criminal secret, nor ever once to pronounce the name of Caroline; I, therefore, forbore to ask him who the object of his attachment might be, or to put any one question which might lead him to speak.[a]

"We had been presented, by our ambassador at London, to several English noblemen and, among others, we one day dined with the Earl of Salisbury. After dinner the toast went round, as you know, Walstein, is the custom in England, and the health of the favorite lady given by each guest. When the toast came to me, my heart named Caroline, and the word rose to my lips. I forbore, however, and begged they would excuse my naming the lady whose health I drank. They joked me on my great discretion, and drank to the health of the fair incognito.[b]

"'I shall not be so discreet as Lindorf,' said Manteul, when it came to his turn; 'I am proud to drink the health of Matilda, Countess of Walstein.'

"The name struck me so forcibly that I scarcely could believe what I heard real; but it was repeated round the table so often that I could no longer doubt it was that same Matilda by whom I had been so tenderly beloved, and whom I had so cruelly offended. It is impossible I should paint the agitation I was in; though, but a moment before, I should not have supposed any human power could have pronounced a name, except Caroline, that might have made an equal impression. Manteul sat too far off for me to ask whether it was Matilda whom he loved; yet, how might I doubt when I beheld his animated countenance, as he repeated, himself, and heard others repeat, her name? I looked and thought him handsomer than usual; he seemed to possess all the qualities of a lover, and, certainly, said I, he is beloved. The letters which gave him so much pleasure are,ᵃ certainly, from Matilda, and his quick return to Dresden, which is to render him so happy, is, also, as certainly, the consequence of her command: he is then to receive her hand whose heart he already possesses!

"These ideas ran in my mind all the afternoon, and accompanied me to the play, whither I was dragged in spite of myself. I wished immediately to have conversed with Manteul, to have learned his secret; reproached myself for having missed the opportunity, and feared lest it might not return; at last, my thoughts were so disturbed that,ᵇ finding myself uneasy in the play-house, where I neither heard nor saw, I determined to quit it and come home. I there waited the arrival of Manteul with an impatience wholly unaccountable to myself. It was not long before he came; my going had alarmed him, and scarcely did I give him time to tell me so, before I asked if the lady whose health he had drunk were the lady he loved, and if she were sister to the Count of Walstein, Ambassador in Russia.

"'Ay, certainly,' replied he, with transport 'she, she herself, your charming countrywoman!ᶜ Are you acquainted with her? It is some time since she left Berlin.'

"'I know her brother,' replied I, eluding his question. 'The Count of Walstein has been to me more than a friend; a father, a saviour,³² the man in the world most dear to my heart.'

"'Ah! dear Lindorf,' said Manteul, embracing me with rapture, 'if you are upon these terms with the Count of Walstein, I may owe all my future bliss to your friendship. She has often protested that her brother, alone, had a right to dispose of her hand; and to him you may speak for me; you may engage him to favor my passion.—Say, will you, Lindorf, will you?'

"'Doubt it not, my friend. Should Matilda, also, find this union that which her heart desires, I then will use all the power of my friendship with the Count to engage him in your interest. But I thought Matilda, in some measure, contracted to the Baron de Zastrow.'

"'Alas! it was that projected marriage which alone determined me to leave Dresden. I was the friend of de Zastrow, and would not become his rival. I, then, was ignorant how much Matilda disliked him; but the letter from my sister, which I found waiting my arrival here, informed me of it, and has given me the most flattering hopes.'

"'And had you none before you received that letter?'

"'None, none. Matilda never testified any thing more than esteem for me, and that friendship which I thought the consequence of her intimacy with my sister; she did not seem even to perceive how much I preferred her to every other woman. Before I left her I myself knew not the strength of my own passion; but my sister's letter, by making happiness possible, has made me feel how much I adore that lovely lady.'

"I most ardently wished to get a sight of this letter he mentioned, and my wish was gratified; he gave it me to read.—'Here, take it, my friend,' said he, 'and see if I have not some reason to flatter myself I am beloved.'—I accordingly took it and, with great emotion, began to read.

"Mademoiselle de Manteul blamed her brother for departing, not following her advice, and openly paying his addresses to the young Countess. The Baron de Zastrow had no right to be affronted; he was hated, and the marriage would never take place. Every thing, on the contrary, proved to her that her brother was beloved; she had remarked it before he left Dresden, and she now had not any doubt. Matilda was very sorry when she heard he was gone, she had even shed tears; her former chearfulness had forsaken her, 'and what convinces me,' said she, 'your absence causes her melancholy, is that it redoubles whenever England is mentioned. She yesterday said, in a pet which made her look more lovely, *I wonder why the men are all so eager to run to that good for nothing England!* This, brother, I should think a tolerably favourable symptom, and, if you want a still stronger, I must tell you she herself has begged me to show her your letters. Profit by this information. You have still time enough to repair the folly you have committed in leaving Dresden. Write me a letter, immediately; not by way of answer to this, but seem to confide the secret of your passion for my young friend to me; entreat me to sound her thoughts; say fear alone occasioned you to go, but that the least ray of hope will bring you back; she will read the letter in my presence: I shall see what impression it makes, and I dare believe the secret of her heart will not escape my penetration. I hope soon to give you more certain information which shall hasten your return.'

"This letter seemed to me a clear proof that Matilda loved young Manteul, and I felt a painful sensation, a spasm of the heart, which I could not account for, and which I endeavoured to conceal.[40] I returned the letter, and confirmed his hopes.—'I have written to my sister,' said he, 'exactly as she prescribed, and I impatiently wait her answer: if, as she thinks, it should be favourable, and if Matilda will permit me to aspire to the honour and happiness of making her mine,[a] you, dear Lindorf, may be serviceable to my interests with the Count, her brother. I may owe my felicity to you, and my friendship for you will thus be increased.'

"This I solemnly promised, but not without a sensation that seemed very like jealousy, which the description he gave of the lovely Matilda augmented. I could not deny I had often seen her before she left Berlin, and he added, 'You would not know her, Lindorf; no, you would not know her. You cannot imagine how much she is altered, how much improved. I know not whether it be possible to find a more beautiful woman; but a more graceful, a more charming one the world does not contain: she has every thing that can seduce and awe the heart. Her features have not a tame regularity; no, each has an expression peculiar to itself; her countenance is continually varying, and is the mirror of a most excellent heart, and a most amiable mind. Never long the same, she is playful, sportive, froward,ᵃ chearful, pretending to take pet, and laughing at the deception she has occasioned. She inspires joy and pleasure in all around her. At other times, mild, fond, and full of sensibility, she would melt the coldest or the hardest heart. Such I beheld her, every day; and how might I resist so many allurements; or what shall be my happiness should she become mine?'

"My secret regret for having wilfully cast this happiness from me was the answer my heart returned to Manteul. And had I!—had I been beloved by this charming lady! And did it once depend only on me to have made her for ever mine! Oh! how little had I merited a gift the value of which too late I knew! What! had she not a right to forget the man who repaid her affection with the blackest ingratitude; neglected, abandoned her, and, on the very first occasion, yielding wholly to the love of another, repelled the heart which fondly had bestowed itself on him, and obliged it to seek a mate more worthy?⁴¹—These ideas rapidly succeeded each other in my mind, and gave me an absent and gloomy air, at which Manteul might well have been surprised; but he was too much interested in the subject of the conversation to perceive it; was too desirous of continuing to speak of his dear Matilda, and his future hopes. It was not possible, however, for me to hear him unmoved; I, therefore, pretended I was not very well, and withdrew.

"No sooner was I alone than I began to inquire what my sensations were, and how I might feel this strange emotion concerning an event which I ought to have foreseen. Since I had not loved Matilda, since I had renounced her heart and hand, what were my rights? Ought I not to be happy that another had been more just, and made reparation for my wrongs? Alas! so far was I from being happy, from thinking thus, that it seemed as if Manteul bore away a treasure which appertained to me alone; nay I was inconsistent, unjust, enough to accuse Matilda of want of constancy, guilty as I myself had been! I recollected every circumstance of our acquaintance, those tender promises, so ingenuous, so often repeated in her letters, to love me, and me only, and exclaimed all women are inconstant; as if I myself had not been an example that men have, at least that I had, very little reason for these reproaches!

"I next reflected on the situation in which I stood with Manteul, and that folly which, a second time, had made me the rival of a friend. Yet durst I not allow myself to say I was his rival, but promised, if he were beloved, as every thing gave me reason to suppose, I would serve him with all the ardor of friendship: this I presently assured him of, and we waited, with equal impatience, the answer of his sister, which was to contain his sentence."

"Well, but Caroline? Is she wholly forgotten; already effaced from that heart where she had reigned with such unbounded sway?"

"From my own experience, Walstein, I am convinced the heart, when it absolutely loses hope, loses, in part, its pain; not, perhaps, in every instance, but in most; and, where love is the passion, whenever a new object is found, that, by any concurrence of circumstances, becomes interesting, the former is presently forgotten; at least, so far forgotten as not to be remembered with the same restless and tormenting sensations. I thought of Caroline, Countess of Walstein, but not of Caroline of Lichtfield, and was most happy to encourage the mutability;[42] my imagination no longer wandered in the gardens of Rindaw, or dwelt in the pavilion, but saw Caroline at Berlin, there in company with the best of husbands, and enjoying her felicity. Happy was I when thus I might remember her without remorse, and, whenever her name rose to memory, the name of my friend was, also, present; while that of Matilda, which Manteul was incessantly repeating, gave me an emotion, the origin of which I, who had had so much experience, could not mistake. Thus, my friend, you see my cure is far advanced; and you soon will learn in what manner I was perfectly restored.

"On our first arrival in England, we designed to have travelled through the different counties; but, supposing we should remain there all winter, intended to have deferred our journey till the spring. Manteul, determined to depart immediately, should his sister's letter recal him to Dresden, entreated me now to go with him and, at least, visit the most famous places. Since I had learned his secret I was ill at ease, and little inclined to rest long in one place. A journey, I imagined, would be some relief, and I willingly consented. We set off, therefore, passed through various counties, and a part of Wales, stopping to examine what was held most curious and interesting. This, dear Count, is not the moment to give you a description of a country where peace and liberty produce abundance, where the productive fields, cultivated by wealthy farmers, are not, like ours, the scenes of bloody battles, and all their direful attendants. Certain of finding them nourishment, the inhabitants fear not to marry and beget children. The towns, villages, and cities, are extremely populous, and every person seems happy; and, as the English nobility pass one part of the year at their country seats, where they contribute to the prosperity of their tenants, those beautiful country seats are built with an elegance, and preserved in a style of grandeur and taste, very different from the gloomy magnificence of our antique chateaus. If we wish to form an idea of the beauties of nature, and the inexpressible charms of a country life, we must go to England."

"You augment the wish I have to see that country," said the Count, "I intend to take my dear Caroline thither; but, till that happens, shall be glad of farther information."

"I know not whether I am capable of affording you any," replied Lindorf, "for we travelled with too much rapidity, and our hearts and minds were too much preoccupied, to remark the numerous things deserving notice. I have only just mentioned what must necessarily strike every foreigner who beholds England for the first time.

"Impatience to receive news from Dresden made us soon turn our faces towards London: I certainly was more uneasy than Manteul. The hope he had conceived contributed much to his happiness, which I rather envied than participated; and the more chearful and animated I saw him, the more did my secret chagrin and gloom increase. I spoke to him, however, continually, concerning Matilda, led him to repeat the most minute circumstances, and was as inexhaustible in my questions as Manteul was in replies. This was our chief subject of conversation, and, every moment, grief, regret, jealousy, and I may add love, acquired new force. Manteul found no letters when we came to London; but, two days after our arrival, as I was rising, intending to breakfast with him, his servant brought me a letter, with my address. Surprised at this, I immediately was going to him, but was informed he was gone out, and would not be home before dinner. My astonishment increased, and I opened the letter, not without emotion, which still became more forcible when I saw the cover inclosed a letter that had been opened, addressed to Manteul, with the post-mark of Dresden, which, by its size, seemed still to contain another. This I supposed to be the answer of his sister, and a letter inclosed from Matilda. But wherefore not bring them himself? In spite of my impatience to see it, I began by reading the few lines Manteul had written in the cover. Here it is," said Lindorf, taking it from his pocket-book, "and imagine what was my surprise."

"I know not whether to the best of friends or most traiterous of men I inclose the letters I have just received; while I thus absolutely cede to the former opinion, I shall prove I wish to find I am not mistaken, however appearances may say the contrary.—And is Lindorf then the lover of Matilda? By her beloved? The husband of her choice, selected by her brother, and acknowledged by her heart? The man to whom she would instantly sacrifice the homage of the adoring world; and is it from herself I learn all this?—Oh! Lindorf, what motive can you have had for the inconceivable mysteriousness of your conduct? I cannot think you capable of base treachery; yet I had some right to your confidence and sincerity.—I am lost in doubt, and own I fear the consequences of meeting you at this moment. Send your answer to the Orange Coffee-house;[43] there can be no reason for longer dissimulation, for, since you are beloved, you no longer have a rival."

Manteul.

"It is impossible to tell you what I felt. Was I—Was I still beloved by the charming, the constant Matilda? Was it for me, ungrateful as I was, that she refused the addresses of de Zastrow, of Manteul, nay of *the whole world!* I opened the letter and found one addressed to me; the hand was well known, and an emotion, almost involuntary, brought it to my lips. I was about to open and enjoy the excess of my happiness when a sudden and bitter reflection stopped me. Again at the expence of a friend must I be happy; and this friend had reason to suppose me perfidious. I could not endure the thought. You, dear Count, are capable of imagining what my feelings were, and the increase they suffered by recollection. This was the second time love had assaulted friendship, and a second time was I desirous friendship should be victorious. I would not read the letters till I first had justified myself to Manteul, and till I had his free consent to read them: I locked them up, and instantly went in search of him to the coffee-house, where he had not yet been, and where the most probable way of meeting him would have been to wait; but waiting at this moment was impossible. I ran to seek him elsewhere. I rather chose speaking to him than writing a letter long enough to have explained all the reasons of my conduct, which little suited my impatience; but, as we might miss each other in the search, I left a line at the coffee-house, saying 'he did me justice in believing me incapable of perfidy; that, certainly, I had many things to reproach myself with, but not that of treachery towards him. Matilda only had a right to complain. I begged him to wait at the coffee-house, and pledged myself to give him every explanation he could require, assuring him I should not take a moment's rest till he had heard me. I had not read, nor would read, a line in the letters he had sent me, and hoped to prove how highly I valued his esteem and friendship!'

"After giving this note to the waiter I continued my search, went to the Prussian Ambassador's, into the Park, to all our acquaintances, but missed him every where; and, returning to the coffee-house, found, to my great vexation, he had been there and was gone, but that he had left a note for me, which was this." (Lindorf read it to the Count.)

"'I wish to see and speak with you,[a] dear Lindorf, but it is not possible. Lord Cavendish has requested me to accompany him to Newmarket,[44] he is setting off immediately, and I scarcely have time to write a word. You know how desirous I am of seeing those famous races, and I was the more ready to accept the offer because my mind is at present in great need of relief. Your note, and especially your eagerness to see me before you have read your letters, tell me all that I at present wish to know. Read them, dear friend, and if you are not, in half an hour, on the road to Dresden you do not merit your happiness. Could any thing disturb, or alter, my esteem and friendship for you it would be to hear you were in London at this time to-morrow. Farewell, dear Lindorf, and be as happy as you deserve; as happy as you must be with the most lovely of women. I will seek another like her, if possible, and whose heart is free. Should the company and sports of Newmarket have the effect I hope, you will soon hear from me. I doubt not but you will write and give me the account you promise, not by way of explanation, it is not requisite, but in the confidence of friendship, and to one who is infinitely interested both for Lindorf and Matilda. She, you say, only has a right to complain—Happy Lindorf!—Fly, behold her, and she will not have that right long.'

Manteul.

"Scarcely had I finished before I flew to the house of Lord Cavendish, hoping still to find him, but they were gone post, and I hesitated, for a moment, whether I should or should not follow; but motives so strong and a desire so ardent drew me elsewhere that I could not long resist. I once more read the note of Manteul, and finding he avoided me, 'Why,' said I, 'should I force the sight of a happy rival on him in the first paroxysm of grief?' Was I in reality beloved by the generous Matilda? Manteul, only, yet, had told me so, and I longed to see the confirmation, I, therefore, returned home, and read the two letters I am going to shew you. You will begin by reading that of Mademoiselle de Manteul, as I did, though most impatient to see the other, which, addressed to me, made my heart palpitate. I trembled to open a paper where each word, traced by the hand of Matilda, must be a reproach to this inconstant heart. She, perhaps, knew not my infidelity; but was I, therefore, less culpable?—Ah! when I did read, how did her ingenuous and affectionate soul, which infused itself into the paper, augment my wrongs, and make me more self-odious! I began with this," said Lindorf, giving it to the Count.

Mademoiselle de Manteul first asked a thousand pardons of her brother for having given him false hopes. Deceived herself, she had believed the thing she wished to be was true, and that he had been the secret object of Matilda's love. "It was your letter," added she, "that very letter I requested you to write, and from which I expected effects so very different, that destroyed all my hopes. No, brother, you are not the beloved man. Matilda has long since yielded her heart. She refuses the homage of de Zastrow, of you, and of the whole world, for the sake of your new friend, that very Baron of Lindorf of whom you speak. She saw but his name in your letter and, instantly, her secret was betrayed: yet it can now be no secret to you, for, being thus intimate with that gentleman, he, by this, has, certainly, made you his confidant; certainly, has told you he has long since been contracted to the young Countess of Walstein. Her brother, the most intimate friend of Lindorf, promoted this union, and their hearts were accordant to his wishes. Matilda declares nothing can break this tie but death; for, though Lindorf should even prove inconstant, she never will. Your passion, therefore, dear brother, for your own sake, you will vanquish, and I think I know you sufficiently reasonable and generous to rest assured it will change to friendship, and that you will take a pleasure at once to serve Matilda and her lover. This you may do by giving him the inclosed letter, which the poor young lady had no means of sending. It is not she that requests this, but I; thinking it the best means of effecting your cure. Tell this Lindorf that his mistress is persecuted by her aunt, who will oblige her to wed de Zastrow, whom she hates; that this will certainly occasion her death; prevail on him to depart instantly, that he may console, deliver, and carry her off, if necessary; and, indeed, I see no other means. What can he have to fear, since he is authorized by her brother? You well may suppose, Charles, I should have been happy had you been the man; but her heart was bestowed before she came to Dresden. Endeavour, therefore, only to contribute to her happiness; and, perhaps, to your sister's likewise."

This latter phrase, which had escaped the observation of Lindorf, made the Count smile, and confirmed him in his former opinion of Mademoiselle de Manteul. He returned the letter to Lindorf, who then gave him that from Matilda—"Read," said he, "and think what must be the impression it made on me!"[45]

Dresden—"Yes, M. Lindorf, Matilda writes to you. Your friend, Matilda. She does very wrong, to be sure; she ought not to be the first to break this excellent silence. Oh! yes, yes; I know I do wrong; but, I likewise know, I cannot help it. There are certain moments in life when the heart speaks louder than reason, and compels it to silence, and my heart says so many many things that I am obliged to listen and do whatever it pleases.[a] It tells me, for example, I shall be less unhappy when I have related all my sufferings to my friend; and I already feel it tells me truth. Since I have begun to write it seems as if my griefs were all changed into so many pleasures; but, alas! these will presently vanish; and no sooner will my letter be ended than my torments will re-commence. My brother still in Russia, Lindorf still in England, de Zastrow still at Dresden, and poor Matilda still persecuted.—My aunt requires impossibilities. Have I two hearts that I may bestow one on de Zastrow? And if I had a thousand, should not I give them all to—to—. Ever since I have begun to write this letter, nay, ever since I first thought of writing it, have I been incessantly torturing my imagination for the best manner of telling you what I feel, and how I might say all I have to say; but the more I think the less I succeed. It will be impossible you should understand me—I will think no more on the matter; I will suffer my hand and my heart to go their own way. I require sincerity, and have a right to give the example—Yes, M. Lindorf (see! see! I am still thinking about the manner). Well then, dear, dear Lindorf! I love you, and shall love you as long as I live!—And be assured, I will live and die either Matilda Walstein, or Matilda Lindorf.—Do not be terrified at this my eternal constancy. No, dear Lindorf, it does not entail itself on *you:* far am I from supposing you under the same obligation. With myself only, not with you, have I entered into this engagement. I have heard men may change as often as they please, without becoming less estimable in their own eyes, or even in the eyes of the women; and it must be true, since my brother, the wisest and the best of men, has changed, nobody knows why, and seems no longer to love his poor sister.— Ah! Lindorf, dear Lindorf, do you supply the place of this brother, who forsakes me; he is so far off I have no means of reclaiming his friendship; but, certainly, yours, Lindorf, will come to my aid. Advise, tell me, how I may avoid a marriage I detest; preserve me for—Alas! if not for Lindorf, for myself.—If it be true he loves another—I ask no questions, I shall know it soon enough; yet it will not alter my present manner of thinking, neither with respect to you, the Baron de Zastrow, nor all the men on earth, for never among them all will I chuse more than one. This I know, and what farther knowledge do I want? Only tell me you will remain the friend of Matilda; the word *friend* will ascertain your sincerity; which will be still farther confirmed by your frankness, and eagerness to answer this, to relieve me from the cruel inquietude your silence, that of my brother, and the absence of you both occasion; from that neglect which resembles offence, forgetfulness, and death, and which certainly will be death, if it continue much longer, to Matilda Walstein.

"P. S. I know not how to direct this letter, nor where to send it. Alas! I know not whether you or my brother neglects me the most; but you both are—What in the world I love the best! Which, I am afraid, is as much as to say, ungrateful."

The Count was affected at reading this letter, and severely reprehended himself for having suffered his passion for Caroline to make him so far neglect his sister. He ought not to have been satisfied with writing a letter; he should have supposed it might be intercepted, and have gone himself. He began to imagine he, only, was in the wrong.—"You may think," said Lindorf, "what I felt from what you yourself feel."—The Count was going to give back the letter.—"No, keep it," said Lindorf, "and, if ever I should be wretched enough to forget it, or give my Matilda a moment's grief, shew me but that letter and I shall instantly repair the wrong.

"I did not hesitate a moment, after I had read it," continued he, "concerning how I must act. To fly to her, to console her, to intreat her to forgive the injuries I had done her, to tear her from the arms of tyranny, and dedicate my life to her happiness, was the first wish, the vow, of my heart. I clearly saw they deceived her, since she still supposed you in Russia. They, no doubt, had intercepted your letters; she was beset with snares, and by people devoted to de Zastrow. The danger was so pressing that I determined immediately to depart; the recollection of Manteul only could have prevented me, and this his note counteracted. *Could any thing disturb, or alter, my esteem and friendship for you it would be to hear you were in London at this time to-morrow.* I determined, however, not to leave England till I had removed every doubt respecting my own conduct, and the mystery

I had made of my engagements with Matilda. I, therefore, sat down and wrote a circumstantial account of what my motives and intentions were, in which I concealed nothing but the name of Caroline, and owned that what he had said of Matilda had more than revived my former inclination for her, but that, feeling she had every right to forget me, I was resolved to make her every reparation I might, by aiding her in this her supposed new passion. My letter was long, and I was still writing when the servant, whom Manteul had taken with him, returned. He, on recollection, had sent him back with another note, which was but a sort of repetition of the preceding one, fearing lest it had not come to hand, and that my departure was by that means deferred.[a] He added new and stronger motives to hasten me, and, that I might not have the least uneasiness on his account, assured me, 'he looked on it as a lucky event; too young, at present, to marry (he is not twenty) no woman but Matilda could have excused his entering into the marriage state. The suspicion of being beloved by her had led him wild, but the conviction of the contrary had restored him to reason and liberty. By these he would profit, would study, and travel for some years, and hoped, when we met again, to find me the happy husband of the most lovely of women. Whatever my motives might have been for forsaking her, he was certain I no longer should be inconstant the moment I saw her. He knew me too well to believe I should not immediately fly to her assistance, though it were but from motives of friendship, and if I even was incapable of love. He concluded by telling me his servant had orders to return to him as soon as he had seen me get into the post-chaise.'

"I sent back the voluminous letter I had written, and his servant departed for Newmarket, at the same time that I left London. The wind was favourable, and we had a quick passage. I found Varner at Hamburg, where he had been several weeks, detained by contrary winds, and at which he had been much afflicted. He gave me your short note, and my banker, the same day, delivered the succeeding letter; both were equally pressing, both requested my immediate return, without explaining your motives. Of this there was no need; the request of Walstein need not fear disobedience, and, had I not been returning, I instantly should have set out. Yet how must I confess that my heart made me take the road to Dresden instead of that to Berlin! I have no excuse unless it were a *presentiment*. I endeavoured to persuade myself that a few days delay could not give you any pain, though it might be of the utmost consequence to Matilda. I was anxious to see her, to persuade her to come with me, and bring her to her brother. Nay, I even interpreted your two so pressing letters into positive orders that related solely to Matilda, and concluded I best was answering your intentions by flying to her aid before I saw you. I therefore stopped only at Hamburg till good horses and equipage could be found. The rest you know; my rencontre with de Zastrow, and my surprise at seeing Matilda leap out of the post-chaise: though I have not yet ventured to tell you, before her, how much the alteration in her person affected, astonished, and enchanted me; how superior she was to the Matilda I had formerly known, to her Manteul had described, or, even, to what my imagination had supposed. Oh! Walstein, how beauteous! how angelic did she seem, embellished as her countenance was by the emotions of her heart! The first words she uttered had something of tenderness, of feeling, of soul, which it is impossible to convey. I see her now fly from the carriage, run with open arms, and hear her utter, 'Lindorf, dear Lindorf, they want to steal your Matilda from you, who is, and only will be, yours!'

"Her native innocence is above all suspicion; she loves, herself, and thinks it most certain she is, herself, beloved. Not a year's silence, not all that others have said, nor all that I have done, could shake her constancy. The moment she sees me they are all forgotten, and not a shadow of doubt remains. Ah! when fainting and feeble she sunk into my arms, pale, inanimate, and with half closed eyes, how interesting was it to my soul! With what ardor did I swear to live for her,[a] and her alone! On her lips, as I bore her into the house, I pronounced the vow which I never can forget, no more than I can the rapturous sensations I that moment experienced.

"My affair with de Zastrow, my wound, the tender care she has taken of me, her understanding, her grace, her ingenuous mind, all have augmented my passion. Yet will I own I felt some emotion at the sight of Caroline; but it was of a very different kind from what I had formerly known.[46] I saw with pleasure, yes, Walstein, with infinite pleasure, you were beloved, and Caroline was to me as a sister, the wife of my friend and brother. And now, dear Count, you know my inmost heart, and, I hope, will not delay to bestow the happiness I so ardently desire, which present conviction tells me I deserve, and which will make felicity perfect."

"My felicity," replied the Count, tenderly embracing him, "will not be perfect till I behold Matilda and Lindorf as happy as I myself am; nor shall it be long before these new bonds of affinity and friendship shall be formed, which will leave me nothing farther to wish."

Walstein, then, related all his past scenes with Caroline. Lindorf shuddered at the idea of the divorce. "Good God!" said he, "could you suppose I would be accessary to such a sacrifice! That I would be happy at the expence of Walstein!"

"It was the happiness of Caroline that was in contest, and neither thou nor I,[b] Lindorf, ought then to recede. The letters I wrote, and which thou wouldest have found on thy arrival, would have removed every scruple: friendship and delicacy must have yielded to motives more decisive. My reasons were good, and my measures well taken, and thou couldest not but have acted accordingly."

"Ask me not how I should have acted," replied Lindorf; "I, fortunately, have not been put to the proof. I am proud of being your brother. You only could deserve Caroline, and she alone could equal your virtues. Matilda, perhaps, is, by temper and nature, better suited to your friend Lindorf."[a]

"She does not know," said the Count, "that Caroline has been her rival?" "She knows every thing," replied Lindorf, with vivacity. "She has a right to know every thing. My heart were unworthy of her had I any secrets. In justice, I was obliged to account for my coolness, my silence, my voyage to England. Might I deceive her? No, impossible; and had I even so intended, no such intention could have been kept. Her noble frankness, her open candor, would irresistibly have ensured like confidence and like sincerity. No sooner were we alone in the post-chaise than she spoke of you and your marriage; and asked if I knew her sister. A full confession of all that had passed was my answer; and, far from feeling jealousy or vexation, I found, as I spoke, she became attached to Caroline, was desirous of her friendship, and determined to imitate her best qualities and virtues. 'Oh! how dearly,' said she, 'shall I love this charming Caroline! How happy will she make my brother! And how gladly shall I learn, from her, to reclaim and fix my rover, my Lindorf!'—Since Matilda has seen her, she has told me, with a tone of sincerity that leaves no doubt on the mind, 'Ah! Lindorf, how perfectly are you justified in your passion! I never could have pardoned you had you seen Caroline with indifference!' Such, dear Count, is your sister; and judge whether I ought not to adore her."

Arrived at Berlin, the first care of the Count was to present his friend and sister to the King, and request his approbation of their marriage; which obtained, the happy family went to the Walstein estate, where Caroline had fled *from* her husband, on the bridal day, and *to* him, on the morning of the projected divorce,[47] and of which Justin was steward. There, in the Count's chapel, was the marriage celebrated, without other witnesses than Walstein, Caroline, the tenants of the Chateau, and some of the villagers. As they left the church, Louisa came to pay her respects to Lindorf, to whom she was presented by Caroline. He beheld both these lovely women, who formerly had raised such commotions in his breast, with perfect tranquillity;[48] and, pressing the hand of the Count who stood next him, "I feel, at this moment," said he, "I am worthy to be the brother of Walstein. I was distracted for Louisa, Caroline I adored, but Matilda I love, and shall for ever love!"[b]

The CONCLUSION.

To those who wish to be informed of every thing that passes we shall further say, that Lindorf continued thus to think; that he made his lovely lady happy,[49] attained to the highest rank in the army, and distinguished himself on several occasions. That Edmund, Count of Walstein, was a pillar to the throne, a friend of the King, a protector of the people, a supporter of the wretched, and that he found, in the constant affection of his dear Caroline, and the good conduct of his children, the full recompense of his virtues; while Caroline, the adored, the beloved Caroline, meeting the admiration she merited, was the happiest as she was the most angelic of women.

We shall likewise add that the young Baron de Zastrow, admiring his Parisian graces, engrafted on a German trunk, finding he pleased only Mademoiselle de Manteul, who pleased not him, returned to Paris and his gaming friends, pursued his theatrical conquests, and made such good use of his time, money, and constitution that, in less than a year, he was ruined, diseased and dead. His aunt, perceiving Matilda had had good reason for her refusal, pardoned, and left her all her wealth.

Mademoiselle de Manteul retired, at first, into a convent; after which she obtained the place of a lady of honor, at court; where, exercising that spirit of intrigue with which she was so liberally endowed, she became perfectly competent to her post.

Her young brother, the well disposed and amiable Manteul, for whom we have been interested, and whom we saw set off to Newmarket, met with Lady Sophia Seymour, who was cousin german to the Count and Matilda,[50] and who greatly resembled the latter. Manteul now found he was far from having suffered a loss, inasmuch as Lady Sophia, no-wise inferior to her lovely cousin, loved him with all the ardour with which Matilda loved Lindorf. The Count, in a voyage he made to London, in company with Caroline, had the pleasure of forming this union, and making two more lovers happy.

THE END.[51]

APPENDIX I

ROMANCE
Accompagné de guitar & de clavecin

La jeune Hortense, au fons d'un verd bocage,
Rêvoit, un jour, seule sur le gazon;
La jeune Hortense au printems de son âge,
Ne connoissoit de l'amour que le nom:
A ce nom souvent elle pense,
Craint & desire un doux lien;
Oh! ma paisible indifférence,
Est-elle un mal, est-elle un bien?

Je vois l'amour dans tout ce qui respire,
Il est partout, excepté dans mon cœur;
Autour de moi, tout aime, tout soupire,
Seroit-ce donc le souverain bonheur?
Tout s'anime par sa présence:
Moi, seule, hélas! je ne sens rien;
Oh! Ma paisible indifférence
Est donc un mal plutôt qu'un bien?

Oui, mais je vois errer dans la prairie
De fleurs en fleurs, le papillon léger:
Abandonnant celle qu'il a chérie,
Ainsi que lui tout amant peut changer;
Vif emblême de l'inconstance,
Tu me dis qu'il faut n'aimer rien;
Oh! ma paisible indifférence,
Loin d'être un mal, est donc un bien.

J'ai vu souvent pour un berger volage,
J'ai vu gémir d'innocentes beautés;
Elle fuyoient tous les jeux du village,
Pour des ingrats toujours trop regrettés.
Moi, je ris, je chante & je danse:
Tous les ingrats ne me font rien;

Oh! ma paisible indifférence,
Vous êtes mon unique bien.

Ainsi chantoit cette jeune bergère;
Amour l'entend, amour se vengera;
Il tient déjà dans sa main meurtrière
Le trait fatal dont il la percera.
Bientôt, jeune & sensible Hortense
En formant un tendre lien,
En perdant ton indifférence,
Tu vas connoître le vrai bien.

APPENDIX II

Un jour pur éclairoit mon ame;
J'unissois l'amour au devoir;
J'osois me livrer à ma flamme,
Ecouter le plus doux espoir.
Mais puis-je m'abuser encore?...
Cet espoir s'éteint dans mon cœur!
Toi qui me fuis, toi que j'adore,
Où veut-tu chercher le bonheur?

Quand tes soins me rendoient la vie,
Je crus les devoir à l'amour;
Je me disois: Je suis chérie,
Je saurai bien l'être toujours.
Mais puis-je me flatter encore?...
Non, l'espoir s'éteint dans mon cœur!
Cruel époux! Toi que j'adore,
Où veux-tu chercher le bonheur?

Quel sort affreux il me destine!
Que ne me laissoit-il mourir ?...
Si tu n'aimes plus Caroline:
C'est là son unique désir.
Mais puis-je m'abuser encore?
Non, l'espoir s'éteint dans mon cœur!
Toi qui me fuis, toi que j'adore,
Où veux-tu chercher le bonheur?

Tu deviendras mon bien suprême,
O le plus chéri des portraits!
Tiens-moi lieu de celui que j'aime!
Viens du moins me rendre ses traits!
Mais puis je m'abuser encore?
J'ai ses traits: je n'ai plus son cœur!
Toi qui me fuis, toi que j'adore,
Où veux-tu chercher le bonheur?

APPENDIX III

On dit que l'amour
Ne dure qu'un jour
Dans le mariage:
C'est un conte que cela.
Si l'on aime on aimera
Toujours davantage.

Ici le bonheur
Redouble l'ardeur ;
On aime au village:
Depuis que je suis heureux,
Je sens s'augmenter mes feux
Toujours davantage.

Plus content qu'un roi,
Quand joue avec moi
Mon petit ménage,
Ma Louise & nos enfans
Attachent nos sentimens
Toujours davantage,

C'est à Monseigneur
Que de notre cœur
Nous devons l'hommage;
Je ne forme plus de vœux:
Comme nous il est heureux
Toujours davantage.

APPENDIX IV

On veut peut-être savoir aussi comment tous les détails de cette intéressante histoire sont parvenus à ma connoissance & à celle du public. Des affaires particulières m'ayant appellée a Berlin, je fus recommandée par M de Karc, gentilhomme Russe, au comte de Walstein, qu'il avoit connu à l'époque de son ambassade en Russe. Le comte me présenta à son épouse et à sa sœur. Cette aimable famille me combla de politesses, & me rendit le séjour de Berlin si agréable, que j'y passai près de deux années. Je vécus avec eux pendant tout ce tems-là, dans la société la plus intime, sans y éprouver jamais un seul instant d'ennui: la conversation du comte, toujours variée, toujours instructive, animée par sa douce philosophie, par l'énergie de son ame, la sensibilité si touchante & si vrai de Caroline, & ses talens enchanteurs qu'elle cultivoit avec soin, la gaîté, la vivacité, la complaisance du bon Lindorf, la charmante mutinerie de Matilde qui faisoit briller son esprit & ses grâces, sans nuire à la bonté de son cœur : toutes ces différentes manières d'être aimable, formoient les contrastes les plus piquans & les plus variés, sans altérer leur union; ils ne se quittoient point à Berlin, ils occupoient dans le même hôtel deux corps de logis différens, & l'été ils se réunissoient dans leurs terres; je fus avec eux à Walstein, à Risberg, à Rindaw.

Une soirée d'automne, nous étions rassemblés en famille, dans le charmant pavillon du jardin ; je demandai l'explication des peintures: le comte me la donna. Caroline, attendrie au souvenir de son amie ne put retenir ses larmes; le comte s'approcha d'elle : il ne lui dit rien: mais il la serra dans ses bras avec l'expression du sentiment le plus tendre: Caroline essuya ses yeux, sourit à son époux, & lui dit, un instant après: "Que ne peut-elle voir comme sa Caroline est heureuse!" Dans un autre coin du pavillon, Lindorf & Mathilde folâtroient avec le fils aîné du comte, âgé de trois ans, & leur fille à-peu-près du même âge; on ne savoit lequel étoit le plus enfant & faisoit le plus de bruit; j'étois au milieu de ces deux groupes! je les considérois avec attention, surprise de voir les caractères de ces époux si parfaitement assortis. Le comte & Caroline se convenoient aussi bien l'un à l'autre que Lindorf & Mathilde; j'en fis la remarque avec eux, & j'ajoutai que la sympathie avoit assurément agi sur leurs ames, & décidé leurs penchans au premier instant qu'ils s'étoient vus. Je le disois de bonne foi, ignorant leur histoire, & jugeant d'après leurs sentimens actuels. Caroline sourit encore, en regardant le comte, qui s'étoit assis auprès d'elle, & lui prenant une main qu'elle serra contre son cœur: Vous aurez donc peine à croire, me dit-elle, que je reçus cette main chérie en frémissant, & que mon premier soin fut de m'éloigner de lui pendant plus d'une année? Et croyez-vous, interrompit le comte, que j'ai sollicité avec instance un divorce, & que je l'ai même obtenu? Si je voulois parler, dit Lindorf, je pourrois peut-être aussi surprendre madame.... Taisez-vous, mon cher, lui dit Matilde, en posant la main sur la bouche, je veux ignorer toutes vos perfidies; laissez-moi raconter à Madame que je suis la seule ici qui n'aie rien à se reprocher: toujours tendre & fidelle comme une colombe, je n'ai pas donné l'ombre de l'inquiétude à ce que j'aimois ; je l'ai dit cent fois: il n'y a ici que moi de bien sage, de bien raisonnable. Très-surprise de ce que je venois d'entendre, je priai mes amis de me développer ce mystère: mais je compris à leur réponse, que ce récit ne pouvoit pas se faire devant tous les intéressés. Cependant ma curiosité étoit vivement excitée, & je persécutai chacun d'eux en particulier. Caroline me jura qu'elle se rappelloit à peine le temps où elle n'aimoit pas son mari, & que souvent elle ne pouvoit croire que ce temps eût existé. Matilde ne savoit presque rien, le comte étoit trop occupé; enfin il me dit de m'adresser à Lindorf, auquel il avoit donné toutes les lettres; il ajouta: nous nous sommes amusés, la première année de notre réunion, lorsque les événemens étoient encore récens, à écrire chacun notre histoire; en disant au plus près de notre conscience ce que nous avions éprouvé dans telle ou telle circonstance. Tous ces papiers ont été remis à Lindorf, qui s'est chargé de les rédiger ; je crois qu'il l'a fait, mais jusqu'à présent il n'a point voulu nous montrer son ouvrage; peut-être aura-t-il plus de déférence pour vous.

Je me préparois à en parler à Lindorf: mais il me prévint ; dès le lendemain il entra chez moi, son manuscrit à la main: Vous avez paru désirer, me dit-il, de nous connoître à fond ; on n'a point de secret pour une amie comme vous, & je vous apporte l'histoire de notre vie & de nos sentimens ; ce manuscrit n'a d'autre mérite que l'exacte vérité, & pour vous, celui que peut lui donner l'amitié; je vous le laisse; emportez-le dans votre patrie: il vous rappellera quelquefois vos bons amis de Berlin, & vous vous croirez avec eux en le lisant.

On comprend combien je remerciai l'aimable Lindorf du présent qu'il me faisoit, & dont je sentois tout le prix. Mais, lui dis-je, pourquoi le comte, Caroline, Matilde, ne l'ont-ils point vus? Ils l'ont vu & composé autant que moi, me répondit-il; je puis vous montrer que j'ai travaillé exactement d'après ce que chacun d'eux avoit écrit; j'ai seulement supprimé les répétitions, donné une suite à ces différens récits, & c'est ce que j'ai craint de leur laisser voir; le comte m'auroit grondé, d'avoir été trop vrai sur ses vertus: vous savez comme il est modeste. Caroline m'eût encore reproché plus vivement d'avoir plaisanté sur son père et sur son amie. Et Matilde... Eh-bien ! Matilde auroit trouvé peut-être son Lindorf bien léger; j'aime mieux qu'elle ignore un défaut dont elle m'a corrigé. Au surplus, j'abandonne le tout à votre prudence; ce manuscrit est à vous, faites-en ce que vous voudrez. Je lui promis de le garder pour moi seule, tant que je serois à Berlin; & j'étois près de mon départ.

Revenue chez moi, je me suis occupée délicieusement à l'arranger à ma manière, & je n'ai pu résister à faire partager au public, une partie du plaisir que cet intéressant petit ouvrage m'a fait éprouver. Je ne sais si mon amitié pour cette aimable famille me fait illusion ; mais il me semble, qu'après avoir lu leur histoire, on les aimera comme moi. La vérité, d'ailleurs, & la simplicité ont toujours le droit d'intéresser. Heureuse si les vertus & le bonheur du comte de Walstein, inspiroient à quelques jeunes gens le désir de l'imiter.

The reader may also wish to know how all the details of this affecting history came to my attention and to that of the public. Some private matters had called me to Berlin, where on the recommendation of M de Karc, a Russian gentleman, I was introduced to the Count of Walstein, whom he had known at the time of the Count's ambassadorship to Russia. The count introduced me to his wife and sister. This good-natured family bestowed so many kindnesses on me, and made my stay in Berlin so agreeable, that I spent nearly two years there. I lived with them during all that time, in the closest of ways, without ever experiencing a single moment of boredom: the Count's conversation was always varied and always instructive, animated by his gentle philosophy and the energy of his soul; Caroline's sensibility was so touching and so sincere, and her talents, which she cultivated so assiduously, enchanted me; Lindorf was cheerful, lively and kind; Matilda was charming in her defiance, which made her wit and beauty shine, without impairing the goodness of her heart. They had all these different ways of being good-natured, which created the most piquant and varied contrasts, without disrupting their accord; they never parted from each other in Berlin, where they lived in two separate apartments in the same house, and in the summer they joined each other on their estates; I went with them to Walstein, to Risberg, and to Rindaw.

One autumn evening, we were gathered as a family in the charming pavilion in the garden; I asked them about the paintings and the Count explained them to me. Caroline, moved at the memory of her friend, could not hold back her tears; the Count went up to her, saying nothing but holding her in his arms with the utmost tenderness. Caroline wiped her eyes, smiled at her husband, and said to him, a moment later: "If only she could see how happy her Caroline is!" In another corner of the pavilion, Lindorf and Matilda were frolicking with the Count's oldest son, who was three years old, and their daughter, who was more or less the same age; it was impossible to say who was the most childlike and made the most noise. There I was in the middle of these two groups! I considered them attentively, amazed at how perfectly matched the couples were. The Count and Caroline were as well suited to each other as Lindorf and Matilda; I said this to them, and I added that sympathy had surely acted on their souls, and decided their mutual inclinations from the first moment they saw each other. I said it in good faith, not knowing their history, and judging by their present feelings. Caroline smiled once more, looking at the count, who had sat down next to her, and, taking one of his hands, which she pressed to her heart, she said: "You will have difficulty believing, then, that I trembled as I received this darling hand, and that, from the first, I took steps to live apart from him for more than a year?" "And would you believe," interrupted the Count, "that I petitioned fervently for a divorce, and that I even obtained it?" "If I might speak," said Lindorf, "I might also surprise you Madame...." "Hush, my dear," said Matilda, putting her hand on his mouth, "I do not want to know about all your perfidies; let me tell Madame that I am the only one here who has nothing to reproach herself for: always tender and faithful as a dove, I have never given my love the slightest cause for disquiet; I have said it a hundred times: I am the only truly sensible and reasonable one here. Astonished at what I had just heard, I begged my friends to divulge the mystery: but I gathered from their reaction that this tale could not be told in front of everyone concerned in it. However my curiosity was greatly excited and I importuned each of them in private to tell me. Caroline swore to me that she barely remembered the time when she did not love her husband, and that often she could not believe that such a time had existed. Matilda knew almost nothing, the Count was too busy; in the end he told me to speak to Lindorf, to whom he had given all the letters, and added: "We amused ourselves, in the first year we were reunited, shortly after the events had taken place, by writing down our stories, each of us recounting, as faithfully as possible, what we had felt in each and every circumstance. All those papers were given to Lindorf, who took it upon himself to edit them. I believe that he has done it, but until now he has not wanted to show us his work; perhaps he will be more compliant with you.

I made up my mind to speak to Lindorf about it, but he anticipated me; the very next day he came into my apartment, manuscript in hand: "You seemed to wish," he said, "for a more thorough understanding of us. We have no secrets from a friend like you, and I have brought you the story of our lives and feelings. This manuscript has no merit save that it is the exact truth, and for you, it will also have that which friendship can give it. I will leave it with you. Take it into your own country. It will remind you from time to time of your good friends in Berlin, and whenever you read it you will believe you are with them.

The reader will understand how much I thanked the good-natured Lindorf for the gift he had given me, and how I appreciated its value. "But," I said, "how come the Count, Caroline and Matilda have not seen it?" "They have seen it and composed as much of it as I have," he replied; "I could show you that, as I worked, I paid scrupulous attention to what each of them had written; I have merely cut out repetitions and put the different accounts in order, and that is what I am afraid to let them see; the Count would have chided me for being too honest about his virtues; you know how modest he is. Caroline would have reproached me even more forcefully for having made fun of her father and her friend. And Matilda... Ah! Matilda might have found her Lindorf very fickle; I would rather she did not know of the flaw in me that she has corrected. For the rest, I leave it all to your judgement. This manuscript is yours, do with it what you will." I promised him that I would keep it all to myself as long as I remained in Berlin; and my departure was drawing near.

Once I had returned home, I busied myself with the delightful task of arranging it after my own fashion, and I could not resist letting the public share in some of the pleasure I had derived from this interesting little work. I don't know if I am deluded by my friendship for this good-natured family; but it seems to me that, after having read their history, the reader will love them as I do. Truth, moreover, and simplicity always have a claim on our interest. How glad I should be if the virtues and happiness of the Count of Walstein inspired young people with a desire to imitate him.

EDITORIAL NOTES

Volume 1

1. *Prussia*: Until 1801, the Holy Roman Empire of the German Nation was comprised of secular and ecclesiastical states, *Reichsstädte* (imperial free cities), and *Reichsritter* (imperial free knights), all of which had representation in the *Reichstag* (Imperial Diet). From 1701, Prussia was a kingdom which, as its borders expanded in the 1740s, formed an increasingly powerful part of this vast empire.

2. *sixteen*: in the French text, Caroline is only fifteen. See I. de Montolieu, *Caroline de Lichtfield*, 2 vols. (Londres: 1786), vol. 1, p. 5.

3. *High Chamberlain*: an official who plays a leading role in the management of the royal court.

4. *he was not only perfectly a courtier ... or a feeling heart*: the text alludes here to the stereotype of the duplicitous, ambitious, highly polished courtier. For radicals like Holcroft, eloquence designed to obscure corruption was a defining vice of the ruling elite, one that many in his coterie tried to counter by advocating, and claiming to practise, plain speech.

5. *unconsciously plucking the leaves of a rose, which she held in her white and virgin hand*: in European literature, a plucked flower would often signify the loss of a woman's maidenhead. In this passage, the Baron of Lichtfield's cunning and deceit might be interpreted as a first assault on Caroline's innocence. In his translation, Holcroft draws attention to her innocence by inserting the adjectives 'white and virgin' to describe the hand that plucks the rose; these adjectives are absent from the French version. Cf. Montolieu, *Caroline de Lichtfield,* vol. 1, p. 8.

6. *(The Baron was charmed to hear his own wit.)*: this parenthetic aside is one of many that Holcroft inserts to consolidate the Baron of Lichtfield's characterisation; they can be regarded as 'stage directions' accompanying his dialogue. In this case, the interpolated line consolidates our impression of his egotism.

7. *King*: the historical detail of the novel suggests that the king in question is Frederick II, later known as Frederick the Great of Prussia. Frederick was a brilliant military and diplomatic strategist, whose highly disciplined army made Prussia a formidable power in Europe. Despite this ruthless territorial expansion and his uncompromising absolutism, Frederick's friendship with Walstein remains plausible, for he was admired by many as a model of 'enlightened despotism'. Frederick was a proponent of religious toleration, promoted universal education, and believed that the welfare of his people took precedence over his personal gain or dynastic interests. An ardent admirer of French literature and culture, he also wrote prolifically on history and politics. In 1789, Holcroft translated

several volumes of his correspondence with writers and *philosophes* such as Voltaire, D'Alembert, Condorcet, and Grimm, along with *Memoirs from the Peace of Hubertsberg, to the Partition of Poland, and of the Bavarian War* (London: 1789), *Political, Philosophical and Satirical Miscellanies* (London: 1789), *The History of My Own Times* (London: 1789), and *The History of the Seven Years War* (London: 1789).

8. *Petersburgh*: in the eighteenth century, St Petersburgh was the capital of the Russian Empire.

9. *Russia*: since Walstein was sixteen at the time of the Battle of Mollwitz in 1741 (below, n. 60) and is now in his early thirties, the action of the novel would seem to take place in the late 1750s. At this time, Russia, allied with Austria and France, was engaged in the Seven Years' War (1756–63) against Prussia. When the Empress Elizabeth died in 1763, Peter II, an admirer of Frederick the Great of Prussia, ended the war. When Peter was deposed by his wife, Catherine the Great, and subsequently assassinated by her supporters, Catherine sought to maintain good diplomatic relations with Prussia, even as she embarked on a project of imperial expansion.

10. *Her natural good sense ... rose leaves she had just been scattering*: Holcroft's multi-clausal sentence expands considerably on the French text. Cf. Montolieu, *Caroline de Lichtfield*, vol. 1, p. 11: 'tout de suite sentant qu'elle en avoit trop dit, elle baissa de nouveau les yeux d'un air confus, sur son tablier' (suddenly feeling that she had said too much, she again cast her eyes on her apron with an air of confusion). Holcroft's additions contribute much to the reader's early impressions of Caroline; we must regard her, not simply as an ingénue, but as a person of 'natural good sense', capable of distinguishing between the dictates of reason and feeling. The analogy drawn between her blushing cheeks and the rose petals typifies Holcroft's tendency to elaborate on Montolieu's sparer prose, but also places renewed emphasis on Caroline's innocence.

11. *For six and twenty*: Montolieu estimates the age of serious reflection at twenty, not twenty-six. Cf. Montolieu, *Caroline de Lichtfield,* vol. 1, p. 12.

12. *Sweet emblem of innocence ... who art thyself all sensibility*: Holcroft contributes to Caroline's characterisation by inserting the descriptions of her as a 'sweet emblem of innocence' and 'all sensibility'. Although the transnational language and culture of sensibility took many forms in the eighteenth century, in this case the term evokes a concept central to sentimental philosophy: that all human beings were innately good and that, uncorrupted by civilization, human feeling could function as a divining rod for the good and the beautiful.

13. *Smelling salts*: chemical compounds containing ammonium carbonate and perfume. Most wealthy eighteenth-century women carried a bottle of smelling salts to revive them if they suffered from faintness or swooning. Although the low blood pressure that causes fainting spells has been linked to the restrictive corsetry fashionable in the period, swooning episodes also became a staple of sentimental literature. Along with blushes, sighs, trembling, and tears, fainting was a physical manifestation of the heroine's finely tuned sensibility, which might denote moral delicacy or physical and emotional frailty.

14. *Berlin*: in the eighteenth century, the capital city of the Kingdom of Prussia.

15. *Though, not so; for still shall I be happy ... he looked in it and durst not*: Holcroft adds the final line of the letter, in which Walstein hopes to gain Caroline's affection, as well as his sorrowful contemplation of his own reflection. The reader might admire the magnanimity of Montolieu's Walstein, but in Holcroft's translation she is also encouraged to sympathize with him.

16. *The Monarch was frank; but, state secrets excepted, Monarchs take little trouble to disguise their thoughts*: Holcroft interpolates this unfavourable characterisation of monarchs as both secretive and insensitive. The interpolation reinforces Montolieu's subtly critical description of the regal character at various points in the text.

17. *Reason to Kings is a superfluous thing, Will is sufficient*: Holcroft inserts the final clause, which emphasizes the detrimental effects of hereditary rule on the moral character of the ruler and reflects his opposition to hereditary rule and privilege.

18. *a most excellent lady, in her way*: Holcroft adds the qualifying phrase 'in her way'.

19. *read novels and romances from morning till night ... for several years*: the reading woman who indulges her love of novels to the detriment of good sense is a familiar figure in novels of the period. Holcroft occasionally makes subtle alterations to the text that sharpen Montolieu's gentle mockery of the Canoness's penchant for romance novels and her tendency to interpret events in light of her reading.

20. *of inanity*: this is Holcroft's interpolation. See above, n. 19.

21. *Quixote*: translates Montolieu's adjective 'romanesque' (romantic) and alludes to Miguel de Cervantes Saavedra's picaresque novel *Don Quixote de la Mancha* (1605–15), in which the protagonist reads so many chivalric romances that he comes to regard himself as a knight-errant bound to seek adventure and revive chivalry. English translations of *Don Quixote* were printed throughout the eighteenth century, and the novel was also parodied, to great success, by Charlotte Lennox in her *Female Quixote* (1752).

22. *if any such quality could reside in a breast so pure*: Holcroft interpolates this clause, emphasising Caroline's innocence.

23. *The Canoness was the daughter of Sensibility ... not often fatal*: the description of the Canoness lists characteristics typically associated with women of feeling. Since 'sensibility' was a mutable term that could incorporate, or conflate, moral, emotional or physical feeling, women liable to heightened emotional response were often portrayed as physically delicate – tears, fainting, and trembling were common occurrences in the sentimental novel. These ideas were symptomatic of a belief current in eighteenth-century medical theory that female bodies were organisms of peculiar sensibility, riddled with obscure but acutely responsive networks of sympathy, and prone to enervation.

24. *for falsehood and Caroline were natural foes*: Holcroft inserts this clause, insisting on the innate virtue of his heroine, despite the need for dissemblance on this occasion.

25. *Hymen*: in Greek mythology, the God of marriage. The concept is inserted by Holcroft.

26. *not all that sweetness and happiness of temper natural to herself*: Holcroft inserts this clause, taking the opportunity to emphasise Caroline's virtue as well as her youth.

27. *flageolet*: a wind instrument rather like a recorder. In its eighteenth-century French form, it was a wooden instrument with four finger holes in the front, two at the back, and a bone or ivory mouthpiece. Holcroft's readership would have been more familiar with the English version, which had six front finger holes and, occasionally, keywork.

28. *the spectacles of Luxury and the feasts of Pride*: Holcroft attributes these particular vices to courtly life. Cf. Montolieu, *Caroline de Lichtfield,* vol. 1, p. 46: 'les spectacles & les fêtes de la cour' (the spectacles and feasts of the court).

29. *a genius of the first order*: in this context, 'genius' denotes innate intellectual capacity. The term was increasingly applied in the eighteenth century to intellectual powers related to the imagination, to poetic or artistic creativity, or original thought.

30. *Virgin timidity she had ... illuminate her countenance:* Holcroft translates these lines with more than usual freedom, apparently intent on connecting the appeal of Caroline's beauty with her taste for literature. His references to 'genius' here connote the powers of

the mind. He is progressive in celebrating the intellect and imagination of his heroine as well as her sensibility. Cf. Montolieu, *Caroline de Lichtfield*, vol. 1, pp. 48–9: 'ses grands yeux bleus foncés brilloient quelquefois de tout le feu de l'intelligence & du génie, & lorsqu'ils étoient baissés & voilés à demi par de longues paupières, ils étoient l'image parlante de sa modestie & de sa sensibilité' (her large dark blue eyes shone at times with all the fire of intelligence and genius, and when they were lowered and half-veiled by her long eyelashes, they were the living image of modesty and sensibility).

31. *To these, her talents, her graces, and her gifts ... must never hope to describe*: Montolieu pays greater attention to sartorial detail than Holcroft, who also changes the colour of Caroline's hair from blonde to auburn. Cf. Montolieu, *Caroline de Lichtfield*, vol. 1, p. 49: 'une robe de mousseline ou de toile, serrée par une ceinture de couleur brune & tranchante, marquoit, sans la gêner, sa taille souple & déliée; un chapeau de paille ombragé de plumes, rassembloit une forêt de cheveux cendrés; les boucles qui s'échappoient, retomboient avec grace sur un cou d'albâtre, dont un mouchoir noir faisoit ressortir la blancheur, & son joli pied n'auroit pas eu besoin du petit soulier noir qui l'enfermoit avec avantage' (a gown of muslin and linen, snugly fastened with a brown belt that showed off, without constraining, her slim and lithe figure; a straw hat decorated with feathers, gathered up a mass of ash-blonde hair; the curls that escaped fell gracefully on her alabaster neck, whose whiteness was emphasized by a black handkerchief, & her pretty foot had no need of the little black shoe that adorned it).

32. *beauteous as Astolpho*: in the French literary tradition, Astolpho (or Astolfo) is one of Charlemagne's paladins. Eighteenth-century readers would have been familiar with the character through Ludovico Ariosto's epic poem, *Orlando Furioso*, of which there were numerous English translations. Holcroft's reference to Astolpho replaces Montolieu's reference to Esplandian, who was the son of Amadís de Gaula (see below, n. 33).

33. *faithful as Amadis*: Amadís de Gaula, the eponymous and idealized hero of a chivalric romance, the first known version of which was written by Garci Ordóñez (or Rodríguez) de Montalvo in 1508. Amadís was not only valiant; he was also handsome and celebrated for his fidelity to the beautiful English princess, Oriana. In his famous parody of the genre of chivalric romance, *Don Quixote de la Mancha*, which was translated into English and read throughout the eighteenth century, Cervantes makes frequent references to *Amadís de Gaula*. It was also the inspiration for a *tragédie en musique*, composed by Jean-Baptiste Lully, first performed in Paris in 1684 and staged several times during the eighteenth century.

34. *tender as Celadon*: the amorous hero of Honoré d'Urfé immense pastoral romance, *L'Astrée* (1607–27), which is set in the fifth century and, with many digressions, narrates the perfect love between Celadon and the eponymous heroine. The novel would have appealed to the Canoness by virtue of its intricate analyses of love.

35. *she would feel a kind of mild melancholy come over her ... perfectly to enjoy*: individuals gifted with refined sensibility were considered prone to melancholy. In the course of the century, melancholy became a fashionable disease, as it signified the sufferer's capacity for a desirable depth and range of feeling. Thomas Warton's graveyard poem, 'The Pleasures of Melancholy' (1765), was frequently reprinted. See also J. G. Zimmermann, *Solitude Considered with Respect to its Influence Upon the Mind and the Heart* (London: C. Dilly, 1791), p. 241: 'Sometimes, indeed, the calm of rural life, and the view of nature's charms, inspires a species of soft and tranquil melancholy. The noisy pleasures of the world then appear insipid, and we taste the charms of Solitude and repose with increased delight.' Where Montolieu describes Caroline as lost in sweet dreams, Holcroft gives her melan-

choly a celestial cast with his reference to 'the guests of heaven', once again laying stress on her purity. Cf. Montolieu, *Caroline de Lichtfield,* vol. 1, pp. 50–1.

36. *Caroline was very desirous of engraving some verses ... not a good poet*: Holcroft alters the sense of this passage. Perhaps influenced by his own experiences as an autodidact, he insists, as Montolieu does not, that poetic talent is learned rather than inborn. Cf. Montolieu, *Caroline de Lichtfield,* vol. 1, p. 59.

37. *Esculapius*: the Greco-Roman god of medicine, also known as Asclepius, Asklepios (Greek), and Aesculapius (Latin). The invocation of a classical deity underlines the neo-classical aesthetic principles evident in the description of Caroline's pavilion.

38. *little Genii sported around her*: in the context of art or sculpture, Genii usually personify abstractions, such as virtues or states of being. These quasi-mythological figures developed from the ancient Roman religion, in which a genius was the tutelary or attendant spirit of an individual, an institution, or a place.

39. *broke the javelin of Death who was seen flying in the back ground*: Since the Middle Ages, death has commonly been allegorized as a ghost-like, shrouded figure who threatens the dying with a javelin or a scythe.

40. *A temple built by inchantment by the wand of a Fairy, or the talisman of a Genius*: although Montolieu introduces the idea of enchantment, Holcroft adds these references to the Fairy and the Genius, enhancing the sense of otherworldly perfection that surrounds Caroline's temple. In this context, the Genius seems to be a spirit capable of enchantment, for a talisman is an object engraved with characters said to endow it with magical powers.

41. *Sylph*: in Western folklore, an elemental being that inhabits the air.

42. *Love*: figured here as Cupid, the Roman God of Love. Cupid is often depicted as a winged infant carrying a bow and a quiver of arrows. Whoever was struck by his arrows would fall victim to love or passion.

43. *Gentle Eugenia ... Bliss the foe!*: for Montolieu's version of this song in the original French, see Appendix I.

44. *the goddess of the temple*: Holcroft introduces this image, which emphasizes the neo-classical aesthetic of the temple.

45. *Noah's flood*: a reference to a biblical myth from the Book of Genesis in which God attempts to rid the earth of evil by sending a flood that drowns most of its inhabitants. Noah and his family are exempt, by their virtue, from this fate, as God gives Noah prior warning to build an ark that will save him from the deluge.

46. *swerd*: a variant of 'sward', a stretch of turf or grass.

47. *Zephyrs*: mild west winds. The word is particularly appropriate in this context because Zephyrus, the personification of the west wind in Greek mythology, also served Cupid, the God of Love, when he carried Psyche to his palace. Holcroft introduces the image.

48. *Ah! How infinite are the charms of Innocence!* : this phrase is Holcroft's addition.

49. *She knew not how to speak ... less communicative*: Holcroft's translation emphasizes that Caroline is largely unconscious of wrong-doing. Cf. *Caroline de Lichtfield,* Montolieu, vol. 1, p. 144: 'L'habitude de cacher un tel secret avoit dû nécessairement la rendre moins confiante' (The habit of keeping such a secret had inevitably made her less confiding).

50. *Gouvernante*: (French) governess.

51. *Moncrief has said that the very act of determining to forget makes us remember*: refers to François-Augustin Paradis de Moncrif (1687–1770), a French writer, poet, and royal historiographer from a family of Scottish origin. Montolieu is probably referring to his poem, *Les Constantes Amours d'Alix et d'Alexis*, in which Alix struggles to forget her

unfaithful lover. See F.-A. P. de Moncrif, *Œuvres de Monsieur De Moncrif, Lecteur de la Reine* (Paris : 1768), vol. 3, p. 214 'Pour chasser de sa souvenance / L'ami secret, / On se donne tant de souffrance / Pour peu d'effet: / Une si douce fantaisie / Toujours revient; / En songeant qu'il faut qu'on l'oublie, / On s'en souvient' (To banish from our memory / The secret love, / We give ourselves so much pain / To little effect: / Such sweet fantasies / Always come back to us; / In thinking we ought to forget it / We remember).

52. *To a heart undisguised and sincere by nature, a heart like Caroline's, this was too much*: Holcroft's translation strives to emphasise Caroline's innate goodness even as she feels herself to be at fault. Cf. Montolieu, *Caroline de Lichtfield*, vol. 1, p. 86: 'C'en étoit trop, beaucoup trop pour Caroline' (This was too much, much too much for Caroline).

53. *(the Baroness was almost as simple and innocent as Caroline)*: Holcroft adds this comment on the Baroness's character.

54. *self-sufficient*: conceited, vain.

55. *your visits will always be well received at Rindaw*: cf. Montolieu, *Caroline de Lichtfield*, vol. 1, p. 100, in which Caroline invites Lindorf to visit that same evening.

56. *She supposed her love for Lindorf was the love of a sister*: according to eighteenth-century standards of female morality, as well as the conventions of sentimental literature, a heroine could not be deemed virtuous unless she displayed a total ignorance of her own nascent sexual desires.

57. *Love stood confessed ... Despair shot them*: the anthropomorphism of Love is less explicit in Montolieu's text; Holcroft introduces the figures of Sorrow and Despair. Cf. Montolieu, *Caroline de Lichtfield*, vol. 1, p. 114: 'c'étoit l'amour dans toute sa force, & d'autant plus violent qu'il se faisoit connoître par les traits les plus aigus de la douleur; si son désespoir en augmenta, elle n'en fut que plus confirmée dans la resolution qu'elle venoit de prendre' (it was love in all his power, and all the more violent for having made himself known by the most acute forms of pain; if her despair increased, she was thereby only more confirmed in the resolution she had just taken).

58. *a Saxon gentleman*: a native of the Electorate of Saxony, a State in the Holy Roman Empire of the German Nation until 1806.

59. *War broke out between Austria and Prussia:* the War of the Austrian Succession (1740–8). Following the death of Charles VI, the Holy Roman Emperor of the German Nation, Frederick II of Prussia challenged the right of Charles's daughter, Maria Theresa of Austria, to succeed him. The war began in December 1740 when Frederick led his troops into Silesia, then an Austrian province.

60. *battle of Molviez*: probably refers to the Battle of Mollwitz in April 1741, in which Frederick II of Prussia led his army to victory against the army of the Austrian Empress Maria Theresa. This was a pivotal victory: the Prussian army overran Silesia and Frederick subsequently formed alliances with France, Bavaria, Spain, and Saxony against the Austrian Empire.

61. *Hussars*: members of the light-cavalry units that formed part of many European armies in the eighteenth century.

62. *Silesia*: a region in central Europe which is now divided between Poland, Germany, and the Czech Republic. In 1742, the Austrian Empress Maria Theresa had ceded Silesia to Frederick II, upon which it became the Prussian Province of Silesia.

63. *Cicely, Joselin, and, particularly, the little Louisa:* in Montolieu's text, Cicely is called Christine; Joselin is called Johannes; Louisa is called Louise.

64. *Erlang*: a German university city, now called Erlangen. The university, at which Lindorf is said to be pursuing his studies, was founded in 1742 in Bayreuth, moved to Erlangen in 1743, and became the Friedrich-Alexander University in 1769.

65. *Poor girl! ... never forsake her*: practised in writing dialogue for the stage, Holcroft has Fritz speak in a rustic English vernacular. Cf. Montolieu, *Caroline de Lichtfield,* vol. 1, p. 150, in which Fritz speaks in standard French.

66. *osier*: willow plant.

67. *scandalize*: in this context, 'to defame'.

Volume 2

1. *One ball had struck him in the face ... neither of them were mortal*: Holcroft omits the gruesome detail, included in Montolieu's text, that half of Walstein's cheek had been torn away. Cf. Montolieu, *Caroline de Lichtfield,* vol. 1, p. 166.

2. *Every circumstance was a dagger to my heart ... capable*: Holcroft intensifies Lindorf's account of the guilt he suffers in the aftermath of his crime. Cf. Montolieu, *Caroline de Lichtfield,* vol. 1, p. 169: 'j'apperçus ce tableau d'un coup d'œil, & je puis attester que la seul impression qu'il me fit éprouver, fut d'ajouter à mes remords' (I took in this tableau with one glance, & I can attest that the only impression it made on me, was to add to my remorse).

3. *Criminal, indeed, most criminal ... see her no more!* : Holcroft omits a sentence at the end of this paragraph; perhaps Lindorf seems too eager, in Montolieu's text, to avoid the memory of his guilt. Cf. Montolieu, *Caroline de Lichtfield,* vol. 1, p. 171: 'je sentois que sa seule présence auroit été pour moi un reproche continuel' (I felt that her mere presence would have been a continual reproach for me).

4. *Yes, it had its effects; but I should ill deserve the sublime friendship of Walstein if I did not lament and execrate them everlastingly*: this is Holcroft's addition, which emphasizes that Lindorf is fully cognisant of the extent and severity of his guilt.

5. *but, no, I would rather follow her to the grave*: cf. Montolieu, *Caroline de Lichtfield,* vol. 1, p. 179, in which Johannes expresses himself more violently: 'j'aurois mieux aimé, je crois, la tuer, que de la lui donner' (I would rather have killed her, I believe, than given her to him). By making this change, Holcroft demonstrates his refusal to construct an avowedly benevolent character who can nonetheless contemplate a violent assertion of patriarchal control.

6. *after a crime for which any other man would have held me in everlasting abhorrence, and have been appeased only by my blood*: Holcroft interpolates this clause, which acknowledges the remarkable saintliness of Walstein's response to his attacker.

7. *I could only testify my gratitude as to a Deity!* : one of several images in the novel that give Walstein a god-like quality in keeping with his unshakeable virtue. These images align him with another demiurge, Rousseau's Wolmar who, in *Julie, ou La Nouvelle Héloïse* (1761) presides over the Swiss pastoral idyll of the Clarens estate.

8. *Dresden*: the capital of Saxony and, in the eighteenth century, the seat of the Electors – and later Kings – of Saxony. The city was renowned for its artistic and architectural splendour, as well as its rich cultural life.

9. The *L E T T E R* of *J U S T I N*: this letter is another instance of Holcroft introducing a rustic vernacular into the text.

10. *You hear the prayers of these good people ... a still superior angel!* : these lines are added by Holcroft.

<u>11.</u> *Nancy*: the maid is named Charlotte in Montolieu's text; Holcroft has selected a name that British readers would have considered appropriate to the maid's class.

<u>12.</u> *A good minister ... the life of a soldier*: cf. Montolieu, *Caroline de Lichtfield*, vol. 1, p. 213: 'il a besoin de bons ministres, autant que de bon généraux; je tâcherai de remplir de mon mieux ma vocation actuelle, & je pense avec plaisir, mon cher Lindorf, que je suis très-bien remplacé pour la précédente' (he needs good ministers as much as he needs good generals; I will try to fill my present role to the best of my ability, & I think with pleasure, my dear Lindorf, that I am very well replaced in my previous one). In Holcroft's translation, Walstein elevates his diplomatic work above his soldiery and emphasizes that he prefers his current work, which he would not have been able to pursue if he were still able-bodied. These subtle alterations make his capacity to forgive Lindorf more plausible.

13. *prevent*: in this context, 'to anticipate'.

14. *apoplectic fit*: in the eighteenth century, 'apoplexy' or 'apoplectic fit' tended to function as a catch-all term to describe sudden and violent symptoms often resulting in loss of consciousness. These symptoms might now be associated with a stroke or heart attack. In George Motherby's popular medical dictionary, an apoplexy is defined as 'a sudden privation of all sense and voluntary motion; the pulse, at the same time, being kept up, but respiration is oppressed.' See G. Motherby, *A New Medical Dictionary; or, General Repository of Physic,* 2nd edn. (London: 1785).

15. *terminate*: 'to complete'.

16. *Potsdam*: during the reign of Frederick the Great, the city of Potsdam was a focal point of intellectual and military activity and, in many ways, functioned as a virtual capital of Prussia.

<u>17.</u> *Oh! how grateful it is to my heart ... not wholly banished from this earth*: in Montolieu's text, Walstein rejoices, not simply to find that happiness is attainable, but to find it attainable instinctively, as it were, by way of sentiment as opposed to rational self-government. Cf. Montolieu, *Caroline de Lichtfield*, vol. 1, p. 238: 'il m'est bien doux que ce soit mon ami ... qui me prouve qu'on peut être heureux sur cette terre, & l'être par le sentiment!' (How sweet it is to me that it is my friend ... who proves to me that we can find happiness on this earth, and find it by way of feeling!)

18. *Sorrows of Werter*: refers to J. W. von Goethe's epistolary novel, *Die Leiden des Jungen Werthers* (1774), first translated into English as *The Sorrows of Werther* (London: 1779). This anonymous translation, which was frequently reprinted, has been variously ascribed to Richard Graves and Daniel Malthus. An early example of *Sturm und Drang* literature, *Werther* was one of the first international bestsellers. Lindorf apparently identifies with the protagonist, Werther, a young artist of exceptional sensitivity tortured by his love for a woman named Lotte, who is engaged to, and later marries, an older man named Albert. The novel was a source of heated critical debate and cultural controversy, as many readers saw it as an apology for suicide, an interpretation that the English translator rejects. The novel was even said to have contributed to a rise in copycat suicides. Montolieu appears to disagree with this reading of the novel, for Lindorf actively seeks, in the pages of *Werther*, the courage and justification to commit suicide, but sees only the despair of those left to mourn the hero. Cf. Montolieu, *Caroline de Lichtfield*, vol. 1, p. 251.

<u>19.</u> *Surely, if Lindorf had been guilty ... expiate all his errors*: cf. Montolieu, *Caroline de Lichtfield*, vol. 1, p. 258: 'Si Lindorf eut des torts, s'il fut la cause involontaire des malheurs du meilleur des hommes, ce qu'il souffroit dans cet instant, suffit pour les expier & pour intéresser tout lecteur sensible à sa situation' (If Lindorf had been guilty of wrongs, if

he was the involuntary cause of suffering to the best of men, what he suffered in that moment, suffices to expiate them all & to interest any feeling reader in his predicament). Holcroft cuts Montolieu's attempt to manipulate readerly responses to her text, in which she implies that failure to sympathize with Lindorf denotes lack of feeling.

20. *Dantzic*: Danzig, the German name for what is now the Polish city of Gdánsk. At the time of Walstein's diplomatic mission, it was part of the Polish-Lithuanian Commonwealth.

21. *(The reader will no doubt here recollect the artifice of the High Chamberlain, and the fears of Caroline for her father's life.)*: Holcroft inserts this line.

22. *(Here Walstein likewise mistook the High Chamberlain's motives.)*: Holcroft inserts this line, exacerbating the guilt of the Baron of Lindorf and diminishing that of Walstein.

23. *Is it in my power, by any means, to give you ease?*: Holcroft inserts this line, perhaps to mitigate further our impression of Walstein's guilt.

24. *his heart was a sanctuary too holy for a guest so vile*: Holcroft's addition; another effort to deify Walstein.

25. *His feelings, ever delicate, were ever averse to give others pain*: Holcroft's addition.

26. *Empress*: the probable dates for the action of the novel (see above, vol. 1, n. 9) suggest that this is the Empress Elizabeth. This would make Walstein's cordial relations with her rather improbable, however, as she was an implacable enemy of Frederick the Great. It may be, therefore, that Montolieu's dating of the action is imprecise, and that the Empress is actually Catherine the Great, who was renowned not only for her ruthless ambition, but also for her liberal views and cultural knowledge.

27. *a bit of green silk, and a ribband, properly disposed, removed that disgust which the loss of an eye might, at first sight, have caused*: in Montolieu's text, Walstein has acquired a false eye made of enamel which, she assures us, is barely distinguishable from the one he has lost; it seems that she could not convince Holcroft. Cf. Montolieu, *Caroline de Lichtfield,* vol. 1, p. 266.

28. *The generous, the philosophic, the capacious heart of Walstein ... detained and repelled*: Holcroft inserts this paragraph.

29. *outrageous*: in this context, 'furious' or 'raging'.

30. *Deign to give me your commands ... for your sake*: Holcroft's translation emphasizes Walstein's willingness to suffer in order to ensure Caroline's happiness. Cf. Montolieu, *Caroline de Lichtfield,* vol. 1, p. 276: 'daignez me prescrire des ordres, des sacrifices: tout me deviendra facile si je puis parvenir à vous rendre heureuse' (deign to give commands, prescribe sacrifices: everything will be easy to me if I can succeed in making you happy).

31. *This husband ... clasped him to her bosom*: Holcroft interpolates this line. In Montolieu's text, Caroline finds her marriage bonds easier to bear, but she does not, as yet, envisage a perfect meeting of minds or an affectionate bond with her husband. Cf. Montolieu, *Caroline de Lichtfield,* vol. 1, p. 280.

32. *Cyrus*: Cyrus the Great, a Persian king. An idealized biography of Cyrus, the *Cyropædia*, was written in the fourth century BC by Xenophon of Athens. The Canoness's allusion is rather apt, as the *Cyropædia* portrays Cyrus as a benevolent despot willingly obeyed by his adoring subjects; Walstein has certainly exerted his patriarchal rights in marrying Caroline, but the Canoness seems eagerly to accept the bonds he has forged for her protégée. Although the *Cyropædia* was widely read in the eighteenth century, many readers of the period would have encountered Cyrus through the Chevalier (Andrew Michael) Ramsay's *Les Voyages de Cyrus* (Paris: 1727), or *The Travels of Cyrus* (London: 1727), a moral-historical romance influenced by Fénélon's *Aventures de Télémaque* (1699) and

Samuel Johnson's *History of Rasselas* (1759). Written to provide entertaining instruction, it is a fictional account of Cyrus's early life. When Stéphanie-Félicité de Genlis, who was a friend of Montolieu, wrote her pedagogical novel, *Adèle et Théodore*, in 1782, she listed *The Travels of Cyrus* as part of Adèle's course of reading. Holcroft translated *Adèle et Théodore* into *Adelaide and Theodore* in 1783.

33. *Oroondates*: the Scythian prince in Gaultier de Coste de la Calprenède's romance, *Cassandre* (1643–50), translated into English by Charles Cotterell in 1652 and reprinted in several editions in the eighteenth century. Oroondates is a hero of great physical beauty and martial prowess but, like Walstein, he suffers for his faithful love for a woman who remains distant.

34. *he merely resembles the present race*: in the eighteenth century, many readers saw, in accounts of classical societies or, in the Canoness's case, the narratives of heroic romance, evidence that humankind had reached the acme of virtue in a Golden Age later lost to the degenerate effects of civilization.

35. *Walstein, indeed, possessed a soul ... the strongest attachment of her heart*: Holcroft alters this line in his translation, explaining and justifying the sudden alteration in Caroline's feelings where Montolieu simply describes it. Cf. Montolieu, *Caroline de Lichtfield*, vol. 1, p. 286.

36. *nor is there a motive ... less wise mortals*: Holcroft expands on Montolieu's text, turning Walstein's duty to king and country into a commitment to improving the lot of the unfortunate. Cf. Montolieu, *Caroline de Lichtfield*, vol. 1, p. 291.

37. *hartshorn*: salt or spirit of hartshorn, another term for smelling salts, so called because ammonia was obtained from the horns of harts (stags). See above, vol. 2, n. 13.

38. *valet de chambre:* a man-servant who acted as a gentleman's personal attendant. The French term reflects the pervasive influence of the French language and culture on the eighteenth-century European aristocracy. This was particularly the case in Germany at the time of Frederick the Great, who was a well-known Francophile.

39. *No, dear Caroline... virtue deceives thee*: Holcroft alters Walstein's reaction to the letter to emphasise the virtuous motivations behind Caroline's request to remain in solitude at Rindaw. In Montolieu's text, he responds simply with an exclamation. Cf. Montolieu, *Caroline de Lichtfield*, vol. 2, p. 29: 'Chère et cruelle Caroline!' (Dear and cruel Caroline!).

40. *Lindorf, wait not a moment ... never return to Ronebourg more*: in keeping with the urgency of the moment, Holcroft has Walstein quickly write a brief letter to Lindorf. In Montolieu's text, the letter is – implausibly – much longer. Cf. Montolieu, vol. 2, pp. 35–6: 'Partez à l'instant, mon cher Lindorf, & faites la plus grande diligence pour vous rendre ici, où votre présence est absolument nécessaire; je vous devrai plus que la vie, si vous ne perdez pas une minute, & si votre promptitude a le succès que j'ose espérer. Lindorf, pourquoi nous avoir quittés? pourquoi vous défier du cœur de votre ami? Mais les instans sont précieux: n'en laissez pas écouler un seul avant que de vous mettre en route; je regrette même ceux que j'emploie à vous demander le vrai témoignage de votre amitié; je vous connois, Lindorf, un seul mot de moi suffit ... Courez jour & nuit; si vous ne me rencontrez pas, venez ici en droiture; si vous me rencontrez, je vous parlerai, & nous ne nous quitterons plus' (Set off this moment, my dear Lindorf, and make the greatest haste to come back here, where your presence is absolutely necessary; I will owe you more than life, if you lose not a moment, & if your promptness brings the success I dare to hope for. Lindorf, why did you leave us? why mistrust the heart of your friend? But the minutes are precious: do not let a single one go by before you set off; I even regret those I employ

to ask you for this true testament of your friendship; I know you, Lindorf, a single word from me will suffice ... Travel day and night; if you do not meet me, come here directly; if you meet me, I will speak with you, and we will never part again).

41. *Happy Lindorf... my loss*: Montolieu has Walstein ask himself whether Lindorf senses the price of his happiness and the sacrifice Walstein is making. Cf. Montolieu, *Caroline de Lichtfield*, vol. 2, p. 60.

Volume 3

1. *and he had the fortitude to imagine Caroline in the arms of another, and not expire at the thought!*: Holcroft alters the sense of this line. In Montolieu's text, Walstein imagines Caroline sacrificing herself to her duty and dying of sorrow. Cf. Montolieu, *Caroline de Lichtfield*, vol. 2, p. 68.

2. *incontinently*: at once, immediately.

3. *Thus did the noble and sympathetic heart of Caroline ... teach her how to estimate his worth*: this clause is added by Holcroft.

4. *Flora*: the Roman goddess of the flowering of plants. Holcroft adds this depiction to the text.

5. *When now no longer starting fears ... Hope cherish in this bleeding heart*: see Appendix II for Montolieu's version of this song.

6. *froward*: peevish; perverse.

7. *Hotel*: denotes a place of residence.

8. *The words are hosts of angels, and the small paper the infinite regions of bliss*: Holcroft introduces this celestial imagery, which does not appear in Montolieu's text. Cf. Montolieu, *Caroline de Lichtfield*, vol. 2, p. 108: 'elle relit encore cette lettre qui est le sceau de son bonheur future, & de l'amour de son époux' (she again re-reads this letter which is the guarantee of her future happiness and the love of her husband).

9. *and when I die she will shed a tear over my tomb*: Holcroft adds this clause.

10. *having drank a third glass*: in Montolieu's text, this is Johannes's second glass of wine.

11. *simple but natural village eloquence* : a counterpoint to the Baron of Lindorf's courtly eloquence. In sentimental literature and philosophy, this kind of plain, unstudied speech is indicative of the sincerity and sensibility of the speaker, which apparently flow from a heart uninhibited by attempts to dazzle or deceive.

12. *allemandes*: Matilda is playing the music for German figure dances. Usually performed by two couples, they involved elaborate turns and intertwining of the arms – a fitting allusion to the interrelated romances of the primary and subsidiary heroines of the novel.

13. *The marriage honey moon ... My dear Louisa and my boys.*: see Appendix III for Montolieu's version of this song.

14. *He had supposed it possible ... he himself now sung*: in Montolieu's text, Justin is said to have composed the new verse of his song while Louisa was singing; Holcroft appears to reject this claim as unrealistic and suggests, instead, that Justin had anticipated this moment and composed the song accordingly. Cf. Montolieu, *Caroline de Lichtfield*, vol. 2, p. 130.

15. *above a year*: in Montolieu's text, Caroline has now been married for almost three years.

16. *He related a thousand traits ... my friend*: Holcroft, perhaps because of his opposition to hereditary rule, cuts from Montolieu's text a claim that the king's goodness is universally acknowledged. Cf. Montolieu, *Caroline de Lichtfield*, vol. 2, p. 136: 'Il lui racontoit mille traits de la bonté du Roi, de cette affabilité qui lui gagnoit tous les cœurs, & le faisoit

adorer de ses sujets' (He recounted a thousand traits of the King's goodness, of this affability which had won every heart, & made his subjects adore him).

17. *not perfectly understanding how a woman might be the cause of all this delirium*: Frederick the Great famously neglected his wife, Elisabeth Christine of Brunswick-Bevern, with whom he had no children.

18. *prodigy*: in this context, a remarkable happenstance.

19. *He certainly feared to meet ... from his imagination*: in Montolieu's text, Lindorf's agitation at this meeting is more pronounced. Cf. Montolieu, *Caroline de Lichtfield*, vol. 2, p. 143: 'en apprenant qu'il alloit revoir Caroline, il s'étoit senti si ému, si peu sûr de lui-même, qu'il avoit tremblé de cette entrevue' (on learning that he was going to see Caroline again, he felt himself so moved, so little sure of himself, that he trembled at the interview).

20. *Opéra House*: the *Opéra* was one of the three authorized theatrical establishments in eighteenth-century Paris and an important social space. Spectators did not attend simply to view performances, but also to be seen – and admired – by other members of the Parisian *beau monde*. De Zastrow's obsession with what Swiss and British authors often depicted as the superficial parade of Parisian theatre culture signals his propensity for decadence and moral degeneracy.

21. *Théâtre Italien*: in seventeenth-century Paris, the *Théâtre Italien*, or *Comédie-Italienne* was set up to accommodate the improvisational, pantomimic, and often ribald performances of the Italian *commedia dell'arte*, as distinct from the neo-classical dramas staged at the *Comédie-Française*, at which the *bienséances* were more rigorously observed. By the latter part of the eighteenth century, the *Théâtre Italien* was primarily associated with *opéra-bouffe* (comic opera).

22. strike: a colloquialism, the modern equivalent of which is probably the verb 'to wow'. The implication is that Matilda would incite admiration in the upper echelons of Parisian society.

23. *(What did Lindorf feel as thus Matilda spoke?)*: Holcroft adds this line, emphasizing how Matilda's constancy chastens her wayward lover.

24. *Better than life! Beyond all thought!*: Holcroft's addition.

25. *(Lindorf with a look petitioned mercy; Matilda smiled and continued)*: Holcroft's addition.

26. *piteous*: in this context, 'compassionate'.

27. *And so you thought I meant to send you to Berlin alone ... a place on the box*: the fugitive noblewoman in disguise was, by the 1780s, a familiar figure of sentimental literature. F. Burney exploited the convention in her novel, *The Wanderer* (1814), in which the mysterious heroine, Juliet Granville, is amongst a group of refugees from Robespierre's Terror.

28. *ducats*: gold coins

29. *my guardian genius*: in this context, the ancient Roman concept of the genius as a person's guiding or attendant spirit appears to have been conflated with the Christian notion of a guardian angel who watches over and protects a human charge.

30. *not yet eighteen*: in Montolieu's text, Matilde is sixteen.

31. *I found a village surgeon to dress my wound*: in Montolieu's text, Lindorf's valet is fortuitously also a surgeon.

32. *Amadis*: see above, vol. 1, n. 33.

33. *Galaor*: a hero of Spanish romance. The brother of Amadís de Gaula, Galaor was the quintessential courtly paladin. Eighteenth-century readers might have encountered him in *The Famous and Delightful History of the Renowned and Valiant Prince Amadis de*

Gaul where he is depicted as a handsome and amorous knight whose 'wonted Custom' it is to seduce beautiful women. See J. Shirley, *The Famous and Delightful History of the Renowned and Valiant Prince Amadis de Gaul* (London: 1702), p. 100. Lindorf and Matilda, however, may be thinking of a passage in Cervantes's *Don Quixote de la Mancha*, in which the protagonist claims that it was Galaor's 'natural disposition' to make love 'to every handsome woman who came in his way', but that he also had 'one mistress, whom he enthroned as sovereign of his heart'. See M. de Cervantes Saavedra, *The History and Aventures of the Renowned Don Quixote*, trans. by T. Smollett (London: 1786), p. 115.

34. *In those times, a woman, with vast* sang froid ... *and he obeyed*: precise reference unknown; however, the motif of the lover enjoined to silence was common in heroic romance. In Charlotte Lennox's *Female Quixote* (1752), the heroine, Arabella, is even more ludicrously prone than the Caroness to interpreting the events of her life according to the conventions of romance novels, and responds with horror to an open declaration of love, which she considers 'a horrid Violation this, of all the Laws of Gallantry and Respect, which decree a Lover to suffer whole years in Silence before he declares his Flame to the divine Object that causes it'. See C. Lennox, *The Female Quixote* (Oxford: Oxford University Press, 2008), p. 32.

35. *balsamic*: a healing or restorative medicine or application.

36. *Hamburg*: a city on the Elbe River in northern Germany. In the eighteenth century, it was a free imperial city of the Holy Roman Empire.

37. *the physician ... had me bled so abundantly that excessive weakness was the consequence*: blood-letting was a common practice amongst physicians in the eighteenth century, whose vague notion that infectious diseases circulated in the blood led them to believe that these diseases could be released from the body by bleeding the patient. In some cases, as in the death of Byron, blood-letting may have contributed more to the demise of the patient than the disease itself.

38. *and that peculiarity of manners which distance and a government so different produce*: Holcroft interpolates this clause, in which national character is regarded, not as innate, but as an effect of environmental and political conditions.

39. *a saviour*: in keeping with his reinforcement of imagery that deifies Walstein, Holcroft translates Montolieu's epithet 'bienfaiteur' (benefactor) as 'saviour', which gives Lindorf's description of Walstein a religious gloss.

40. *I felt a painful sensation ... which I endeavoured to conceal*: in Montolieu's text, Lindorf's pain is accompanied by anger. Cf. Montolieu, *Caroline de Lichtfield*, vol. 2, pp. 212–3.

41. *a mate more worthy*: in Holcroft's translation, Lindorf's dialogue is subtly altered to make him sound a little more self-critical than in Montolieu's text, where he describes Matilde seeking 'un autre objet d'attachement' (another object of attachment). Cf. Montolieu, *Caroline de Lichtfield*, vol. 2, p. 214.

42. *From my own experience, Walstein ... happy to encourage the mutability*: Holcroft makes significant alterations here to Lindorf's account of his present feelings for Caroline. In Montolieu's text, he claims that he still thinks of Caroline more than he would like, but that his efforts to forget her are finally bearing fruit. Holcroft's Lindorf is more effectually 'cured' of his love for Caroline when he asks for Matilda's hand in marriage, which makes him seem at once more changeable and more wholehearted in his commitment to the latter. Cf. Montolieu, *Caroline de Lichtfield*, vol. 2, p. 216: 'Non, mon ami, Caroline est présente à mon cœur, à ma pensée, plus que je ne voudrai; j'écarte autant qu'il m'est possible ce dangereux souvenir; & depuis quelque temps, je pense plus à Caroline de Walstein, qu'à Caroline de Lichtfield' (No, my friend, Caroline is present in my heart,

in my thoughts, more than I like; I suppress the dangerous memory as much as I can; & for some time, I have been thinking more of Caroline of Walstein than of Caroline of Lichtfield).

43. *Orange Coffee-house*: each of the London coffee-houses had a defining character and clientele. The Orange Coffee-house was a meeting place for foreigners in London.

44. *Newmarket*: a town in Suffolk established by the patronage of Charles II as the celebrated headquarters of English horse racing. Holcroft became a stable boy at Newmarket in 1757.

45. *"Read," said he, "and think what must be the impression it made on me!"*: Holcroft here condenses Lindorf's dialogue. Cf. Montolieu, *Caroline de Lichtfield*, vol. 2, pp. 227–8: 'lisez, lui dit-il, & voyez quelle impression dut faire sur mon cœur cette ingénuité si touchante! il étoit impossible que ce cœur sensible & reconnoissant ne se donnât pas entièrement à celle qui, malgré tous mes torts, m'avoit conservé le sien' (read it, he said, & imagine the impression this touching ingenuousness made on my heart! it was impossible that this feeling and grateful heart should not give itself entirely to the woman who, despite all my wrongs, had kept hers for me).

46. *Yet will I own I felt some emotion ... a very different kind from what I had formerly known*: Holcroft cuts an extra line here. Cf. Montolieu, *Caroline de Lichtfield*, vol. 2, p. 237: 'un regard de Matilde l'eut bientôt dissipée, & j'ose assurer que ce sera la dernière' (a look from Matilda had soon dissipated it, & I dare affirm that it will be the last time).

47. *where Caroline had fled* from *her husband, on the bridal day, and* to *him on the morning of the projected divorce*: Montolieu's text reads simply, 'où Caroline étoit allée le joindre' (where Caroline had gone to join him); Holcroft emphasises the irony of separation on the wedding day and union following divorce.

48. *He beheld both these lovely women ... with perfect tranquillity*: in Montolieu's text, this moment is described as another 'épreuve' (trial). Lindorf's preference for Matilde is also described in terms of a general human tendency to respond more powerfully to recent than past emotion. Cf. Montolieu, *Caroline de Lichtfield*, vol. 2, p. 240: 'le dernier sentiment qu'on éprouve, est toujours celui qui paroît le plus vif' (the last feeling one has felt is always that which seems the strongest).

49. *To those who wish to be informed of every thing ... he made his lovely lady happy*: Holcroft cuts an additional clause here, in which Montolieu blithely acknowledges that Lindorf continues to be somewhat fickle in his attachments. Cf. Montolieu, *Caroline de Lichtfield*, vol. 2, p. 241: '& que, malgré sa légereté naturelle qui l'entraîna peut-être à des infidélités passagères, il fit le Bonheur de son aimable compagne' (and that, despite his natural inconstancy, which perhaps led him into passing infidelities, he made his amiable companion Happy). In her adaptation of *Sense and Sensibility*, Montolieu redeems Willoughby at the end of the novel by having him marry the second Eliza, who has borne his illegitimate child. His redemption does not, however, demand total fidelity: 'Elle le fixa autant qu'on pouvait le fixer' (She kept him as faithful as anyone could). See I. de Montolieu, *Raison et Sentiments*, ed. H. Seyrès (Paris: L'Archipel, 2011), p. 571.

50. *cousin german*: a first cousin, the child of a parent's brother or sister.

51. *making two more lovers happy .;.. T H E E N D*: Holcroft cuts a substantial section at the end of the novel. See Appendix IV.

SILENT CORRECTIONS

Volume 1

p. 32, l. 38, not the foe.] not the foe

p. 37, l. 38, dies alabaster scarlet] dyes alabaster scarlet

p. 61, l. 40, in all proability] in all probability

p. 63, l. 17, hussars] Hussars

p. 67, l. 24, When I sat out for the farm] When I set out for the farm

p. 68, l. 22, I should ra- see her the mistress of a great Lord] I should rather see her the mistress of a great Lord

p. 74, l. 26, songs and and flageolet] songs and flageolet

Volume 2

p. 90, l. 30, He often spoke of her to me, at Rindaw] He often spoke of her to me, at Ronebourg

p. 101, l. 17, happipiness] happiness

p. 115, l. 38, yet had she, certainly, began] yet had she, certainly, begun

p. 119, l. 30, confirmed the allusion] confirmed the illusion

p. 143, l. 9, Neither did he dobut] Neither did he doubt

Volume 3

p. 176, l. 31, he remembers there pugnance] he remembers the repugnance

p. 178, l. 20, wait his return.] wait his return."

p. 185, l. 38, its my opinion] it's my opinion

p. 187, l. 37, with the Count the Countess and the bottle] with the Count, the Countess and the bottle

p. 189, l. 16, though I do think, my Lady] "though I do think, my Lady

p. 194, l. 39, so inestimable!] so inestimable!"

p. 195, l. 19, It is almost as singular, said she, to her brother, as the fine tales you used to tell me when I was a very little, little girl] It is almost as singular," said she, to her brother, "as the fine tales you used to tell me when I was a very little, little girl

p. 195, l. 33, To morrow they will clip thy wings] To-morrow they will clip thy wings

p. 209, l. 21, at the sight of De Zastow] at the sight of De Zastrow

p. 210, l. 16, was to have married me to day] was to have married me to-day

p. 218, l. 37, to Hamburg] from Hamburg

TEXTUAL VARIANTS

Volume I

4a   to comprehend to what this his preface tended] to comprehend to what this preface tended *1795*

5a   brought thee hither] brought thee thither *1795*

9a   He reflected that this would even be the wisest course] He reflected that this would certainly be the wisest course *1786 2ⁿᵈ edn, 1797, 1798*

9b   from which the timid Caroline would not dare recede] from which she would not dare recede *1798*

9c   to hear reason at present] to hear reason at that instant *1786 2ⁿᵈ edn, 1797, 1798*

10a   How desirous to see me happy!] How desirous is he to see me happy! *1786 2ⁿᵈ edn, 1797, 1798*

10b   the same infantine graces with which he was daily received] the same infinite graces with which he was daily received *1795*

14a   to find her tolerably calm and resigned] to find her totally calmed and resigned *1795*

15a   supported the jaunt exceedingly well] supported the journey exceedingly well *1798*

15b   added a fresh pang] inflicted a fresh pang *1786 2ⁿᵈ edn, 1797, 1798*

15c   and read as follows] and read *1786 2ⁿᵈ edn, 1797, 1798*

15d   I dare expect and hope benevolence] I dare ask and hope benevolence *1786 2ⁿᵈ edn, 1797, 1798*

16a   you will inspire gratitude inexpressible] you will ensure gratitude inexpressible *1798*

16b   the just reproaches you have a right to make me] the just reproaches I merit by acting thus *1786 2ⁿᵈ edn, 1797, 1798*

17a   A mirror was over the table] A mirror hung over the table *1786 2ⁿᵈ edn, 1797, 1798*

17b   whose face has been disfigured by wounds] whose face is disfigured by wounds *1798*

19a   he really understood nothing of the education of a daughter] he really knew nothing of the education of a daughter *1786 2ⁿᵈ edn, 1797, 1798*

19b   but, a few ridiculous singularities excepted] but, no; a few ridiculous singularities excepted *1786 2ⁿᵈ edn, 1797, 1798*

20a   every person she saw instantly became her dearest intimate] every person she saw might soon become her dearest intimate, *1786 2ⁿᵈ edn, 1797, 1798*

20b   she herself knew not whether it were better to rejoice or weep] she scarcely knew whether it were better to rejoice or weep *1786 2ⁿᵈ edn, 1797, 1798*

22a   which she certainly did not greatly embellish] which she undoubtedly did not much embellish *1786 2ⁿᵈ edn, 1797, 1798*

24a we will not pretend [...] unfortunate one] we will not pretend to affirm he did not even think the caprice of his young bride very fortunate *1786 2ⁿᵈ edn, 1797, 1798*

26a only desired to remain as she was] only desired to remain where she was *1798*

26b This was a very different kind of sensation from that which her marriage had occasioned] This was a very different sort of sensation from that which her marriage had occasioned *1786 2ⁿᵈ edn, 1797, 1798*

26c No, however natural such a thought might be] However natural such a thought might be *1786 2ⁿᵈ edn, 1797, 1798*

27a Is it for sixteen to fear a whole six months before it shall happen?] Is it for sixteen to fear an evil six months before it shall happen? *1786 2ⁿᵈ edn, 1797, 1798*

36a remain she must with all her fears and inquietudes] remain she must with all her anxious inquietudes *1786 2ⁿᵈ edn, 1797, 1798*

37a these all are fled] that and these are fled *1786 2ⁿᵈ edn, 1797, 1798*

37b If I had left the window, he would not have pulled off his hat, and his horse would not have been frightened] If I had left the window, he would not have been frightened *1795*

39a All these things had the furtive glances of the beauteous Countess presently remarked] All these things had the furtive beauteous Countess presently remarked *1798*

39b all her fears and inquietudes during those two dreadful days of rain] all her fears and apprehensions during those two dreadful days of rain *1786 2ⁿᵈ edn, 1797, 1798*

41a as she sauntered towards the pavilion] as she sauntered near the pavilion *1786 2ⁿᵈ edn, 1797, 1798*

42a which she was very industriously spoiling] which she was industriously spoiling *1798*

48a and that him whom your respectable friend has deigned to honour with her protection will] and that him whom your respectable friend has deigned to honour with her protection may *1786 2ⁿᵈ edn, 1797*

48b still esteemed and respected] still esteemed and still respected *1798*

49a thus began to dictate] thus began *1786 2ⁿᵈ edn, 1797, 1798*

50a she has therefore desired me to write in her name, and to inform you, Sir] she has therefore desired me to inform you, Sir *1798*

50b a thousand sensations to communicate] a thousand things to communicate *1795*

50c expected him with somewhat of impatience] expecting him with somewhat of impatience *1795*

52a with a tone more than usually animated] with a tone of voice more than usually animated *1798*

53a the rays of the setting sun with gold and purple decorated the horizon] the rays of the setting sun with gold and purple beamed over the horizon *1786 2ⁿᵈ edn, 1797, 1798*

54a some noise suddenly drew her from the profound revery in which she was plunged] some noise drew her from the profound revery in which she was plunged *1795*

54b already he is testifying] already testifying *1798*

55a observed her with eyes alternately expressive of tenderness, hope, and fear] observed her eyes alternately expressive of tenderness, hope, and fear *1795*

55b and my destiny shall be eternally decided!] and my destiny shall be decided! *1795*

56a Virtue pronounced it; but her heart could not forbear weeping while it was pronounced] Virtue pronounced it; but the heart of Virtue herself must bleed while it was pronounced *1786 2ⁿᵈ edn, 1797, 1798*

56b the sun rising in all his splendour] the sun rising in all its splendour *1797, 1798*

57a   he rose, flew to catch her, fall at her feet, and utter] he rose, flew to catch her, fell at her feed, and uttered *1786 2nd edn, 1797, 1798*

57b   till you have told me what my destiny is to be] till thou hast told me what my destiny is to be *1786 2nd edn, 1797, 1798*

59a   Lindorf stood [...] long he stood] Lindorf remained with his eyes fixed on the earth, his arms crossed, his faculties wholly absorbed, and in thought so deep as to seem almost lifeless; long he remained *1786 2nd edn, 1797, 1798*

59b   Imagine what the condition was, what the feelings were of Caroline] Imagine what the condition, what the feelings were of Caroline *1786 2nd edn, 1797, 1798*

61a   Lindorf observed her excessive paleness and dejection] Lindorf observed her successive paleness and dejection *1795*

63a   'I remit him, Sir,' said he] 'I commit him, Sir,' said he *1786 2nd edn, 1797, 1798*

63b   he has partook my peril and my glory] he has partaken my peril and my glory *1795*

64a   my dear little Matilda] my dear Matilda *1795*

65a   granted, though with pain] granted, though reluctantly *1786 2nd edn, 1797, 1798*

65b   his eyes were the very mirror of his mind] *1786 Dublin edn, 1795, omit*

65c   nor is it possible to convey the pleasing sensations that the symmetry of his person and his whole appearance inspired] nor is it impossible to convey the pleasing sensations that the symmetry of his person and his whole appearance inspired *1798*

65d   comprehended whose it once was] comprehending whose it once was *1786 Dublin edn, 1795*

65e   an emotion that augmented at every line] an emotion that augmented every line *1786 Dublin edn, 1795*

66a   They were not forgotten, and he was more on the footing of a friend than of a domestic] They were not forgotten, and he was esteemed rather as a friend than as a domestic *1786 2nd edn, 1797, 1798*

67a   her black gown] her black vest *1786 2nd edn, 1797, 1798*

70a   'And what, in the name of God,'] 'And what, in the name of heaven,' *1786 2nd edn, 1797, 1798*

71a   The Count observed, and saw what was passing in my mind] The Count observed me, knew what was passing in my mind *1786 2nd edn, 1797, 1798*

71b   and now I feel, too powerfully for me] and now I feel, too powerfully feel *1786 2nd edn, 1797, 1798*

72a   it's quite piteous to see her, my Lord] 'tis quite piteous to see her, my Lord *1786 2nd edn, 1797*

72b   yet was she not spinning, and, leaning on her elbows, she had covered her eyes with her handkerchief] yet was she not spinning, but, leaning on her elbows, she had covered her eyes with her handkerchief *1786 2nd edn, 1797, 1798*

72c   while I covered them with kisses] while I devoured them with my kisses *1786 2nd edn, 1797, 1798*

73a   what then could be your intention by this secret visit?] what then could be the intention of this secret visit? *1786 2nd edn, 1797, 1798*

73b   looked steadily at him] looked stedfastly at him *1795*

75a   after pressing him a good deal] after pressing him repeatedly *1786 2nd edn, 1797, 1798*

76a   living and dying for her] living and dying with her *1795*

77a   to have obtained the so much desired consent to go off with me] to have obtained her so much desired consent to go off with me *1786 2nd edn, 1797, 1798*

Volume II

81a   One ball had struck him in the face] One ball had struck him on the face *1786 2ⁿᵈ edn, 1797, 1798*

81b   A sole word will for ever deprive you of my friendship] A sole word will for ever deprive thee of my friendship *1797, 1798*

86a   I was alone with Louisa only for a moment] I was alone with Louisa but a moment *1798*

87a   the absence of Fritz] the disappearance of Fritz *1786 2ⁿᵈ edn, 1797, 1798*

87b   Louisa had been, all day, at the village with a relation] Louisa had been, all day, with a relation *1786 Dublin edn, 1795*

88a   though he certainly would be somewhat lame] though he certainly would become somewhat lame *1798*

88b   the charms of this kind of occupation] the charms of this occupation *1798*

89a   then, laying it close to her elbow, she again took up the manuscript] after which, laying it close to her elbow, she again took up the manuscript *1786 2ⁿᵈ edn, 1797, 1798*

90a   holding out his hand] *1798, omit*

90b   He often spoke of her to me] He had often spoken of her to me *1798*

91a   the regular and striking features of Louisa] the regular or striking features of Louisa *1795*

91b   May I soon call you brother?] May I hereafter call you brother? *1786 2ⁿᵈ edn, 1797, 1798*

92a   I had no great difficulty of obtaining it from her, and, under the promise of secrecy, of taking a copy] I had no great difficulty in prevailing on her, under a promise of secrecy, to suffer a copy to be taken *1786 2ⁿᵈ edn, 1797, 1798*

92b   the beauteous mind which once animated that beauteous form still exists] the beauteous mind which animated that once beauteous form still exists *1786 2ⁿᵈ edn, 1797, 1798*

92c   Yet, Caroline, should you detest his wretched assassin, forget not his remorse;] Ah! Caroline, you must detest his wretched assassin, but forget not his remorse; *1786 2ⁿᵈ edn, 1797, 1798*

93a   as often as the multiplicity of affairs in which he was going to engage would permit] as soon as the multiplicity of affairs in which he was going to engage would permit *1795*

94a   shall I not vex you, dear Lindorf, when I say I believe Matilda has at least as much feeling as my young friend?] shall I not vex you, dear Lindorf, when I say I believe Matilda has at least as much feeling as my friend himself? *1786 2ⁿᵈ edn, 1797, 1798*

95a   written with such simplicity of heart] written with such sympathy of heart *1795*

98a   Is it not a shocking thing to be obliged to set off without seeing you?] Is it not a shocking thing to set off without seeing you? *1798*

99a   the very moment you feel certain some other woman may render you more happy] the very moment you are convinced some other woman may render you more happy *1786 2ⁿᵈ edn, 1797, 1798*

102a   the few remaining moments in which I would conduct you to happiness] the few remaining minutes in which I would conduct you to happiness *1786 2ⁿᵈ edn, 1797, 1798*

102b my mother especially, who loved me with most affectionate tenderness, found herself sensibly better] my mother especially, who loved me with affectionate tenderness, found herself insensibly better *1786 Dublin edn, 1795*

103a which struck me at the moment of reading] which I remarked when I read it first *1786 2ⁿᵈ edn, 1797, 1798*

103b than I should have done at any other moment] than I should have done at any other time *1786 2ⁿᵈ edn, 1797, 1798*

104a asked me, with an affecting openness [...] less riches and more happiness] and asked me, with an affecting openness of heart whether it were not a thousand times better to have less riches and more happiness *1797, 1798*

110a his fiat formed you for each other] his fiat formed ye for each other *1786 2ⁿᵈ edn, 1797, 1798*

118a first had the idea of this marriage] first projected this marriage *1786 2ⁿᵈ edn, 1797, 1798*

118b might these two dreadful months have thrown in the way of happiness!] might these two months have thrown in the way of happiness! *1798*

119a I had feared lest her residence at court might have tainted] I had feared her residence at court might have tainted *1795*

120a in characters most affecting] in language most affecting *1786 2ⁿᵈ edn, 1797, 1798*

120b fell from his cheek] fell down his cheek *1797, 1798*

121a we will speak on these matters another time] we will speak on these matters some other time *1795*

121b a most amiable, as well as a most instructive companion] a most instructive companion *1798*

121c While he spoke no person remembered his person] While he spoke no auditor remembered his person *1786 2ⁿᵈ edn, 1797, 1798*

123a the deep and lengthened sigh heaved in his bosom] the deep and lengthened sigh heaved in his bosom, and silently escaped *1786 2ⁿᵈ edn, 1797, 1798*

123b sighed bitterly, and gave it back without speaking] sighed with bitterness of spirit, and gave it back *1786 2ⁿᵈ edn, 1797, 1798*

124a equally angered by your long and obstinate disobedience] equally irritated by your long and obstinate disobedience *1795*

124b understood all he said literally] understood all he wrote literally *1786 2ⁿᵈ edn, 1797, 1798*

126a its highest ornament] its brightest ornament *1786 2ⁿᵈ edn, 1797, 1798*

126b assume the name, the title, and the rank, of the Countess of Walstein] assume the name of the Countess of Walstein *1786 Dublin edn, 1795*

127a far was she from suspecting what she was about to be told] far was she from imagining what she was about to be told *1786 2ⁿᵈ edn, 1797*

128a Fault, poor girl, it would be no fault of thine; but thy struggles will all be in vain] Fault, poor girl, it would be in vain *1795*

129a In proportion as Lindorf lost ground, in her esteem] In proportion as the fickle Lindorf sunk in her esteem *1786 2ⁿᵈ edn, 1797, 1798*

129b and heard to what excess he had carried generosity and friendship] and to what excess he had carried generosity and friendship *1786 Dublin edn, 1795*

131a before he would make so cruel a determination?] before he would make such a cruel determination? *1795*

132a I wish to live here forgotten] I wished to live her forgotten *1797*

134a   Surprise, gratitude, tears, faintings, if these were wanting the scene must have been insipid] Surprise! Gratitude! Tears! Faintings! If these were wanting the scene must have been insipid *1786 2nd edn, 1797, 1798*

135a   presently would I forget other and stronger passions] presently should I forget other and stronger passions *1786 Dublin edn, 1795*

135b   thou hast no person] thou hast no creature *1786 2nd edn, 1797, 1798*

136a   with infinite satisfaction] with infinite pleasure *1786 2nd edn, 1797, 1798*

136b   and she drops] and she droops *1798*

141a   whom I shall ever love] whom I shall forever love *1798*

146a   almost mechanically] most mechanically *1795*

146b   yet, having read it, was it possible to remain insensible to its contents?] yet, having read, it was impossible to remain insensible to its contents *1786 2nd edn, 1797, 1798*

146c   I now find my error] I find my error *1795*

149a   where, where art thou] where art thou *1786 Dublin edn, 1795*

149b   This dreadful incertitude was every moment increased] This dreadful incertitude was every moment increasing *1798*

153a   tell her all he meant to do] tell her what he meant to do *1798*

153b   I, I alone wish, I alone ought, to suffer] I, I alone ought to suffer *1795*

155a   knowest not my loss] knowest not thy loss *1795*

157a   the woman I love is for ever mine] the woman I love is mine *1798*

157b   it depends for ever to separate or unite them] he depends for ever to separate or unite them *1795*

Volume III

161a   It could not be long before Lindorf would arrive] It would not be long before Lindorf would arrive *1795*

164a   which he so soon was to renounce] which he soon was to renounce *1786 Dublin edn*

165a   such like fears torment him that scarcely could reason sustain the conflicts of the heart] the like fears torment him that scarcely could reason sustain the conflicts of the heart *1795*

165b   written to conjure his friend to return] written to conjure his friend's return *1786 Dublin edn, 1795*

165c   whether she really wished to leave Ronebourg] whether she wished to leave Ronebourg *1795*

166a   at Berlin, for some months. In less time than that Walstein [...] relative to where Caroline should remain] for some months, and probably in less than that time Walstein and Caroline's future fate would be decidedn In the mean while, wholly unknown in her house at Walstein, no one should visit her only he and the High Chamberlain. This was perhaps his motive for consenting so freely; all seemed easy, provided he was not obliged to quit the object of his love, 'till the hour of final separation should come. The sage in love is mo more than man. The Count no longer saw impediments to Caroline living in his house, and in seeing her was perfection of bliss; and, though he still destined her for a man he supposed she loved, though still determined carefully to conceal his own passion, he could not refuse himself this intermediate enjoyment of happiness; which, beside, would remove every difficulty, relative to which her present habitation became improper. *1786 Dublin edn, 1795*

167a   The day of departure was, therefore, fixed [...] every thing that might bring Lindorf to memory] The day of departure was therefore appointed; and the gentle Caroline beheld it come with transport: she could no longer remain in Lindorf's house. As it was with a beloved husband she was going to pass her life, she considered her fate as irrevocably fixed, and flattered herself with a hope of soon effacing, by the most studied excesses of tenderness, her capricious and erroneous conduct, which her heart, at present, disavowed, and which she herself could not pardon. Walstein, attentive to every action and look of Caroline, perceived she went with pleasure; but this pleasure he ascribed to virtue, and to the desire she had, hitherto, of avoiding every thing that could bring Lindorf to memory. *1786 Dublin edn, 1795*

167b   These, all conspiring, contributed but to augment that emotion which she no longer could conceal] These, all compounded, contributed but to augment that emotion which she no longer could conceal *1786 Dublin edn, 1795*

167c   but we have before seen the motives by which he was withheld] but we have before seen the motives by which it was withheld *1795*

171a   by which he was continually assaulted] by which he was assaulted *1786 Dublin edn*

172a   earnest to hear the words] eager to know the words *1795*

172b   he looks, he listens, and presently the shadowy pleasure of doubt itself vanishes] he stops, he listens, and presently the shadowy image of doubt itself vanishes *1786 Dublin edn, 1795*

172c   Caroline laid her guittar [...] always carried concealed in her bosom] Caroline laid her guittar in her lap, and untied a small ribband which she always wore about her neck. Till then, the Count had supposed it to be only an ornament, but he saw now that a miniature picture was pendent to it, and which Caroline always carried concealed in her bosom. *1786 Dublin edn, 1795*

172d   he yet could see] he only could see *1786 Dublin edn*

172e   The tears ran down her cheeks] The tears fells down her cheeks *1786 Dublin edn, 1795*

177a   Caroline had been silent so long] Caroline had been idle so long *1795*

177b   he will pardon me, will dispel my fears] *1795, omit*

178a   will he not call me by his name?] will he not call me by my name? *1786 Dublin edn*

178b   Souls of sympathy, that now with Caroline remain in fearful suspense, imagine a paper] Souls of sympathy, that, although Caroline remain in fearful suspense, imagine a paper *1786 Dublin edn*

178c   a hope that the hand of death is upon her] a hope that the hand of death is near *1786 Dublin edn, 1795*

179a   She looks at the direction of those letters] She looks at the reality of those letters *1795*

179b   will exist for him, with him, by him, and never, while life endures, will leave him more!] will exist for him, with him, and never, while life endures, will leave him more! *1786 Dublin edn, 1795*

184a   the timidity by which she was restrained] her timidity by which she was restrained *1786 Dublin edn*

188a   to hear his Louisa sing] to hear Louisa sing *1795*

189a   her husband appeared a supernatural being, a benevolent Deity] her husband appeared a supernatural benevolent Deity *1795*

190a   is this moment in distress, when I am so happy; and I myself am the cause of her affliction!] in this moment in distress, when I am so happy! *1798*

190b   with earnestness] with eagerness *1795*

190c   above a year] about a year *1786 Dublin edn, 1795*

191a   While she was last at Berlin] While she was living at Berlin *1786 Dublin edn, 1795*

191b   I should no longer remain so childish?] I should no longer remain childish? *1797*

193a   a merry, unpolished, country fellow] a very unpolished country fellow *1795*

199a   it is he, he himself] it is he, himself *1795*

201a   I will love none but Lindorf] I love none but Lindorf *1795*

209a   instead of in England] instead of being in England *1795*

210a   you, certainly, Sir, must have met a young lady, alone, very handsome, driving full speed!] you, certainly, Sir, must have met a young lady, alone, driving full speed! *1798*

214a   I have very strong doubts concerning those proofs] I have strong doubts concerning those proofs *1797*

218a   such features and such colours as could affect the heart of Caroline] such noble features and such colours as could affect the heart of Caroline *1798*

220a   to put any one question which might lead him to speak] to put any question which might lead him to speak *1786 Dublin edn*

220b   the fair incognito] the fair incognita *1795, 1797*

221a   The letters which gave him so much pleasure are] The letters which gave him such pleasure *1798*

221b   my thoughts were so disturbed that] *1798, omit*

221c   she, herself, your charming countrywoman!] she herself, your charming countrywoman! *1786 Dublin edn, 1795*

222a   the honour and happiness of making her mine] the honourable happiness of making her mine *1795*

223a   forward] forward *1797, 1798*

226a   I wish to see and speak with you] I wish to hear and speak with you *1795*

228a   my heart says so many many things that I am obliged to listen and do whatever it pleases] my heart says so many things that I am obliged to listen and do whatever it pleases *1798*

230a   my departure was by that means deferred] my departure was thereby deferred *1798*

231a   did I swear to live for her] did I swear to live with her *1797*

231b   and neither thou nor I] and neither you nor I *1797*

232a   Matilda, perhaps, is, by temper and nature, better suited to your friend Lindorf] Matilda, perhaps, is better suited to your friend Lindorf *1786 Dublin edn*

232b   and shall for ever love!] and shall for ever! *1786 Dublin edn, 1795*

For Product Safety Concerns and Information please contact our EU
representative GPSR@taylorandfrancis.com
Taylor & Francis Verlag GmbH, Kaufingerstraße 24, 80331 München, Germany

www.ingramcontent.com/pod-product-compliance
Lightning Source LLC
Chambersburg PA
CBHW071449110726
47908CB00003B/573